# Taste of Forever

## Vampires of Sanguine
### Book 3

Sophie Ash

# Content warnings

- Bloodplay/blood in sexual situations
- Kidnapping
- Stalking
- Moderate descriptions of torture
- Mentions of self-harm
- Drug use
- Explicit sex

# Prologue

## Heather

### Four months earlier

"**O**h, thank God." Relief urged my aching feet into the forest clearing, where two people in wide-brimmed hats tended to neat rows of plants.

Right then, I didn't care if people were farming in a protected wilderness area known for hiking, camping, and bike trails. I had run out of water hours ago and my throat felt like sandpaper. My dry tongue dragged over cracked lips while my feet screamed in pain as I hobbled out of the tree line.

Yes, it was a dumbass move to go off-trail on my hike this morning. With an uncharged, now-dead cell phone, no less. But at least I'd found a fellow human before running into a bear or a pack of wolves.

"Hello!" I waved my arms as I approached the two figures. "Hi! I'm so sorry to bother you, but I need help."

The two people stopped working to watch me,

squinting under the brims of their hats. It was late afternoon and the harsh sun cast their faces in shadow.

I had left home in an angry huff after yet *another* fight with Justin, and I hadn't thought to grab a hat myself. It wasn't like I expected to get lost hiking in an area I knew like the back of my hand.

"Would it be possible to get a ride to the nearest ranger station?" I shielded my eyes against the sun. "I got lost on a hike and haven't been able to find my way back."

The two people, a man and woman with deep, weathered lines in their faces, glanced at each other before staring at me again. Neither said a word, and I got the first prickle of warning that something was not right.

Their shirts looked hand-sewn from fabric that had been worn thin long before it became clothing. The pickup truck at the far edge of their planted field was some rusted out 1980s model. Even their jeans, boots, and hats looked handmade, and not from the current decade.

But farm laborers weren't exactly expected to wear the latest fashion. More importantly, I was exhausted, dehydrated, and sunburned. I would have offered a kidney for a cup of water.

"I'm so sorry. I really hate to be a bother." My attempt at a smile felt more like a grimace. "I'd just like to get back home."

"Where are you from?" the woman asked.

"Eureka. I'm a local," I said.

She stared blankly, not a glimmer of recognition at the word. Unease prickled my scalp. I couldn't have wandered *that* far from home, could I?

"Are we still in the Mckay Community Forest?" I asked tentatively.

The man leaned close to the woman, muttering something I couldn't hear. I thought I caught something like "human world," but must have misheard. She answered with rapid whispers that were lost on the breeze.

"Look, I don't want any trouble." It hurt to speak and my voice cracked with a dry ache. God, I would kill for some water and the chance to get off my feet. "I won't alert anyone that you're here. I just want to go home."

It was becoming clear to me, through their nervous glances and hushed arguing, that these people weren't supposed to be here. And they certainly hadn't expected to be found.

The rows of plants in the neatly tilled soil looked unassuming enough, but maybe they were growing coca or kratom or some other illegal operation. I didn't know and I didn't care.

My feet were on the verge of giving out on me, butt already on its way to the ground, when the woman turned toward me.

"We'll help you out, miss. Are you thirsty?"

She had an accent I couldn't place, but that was the last thing that mattered.

"Oh God, thank you so much. Yes, please." My battered body somehow remained upright as I followed the couple to their truck. Maybe I should have been more vigilant, but I was desperate and they were angels who were answering the prayers of an atheist woman.

The man lowered the tailgate and handed me an old-fashioned canteen. It was the kind I had seen in Western movies—a circular, metal container with a small screw-top, encased in leather with a shoulder strap.

I muttered a string of fast "thank you"s before tipping back the canteen and messily gulping down the liquid inside. The water was warm, but it was some of the freshest and cleanest I'd ever tasted.

I drank until my belly was near bursting and the canteen was empty. The man only looked amused when I set down the container with an apologetic expression.

"S'alright. Go ahead and have a seat." He patted the tailgate with a rough, weathered hand. "We'll get you where you need to go."

I obliged, surprised when he gestured for me to scoot backward and then closed the tailgate. Without another word, he got into the driver's seat of the truck, next to where the woman was already seated and waiting.

The engine turned over with a rattle, and I grabbed the metal sides of the bed as the truck started moving.

*Okay. I guess they* are *giving me a ride.*

I hadn't ruled out the possibility that they were taking me to a drug processing work camp, but I planned to worry about that when I had to stand up again.

The area of cleared forest stretched on as we drove. We passed a surprising number of tilled fields and growing patches of various sizes. I spotted corn, different kinds of squashes, tomatoes, hops, and even spied a small orchard of fruit trees. Definitely normal, not illegal crops.

I shook my head in disbelief as I took in my surroundings. Later, I'd have to find this place on a satellite map. How many miles must I have wandered around aimlessly to wind up on someone's farm? I'd been trying to find my way back to the trailhead by following the sun. Great navigation skills, Heather.

The truck had only gone a mile or so before pulling up to a cluster of structures. Some were mobile homes that had seen better days, but I spotted cabins and more permanent structures too. All worn and aged like they'd sat here for decades.

*Someone from here will drive me to the parking lot,* I figured as the man parked the truck in front of the largest cabin and got out.

"Wait here," he said, exiting the vehicle.

The woman remained in the passenger seat, watching me through the rearview mirror. I pretended not to notice while I took in the surrounding buildings. It looked like a commune or settlement of some kind. Maybe temporary work and living spaces for farm laborers? For such seasonal work, it would make sense.

After about ten minutes, the man emerged from the cabin with another man at his side. They came around to the back of the truck together, and the first man lowered the tailgate.

"Come on out, miss." He offered his hand as if to assist me.

I scooted to the end of the truck bed and accepted his hand, not trusting my own feet to hold me steady when I got out.

The other man came to my opposite side, and I assumed he'd steady my other arm. Shock hit me like a cold wind when he grasped my upper arm and proceeded to drag me from the truck.

"Hey! What the hell?"

I tried to pull my arm away, but he held fast, and the first man took hold of my other arm. Before I realized what was happening, the two men had restrained me between them and were dragging me around to the back of the large cabin.

"Hey, stop!" I kicked and ground my heels into the dirt,

trying to find some purchase. But they only lifted me higher so that I kicked at air.

"Let me go!" I hollered, twisting and struggling to no avail. "You said you'd help me!"

"We are," said the second man. "It's safer for you this way." He actually managed to sound regretful.

"I'm being kidnapped!" I yelled at the top of lungs to the onlookers who began to stare curiously. "Someone call the police! Fuck, someone help me!"

"We won't hurt you," said the first man. "But where you're from, you don't understand how things work around here."

"What the hell are you talking about? I'm from the United States! I'm a citizen, I have rights! I *work* for the fucking government!"

"Sorry, but none of that matters here."

The first man opened one of two doors leading into a smaller cabin. Both men gave me a hard shove into the building, sending me sprawling onto a hardwood floor.

"Hey!" I got to my feet as quickly as I could, but in my weakened and panicked state, I moved in an unsteady wobble that cost me precious seconds.

By the time I made it to the doors, the men had already closed and locked them from the outside.

"Come back!" I screamed through the wood. "Don't leave me in here!"

Pulling and jiggling on the doorknobs was useless. Pounding and slamming against the hard surface only hurt my hands and gave me splinters.

"Fuck!" I spun around to figure out my other options.

The cabin was a single room that looked like it was meant for meetings or town halls. It was sparsely furnished with a single desk, a couch, and a few folding tables and chairs. The ceiling was high and vaulted, with skylights and high windows near the roof line.

Meaning I would not be able to break a window to escape.

Still, I walked along the walls, my mind running on overdrive to find a solution. I was a scientist, goddamn it. If there was one thing I was good at, it was finding solutions.

After roughly an hour, my butt sank to the floor in defeat. There was truly no way out.

I could stack every piece of furniture on top of each other and still not reach a window. There was no chimney or any other type of vent to crawl through. I dug through the couch cushions, tore through every drawer in the desk, and even inspected the floorboards. No sign of a key, or even a tool I could use to break through the drywall.

Or defend myself against these wackos.

I let the back of my head rest against the door, exhaustion settling heavily over me. This morning, I'd been on the verge of breaking up with Justin. Now I would have given anything to see his face. I'd even settle for the back of his head, which was becoming my usual view of him, since he seemed to prefer gaming over spending time with me.

A mirthless laugh escaped my lips. Even now, our arguments were the first thing to pop into my mind. They felt so petty compared to being kidnapped by weirdos. And yet, I couldn't help but feel like I wouldn't be in this situation if he had cared enough to listen.

*He'll call the police when I don't come home. Maybe he already has. If I'm still here by Monday, work will start making calls too.*

*Someone will find me. It's only a matter of time.*

———

I must have fallen asleep for a few hours. The next thing I knew, the cabin was dark and something, like a set of keys, was rattling in the door.

My first instinct was to hide. I darted across the room to the desk, only realizing too late that I should have stayed by the door and taken the chance to escape.

"Hello?" A woman's voice called out as she flicked on a light switch.

A dusty chandelier flickered to life. The woman, in her forties with short brown hair, peppered with gray, scanned the room. When her eyes landed on me, crouched next to the desk like Gollum from Lord of the Rings, she smiled.

"Hi there. I thought you'd be hungry."

She carried a plate that I realized smelled *amazing*. Grilled chicken thighs on a bed of rice and vegetables. My stomach growled with an echo that filled the cabin, though I refused to move.

"I'm gonna put this here for you." The woman set the plate down on one of the tables, along with a knife and fork, a cloth napkin, and a mason jar filled with water.

My gaze went straight to the knife and she immediately clocked it.

"I have no intention of hurting you, so I hope you'll treat me with the same courtesy." She began to approach me with slow, careful steps. "What's your name, hun? I'm Robin."

"Look, I won't go for the knife if you promise to let me go."

Robin gave me a sympathetic look that actually seemed sincere. "I'm really sorry, but we can't do that. Especially not at night." She glanced upward at the half moon peeking through clouds in the skylight. "I know this is strange and confusing. I'll see what our council says about returning you to your world during the daytime."

"My *world*?" I repeated. "What are you on about, lady?"

"You got lost in the woods, yes?" She perched a hip on the edge of the table. "Thought you knew where you were going, but unable to find your way back?"

"Yeah."

She nodded knowingly. "We get people like you stumbling upon us every few years. It doesn't seem like it, I know, but in our world, wandering around alone is far more dangerous than in yours. We lock you in here for your own safety."

"Safety from *what*?"

Robin hesitated. "From the vampires."

# Chapter 1

## *Heather*

### Present Day

"I can't believe I'm actually saying this." With a glance at myself in my phone screen currently recording video, I let out a big breath. "But I'm going to let a vampire bite me. Let's hope I'm still alive afterward."

If I had said that out loud six months ago, it would have been a joke. A Halloween prank, maybe. But right then, as I walked through dense woods under the cover of night, I was dead serious.

I stopped recording and slid the phone into my leggings side pocket. It would be too dark to capture anything until I reached my destination, the vampire world of Sanguine.

Four months after stumbling into this supernatural world and seeing a real vampire with my own eyes, I couldn't get those creatures out of my mind.

The strange group of people out in the woods released me after three days and endless insistence that vampires were real and prowling in the night. Kidnapping and strange beliefs aside, I had been fed and well-taken care of.

Regardless, I was eager to get home and put the whole experience behind me. I had sobbed with relief when I found a hiking trail that led me back home.

The night before I left, one of *them* had come to the settlement. He rode up on a motorcycle, a woman climbed on behind him, and they left together as if they were a couple. The entire community of humans seemed to hold its breath until he was gone.

Even from a distance, I knew the fangs and red eyes weren't part of a cheesy costume. Just the sight of him sent my instincts prickling, some kind of warning deep in my DNA sounding off at this nearby predator. He wasn't human. I knew that as certainly as I did my own name. There was some uncanny valley disconnect in the way he moved and how smooth his skin was.

I made it home the next day, but Sanguine never truly left me.

For months I'd scoured the internet, finding vague references to Sanguine and another place called Vargmore on cached archives of long-dead blogs and websites. My notes became messy, disorganized scribbles, so I started a blog of my own for easy reference and, potentially, to connect with other people who had stumbled into Sanguine.

At least, I attempted to start a blog a few times. Every single one mysteriously disappeared after a few posts. First, my password wouldn't work. And when I reset it, everything I posted was gone.

Talking about things out loud helps me process information, so I had tried starting Youtube channels after that. Those also got taken down.

Someone clearly didn't like me talking about the possibility of actual vampires living in a parallel world, no matter how vague I was. Eventually, I was forced to keep everything offline, backed up by at least two different hard drives. I didn't trust cloud storage at that point.

I knew I wasn't losing my mind. I *knew* what had happened to me and what I saw. Even so, I couldn't fully trust my memories until I attempted to find Sanguine again.

And find it I did.

It was a completely different hiking trail in another part of the local community forest. Maps showed nothing but more wilderness, but the trees eventually thinned out to what looked like the fringes of a small city, or maybe an older suburb. Aged brick and concrete buildings lined streets of cracked pavement and in some areas, cobblestone. There was enough wear and tear on the structures to make it clear they'd been standing for decades, if not longer.

If the lack of any mention on a map wasn't weird enough, I felt a strange heaviness in the air when I spotted the city. Something like humidity, but not quite. It made the small hairs on my body stand up and instincts of danger prickle like I was being watched.

I'd turned back and went home immediately, too scared of possibly being captured again, or worse. The city had been utterly still, empty and quiet to the point of creeping me out. Later, I slapped my forehead in a *duh* moment. Vampires were nocturnal and I'd gone looking during a day hike.

As a scientist, I really should have known better. To replicate results, everything, especially environmental factors, had to remain consistent. If I really wanted to prove myself not crazy, I'd have to go at night.

My next visit to Sanguine was my third, and I watched the silent city come to life.

Red-eyed people with flawless skin went about their business. They talked to each other and laughed, drove cars and rode motorcycles, entered and exited buildings like normal people. Humans were among them, as well as less vampiric-looking people with black eyes and smaller fangs.

Again, I people-watched for a few minutes and then went home, this time to come to grips with the reality that I had seen.

Vampires were real. And the world they lived in was a short drive and walking distance away.

Which brought me to tonight, and my plan to go into that world and record some evidence of their existence. What better proof than being bitten? Assuming I didn't die from it, of course. Stranger things had happened in the name of scientific discovery, right?

What did I plan to do with the recordings? I wasn't sure yet. Putting it online didn't feel right, even if it didn't get immediately removed. I thought of sharing my findings with Justin, but had the sinking feeling he'd be dismissive even if faced with proof. It had been a long time since he validated my feelings about pretty much anything, and I didn't want this to become another desperate bid for attention.

Sharing with a colleague from work would be another option but considering we all worked in a secure, state-funded lab, that felt a hair too close to alerting the government. Which could either open a can of worms in terms of research and ethics or get me blacklisted as the crazy conspiracy theorist lady.

*Mom and Dad would have heard me out.* A brief pang of longing clenched in my chest, as it always did when I wished my parents were still around.

But they weren't, so I'd have to be satisfied in finding the proof for myself. To have in case I ever doubted my own mind again. Evidence was the basis for reality. I needed to know I wasn't losing touch with the real world.

I followed the now-familiar trail by flashlight, heading off-trail when I reached the tree that served as my personal landmark. It was a few minutes of walking through wild, untamed wilderness before the brush and forest started to thin out.

Emerging from the trees brought me to the top of a gently sloping hill, where I could see the lights and activity below. Dusk had fallen maybe twenty minutes ago, and I could see the small city rousing, waking like some nocturnal beast.

I clicked off my flashlight, then whipped out my phone and took a few still photos of the view. It was no sprawling metropolis, but quaint in an older, small-town way. Most of the buildings were single story, except for a couple that looked like nightclubs and one stark white building that appeared to be a hospital. That one in particular stood out like a sore thumb, and I'd remembered it from my previous visits.

The white building said *BLOOD BANK* on the side, and I wondered how literal that was. Could I give blood like at a normal blood bank, sitting with a tube in my arm and cookies and juice afterwards? Or was it more of a place that my corpse would be delivered to and never leave?

The humans I'd seen the other night seemed to walk around freely with the vampires, but the people in the commune had acted...not exactly scared, but certainly wary. They seemed very proud of being an exclusively human community with very little interaction with their fanged neighbors.

It almost sounded prejudiced, if I was being honest. But what did I know?

Before I could formulate a plan, hushed voices and the sounds of footsteps made their way up the hill. Four heads popped into my vantage point as the small group climbed up from the opposite side of the slope.

There was soft laughter, both male and female voices. They didn't notice me right away, but they looked like teenagers. Two boys and two girls of about high school age, all lanky limbs and youthful exuberance. One of the girls unfolded a picnic blanket and laid it on a relatively flat spot. The boys had their heads bent, examining something between them.

"Are you gonna share, or what?" asked the other girl, who flopped down on the blanket and stretched her legs out in front of her.

"You'll have to be careful, these are the strong ones." One of the boys held up something that looked like a cigar. "Nicked it from my dad's top shelf," he added proudly.

"My mom smokes those every day," said the girl who had carried the blanket, unimpressed.

The other boy suddenly lifted his head, inhaling deeply. "Someone's here. A human."

All the teens whipped around and in the next instant, I was being stared at by four pairs of very distinct red eyes.

Even though all of their eyes were all red, the variation in them was fascinating. One of the boys had irises that were nearly purple. The girl sitting on the blanket had a bright red, almost pink gaze.

"Uh, hi guys." I waved awkwardly, hoping that teenage vampires were the least dangerous kind. "Not trying to crash your party or anything, I'm just..." My mind blanked. Just *what?* Lost? And give them an opportunity to pounce, if they even did that?

The kids instead seemed to relax when they realized I wasn't a threat. Or a tattle-tale, which was probably worse in the eyes of teenagers sneaking off to smoke their parents' stash.

"Hi. You from Shadowburn?" asked one of the girls.

"Ah, yes," I lied, hoping it was the right thing to say. "Just visiting...Sanguine." If there was any awkwardness in how I delivered the name of their world, the teens paid no mind.

"Welcome," said the boy with the stolen cigar. He gave a polite smile, showing fangs that were almost too big for his mouth. "Where you trying to go? Need directions or anything?"

"Um, well." I waffled for a few moments, then decided to just go for it. "Can you tell me how the blood bank works?"

"Oh, sure. Humans go in through the donor entrance—it's on the left side." He pointed at the corner of the building in the distance. "It's very above board, clean and sterile, all of that. You never see who you're giving blood to and they never see you. It's totally anonymous to keep you safe. Feeding's always from the wrist. I heard they pay pretty well too, if you're in a bind."

"The wrist," I repeated. "You mean a bite?"

"Well, yeah." The teen grinned, his overly large fangs sending a shiver of fear down my back. "That's typically how we do things. Hope you're not squeamish."

Considering my job was testing evidence from crime scenes, I was as far away from squeamish as you could get. Blood was the least offensive bodily fluid I worked with. If anything, I found it fascinating. Blood told stories about the person it came from–their diet and overall health, diseases they had or were predisposed to, any substances used, antibodies from lingering or past infections. Blood was data, a wealth of information running through every living creature

"And they'll pay?" I asked. "For my blood?"

"Yeah." He shrugged. "Only seems fair. Humans have to buy all of their food. Sometimes vampires have to buy theirs."

It did make sense when he put it that way.

"How much blood do they take?"

"I dunno. I think it depends."

"It's totally safe for you," one of the girls chimed in. "My mom's best friend goes to the blood bank all the time. She feeds from the same human male every week."

I turned to her. "How does she know, if it's anonymous?"

"We can taste it in the blood," the other girl said with a shrug. "Sometimes they'll set up regular appointments from the same source if you have a preference."

"I see."

A regulated, clean environment sounded much better than asking some random vampire on the street if they wanted to bite me, and then finding a way to discreetly record it. I didn't exactly have a plan for getting bitten, but this blood bank place seemed like my best option.

"Don't look so scared," the other boy teased. "I don't know how many vamps there are in Shadowburn, but we're way less scary than dragon shifters."

I wasn't sure if I schooled my facial features quickly enough, but I forced away the wide-eyed shock with a laugh. "Right. Yes, of course. Well, thanks for your help. You all have a good night."

The four of them waved and said goodbye as I started down the hill toward the vampire city. Nice kids, all things considering.

When I hit the street below, my hand slapped my thigh,

over the pocket where my phone was. "Shit!" I hadn't recorded a single word of that conversation.

With a huff, I turned on the audio recorder before shoving the phone back in my pocket with the microphone facing up. In all honesty, it didn't feel right to record kids without their knowledge. But I needed real, physical proof and this time, I'd get it.

My blood pounded in my ears while I tried my best to act completely normal and like I belonged in this world. While vampires of every size, shape, and ethnicity passed me on the street, I fought the impulse to stare at them as I headed straight for the blood bank.

# Chapter 2

## *Heather*

The strangest part about walking into the blood bank was how eerily familiar it was. From the reception desk to the tiled floor to the chairs against the walls, it could have been any doctor's office or walk-in clinic.

A mid-twenties-looking man wearing dark blue scrubs stood at the reception desk. I saw his side profile first, his dark brown hair and glasses making him look utterly normal, even approachable. A human, hopefully.

My nerves relaxed as I approached the desk, but after two steps, my heart crashed against my ribs. He turned to face me, offering a smile that was full of fangs. The whites of his eyes were completely black. His dark brown irises were almost lost among the blackness.

"Hi. Did you have a donation appointment?"

"... What?" The noise he made reached my ears but the question didn't register. I couldn't stop staring at his strange eyes.

"Do you have an appointment, or just walking in?"

"Oh... Um, walking in. If that's okay."

"Of course it is." He tapped a button on the computer before angling his head toward me with a small smile. "First time in, I take it?"

"Uh, yes. I'm visiting." I forced my head to nod, leaning on the same story I'd told the kids on the hill. "From Shadowburn."

"Ah, welcome," he said casually, gathering a few sheets of paper and a pen on a clipboard. "Have a seat and fill these out. Then we'll run a few tests to make sure you're a good candidate for donation."

"Tests?" I accepted the clipboard absently. "What kinds of tests?"

"We'll prick your finger for a small blood sample to check your iron levels and any other abnormalities that may disqualify you for donation." The man smiled at me in a way that was probably supposed to be easygoing and friendly, but all I could see were those long canines and his black eyes. "If you're generally healthy, you don't have anything to worry about. We just want to make sure recipients get high-quality blood during their feedings. Our high standards keep the blood bank in business."

"Right." I realized I was staring at his eyes more than was considered polite and jerked my gaze down to the clipboard. "Okay, thanks."

He gave a slight chuckle. "Don't see many brusang in Shadowburn, huh?"

"What?" I looked up, once again caught off-guard by his eyes.

"Brusang." He pointed at his eyes. "That's what I am."

"Oh. You're not a vampire?"

"Not exactly. I was born human and got turned. So I'm a little of both." He smiled again, turning back to the computer. "Welcome to Sanguine. There are dozens of us here."

"Oh, I see." I gave an awkward laugh, unsure of what the appropriate response should be.

"Make yourself comfortable." The brusang man nodded at the row of chairs. "Let me know if you have any questions. There's water and juice in the dispensers. No coffee, I'm afraid. It bitters the blood."

I sank into a chair and scanned the forms he'd given me. The questions were incredibly normal, asking about general health history, diet, drug and alcohol consumption, and any potential blood disorders or genetic conditions. It was strange how normal the form was, considering I was in a hidden, parallel world, about to donate my blood to a freaking vampire.

The second page asked more personal questions, including age, height, hair and eye color, gender, and sexual orientation. I scanned all the questions several times before hesitantly filling it out. The final page was a consent form and an explanation of their anonymity process. At least I had some protection in that regard, right?

After finishing the forms, I discreetly checked my phone to make sure it was still recording, then returned to the front desk.

"All set?" The man, brusang, whatever he was, took my clipboard and released the forms.

"I had a question about the second page, actually."

"Yes?"

"Why do you take this information?" I ran my finger down the list of questions. "The first page makes sense, but what do my eye color, hair color, and sexual orientation have to do with giving blood?"

"Our recipients sometimes have preferences. Taste is a

very subjective thing, and we try to match recipients with donors that align closely with their preferences. We've also noticed that compatible sexual orientations tend to have the most satisfying feedings. So"—he glanced at my sheet—"you will most likely be paired with a heterosexual male."

"But this is purely about blood, right? Nothing...sexual." These so-called preferences made me uneasy. Human blood, down to its molecular components, was by and large the same stuff in every single person. What did physical traits and sexual orientation have to do with it?

"Yes, absolutely." The brusang nodded emphatically. "Our job is to facilitate a safe feeding ground for both donor and recipient. Nothing goes on here besides providing a basic biological need. As the third page says, staff members are present at all times on both sides of the room. Your identity is kept secret during the whole process."

My phone felt like a brick in my thigh pocket. Conversations about blood donation were one thing, but I needed proof of an actual feeding. It was now or never.

"Okay," I said with a nod. "What's next?"

"Great! Come on back." He walked out from behind the desk, opening a door for me as he scanned my paperwork. "Nice to meet you, Jamie. I'm Cedric."

I smiled to acknowledge the fake name I had written on my form. "Thanks for helping me out with this."

"No problem. Sanguine is pretty small, so we don't get many new donors these days. It's nice to shake things up once in a while."

Cedric led me down a hallway to a small, typical doctor's office-looking room, complete with an exam room chair covered in a layer of tissue paper. I sat there while he took the rolling stool and pulled on a pair of nitrile gloves.

Nerves settled in and made me fidgety. My fingers

played in my lap while my gaze bounced all over the room. The stretching sound of gloves over fingers and wrists became deafening in the otherwise silent room. I blurted out the first thing on my mind in order to fill the silence.

"So, how did you end up becoming a brusang?"

Cedric froze in the middle of opening a drawer. "Um, well." He gave an awkward laugh. "I got hit by a car and died."

Horrified, I slapped a hand to my open mouth. "Oh my God! That's awful." I cringed, realizing my mistake. "That's not really something people go around asking, is it? I'm so sorry."

"It's all right. You didn't know any better." Cedric closed the drawer and finished assembling the device he'd taken out. "But yeah, it's not really polite conversation. All brusang are humans who were near death or had recently died before being fed vampire blood. Then, if we're lucky, we wake up looking like this." He gestured to his face, grinning broadly to show off his fangs. In the brighter lights, the contrast between his brown irises and the black areas of his eyes was more apparent.

"I'm sorry," I repeated. I was morbidly curious about how that process worked but didn't want to risk being rude again. He'd already given me one pass. "For being inappropriate and, um, for your death too."

"Ah, it's fine. That was almost thirty years ago now. It doesn't haunt me like it used to."

Thirty years? He looked barely thirty himself.

"I'm going to take a blood sample now, if you don't mind." Cedric held up the device he had put together, which just looked like a die with one side missing. "It'll just be a little poke on your index finger."

"Okay."

He wiped the tip of my finger with an alcohol swab, slid the cube over my fingertip, then pulled it away as I felt a single sharp prick. I got a band-aid over the small cut, and that was that. It was all very efficient and professional.

"Great. Now let's see what your blood has to say."

Cedric inserted the cube into another device that sat on the desk, and watched the computer screen as my sample was analyzed.

I fought the burning curiosity to peek over his shoulder, to rummage through the drawers and inspect the machinery for myself. Was it comparable to what we used at work? The laws of physics seemed to work the same in this world, so the equipment had to be similar. The rapid-testing machine Cedric used looked almost familiar, something I could probably figure out, but I had never seen or used that exact model before.

"Your blood looks good," he mused, scrolling through the onscreen results. "All within normal ranges. Your vitamin D looks a little low for someone from Shadowburn, though." He gave me a teasing look. "The dragons don't let you outside that much?"

I forced a laugh. At some point I'd have to find out what these so-called dragon shifters were. Surely not *actual* dragons, right?

"Yeah, I work inside a lot." That wasn't a lie, at least.

"Well, everything looks great. I'll get your file and blood profile into our system." Cedric made some notes on my paperwork. "Then we'll see who we have waiting to feed and find a compatible recipient for you. Sound good?"

"Uh, yeah." I swallowed and manipulated my lips into a smile. "Awesome."

"I'll be right back, Jamie. Sit tight."

The moment he left the room, I whipped my phone out and stopped the audio recording to shoot video.

"What the hell is this?" I whispered, crossing the small room to hold my phone in front of the machine that analyzed my blood.

After a few seconds, I brought my phone to the computer monitor, squinting as I tried to make sense of the results on the screen. Based on the numbers displayed, I could make educated guesses of what each line was, but the words were in a language I didn't understand. The characters looked almost runic, or like simple pictographs.

I stepped back from the computer and held my phone up as I turned in a small circle to capture the whole room. "Looks like a regular doctor's office," I commented. "But something is very weird about this place."

Once I had footage of the whole room, I stopped the video, went back to audio recording, and stuck the phone back in my leggings. I had no idea when Cedric would be returning and didn't want to risk getting caught.

My hasty recording ended just in time, because he knocked and poked his head in the door not a minute later.

"We've got a recipient ready for you, Jamie." He widened the doorway. "If you'll follow me."

I stepped out into the hallway after him, passing by other staff wearing scrubs of various colors and styles.

"Next time you come, this'll all go a lot faster," Cedric said, keeping pace with me. "You can keep a standing appointment if you'd like, or just drop in whenever. But if you have a preference for a certain recipient and they like your blood in return, we'll do our best to keep you paired up for each feeding."

"Why would I have a preference?" We passed another

brusang in the hallway, a woman with pale blue irises set in black. This time, I knew better than to stare for too long.

"Just as the taste of blood is subjective, so is the experience of providing it," Cedric explained. "On your end, sensations can range from mildly uncomfortable to euphoric and pleasurable. It may take some trial and error, but we strive to make it the best experience for both parties." He opened a door for me. "Here we are. Go ahead and have a seat."

A chair matching the ones in the waiting room was set next to a blue folding screen that divided the room in half. Next to the chair, a bit lower than shoulder height if sitting, was a softball-sized hole in the screen.

The donation process had been spelled out in the form I'd read, but seeing it with my own eyes was a completely different experience. I could read words and tell myself it was fiction, but there was no denying reality.

Moments after lowering myself into the chair, I heard a door open on the other side of the screen where I couldn't see. Heavy footfalls crossed the room, and I felt a sizable presence drop into the other chair mere inches away. We could have been sitting on the same couch, if not for the screen between us.

"Hey, how's your night going?" a warm, smooth voice asked.

"You don't have to talk to him," Cedric said before I could respond. "We'll always protect your anonymity, but how much personal information you want to divulge is up to you."

An indignant huff came from the other side of the screen. "I asked how their night was going. It's just making conversation."

"This donor is new to the process," Cedric retorted. "I'm just reassuring her of her safety."

"It's okay," I piped up before the male chest-thumping could get out of hand. "My night's going well, thanks. How's yours?"

There was a slight shuffle of movement, like he was adjusting his posture in the chair. "Just peachy."

The two words in that low timbre had a sarcastic tone that piqued my curiosity. Everything about this situation was like a strange dream. Some anonymous, silky-voiced vampire was about to bite me and drink my blood. I heard his voice, could glean his general mood from the way he spoke, but would never see the face or know the name of this person.

"We're ready whenever the donor side is," said a woman's voice from the other side of the screen. I heard what sounded like gloves being put on.

"Go ahead and put your forearm through the screen," Cedric told me. "You can rest your elbow there." He nodded at a raised, padded cushion attached to the side of the chair.

I steeled myself with a breath and put my hand and wrist through the softball-sized hole in the screen, feeling like I was voluntarily dunking my arm into shark-infested water. In hindsight, I probably should have asked more questions about the safety of sticking my arm out for some random vampire to take a bite. What would really prevent him from draining me dry? Or ripping my arm from its socket?

"Sorry if I'm shaky." The apology sounded ridiculous as it tumbled out. Did a gazelle say sorry to a lion for its fear?

"Don't worry. I've got you."

The honeyed voice took on a gentler tone than I

expected, and then I felt the warm contact of someone's skin against mine. Fingers supporting my wrist. I could see them through the hole in the screen. Long masculine fingers with short, clean nails and skin slightly paler than mine. His hand felt big.

"Are you comfortable?"

The question, and the concern it conveyed, were more surprises.

"Yes, thank you."

Something else touched me—a cool jelly-like substance on the upturned underside of my wrist applied with a gloved finger.

"Give it about thirty seconds to take effect, and then he'll feed from your wrist," said the female staff member I couldn't see.

Right, this was the numbing gel mentioned in the form. They applied it to prevent any pain during the initial bite.

This was it. This was actually about to happen. If my phone wasn't picking up clear audio, I was going to be really pissed about going through all this for nothing. Assuming I survived.

"Okay," I said, trying not to let my nerves show.

"You don't have to be afraid," said the man about to drink my blood. "I'm actually pretty good at this. I've been a vampire my whole life."

Somehow, the unexpected humor broke through my fear and pulled a laugh out of me. "Oh, really?"

"Yes, and I do come here often. I don't even need an invitation."

A vampire making vampire jokes? What kind of alternate universe was this? The whole absurdity of this experience had me giggling, because what else could I do but laugh?

My giggling fit ended just as the female employee wiped the excess numbing gel from my wrist. "It should be set by now."

A firm grip wrapped around my wrist and forearm. It didn't hurt, but also ensured I wasn't going anywhere. After his effort to ease my nerves with laughter, the hold felt secure, almost comforting.

"This won't hurt you. I promise."

I already knew it wouldn't. That was what the gel was for. But I absolutely did not mind that silky voice reassuring me, even promising me.

"Okay," I said, bracing myself with deep breaths. "I'm ready."

A few seconds passed before I felt the soft pressure of lips on my wrist. I tensed at the contact only because I was expecting much worse, but it almost felt like a soft touch of affection. Not quite a kiss, but almost.

Next came the sharpness of what could only be his fangs. I felt no pain, but he pierced through my skin like a knife through butter. When he pulled at my vein, the last thing I expected was a rush of sensitivity.

It was a full-body shiver that made me aware of everything, from the toes inside my socks to my pulse in my lips. Actually, I could feel my pulse in more places. Even between my legs.

*Been a while since I felt anything down there.*

The vampire took a few more draws at my wrist before I realized my pulse was pounding harder, and the sensitivity all over my body was ramping up. I clamped my thighs together in an effort to ease the ache between them. My skin felt hot, my clothes too scratchy. The mouth on my wrist pulled in a tight seal and I fought the urge to squirm. I craved friction. Frustration and aching need coiled within me, building an urgent desperation for release.

When my breaths turned to pants and I found myself stifling whimpers and moans, the realization hit me like a brick wall.

I was turned on. *Really* fucking turned on, like I never had been before in my life.

A creature I had never believed to be real was currently drinking my blood and I felt moments away from an orgasm because of it.

The absurdity of the situation left my mind and was replaced by an all-consuming need. Every pull of the vampire's mouth felt like a teasing stroke of fingers against my clit, winding me up, but never enough to reach my destination. I needed more, like his mouth on me down there. I needed something thick and solid to fill up this ache inside me, to pound me roughly while I tasted sharp, fanged kisses...

Then, all at once, the delicious sensations were ripped away. My pulse still pounded insistently, my breaths short, but the vampire's mouth was gone from my wrist.

The same voice that had gently reassured me now growled, "Get your fucking hands off me if you want to keep them."

Things were happening around me quickly, and my lust-drunk brain was struggling to catch up. Someone grabbed my arm, urging me to stand up. I rose on wobbly legs and then was pulled through an open door into a hallway.

"Jamie? Jamie, are you alright? Can you hear me?"

"Who the hell is Jamie?" I muttered.

"It's okay. We have a recovery room if you're feeling faint. Just follow me."

I blinked, the hallway and Cedric's face coming into focus. Everything slowly filtered in, and the more I processed what had just happened, the more horrified I felt.

"Oh, God." I held up my wrist and stared at the two small puncture marks left behind by the vampire's fangs.

It really happened. And it really made me feel like...*that*.

Cedric said something, probably asking if I was okay again, but all I heard was noise.

"I can't stay here. I have to go home."

No one tried to stop me as I turned and went down a hallway, then pushed on a door marked *Donor Exit*. The cool night air against my heated skin felt like the slap of reality that I badly needed.

Another man had brought me to the brink of orgasm.

Not only that. I had been really, *really* into it. I didn't want it to stop.

Guilt sat heavily in my chest as I started toward home, where my boyfriend of five years would be waiting for me.

## Chapter 3

*Heather*

I didn't check the audio and video recordings until I was safely in my car with the windows locked. Relief flooded me as I listened to and watched what I'd captured. Everything was there. Not all of the audio was clear, but that could be cleaned up with some editing software.

Vampires were real. And now I had proof.

Despite the guilt riding me, I turned up the volume when the anonymous vampire was speaking to me, trying to recapture the memory of that voice. I could still feel his fingers wrapped around my forearm, the warmth of his lips sealed to my wrist.

Just as abruptly, I stopped listening and tossed my phone into the cup holder. With a shake of my head, I started up my car and began the short drive home.

*I didn't do anything wrong,* I told myself. *I did not cheat on Justin.*

It wasn't like I expected to become so turned on by the blood-drinking. I was still trying to wrap my head around my own response, but surprise horniness alone wasn't a reason to feel guilty. Right?

My thoughts churned as I drove home. I felt more guilty about the fact that I kept thinking about the vampire's voice, and that I couldn't stop wondering what he looked like. I saw only a glimpse of his hands and was now trying to imagine how the rest of him was built.

He had a presence on the other side of that screen. His footsteps had weight to them. He felt like he took up a lot of space, like he was probably tall. Or strong.

But there was no point to wondering, no reason to fantasize. Getting turned on had to be due to some kind of vampire evolutionary thing. Something to make their victims more compliant. Cedric had mentioned potential euphoric or pleasurable sensations, which still seemed like a far cry from orgasms. Had I misunderstood?

"Damn it. Of course." I muttered curses as I entered my apartment complex and spotted no open parking spots near my building. Justin's car was in our designated spot, not that he needed it, since he worked his IT job from home. It always turned into a fight if I asked him to let me have the parking spot, so I let it go.

After circling the complex a few times, I gave up and decided to park on the street a block away. Thanks to working overnights at the crime lab, I usually came home when everyone else was leaving for work, and parking usually wasn't an issue. I was not thrilled to walk a block home alone in the middle of the night.

I grabbed my phone and shoved it in my pocket, resisting the urge to listen to the vampire's voice once again. The sooner I copied it to a hard drive, the better. And then...I didn't know exactly what to do with it. But, as a most-of-the-time happily attached woman, I definitely wasn't going to listen to it repeatedly like a psycho.

The walk home would be short, but I kept my pace brisk. Why I felt safer hiking in the woods at night than walking in my own neighborhood, I had no idea. We didn't live in the best part of town, but it wasn't the worst either. Maybe it was something about this area, with all of its apartment complexes and parked cars. So many people living in such close quarters almost guaranteed I was being watched, no matter how late it was.

That was the feeling I couldn't escape, like there were eyes on my every move.

I had only walked a few yards when I decided to pull my phone out. Better to have 911 at the ready than not.

My senses were on high alert as I quickened my pace. My phone was in my hand, but my gaze swept widely in front of me. I felt ready for anything, and yet somehow I wasn't fast enough for the car door that opened just ahead of me, and the man stepping out of the passenger seat.

He started in the opposite direction and bumped into me so hard that I stumbled backwards.

And dropped my phone.

"Oh shit! I didn't see you there. Are you okay?" He put a hand on my arm to steady me.

It happened so quickly, I just blinked up at him dumbly. The nearby streetlamp cast harsh shadows on his face, but I could still tell that he was good-looking. Clean-shaven, early thirties maybe, with a crew cut. He was tall and muscular, and had *active duty military* written all over him.

"I'm okay," I said after catching my breath. "But I dropped my phone."

The man cringed as he released my arm. "I'm really sorry. I can replace your screen or anything if it's damaged."

He bent to retrieve the phone, turning it over quickly to look at the screen and the back. "Hey, look at that." He smiled as he handed it to me. "Seems it survived."

Luckily, I did protect my electronics well. The selfie of Justin and I, taken over a year ago, smiled up at me from my perfectly intact lock screen. No cracks in the glass or distortion in the image. The only damage I could see was some scuffing on the corner of the phone's case.

"All good?" the man asked.

"Yeah. Saved by the case," I said with an awkward laugh.

"Glad to hear it. Sorry again for running into you. Have a good night." With that, he turned and continued on in the direction he was heading.

I paused for a few seconds, willing my heartbeat to slow down before resuming my hurried walk home. With a glance over my shoulder, I watched the man's back as he walked away. As far as things happening at night to a woman alone, it certainly could have been worse.

The apartment was dark when I walked in, with only the glow of a computer screen lighting up the small living area. Of course Justin was still up, gaming with his buddies.

"Hey," I said, taking off my purse and coat to hang on the hooks by the front door.

I got no response. Not even a glance as I walked in. Justin had a headset on, talking into the attached microphone to whoever he was gaming with.

His eyes didn't even flicker from the screen as I crossed the room to the mantle shelf, where I touched the framed photo of me and my parents. It had been years since they passed away, but I still touched their photo every time I came home. It was my little ritual, my way of greeting them every day.

When I turned back to Justin, his eyes were still focused on the screen in front of him like he'd never looked up. At this point, I should have been used to it, but the lack of any reaction from the guy who was supposed to love me still stung. He'd definitely heard me unlock and open the door. Every time I brought it up, he made it sound like some huge ask to just be acknowledged when I came home.

I smothered the spark of anger as I kicked off my shoes. I seemed to be doing that a lot lately, suppressing my own feelings to make *his* life easier. But I hated arguing, hated always being made out to be the bad guy and he the victim. I wanted peace in our relationship, and I missed the version of my boyfriend who once made me feel loved.

I walked up behind Justin's chair, my palm coming to rest on his upper back. Only then did he look up at me, pulling one side of his headphones off of his ear.

"Hey, babe. Home from work early?"

The angry spark I'd smothered moments ago reignited. "I told you I wasn't working tonight. I went for a night hike at Ryan Creek."

"Oh, right." He laughed sheepishly. "My shitty memory."

With that, he replaced his headphone and returned his attention to the computer, effectively dismissing me.

No, *How was it?*

*Did everything go okay?*

*Were you safe?*

*By the way, I finally washed that load of laundry you've been reminding me about for the past week.*

And, shitty memory? Evidently, it was only shitty when it came to me. He forgot my days off, but he never missed a raid night.

"Resentment is the relationship-killer," our couples

therapist had told us at one of the few sessions I'd managed to drag Justin to. "The two of you need to be a united front against all hardships, even if that hardship is the relationship itself. If you turn against each other, there won't be a relationship to save."

I took deep breaths through my nose, each one a battle with that word: *resentment.*

We wouldn't last if I let the resentment win. We'd never go back to how happy we used to be if I got offended by everything he did. I had to prioritize *us*, not just me.

My hand returned to Justin's back, where I rubbed in wide circles. I added pressure, making it more of a massage as I leaned in closer.

"When are you going to bed?" I asked, letting my voice drop, low and sultry.

"Mm, I dunno. Few hours, at least." His dismissive answer was punctuated by rapid mouse clicks and aggressive key strokes.

I brought my hands over his shoulders and ran them down his chest. "Is there any way I can convince you to come to bed sooner?" Dodging his headphone cord, I kissed his neck.

"I mean, I can try, but we've been planning to raid this dungeon all week. This is the only time we could get this many people together. The party needs me."

*And your girlfriend is trying to fuck you. Is this really where your priorities are?*

I smothered the voice of resentment, which I was starting to think of as a little demon on my shoulder, and tried one more time.

"I miss you, Jus. We haven't gone to bed together in weeks." I kissed his neck again, flicking my tongue in a way that used to drive him wild.

It wasn't even sex that I was after, although that would be a bonus. I missed the intimacy we used to have, our nightly routine of cuddling in bed and kissing goodnight before falling asleep.

Now, Justin leaned away from my touch, rolling his shoulder to break contact. "Should've thought of that before you started working night shift. We're on totally different schedules now."

I straightened, hurt shooting through me like ice water. "And whose idea was that? I moved to nights for the shift deferential because we were struggling. I was worried about never seeing each other, but *you* suggested it. Remember?"

His response? A shake of his head and a sigh. "Yeah, DimeBag, I'm still here," he said into the microphone.

"Unbelievable," I groaned, heading for the bedroom.

After a shower and brushing my teeth, I flopped into bed and stared at the ceiling. Sleep wouldn't come for hours. My work schedule had turned me into a night owl, so I was wide awake to stew—to listen to every whisper from that little resentment demon on my shoulder.

*What kind of man turns down sex to play a computer game? He doesn't even pretend to care anymore. Why do I even bother?*

*Is he getting his needs met somewhere else?*

That last thought made me flop violently onto my side, facing my nightstand where my phone lay charging. No, Justin wasn't a cheater, despite all his faults. I was just projecting because it felt like *I* had come dangerously close to cheating tonight.

I reached for my phone without thinking, but stopped short of picking it up.

*A vampire drinking my blood showed me more concern*

*and care than my own boyfriend tonight. How messed up is that?*

I had been nothing but an anonymous, faceless blood donor, and he'd made me laugh to relax me. He told me not to be afraid, assured me he wouldn't hurt me.

And he hadn't.

He'd made me feel incredible.

My skin heated at the memory. Not just at the physical pleasure, but the sound of his honeyed voice. The weight of his presence—so close to me but impossible to see. Who was he? Did all vampires have that effect when they walked into a room? His presence seemed to demand attention, demand respect.

But I hadn't felt afraid. The whole situation was strange and scary, but *he* wasn't. He'd made me feel comforted, like he would shield me from harm. And then fuck me into oblivion after he finished drinking my blood. Or maybe *while* he drank it.

I rubbed my eyes with a sigh. It had been so long since I'd felt desired that my mind was truly spiraling, thinking of blood and vampires as sexy. Ugh, absolutely not.

Justin really didn't need to do much to show me that he cared, that he still loved and desired me. I wanted to believe that he did, that he was just comfortable in the relationship and didn't see the need for romantic gestures anymore. It wasn't like I was asking for flowers or even a date night—a spontaneous kiss would have made me swoon. A, "Hey, how was your night?" would make me feel I mattered.

*Really?* asked the resentment demon on my shoulder. *You think a starving woman will be satisfied with sprinkles of breadcrumbs?*

Well, no. Maybe not satisfied. But it would be better than how things were now. A step in the right direction.

Minutes crawled by and I was no closer to falling asleep. Justin swore and yelled at his teammates in the living room, oblivious to the real world. And the real world had vampires in it. I was still wrapping my head around that.

Justin had been mildly concerned when I had been held captive for three days at the prepper village, but we'd fought about something stupid right before. When I finally returned home, he figured I'd been staying at a friend's place to cool off.

"You didn't try to call me? File a missing person's report?" I demanded when I returned home. "Or even check in with my friends or coworkers to make sure I was okay? I could've been dead in a ditch or something!"

"Well, you're obviously not," he'd said. "I figured you wouldn't answer if I called. You're the one who stormed out."

*Always your fault,* mused the resentment demon. *Even your own disappearance. Your boss called because you missed a day of work, but your boyfriend? Not a peep.*

I rolled to my side with a frustrated groan and yanked my phone off the charger. I wouldn't make a habit of this. Seriously, I wouldn't. But if there was a chance that the vampire's voice could relax me enough to sleep, I'd take it.

My eyes half-closed when I hit the play button on the audio file. I wanted to immerse myself in that room again and recall every sensation. How strange that I'd rather be there again instead of in my own bed.

But instead of hearing recorded voices, I got nothing but static.

"What the hell?" I opened my eyes and dragged the slider to different parts of the audio file. It was all static.

I sat up, confused and frantic as I swiped through my recent files.

"No! What the fuck?"

The video and still images I'd shot were corrupted too. Nothing could be made out through the dead pixels and random lines of distorted color. Everything I'd recorded that day, all the proof I had of vampires' existence, was completely unusable.

How? I had checked everything when I got to my car. It had all been there.

My head shot up, recalling the guy who'd bumped into me. Something must have broken when I dropped my phone.

I turned on my bedside lamp to inspect my phone more closely. Maybe I missed something because of how dark it was outside. I popped the phone from the hardshell case and brought both pieces right in front of my nose.

Nothing. Every dent or scratch had either been there before or was entirely too small to cause any internal damage. The same scuff on the case's corner I'd noticed before was the only visible damage that I could attribute to dropping it.

"Damn it," I sighed, replacing the case and checking my files again. Just for good measure, I powered the phone off and turned it on again. No change. All the files from earlier today were corrupted, including photos I'd taken of the tiger lilies I grew on our back patio. At least those would be easy to re-take.

I held the phone next to my ear and shook it, expecting to hear some loose component rattling inside, but there was nothing. At a loss, I tossed the phone back onto the nightstand and flopped down onto the pillow.

It seemed really weird that dropping my phone on a

sidewalk would corrupt only my most recent files, but I supposed stranger things had happened. Like finding a hidden world full of vampires, getting bitten by one, and nearly having an orgasm as a result.

Without those files, I realized, I had no proof of vampires. That was the whole fucking point of me going there.

"Shit." I rubbed my forehead.

My brain was locked on to the vampire world like a target. I *needed* proof—for my own peace of mind, if nothing else. I needed to know that I wasn't completely losing it.

Which meant I had to return to Sanguine once again.

# Chapter 1

## *Laith*

"You need to stop," Des warned, grabbing at my sleeve. "The blood bank is gonna blacklist you if you keep this up."

"I know, but what if she's the one?" I jerked my arm out of his grip and kept walking, heading across the street to the blood bank's donor exit. "Hey there, sweetheart. Can I ask you something?"

The night was young with a full moon casting plenty of illumination, and the human woman still jumped, startled at my approach. It always surprised me how dulled their senses were compared to ours. I wasn't trying to sneak up on her. Vampires just moved quietly. Even so, I figured my head of pale blond hair would stand out in the darkness of night.

When the woman recovered, she gave me an assessing look. "Yes?"

"Did you happen to donate blood here two nights ago?"

"No. I donate about every two weeks, usually on Thursdays." Her posture relaxed and she smoothed a hand over her hair. "If you're wondering."

My hope deflated as my gaze wandered over her fingers and arm. There was no sign of purple nail polish or a forearm tattoo.

"No, thanks. I'm good."

I turned abruptly, returning to the bench across the street where Des waited for me, shaking his head at me yet again.

"Not her." I dropped onto the hard surface with a sigh.

"Color me shocked," he muttered.

We sat outside of a darakt shop, watching the busy night pass by. For me, that entailed staring at the donor exit at the blood bank and approaching every human female who walked out.

It had been the first and last place I'd tasted my blood mate.

My tongue ran over my teeth, seeking the memory of her rich, beautiful blood filling my mouth. I recalled how her scent filled the air, feminine and floral. Her quickening pulse in my ears and her ragged puffs of breath before she was ripped away from me.

Apparently I'd gotten too enthusiastic in my feeding. I'd taken from her too quickly, became too aroused. Too possessive of that sweet, soul-quenching blood. Once her taste hit my tongue, I couldn't get enough. The moment someone tried to make me stop, I'd made threats. And then they'd separated us. For good.

Aside from how she tasted, her purple nail polish and the tattoo on her forearm were all I had to go off of. Needle, meet haystack.

And with the blood bank's strict privacy rules, my best bet at finding out her identity was outside of the facility. Like, *immediately* outside the facility. For the past two nights, I'd been walking up to every human woman who came out of the donor exit.

Would such an approach be frowned upon? Absolutely. Was it illegal? Technically not. Did I care either way? Not really.

The blood bank could only maintain donor anonymity on their own grounds. Once off their grounds, in public, anyone was fair game. It was no different than walking up to someone and asking their name. I'd even heard of some people being paired at the blood bank, having a connection at the feeding, and agreeing to meet each other formally after it was done. If two people wanted to know each other, it wasn't like the blood bank could prevent it.

The longer I thought about that, though, the more a certain question nagged at me. *What if she doesn't want me to know who she is?*

My foot bounced on the ground, eyes glued to the exit door across the street. How could someone not want to meet their blood mate? For me, being without her sucked extra hard because now any other blood would taste foul and disgusting compared to hers. Once my brain locked onto the perfect source, it would accept nothing less. So, it would be great to not only find my life partner, but also not starve to death.

But for a human? I guessed she wasn't suffering at all without me. Did she even know what this connection was? What it meant? The male staff member on her side had said she was new, so maybe she didn't know.

"You need to chill the hell out. Here." Des shoved his tin of darakt gummies in my face.

"No, thanks." I waved his hand away and took out the fresh pack of cigarettes I'd just bought at the shop behind us.

Darakt was most comparable to tobacco for humans, but had some cannabis-like effects as well. It was a mixture of powdered blood and herbs native only to Sanguine. There were endless blends, flavors, potencies, and ways to consume it. Humans didn't care for it, but the stuff was a staple for vampires. Just as essential as coffee for most people.

Now that I'd tasted my blood mate, I figured edible darakt was out for me. Smoking would be the only way to get my fix. Fortunately for vampires, we healed too quickly for any significant lung damage to take effect.

Unless you were Thorne, I imagined. The head of Blood 'til Dawn smoked so damn much, he would probably be the first vampire on record to get emphysema.

I had just lit up when the blood bank's exit door swung open. Like a strung puppet, I got to my feet and started walking, ignoring Des's groans and his yelling for me to come back.

My reaction was so automatic, I didn't take note of *who* had come through the door until I met Rebecca's withering glare.

"Hey, Becks." I tossed the blood bank employee a casual smile, acting like I had every right to be there. "Out for a smoke break?"

"You know you can't be doing this, Laith," she said. "You're making our donors feel unsafe, hovering outside their exit like this."

"I'm not harassing anyone, I swear." I held up both hands placatingly. "I'm just trying to find *her,* that's all."

"She obviously didn't want to be found by you. You need to drop it, or we're..." Rebecca hesitated, like she didn't want to follow through on that thought. "I'm sorry. I don't want to, since you're part of Blood 'til Dawn, but protecting our donors is of utmost importance. If you don't stop this, we'll have to blacklist you from our services."

I shrugged. "Blacklist me, then."

She blinked, staring at me dumbfounded. "You can't mean that."

"I fed from my blood mate, Becks." My arms spread wide. "I'm ruined for all other blood sources. I can't take from anyone else ever again."

"We do have ways around that," she said hesitantly. "We can give you blood through an IV so you won't have to taste it. But you have to respect our rules, Laith."

"Nah, I'll take my chances." I finished my cigarette on a long drag and crushed the butt under my boot. "She's out there and I'm not giving up on finding her."

Rebecca sighed. "I didn't want to do this, but calling Thorne is my last resort and I *will* take it."

I frowned. "You'd really do that? Tell my dad on me?" Thorne wasn't my actual dad, but as head of the ruling clan, he was basically everyone's dad.

"Unless you go somewhere else and leave our donors alone."

"No can do, Becks. This is fate. Temkra's chosen someone for me, and has challenged me to find her." I brought a hand to my chest. "I'm on a quest from the goddess. You wouldn't deny me fulfilling my destiny, would you?"

"God, I hope your mate teaches you something about ego." Rebecca turned with a huff, heading for the door. "I'm calling Thorne."

"Fine. But just remember, tattlers get...rattlers!"

She slammed the door closed before my rhyming skills could really land.

I returned to the bench with a bemused Des staring at me.

"Tattlers get rattlers, huh?"

"Yeah, you know. Rattlesnakes. They're all over Shadowburn." The dragon shifter territory was essentially one big desert, which I avoided going to whenever possible. Too much damn sunlight, thank you.

"I believe the original saying is snitches get stitches," Des informed me.

"I know but she's just a human. I didn't want to come off too threatening."

"A rattlesnake bite is less threatening than a wound that needs stitches?"

"Not a bite necessarily, just the presence of the snake itself. Doing its hissing, rattling thing. Scary, but not life-threatening."

"Does your little rhyme differentiate between the two?"

"Sure it does. It's not tattler-mites get rattler-bites."

"Ah. Well I'm sure Rebecca interpreted that as you intended it."

"She totally did."

My phone rang just then and Des chuckled when he saw Thorne's name across my screen. "You're in trouble."

"No way. I'm his favorite." I answered the call. "Hi, Dad."

"Get away from the blood bank or I'll post you at Sapien for a week straight," Thorne drawled. "If you want to stare at humans so badly, I can certainly arrange that."

"Dad, come on," I protested. "I have to find my blood mate. You know how important this is."

"Stop calling me Dad. This isn't a human sitcom," he groused. "You'll find her again if it's meant to be. But the blood bank provides an important service and you're stressing them out."

"But what if I miss her?"

"You'll live another day. But right now you're fucking with the balance of Sanguine. You're hampering other vampires from getting the blood they need. So quit camping out, or I will drag you away behind my motorcycle. Am I clear, Laith?"

Such a Dad thing to say.

"Yes, Da—Thorne."

"You really are a child," he groaned. "No wonder she split right after you fed from her." With that final heart-warming sentiment, he hung up.

"Hey." Des smacked my arm as I put my phone away. "What if she's from Sapien, like Amy and Tavia? She might've snuck away to get a taste of the *real* Sanguine and had to hurry back before she got caught."

I considered that, but it didn't feel right. The all-human community on the fringes of vampire territory was, frankly put, weird as hell. Cultish, even. They shunned any kind of integration with vampire society, despite the many other humans living well among us. Tavia and Amy had been lucky to get out. They had both found their mates and now seemed extremely content with their lives.

I could make someone content too. Even happy.

If my mate was cut from the same cloth as Tavia and Amy, she could possibly be from Sapien. But those two seemed to be the exception, not the norm.

"I don't know," I said to Des. "My gut doesn't really feel like she's one of them."

"The only thing your gut knows is wine and cherry danishes."

"Hey, I'm picky about my wine!" He was right about

the danishes, though. I was one of the few vampires with a sweet tooth.

"Everyone loves Tavia's wine, doesn't mean you're picky."

"Well I can definitely tell when one isn't made by her." My foot started bouncing again, so I stood from the bench. "Come on. Let's leave before Thorne makes good on his threat to peel my skin off with the road."

"Never thought I'd see the day." Des hopped up and followed me down the sidewalk. "Now where we going? Gonna stalk women at the market?"

I chewed on that thought and let it go just as quickly. "Nah. I don't think she buys food there."

Des guffawed. "How in Temkra's name would you know that? You don't know a single thing about her."

"It just doesn't feel right to me." I shrugged. "Maybe it's her blood telling me. I've fed from a few humans from around here and she doesn't taste like any of them. She tastes—"

"Like night-blooming flowers, cherry danishes, and an orgasm in your mouth. Yeah, I know. You've only gone on and on about how she tastes nonstop for the past two days."

I smirked. "Can perfection ever be adequately described with simple metaphors?"

"Well, hold on, Shakespeare. That poses another question." Des popped another darakt gummy in his mouth. "If she doesn't shop at the market, is she not from around here? Maybe Shadowburn or the human world?"

I considered the human world, but the chances were slim. It was rare that a human stumbled into the supernatural world with zero previous contact. Most of them weren't sensitive to the magic that kept our world hidden, having never been exposed to it before. The majority of humans in Sanguine had been here for generations and chose to stay.

"More likely Sapien, where they grow their own food," I conceded. "Or one of the forbidden territories. Maybe she got sick of angels and werewolves, or she's escaping them."

"Great, just what we need. Werewolves on our asses for sniffing out one of their humans."

"I really don't know, though." I ran a hand through my hair, tugging the short strands at the base of my skull. "The blood bank was the only place I knew where to start looking. Beyond that, I'm fucking clueless."

Forget finding a needle in a haystack. I was trying to find a needle among needles. It just needed to be *my* needle.

"Wait a second." Des grabbed my shoulder, pivoting around to stand in front of me. His eyes were dilated, probably as a result of the darakt gummies. "We've been doing this all wrong. We've got to Cinderella this shit."

I stared at him for a beat. "I don't follow."

"Cinderella!" he repeated. "You know, the whole deal with the glass shoe? She had to run off before midnight because she'd turn into a banana tree or something, but she left one glass shoe behind."

"Okay?"

He slapped my chest. "The prince didn't get her name, and I think it was a masquerade ball or something because they danced all night and he didn't know what she looked like. The glass shoe was the only thing he had of hers."

"So?"

"So! Only his dream woman would fit into that shoe, right?"

"Unless another woman was the same size."

"Not the point. Just go with me here. Everyone wants to marry a prince, right?"

I shrugged. "Can't say it's my thing, and I don't want to speak for anyone else—"

"*Anyway*, they put it out to the entire kingdom that the prince was looking for the owner of this shoe. And the women flocked in droves to try it on because they wanted their chance at becoming a princess. You see where I'm going with this?"

"Not really," I admitted. "Seems dishonest. Those women had to know the shoe wasn't theirs."

"Dude!" Dez slapped my shoulder, then poked me with his index finger. "You're the prince in this scenario. Part of Blood 'til Dawn, the ruling clan of Sanguine. You're a catch. Lots of women would love to be your mate."

"Aw, thanks buddy. But I only want one person."

"Obviously," he snorted. "Bringing the women to us is just an easier process of elimination. We don't have to go all over the territory. We put the word out and let them come to us instead. And, hopefully, your mate is among them."

I nodded, scratching my chin. "That would make it easier. But what's my glass shoe?"

"The taste of her blood. And the window of time she was at the blood bank." Des gave me a sympathetic look. "But to make sure, you'll probably have to feed from some women who are definitely not her."

The thought made me shudder, but he had a point. If my blood mate changed her nail polish or her strange tattoo wasn't visible, the taste of her blood would be the only way of knowing.

"That's fine. I'll do whatever it takes to find her. So how do we do this? The text alert system?"

"Yeah, and word of mouth. We'll be very specific about the criteria."

"Good." I nodded, feeling optimistic for the first time since her flavor danced over my tongue. "The blood bank has, what, a dozen donors at any given time? There aren't that many people it could possibly be."

"Huh, famous last words."

"Why do you say that?"

Des pointed at me again. "*You* may not want to marry a prince. But do not underestimate the amount of human women who do."

# Chapter 5

## *Heather*

All week during work, while running tests on crime scene evidence and compiling toxicology reports, I couldn't stop thinking about vampires.

Well, one vampire in particular. The one that bit me. And how I wouldn't mind being bitten by him again. Just him, though. No one else.

There was something about that whole experience, and my reaction, that felt too intimate to share with anyone else.

Just as quickly as my daydreams took me back there, guilt would snap me back to reality. I had a serious, long-term boyfriend, for shit's sake. I had zero reason or excuse to be fantasizing about another person. Especially someone whose face I had never seen. Someone who wasn't even human.

Justin and I were doing better this week, which made me feel even guiltier. I could tell he felt bad about blowing me off that night I came home from Sanguine. There were little things I noticed, like setting the timer on the coffee maker to start brewing when I got up for work. The laundry

I'd been nagging about finally got sorted, washed, dried, and put away.

When I came home from work at six a.m., he'd pull his headphones aside, say, "Hey babe. How was it?" and we'd get ready for bed together.

One morning while we'd been brushing our teeth before bed, he took hold of my wrist and examined the two puncture wounds that had begun to scab over.

"What happened there?" He'd asked, concern in his tone.

My mind stuttered with a rush of panic and guilt. I'd never expected him to notice or care. How fucked up was that? This was my partner, the man I loved. Here he was, expressing worry over my injury and it shocked me into scrambling for an answer.

"Oh! Just...hit a thorny bush on a hike."

I'd never been good at lying. My already-heavy guilt folded over on itself, doubling in mass and density. If Justin sensed my bullshit, he didn't comment on it.

He'd fall asleep immediately when we went to bed together, which meant sex still wasn't happening. Still, these quiet, domestic moments were the most intimacy I'd had in recent months.

*Breadcrumbs*, my resentment demon whispered in my ear. *He's doing the absolute bare minimum. Tossing you breadcrumbs. And look at you, eating them up so gratefully.*

The resentment wasn't as strong over the past few days, so it was easier to ignore that voice. I was happier with the effort Justin was putting in. Besides, it wasn't fair to expect perfection.

Lots of guys weren't romantic. Plenty of men didn't want to get vulnerable and talk about their feelings. That didn't mean they were bad partners. They did their best, and I knew Justin was trying. I had to remember to appreciate the small things.

It took two to tango, as the saying went. I had to open myself up to him too. Months of arguments, rejections, and ruts had closed me off emotionally. If we were going to reach a better place in our relationship, I had to take accountability for my part.

A good girlfriend didn't receive almost-orgasms from other people, period. A good girlfriend didn't lie about wounds on her wrist. A good girlfriend would put a gag on that annoying little demon and address issues before they became resentment.

My obsession with that vampire and that world was a symptom of trying to run away from my relationship issues. Why was it so important to prove it was real, anyway? Because I needed something real and concrete to hold onto when it felt like Justin was slipping away?

Maybe some things were better off as mysteries. Blips and anomalies happened during scientific observations all the time. I was too curious for my own good, and maybe the two worlds were never meant to overlap. It would certainly be safer to leave well enough alone.

I closed my eyes to the sounds of Justin snoring softly next to me. My decision was made.

No more looking for escape from my own circumstances. No more searching for a vampire world.

———

It only took a week for everything to fall apart.

I was putting on makeup in the bathroom, excited for our first real date in months. Justin and I planned to check out a new restaurant for dinner, maybe go for a walk by the water if the night wasn't too chilly. Something simple and lowkey, but another chance for us to reconnect and find the spark we'd lost.

So when he called out, "I'll see you later, babe!" from the living room, I was utterly confused.

"Wait. What?" I came out of the bathroom laughing, because this had to be a joke. "Where are you going?"

Justin was putting on his shoes by the front door and looked irritated by the question. "Poker tournament at Mike's. The same one I go to every month."

My mouth fell open. "Are you kidding me? That's tonight?"

"Uh, yeah."

"Did you forget that we also made plans for tonight?"

"That's tomorrow, isn't it?"

"No, Justin. We agreed on Saturday. You said you had nothing else going on."

"Oh." He had the nerve to wince. "I didn't realize."

"We talked about it on Tuesday. I literally had my calendar out on my phone and asked if you were *sure*."

"Yeah. Sorry, babe. I just didn't think."

A long, tense silence passed. I crossed my arms, waiting. Surely he would do more than say a lame *Sorry, babe*. Surely he would take this opportunity to make his priorities clear.

After a few more seconds of awkwardly staring at each other, he broke eye contact to tie his shoes.

"You're still going?!" I cried out in disbelief.

*Are you really surprised?* my resentment demon whispered.

"I paid my buy-in already," Justin argued. "I'll lose money if I don't go."

"Not as much as you'll lose when you show up to play."

"Oh, come on." He finished with his shoes and stood to full height. "I don't always lose. You sure don't complain when I come home with an extra three hundred bucks."

"Oh yeah. *Wow*, three hundred whole dollary-doos." I widened my eyes to lay on the sarcasm even thicker. "That'll go a long way toward getting us out of this apartment and into a house. Oh wait. Actually it won't because that money will go right up in smoke in the next poker tournament."

Justin only muttered something under his breath that sounded like, "I don't need this shit," as he shrugged on a jacket.

"You're actually doing this?" I said. "Playing cards with your buddies over the dinner that *we* planned?"

"I seriously thought it was tomorrow," he said, like that excused his actions right then.

"Because you were tuning me out while I set the date! Is it so hard to just listen to me? To prioritize me?"

"When you're being like this," he flung an arm in my direction, "yeah, you make it kind of hard."

I turned my back to face him so he wouldn't see the hot, angry tears brimming in my eyes. "Whatever. Just go."

I didn't have to tell him twice. The door opened and then closed behind him without another word.

With him gone, it felt slightly easier to breathe. My chest didn't feel like it was going to explode with every moment of disappointment I'd swallowed in this relationship. But I was restless. Angry. I had pent-up frustration that I needed to let out.

And I was all dolled up with nowhere to go.

Moving on autopilot, I put on my hiking shoes and grabbed my longest coat from the closet. An hour later, just after dusk, I stood at the base of the hill, watching the lively vampire city wake from a daytime slumber.

I barely remembered driving or trekking through the woods. In my blinding frustration at Justin, it almost felt like the vampire world put me in a trance and drew me here with the tug of a gentle string. I fully intended to stay away from this place. But I couldn't stay in that apartment, and I was already here. Exploring would certainly burn off some energy.

Turning to a shop window, I did a quick check of my face and hair to make sure I didn't get dirt anywhere embarrassing.

"You look lovely, darling."

I startled at the voice, then tried to smooth over my embarrassment with a laugh. "Oh, thank you."

The speaker, a woman with dark red, almost burgundy eyes, smiled broadly as she unlocked the door of the shop where I'd been checking my reflection. She looked middle-aged and her grin was full of fangs.

"Whoever drinks from you tonight is a lucky one. Have a nice evening."

She went inside before I could reply, flicking on a light switch that powered a red neon sign in the front window. The sign read *Costanza's Finest Darakt.*

*What the hell is darakt?* I wondered, watching as she turned more lights on inside. I gathered it was some kind of tobacco or marijuana product from all the smoking paraphernalia on display.

I kept walking, trying to keep track of where I was going, and not get so distracted by my surroundings that I ended up lost. Luckily the blood bank was a good landmark, being the tallest and brightest structure in the general area.

Keeping the stark white building in my periphery, I

made my way deeper into the city. Buildings became smaller and more packed together, the sidewalks and streets narrower. I sidled my way past dozens of red-eyed vampires, hardly any of them giving me a second glance. Some were smoking cigarettes that produced red smoke with an herbal and metallic smell. It wasn't a bad smell, but I couldn't shake the idea that blood was in those rolled-up pieces of paper.

The area was well-lit thanks to tall street lamps and the various shops and businesses throwing off their own lights. Some restaurants had outdoor patios with fire pits and string lights around their perimeters. Whether by all the lights or the weather or the hundreds of people out and about, the night air was comfortably warm.

"Coming up on your right!" someone called over the roar of a motorcycle engine.

I looked behind me and darted away from the edge of the sidewalk just as the bike and its rider zipped past me. The vampire driving glanced over his shoulder at me with a quick, fanged smirk before facing forward again.

My hand came to my chest as I tried to get my heartbeat under control. I had to be aware of my surroundings without being so jumpy. Getting off the street and sitting down somewhere would definitely help with that.

Ahead of me on the next block was a place called Pulse Point Club and Lounge, which seemed to be exactly what I was looking for. It was one of the few places besides the blood bank that had a second level. I glanced behind me, making sure I could still see the hospital-like building before I crossed the street.

I walked inside to even warmer air and a large, dimly lit room. A well-stocked bar took up the center space, with intimate booths along the walls and a dance floor with a DJ table taking up the rest of the floor. A wide staircase led up to the second floor, which was a loft set up with comfortable furniture and its own miniature bar. The VIP area, I assumed.

There were more people here than I expected, considering it was probably mid-morning for vampires. Couples and even a few throuples cozied up in the booths along the walls. At the bar, people leaned in closely to talk over the bass-heavy music.

The dance floor was mostly filled with women. Human women, I realized after a second glance.

"'Scuse me." Someone, another human woman, squeezed past me from behind and headed straight up the stairs to the loft section.

After realizing I'd been taking in everything from the doorway, and therefore blocking the entrance, I took a few steps forward. My nerves eased at seeing so many humans around and I gathered enough courage to slide into an empty seat at the bar.

"Be right with you," said the bartender, who I was pretty sure was a vampire. I couldn't see their eyes, but there was something in the quality of a vampire's skin that was almost too perfect to be human.

I looked up at the loft section as I waited, noting several human women up there too. Most of them stood around, as if waiting for something. A few had drinks in hand but most didn't. All were beautiful, varying from girl-next-door to ethereal supermodel. Through the spaces between their bodies I saw two men lounging on a couch, although I was too far away to tell if they were vampires or not.

"What can I get you?" The bartender stopped in front of me, red eyes bright. They had an androgynous look with a slender, feminine face, short hair, and dark slacks held up by suspenders over a white buttoned shirt.

"Forgive me if this is a stupid question," I started. "But you do have drinks without blood in them, right?"

The bartender grinned, stopping just short of laughing. "Yes, we definitely do. Almost anything you can get in the human world, you can get here. Unless it's really limited or seasonal."

"Okay, I would love a gin and tonic, then."

"You got it."

As they started making my drink, I suddenly panicked over how I would pay for it. Would a debit or credit card even work here? Did they use dollars or some other currency?

"Um, what kind of payment do you take?"

"Blood."

At my panicked face, the bartender burst out laughing as they set the drink in front of me. "Temkra, I'm kidding. We take all kinds. It costs five, or I can start a tab."

"Five what?"

"What have you got?"

"Uh, dollars?"

"Sure. But if you need change, it won't all be the same currency."

I stared at them for a beat. "What do you mean?"

"So, say you give me a ten. I'll give you back five like this." They opened a drawer and placed a five euro note on the bar. "Or like this." Taking back the five euros, they replaced it with a five British pound note. "Or like this." They placed a US dollar, a Canadian dollar, a Fijian dollar, a Dominican peso, and an Egyptian pound below the British fiver.

"No way, you're kidding." I picked up one of the foreign bills to examine more closely. "This is how you use money here?"

"Yeah." The bartender shrugged. "As long as it's got the right number on it, we take it."

"This is wild. Do you take Monopoly money?"

"No." They laughed. "I'm pretty sure it has to have been legal tender at some point in time."

"How did you even get so many different kinds?"

"From humans like you, venturing from your world to ours."

I glanced at them over the Fijian dollar in my hands. "I'm that obvious, huh?"

"Just a little." They pinched their thumb and forefinger close together.

"And you're okay with that? Us coming to your world."

The bartender placed a forearm down and leaned toward me. "No offense, but I think we could take you guys if we had to."

I let out a laugh. "Yeah, that's probably true."

"And anyway, most humans who end up here don't come with bad intentions. They usually end up staying."

"Really?" My eyebrows went up. As fascinating as this world was, I couldn't imagine leaving my whole life behind.

"Yeah I'd say eighty percent, roughly." The bartender leaned back, grinning wryly as they returned the money to the drawer. "I'll let you enjoy your drink and check on you in a bit. Just flag me down if you want to start a tab or close out right away."

I appreciated the peace to sit with the new information I'd learned. It seemed I wasn't the first human to randomly stumble upon Sanguine, nor would I be the last.

The prepper community I'd run into my first time seemed like they'd been here for several generations. A couple hundred years or so. I wondered if their ancestors had been occultists or something, searching for a supernatural world. Or if they had been like me, and stumbled their way into Sanguine completely by accident.

After sipping my drink for a few minutes, a commotion drew my attention toward the VIP loft. The women were raising their voices, shouting and arguing loud enough to be heard over the music. They appeared to huddle around something, packing in tightly with their backs facing me. The couch where the two men sat was now completely hidden from view.

All at once, something made the women draw back with a collective gasp. A man surged to his feet, his head and shoulders visible above the crowd closing in on him once again. My muscles locked with tension at the sight of his face. Even from a distance, I could tell he wasn't human.

The sight of him stopped my breath. He was definitely a vampire. Even taking that into account, he was...something else.

His eyes were on the lighter side of the red spectrum, a bit more magenta than true red. He was tall, with bone structure that looked straight out of an illustration or a Greek statue because it was too beautiful to be real. His hair was a pale ash blond, cut close to his scalp with longer, messy waves on top.

I couldn't stop staring, and not only because he was beautiful to look at. My instincts prickled on high alert, and I didn't want to take my eyes off of what was surely a predator.

There was something feral about him, an untamed wildness in his gaze. A sharpness to his features that indicated hunger and struggle. He wasn't gaunt by any means, but this vampire almost looked more animal than human.

Whatever he hungered for didn't seem to be in the beautiful women surrounding him. His lips peeled back in a snarl, exposing long, white fangs. I could almost hear the growl rumbling in his throat. A feminine hand reached out to him, looking like it was going to caress his jaw or neck, but he smacked the hand away like it was a fly buzzing around his head.

The effect rippled throughout the crowd of women. Some drew back in fear while others made their way closer to the vampire, willing to take their chances. The more they crowded him, the more agitated he seemed to become. His friend, a darker-haired vampire stepped in, spreading his arms to create space as he tried to placate the women.

Then the feral vampire looked up.

Magenta eyes locked onto mine with laser focus and an intensity I couldn't escape. He stared at me like the women surrounding him didn't exist.

I knew then that the predator had sighted his prey. He'd found what would curb his hunger. That gaze showed no intention of letting me go.

Deep, hindbrain instincts told me to run. And yet, I couldn't bring myself to move. I couldn't help but wonder what would happen if this beautiful, dangerous creature captured me.

The vampire pushed his way past the crowd of fawning women as if they were curtains in a doorway. He gripped the railing at the edge of the loft, large hands and broad shoulders bunched with tension as he stared down at me.

He only stared for a few seconds before he vaulted *over*

the railing, the movement as quick and fluid as an Olympic athlete. Before I could make a sound or react in any way, he landed lightly on his feet.

Red eyes ablaze and a fanged smirk on his mouth, he started toward me.

# Chapter 6

## *Laith*

After two weeks of my glass slipper prince bullshit, I felt like I was losing my Temkra-loving mind.

Women came to Pulse Point every single night, swearing they had been at the blood bank that night and were sure they were the one I was looking for.

Their faces blurred in my mind, all meaningless and a waste of time. My body rejected the wrong blood with every cell and never failed to let me know. I was fatigued, sluggish, yet couldn't sleep restfully. My fangs throbbed with a constant ache. My stomach cramped and roiled with every wrong mouthful of blood I choked down.

I hated this. Hated every minute of it. Hated the fakeness of the women trying to get a cushy life as a mate to someone in the ruling clan. Hated being the asshole who said, "No, I'm sorry. It's not you," hundreds of times.

Some women actually had the gall to argue with me.

"Taste my blood," one said, thrusting her wrist insistently toward my face. "Taste me and you'll remember. You'll see."

"You don't have a tattoo on your arm," I said. It was

gentler than telling her she just didn't smell right. None of them did.

"That wasn't a real tattoo. I put on a temporary one for a party."

"Okay. What was it again?"

She paused for a bit too long. "A rose."

I shook my head, suppressing a growl then rubbed my temples. "No. Next."

Des had taken her firmly by the shoulders and turned her toward the stairs of the VIP loft. And on and on it went.

The nights had started out optimistic. *Maybe this time she'll really come,* I thought. *Maybe this is the night she'll be here.* I couldn't picture her face or body, but my imagination conjured up a fuzzy fantasy. She'd waltz in and our eyes would meet. She'd smile playfully, and both of us would instantly know.

"Sorry I took so long," she'd say.

"You're worth the wait," I'd answer.

Then I'd take her in my arms, Des would usher all the other women out, and we'd spend the entire night in the VIP loft getting to know each other properly before I took her back to the Blood 'til Dawn compound. There, she would meet everyone and become friends with Tavia, Bea, and Amy. Even the surliest of us, Thorne and Rhain, would be charmed by her.

My mate would have everything she needed, whatever her hobbies and interests were. Cyan thought he was hot shit by planting a vineyard and cider orchards for Tavia? If my mate liked flying planes, I'd build her a hangar and a fucking runway. Top that, Cyan.

All I needed in return was her blood. If she ended up loving me, that'd be great too. Blood mate bonds aside, I knew those feelings couldn't be forced. I was idealistic, not naive.

But nights passed. Faces and names blurred into each other. My hope dwindled and my desperation grew. The women who approached me began to look more fearful, or at least cautious. Over time, I could feel myself devolving into a snarling, hungry beast. My jokes and ability to carry on conversations were replaced by short, irritable words and gnashing of my fangs. My thoughts became jumbled and gaps formed in my memory.

I was fucking losing it. And the reality that I might actually die if I didn't find her hung around my neck like an anchor.

Why didn't she come? We put messages out as far and wide as possible, even sending feelers out into other territories and the human world. Des used a site called Craigslist and posted in the missed connections section. It sounded far-fetched to me, but he insisted it was something lots of humans used.

"Don't worry, it's vaguely worded. But if she reads it, she'll know," he said when he set it up.

"Any hits on that post?" I asked, my voice raw with hunger and exhaustion.

"No, nothing viable." Des scrolled through his phone, his expression passive. "Lots of human men sending dick photos, though."

"Why do they always do that?"

"No idea." Des shook his head and shuddered. "That one definitely needs a doctor," he muttered, swiping and deleting.

I slouched on the loveseat, ignoring the many voices of women trying to get my attention. They were nothing but noise to me. Noise and pheromones that smelled wrong.

Blood that tasted wrong. My stomach gave a shuddering little gurgle at the thought of tasting another one of them tonight.

Bone marrow from a mukrot was the only thing that helped with symptoms of starvation. Marrow was rich in nutrients and, when freshly prepared by a Marrower vampire, soothed my stomach and temporarily eased the ache in my fangs. But, as a replacement for actual blood, it could only go so far.

By the fourteenth night of scenting, tasting, and being lied to by dozens of human women, I'd had enough.

I was sick of searching faces, of breathing in scents that weren't hers. This whole fucking Cinderella thing was pointless. All it did was expose how much humans were willing to lie for their own gain.

If I was a different kind of vampire, I might take my pick. Settle for the one who tasted the least revolting. Maybe even take a few home. The days of having harems of blood pets were mostly gone but some still did it, as long as their care could be afforded and the arrangement was consensual.

But that wasn't me. I wanted none of them.

"Fuck this," I growled, rising to my feet.

The sudden movement startled the surrounding women, making them draw back with a collective gasp. If I were well-fed I'd apologize, crack a joke, make an effort to make them feel comfortable. But all I could feel was frustration clawing under my skin. So many unique blood sources and all of them were wrong.

On the bright side, being taller than them allowed me to suck in a lungful of fresh air. Air that wasn't tainted by the scent of wrongness, but carried a hint of something sweet and floral.

All my senses sharpened. I *knew* that scent. How could I forget when it floated over so gently from the far side of a privacy screen, and had been accompanied by the sweetest blood I'd ever tasted?

She was *here.*

My jaws parted, fangs hitting their maximum length as if her scent itself could nourish me. *Where is she? Where—*

Movement at the corner of my eye threatened to invade my space, and I smacked it away with an animalistic snarl. There were still too many wrong scents here, threatening to overpower the right one. If only I could see her.

*There.*

There was no second-guessing with blood mates. It was instant. Instinctual. I knew who it was the moment I laid eyes on her.

A woman sitting at the bar on the lower floor. Wavy hair the color of dark honey spilled over her shoulders. Lush lips parted in a soft gasp when her wide blue eyes met mine.

She recognized me too, even if she didn't know how or why yet. I saw it in how still she became. She knew I was a predator, but she wouldn't run. Her instincts knew her blood was meant to nourish me.

My blood mate had come after all, and for the first time in many very long days, hope re-emerged.

I decided to not bother with the stairs and jumped over the loft railing. My gaze remained locked to hers the whole time. I could barely feel my feet move as I approached her. She might as well had been drawing me in with a homing beacon.

Her scent became stronger the closer I got. It felt like I had been trapped in a dank cellar and was now taking deep, refreshing breaths for the first time in weeks. I wanted, no, *needed* her in my lungs, my pores, on my tongue, and sinking into every groove in my brain.

I came to a stop in front of her and realized I should say something before gorging myself on her blood.

"I recognized your scent," I choked out. Her forearm, with its odd geometrical design, caught my eye. "And you have the tattoo."

"Oh?" She looked down at her arm like she'd forgotten it was there.

"You still have the marks." I moved slowly to not startle her, bringing my fingertips the points on her wrist where my fangs had been. "I didn't get the chance to heal them closed."

It felt like a lame excuse. I was supposed to take care of my blood mate, and that included licking her wounds closed so they would heal faster and not become infected.

Her large blue eyes widened in surprise, giving her a doll-like appearance. Fuck, she was pretty. *So* pretty.

"You," she said, realization lighting up her face. "*You're* the one who fed from me?"

"Yes."

There was so much I wanted to say, so many ways I'd imagine this moment would go. But my mind was blank with awe, filled with her delightful scent but not a single coherent thought. Her heartbeat picked up speed in my ears, making my fangs ache with the memory of her perfect blood.

"I've finally found you. My blood mate." I could only marvel as I drew closer, needing another inhale of that scent like a drug.

She was finally here. Finally mine.

"I'm your what?"

A chuckle escaped as I pulled her flush to me. She was

funny too. It was cute how she pretended to have no idea. Why else would she be here?

I bent to kiss her and the world melted away.

Her mouth was so soft, and the soft gasp of breath lit up all my senses. I dipped my tongue between her parted lips and tasted gin, tonic water, and a hint of lime. The inside of her mouth was a cocoon of warmth I wanted to savor and sink into.

My mate's mouth didn't move, so I pulled lightly at her top lip, encouraging her to explore and respond. I wanted to learn how she kissed, to find out what she liked best so I could give it to her over and over.

The next thing I knew, palms shoved hard at my chest and she broke away.

"What the fuck are you doing?" she demanded loudly.

Nearby conversations stopped and I sensed heads swiveling in our direction.

I attempted a smile, but panic stormed inside me. Where had I gone wrong?

"It's just a kiss," I said. "We don't have to go any further. Unless you wanted to, that is. Which I am extremely down for, by the way." I lifted my palms in a surrendering gesture. "But totally good if you're not."

Her eyes that had been wide and doll-like a moment ago narrowed into slits of anger. "Why would I do that? I don't even know you."

"Because you're my blood mate." What sounded obvious to me seemed to be lost on her. "That's why you came here, isn't it?"

"No. I don't even know what that means."

"You don't?"

"No! Why would I?"

"You don't know who I am? What clan I'm part of?"

"Again, no. But if you could clue me in on all of that, that'd be great."

She crossed her arms, frustrated, while mine fell limply to my side in disbelief. Holy fucking Temkra, she had no idea. She'd never seen any of the territory-wide text alerts or the Craigslist posts. She was just a human getting a drink at the bar.

I rubbed the back of my neck, which felt uncomfortably tight. "I feel like we need to start over. I'm Laith, and I'm sorry about the kiss. I really thought we were on the same page."

The woman was quiet for several long seconds. "I'm Heather."

Heather. Even her name was so soft and pretty in my mouth. "Can I ask where you're from, Heather?"

Another long silence. "California."

"Ah, human world." I nodded, trying to recall what I knew about the United States, one of the biggest countries. "That's the one with Hollywood and avocados and shit, right?"

Her lips twitched like she was suppressing a smile. "Not exactly in my neck of the woods, but close enough."

"Okay. Do you know where you are now and what I am?"

"Sanguine. And I assume you're a vampire."

"Great." I smiled and for the first time in my life, felt self-conscious of my fangs. Her eyes went right to them with a mixture of curiosity and fear. "Just trying to find out where your baseline of knowledge is."

"I don't know much, but this isn't my first time in this world." She gestured toward me. "I mean, obviously you know that."

"Right." I gripped the back of a stool and stared blankly

at the bar. This was not how I'd expected this to go, and I'd have to rethink my whole approach. "Can we sit down somewhere, Heather?"

Her stare became suspicious. "Sit down where? Why?"

"To explain the whole blood mate thing. No kissing, I promise. Though, if you want to kiss, you can lay one on me whenever you want."

She didn't seem thrilled by the offer, but not entirely repulsed by it either. Her elevated heartbeat had calmed. Those wide eyes darted all over me with an analytical curiosity, like she was filing away data to comb through at a later date. There was a sharpness about her that intrigued me greatly.

"So." I slid into the barstool next to her, angling the chair to give her a bit more room. "When I fed from you, did you feel anything?"

"No."

Her heartbeat quickened just before she said the word, and I could almost taste the blood rising to flush her neck and face. *My little liar,* I mused.

She didn't want to admit being aroused by the feeding. Why? Because I was essentially a stranger to her?

I let it go for now.

"Humans aren't my usual preference," I said. "To my kind, your blood tastes watered down. Bland."

Heather's brows knitted together almost like she was offended. "What else do you feed on?"

"Other vampires are most common. The flavor of our blood varies, but we usually find it very hearty and comforting. Dragon shifters from the neighboring territory have a rich, spicy taste to them. Do you know what a brusang is?"

"Uh, yes." Heather nodded. "A human who was given vampire blood shortly after death."

"Correct." I grinned, pleased with how much she knew already. "They taste a bit like watered-down vampire. Not quite as bland as a human, but not as potent as my own kind."

"I see." Heather's shoulders were tense. Her gaze continued flitting over me, but also toward the exits.

"I'm not going to hurt you." I could sense her fight or flight response like it was a neon sign. "We don't harm humans here, even when feeding outside the blood bank. Vampires recognize you as a fellow sentient species."

That had been a fairly recent development in vampire society, but she didn't need to know the gory details of the past.

"I'm not worried about that." She frowned like she was confused by her own admission. "I mean, I can't believe I'm having this conversation. This doesn't feel *real*."

"You had my fangs in your wrist. This is very real."

"I know. Just letting it sink in, I guess. Anyway, go on." She met my eyes, resting her forearm on the bar. "You were saying I tasted bland?"

"No, that's the thing. I expected you to, but you tasted incredible. The best blood I've ever had."

My mouth watered at the memory, and my stomach growled with hunger. Every instinct screamed at me to just grab her. Find a vein and quench this burning thirst. But she was more than just a meal. I wanted her to trust me. To understand me.

"Your flavor was indescribable," I went on. "I couldn't get enough. It didn't really hit me until your wrist was taken away, but I felt like...like I would kill to taste you again. And that was when I knew."

Heather tensed again, her heartbeat elevating as she leaned back slightly. "Knew what?"

"That you were my blood mate. Your blood, and yours alone, is suited perfectly to my needs. My brain recognized it before I did. That was why you tasted so good. My body, instincts, whatever you call it, had found the perfect source and now nothing else will satisfy." I grinned, the utter joy and relief of having found her washing over me again. "So, what do you think?"

"Hold on. Pause." Heather held up a palm while pinching her nose bridge with the other hand. "What do you mean, it perfectly suits your needs? What is it about my blood in particular?"

I shrugged. "I don't know. All I can say is, whatever's in your blood, in whatever ratios or amounts, tastes like a fucking dream and makes me feel...like I've never felt before."

Heather stared at me like I'd begun speaking a foreign language. "I'm sorry, but that's literally impossible."

"It is a rarity. Well, two other people I know found their blood mates pretty recently, which might have been a fluke. But now that it's happened to me"—I let my grin spread wide—"it feels like a blessing."

"Listen, Laith." She paused, crossed her legs and I enjoyed the brief lull, soaking in the way she spoke my name. "I actually know blood pretty well for a human."

"Do you?"

"Yes, I test and analyze it and make reports based on my findings all the time. It's part of my job."

"Really?" I couldn't help but lean into her, fascinated. "What do you do?"

She hesitated. "I work in a crime lab. I test evidence from crime scenes."

Oh shit. She was smart. Like *smart* smart. Which meant I was fucking doomed.

Remembering to give her space, I drew back. "Wow. So you're, what, like a science person?"

She gave a humble little shrug and nodded. "Forensic scientist is my official title, yes."

"Damn, that's...impressive."

What I really wanted to say was, *that's so fucking hot,* but I had a feeling she wouldn't be receptive to it. Not yet anyway.

"Thank you."

Her eye contact shifted away briefly while she played with a lock of her hair. Someone wasn't accustomed to receiving compliments. Interesting.

"Anyway my point is, human blood is basically all made up of the same components. The little variance that does exist from person to person would not be enough to determine if I was your...your blood mate."

"But human blood is only one half of the equation," I pointed out. "You don't know vampire blood. Or any vampire anatomy, I imagine. How do you know there isn't something in my biology that recognizes an ideal food source in yours?" When Heather gave no answer to that, I said, "See? Not as dumb as I look."

"You don't look dumb," she blurted out and blushed.

"Aw, that's the sweetest thing anyone's ever said to me."

She actually laughed into her hand that time, then shook a finger at me. "That's right. I remember you've got jokes."

"That's not the only thing I got."

She shook her head, fighting a grin. "I can see where this is going and I'm not walking into it." Before I could deliver a witty comeback, she sobered. "Okay, so assuming this blood mate thing is real, what then? We set up regular appointments at the blood bank or what?"

"No." I stifled a laugh. Her naivety about my world was an adorable contrast to how intelligent she truly was. "No, blood mates are so much more than that. It's not just finding an ideal food source. It's...a bond. A connection that goes deeper than taking blood. In exchange for your blood, I'm expected to take care of you. To provide for you, keep you comfortable and happy. Satisfied."

Heather became statue-still as I spoke, but her heartbeat quickened at a rapid rate.

"Do you get what I'm saying?" I asked during her silence.

"That sounds..." She wet her lips on a deep breath and started over. "That sounds an awful lot like a romantic relationship."

"Oh, it absolutely is." I nodded. "Blood mates stay bonded for a lifetime and they're exclusive partners in every way."

I didn't know Heather's eyes could get any bigger, but impressively, they did. "And that's what you expect out of... this?" She gestured between the two of us.

"Well, we can take things slowly. I have all the time in the world, and I would like to get to know you." I gave my best non-threatening smile, which was quite a feat with hunger making my fangs so long. "This is strange to you and I get that. We can figure something out, and then seal the deal with a ceremony whenever you're ready."

"No, I'm sorry." She shook her head and began fidgeting in her chair, making subtle movements like she wanted to leave. "You seem nice and all, but I can't do anything like that. I'm already with someone."

"Oh." The solution was clear to me. "Well, obviously, you have to break it off."

Heather blinked and then her eyes narrowed. "What?"

"You have to end it. This is with a human partner, I assume?"

"Yes." The word dropped harshly from her mouth. "I'm not leaving my boyfriend of five years. We're serious. We live together."

"Serious?" I couldn't help but laugh at that. "I've seen your TV shows. You make vows to each other for life, then split within a decade. You promise to love in sickness and in health, then sneak around with affairs and gambling debt. You marry for health insurance, citizenship of another country, status, wealth. Serious?" I laughed again. "Humans don't know what serious means."

"We're not all like that," Heather shot back. "TV doesn't always reflect real life. There are plenty of humans in happy, lifelong relationships."

"What's your divorce rate again? Fifty percent, was it?"

"And dropping. What's yours?"

I grinned. "Zero, because we don't get married."

"And you say humans don't take relationships seriously?"

"Nothing is more serious and committed than blood mates," I said. "But what makes a mated pair is out of our control. It's one part biological compatibility, one part divine fate."

Heather gave me an incredulous look. "Fate? Really?"

"Yes." I held up my hands and wiggled my fingers. "Call it magic, divinity, whatever you want. But it's true that our matron goddess Temkra has a hand in choosing mate pairings. Quite a matchmaker, she is."

"I don't believe in magic," Heather deadpanned.

"It doesn't matter what you believe. It simply *is*."

"All right, well." Heather slid from her barstool, careful to not brush against any part of me as she shouldered her purse. "This has been a fascinating conversation, but I've had enough for one night. Nice to meet you, Laith."

With a determined stride, she started toward the door.

"When will you be back?" I called before she could get too far. "I kind of need your blood to live, remember? You wouldn't want my death on your hands."

She paused and looked at me over her shoulder. "I'm sorry, but I didn't sign up for this blood mate thing. I wish you the best."

"At least admit I'm funnier than your boyfriend!"

She carried on without looking back, despite my yell across the room. I only saw a flash of her side profile as she went out the front door and turned onto the street, but I swore a smile curved her lips in that moment.

*She's going back to him,* I thought bitterly. The human she chose years before she even knew I existed.

The thought of her with someone else soured my stomach almost as much as all the rancid blood that wasn't hers. But it truly didn't matter that she had another partner at the moment. Heather was still my blood mate. Her care and safety was my responsibility.

I only waited a beat before leaving the club, and began to follow her from a distance.

# Chapter 7

## *Heather*

I walked to the edge of the vampire city, up the hill, and through the woods as if in a trance. My body was on autopilot but my mind was back in that club, sitting with Laith at the bar. From the moment I walked out to when I reached my car, I asked myself several times why I had been so quick to leave.

The logical answer was simple. I had a life. A job I worked hard for, and a partner I hoped to spend the rest of my days with. It would be insane to give up everything I had to become a vampire's wife-slash-meal.

And yet there was a discomforting tug pulling me back in the direction of Sanguine. Back to the tall vampire with an angel's face and a demon's teeth.

Laith was deadly, there was no doubt in my mind about that. My instincts had been on edge throughout our entire conversation, like something deep in my DNA recognized him as a natural predator.

That kiss, brief as it was, felt like licking honey off the edge of a knife. Sweet and a little dangerous. I could still feel the press of his lips and the long fangs just inside his mouth. His tongue flicking inside for that curious, playful moment had done too much to me for such a small action. Sensation had rippled over my whole body during that kiss, and that was exactly why I'd stopped him. Exactly why I didn't stay.

I left because I had to. Because talking to him felt too much like flirting, which felt like a betrayal. Because in the brief few times he touched me, my physical response had been more intense than it had been in years with Justin.

It wasn't until I'd been sitting in my car for a few minutes that I realized I had completely forgotten to take any pictures or video.

"Goddamn it," I groaned, scrubbing my hands over my face.

Even before I'd seen Laith, documenting had slipped my mind. I was too fascinated by my surroundings, like all the mismatched currency the bartender had shown me. And after Laith and I began talking? It felt like nothing existed outside of him and me.

Just another reason why I had to remove myself from the situation.

My fingers drummed on the steering wheel as I started the drive home. If I went back to Sanguine again to document proof, chances were good I'd run into Laith again. He seemed like a dog after a bone. A little obsessive, to put it lightly. The guy basically said we, despite being total strangers, were destined to live happily ever after, and he was more than ready to start our life together.

As if that wasn't a blinking neon sign to stay the hell away. Not just from him, but Sanguine altogether.

The whole concept of blood mates was crazy to me. Absolutely bananas. Not to mention presumptuous as hell. How were two complete strangers supposed to deal with the fact that they were expected, even predestined, to become life partners? It sounded like disaster and a lifetime of misery waiting to happen.

And strangely, I wasn't as pissed off or horrified by the idea as I expected myself to be. I could probably do worse than someone as hot and funny as Laith.

A smile broke out across my face, remembering his silly little quips and comments. The playfulness in his magenta eyes and those fanged smiles that made my heart skip a beat, and not entirely out of fear.

Yeah, I could certainly do worse. The fact that he seemed all-in, ready to do the vampire equivalent of walking down the aisle and saying vows, was oddly flattering.

But he didn't even know me, so how could any of it be genuine?

*You're flattered by the attention of a stranger because your relationship hasn't moved toward real commitment in years.*

Ah, there she was. My little resentment demon back to haunt me again.

"I love Justin," I said out loud, as if that would make the declaration more real. "We may not be married yet, but we *are* serious about each other, no matter what some vampire says. We're committed. And I won't do anything to jeopardize that."

*Keep telling yourself that,* my resentment demon said. *And are you 100% sure Justin feels the same way?*

"Course he does," I muttered.

Still, the doubts lingered. They came and went in waves throughout our whole relationship, but were more frequent over the past year. Since we'd moved in together, honestly. But was there a single couple out there who had zero doubts of their partner's feelings? No one was *that* certain about their relationship, were they?

I pulled into my apartment complex, feeling victorious about seeing our covered spot open until I remembered that Justin would be gone all night playing poker.

Part of me felt relieved. The other part was filled with longing. I missed us, how close and loving we used to be. While I enjoyed having our place to myself, I couldn't shake the feeling that he'd rather see his friends than spend time with me.

We might need to have a talk. Again.

I should have been more vigilant as I got out of the car. Even though I could see the front door from the parking spot, I should have been watching the shadows.

Then I might have been able to see him coming.

"You don't know when to quit, do you?"

By the time my head snapped around in the direction of the voice, he'd already clamped a hand on my upper arm and roughly spun me to face him.

I stared in confusion and rising fear, recognizing the man who'd bumped into me last week. He still had that clean-cut, all-American look, but his eyes held annoyance, even contempt. His lips pressed together into an aggravated line.

"Excuse me?" I tried to pull my arm away, but his grip was unrelenting. "Let go of me."

I was alone in the middle of the night, but surely someone in the apartment complex would hear me if I screamed.

"You need to stop visiting that place. It's not safe for civilians." He leaned in, crowding my personal space. "This is your only and last warning."

"What are you talking about?" I demanded.

"Don't play dumb, Heather. You know I'm talking about the hidden place you've been to multiple times. You're messing with something way too dangerous to comprehend."

*He knows about Sanguine?* He wasn't a vampire or a brusang, but one thing was clear. *He knows and he* really *doesn't like that I know.*

"Why's it dangerous?" I demanded. "And how do you know about it?"

He opened one side of his jacket to flash a badge attached to the inner pocket. "The federal government pays me to gather intelligence on that place and other phenomena like it. This is a matter of national security."

"National security?" I repeated. A few puzzle pieces clicked together in my brain. "Did you corrupt those files on my phone when you bumped into me?"

"And took down your blogs and Youtube channels, yes," he said. "Just leave this alone, Heather. Stop the internet searches. Stop going back there. Leave it up to the professionals."

"Hold on." I raised my free hand. "Are you spying on me?"

The man grabbed both of my arms then, and shoved me backwards until I was pressed against the wall of the building. His fingers dug so deeply into my flesh that I whimpered from the pain. Part of me was in disbelief, feeling a strange disconnect from my body. I was too shocked to struggle, not that it would have done any good. He held me pinned to the wall like a butterfly in a shadow box.

"Please, stop. You're hurting me." I wanted to scream, but my voice came out small and terrified.

"Spying is the last thing you need to worry about, Heather," the man hissed. His eyes were so cold, they almost looked dead. "You know how easy it was to make your digital footprint disappear? I can just as easily make *you* disappear if you don't stop fucking around."

Panic made all my systems freeze. I still couldn't find my voice except to mumble, "Okay. Okay."

"I need your verbal confirmation that you won't go back there again."

"Okay, I won't."

"Won't what?"

"I won't go back to...to that place again." I couldn't bring myself to meet his cold, dead eyes, so I stared at his throat column instead, silently begging for this to be over.

Finally, he released his iron grip on my arms. "We'll be watching you." He turned and headed swiftly down the sidewalk.

I hugged myself as soon as he was gone, shocked and unable to move for several long moments. My arms were sore from where he grabbed me, and I was almost certainly bruised.

"What the fuck?" I whispered through my uneven, panicked breaths.

Government operative or not, that guy was a fucking psycho. I was ten times more afraid of him than Laith or any of the people in Sanguine.

And if he really was spying on me, not even the inside of my apartment was safe. But where else could I go? The only place that felt safe was inside those four walls.

I went to my front door, fumbling for my keys with shaking hands. Where the fuck were they?

"Damn it." I dug out my coat, my phone, sunglasses, pens, everything that could possibly get lost in the abyss of a huge purse. Where the hell were my keys? My mind felt like a scrambled mess. I couldn't have driven here without them.

"Heather?"

My head jerked up, and then I froze like an animal trapped in headlights. Laith stood at the end of the walkway, a leather jacket bulking up his frame slightly. A sleek, black motorcycle idled behind him in the lot, rumbling with a low growl.

"What are you doing here?" My back flattened against the door. "Did you follow me too?" I had been so rattled by the guy in the shadows that I hadn't even heard a motorcycle approach.

Laith's eyebrows lifted. "What do you mean, *too?* Did someone else follow you?"

I shook my head, shutting my eyes. All of this was way too much for one night. One lifetime, even.

"How are you even here? *Why* are you here?"

"I wanted to make sure you got home safely." He said it so earnestly, like we'd been on a first date and he was doing the gentlemanly thing of seeing me to my door. "Heather, are you okay?" Laith started toward me. "You're shaking like a leaf. Did someone—"

"Stop." I held my palms out in front of me. "Don't come any closer. Do not fucking touch me."

If I got manhandled again by a stranger, I would lose my everloving shit.

To his credit, Laith stopped short a few feet away from me. His angelic face looked torn, like he wanted to blow past the boundary I set, but chose to restrain himself.

"What happened?" he asked in a soft tone.

"Just some creepy guy. He's gone now, though."

Mentally, I chided myself. Was Laith not just as creepy for following me home from Sanguine? The two situations felt different, although I couldn't place how. Part of me was glad that Laith had showed up. If only he had gotten here a moment sooner.

"How did you even follow me on that thing?" I asked again, nodding at the idling motorcycle.

"Your scent and your heartbeat," Laith said as if it were obvious. "I followed you on foot at first, then had to run back for my bike when I saw you had a vehicle." He frowned and rubbed the back of his neck. "I did get a little lost at first and didn't know which direction to go. But then it was like...I could sense your distress. Something was wrong and your heart was going crazy. I followed that feeling to here." A grin pulled at one side of his mouth. "Told you there was a bond between us."

I chose to ignore that part. "And you can just come here, to this world, whenever you want?"

"Not during the daytime, obviously. But otherwise, yeah. Why not? As long as no one sees my eyes or teeth too closely, I can slip in and out just like you can." His grin grew wider. "There are more of us popping in and out of your world than you realize."

That was not a comforting thought. Especially considering there was some shadowy government agency collecting intelligence on vampires.

Exhaustion sank into my bones. I'd had quite enough for one night. My front door was doing more to keep me upright than my own two feet.

"Well, thanks for looking out for me, I guess. Goodnight, Laith."

I started a half-hearted rummage through my purse again for my keys while Laith continued to stand there. His magenta eyes did not seem to miss anything. Were bruises forming on my upper arms? They sure as hell felt like it.

"Is your boyfriend home?" he asked after a moment.

The smart thing to say would have been a lie. *Yes, he's home and we have guns. Or holy water. Garlands of braided garlic all over the kitchen. Whatever the hell deters vampires.*

Instead, I spoke the truth. "No, he's not home."

Laith gave a small nod. "I should stay with you so you're not alone." He looked toward the eastern sky. "I have to leave before dawn, though. Unless you have a lightproof room I can spend the day in."

"No." I shook my head. "Absolutely not."

"No touching, I promise." Laith brought up his hands, wiggling his long fingers, then brought his wrists together in front of him. "You can even tie me up. Actually..." He let his hands fall to his sides. "Maybe not a good idea. I might enjoy that too much."

For once, my nerves were too frayed and my exhaustion too deep to crack a smile. "You're not coming into my house."

It didn't matter that he was right. That I didn't want to be home alone. Maybe that was the reason I was still out here talking to him. But, whatever the case, letting him into my place was a step too far.

In my mind, bringing Laith inside crossed a bigger line than him kissing me. It was way more than nearly having an orgasm while he drank my blood. Worse than talking to a handsome stranger in a bar.

This was the home I shared with Justin. We made memories within those walls. We made plans, had arguments, and made up from arguments. No matter the cracks in our relationship, it was between us and no one else. This vampire was not part of our life.

Going to the blood bank and then the club had been a mistake. Meeting Laith had been a mistake. He was just a convenient distraction. It was probably better for both of us to never cross paths again.

He didn't push the issue, instead shoving his hands into his jacket pockets. "There's no need to be embarrassed about your secret Beanie Baby collection or whatever you're hiding but, fine." He turned to lean against the exterior wall, propping one booted foot behind him. "I'll keep watch from outside."

Again, I was too exhausted to respond to his joke and felt my teeth grinding. "No, you need to leave. And don't come back here."

His smirk was infuriating. "Worried I'll scare your boyfriend off?"

"No, just... whatever, I don't care. Stay out here or go, just leave me alone."

I patted my jeans pockets and...there were my keys, for fuck's sake. Heaving a sigh of relief, I turned my back on Laith to unlock the door.

"I'm staying." His tone was serious for once. "Sleep well, Heather. No one will bother you until I have to go before sun up."

I didn't respond as I went inside. Didn't even meet his eye as I turned to shut and lock the door.

He would keep his word and stay out there all damn night. For some reason, I knew he would do exactly as he said: keep watch like a loyal bodyguard until he retreated with the darkness of night.

Guilt stabbed through me. Now I felt like an asshole for not letting him in. You were supposed to keep stray animals out of your house, not people trying to help.

I raked my fingers through my hair, blowing out a long breath. "Don't be stupid, Heather," I muttered, digging through my purse for my phone.

Laith's behavior was weird and obsessive. He shouldn't have followed me home, shouldn't have kissed me, shouldn't have insisted on staying all night to protect me. If he were human, I would have called the cops.

So why did I feel a little bit calmer, knowing he was out there? Why did I carry a smidge of regret for not letting him inside?

Once I located my phone in the great purse abyss, I called Justin. His phone rang several times before going to voicemail. Not surprising, but disappointing all the same. I ended the call and typed out a text message.

> Me: Hey, let me know when you're coming home.

I almost added 'miss you' at the end, but ended up deleting the words before hitting Send. I was already needy enough to be texting and calling while he was out with friends.

At least someone wanted to be near me all night. Even if that someone wanted to spend forever drinking my blood.

# Chapter 8

## *Heather*

Drew, my longtime office partner, turned to me in the taco truck line. "Did you hear that Munroe is retiring?"

I was only half listening, my stomach growling at the promise of rich, savory food. "Oh, no kidding? Finally letting go of that cushy supervisor job, huh?"

"More like it's being ripped away because he can't dig his claws in any deeper. I lost count of how many times he's been caught sleeping at his desk. It's a miracle he stayed in for that long."

I snorted. "You applying for it?"

"Nah, I don't think I'd get it. Sergio and Frost have more seniority than me. It'll probably go to one of them."

"And then they'll probably camp there until retirement before letting one of us have a chance at it."

"Yep, that's how it goes."

The mundanity of my every day life was so bizarre compared to everything else. Was it just a few days ago that I had drunk at a bar in the vampire world, then a scary man from a shadowy government organization threatened me to stay away? And then the aftermath, when Laith spent the whole night guarding me from outside.

He'd been long gone by when I woke up late the next morning. I slept better than I'd expected, probably because I knew I wasn't truly alone.

Justin still hadn't come home by then, but I'd received a text saying he spent the night because he didn't want to drive drunk. I almost texted back, *It's okay, it wasn't like I needed you after some guy stalked, grabbed, and threatened me.*

Now, it was a normal Wednesday night shift. Drew and I were on our two a.m. lunch break, gossiping about work while waiting in line for food.

How did a world like this exist alongside one filled with vampires? I had the impulse to turn to Drew and say, *Forget Munroe's retirement. Did you know there's a hidden vampire world less than an hour away? Oh, and a vampire is sort of obsessed with me and I kind of like it even though I shouldn't. Don't look at me like that, vampires are totally real. The government knows about them, and they're harassing me too.*

I was so damn tempted to let it all out. But instead, I stepped up to the window and ordered a chile verde plate with rice, beans, and extra tortillas.

"You and Justin doing anything this weekend?" Drew asked after we paid and stepped aside to wait for our food.

"Uh, no. I don't think we have any plans. How about you guys?"

"Baby shower," he groaned. "Stacy's cousin or somebody, I don't know. I'm just there."

*That's more than I can say about Justin,* I thought. We barely spent time together in the same room anymore. And when we did, I might as well have been alone. Every waking moment seemed to be spent on his phone or gaming with his friends.

Come to think of it, I hadn't seen him logged into his work portal in a while.

*No, don't go there. He'd tell me if something happened with his job.*

*Oh, would he?* My resentment demon mocked me. *Would you bet on it? It doesn't seem like he tells you much of anything lately.*

In an effort to shove my own thoughts away, I nudged Drew with my elbow. "Ah, you'll live."

"Playing those weird baby games?" He shuddered. "I don't know. If I'm not here Monday, you'll know what happened."

I laughed. "You're leaving your purple sticky notes to me in your work will, right?"

"Of course, but I promised my red stress ball to Dinaj."

"That's fair."

A silence lulled between us as we waited for our food. Six more people stood in line to order, and for good reason. This truck had the best local Mexican food. We were lucky they were willing to come out so late for us night-shift workers.

Voices and conversations mixed with the sizzling of the grill. Food orders and workplace gossip. A comforting, familiar bubble that I was once fully encased in.

"Hey. I'll take the carne asada tacos. Thanks."

*Oh fuck.* That voice.

My blood froze and I turned stone-still. Only my eyes moved, inspecting the people in line. No, I hadn't imagined the voice. There he was, the government guy from that night just before Laith showed up. He handed cash to the chef and waited patiently to receive change.

Casually, and yet so deliberately, his head swiveled in my direction with a sly grin. "Hey, Heather. Nice to see you again."

I couldn't speak, couldn't respond in any way, but my mind raced with panic. It had only been four days and I had done everything he told me to do. I hadn't gone back to Sanguine, nor searched online for anything vampire-related. The bruises on my arms were covered by my lab coat, but they throbbed painfully at the memory of him grabbing me and shoving me against the wall. What did he want? Why was he here?

He meandered over slowly, casual and non-threatening in his non-descript jeans and dark bomber jacket. No wonder the government hired him to sneak around. He could blend in anywhere.

"Can I borrow you for a quick minute?" The polite phrasing of the question, along with his classical good looks, would make anyone want to say yes. I only did because I knew there was no other option.

"Sure," I said through a nervous smile that was holding back a scream.

"I'll see you inside," Drew said, oblivious to the hidden danger in front of us. He gave a quick nod to the man, probably assuming he was someone who worked in a different department, then grabbed his Styrofoam container at the pickup window before heading inside.

"Relax," the operative said, standing in Drew's place next to me. "You're not in trouble."

"Then what do you want?" I kept my gaze forward, refusing to look at him.

He was quiet for a few moments, like he wanted to savor my discomfort. "I noticed you had a visitor the other night. Right after we last spoke."

My throat tightened with discomfort. "I never asked him to come see me. I swear."

The guy angled his head toward the food truck. "Chicken chile verde plate with extra tortillas, isn't that you?"

I stole a glance at his smug face before willing my feet to move. Somehow I made it to the pick-up window, got my food, and even left a cash tip in the jar, all while he followed a few feet behind me. I hated having him at my back, hated that he was still following my every move while I went through the motions of normal life.

He got his tacos right after my food came out, then jerked his head to a nearby picnic table. "Let's sit."

I headed in that direction like a robot, marching without a single word. This guy had to be messing with me, and I hoped my lack of reaction would get him to leave sooner. He seemed to be in no hurry, though, and dug into his tacos the moment we sat down. I, on the other hand, had lost my appetite.

"So what's this about?" I asked.

He chewed his food slowly, then his throat bobbed as he swallowed. "I feel like we got off on the wrong foot the other night. I'm Soren, by the way."

I let the silence drag out, my expression blank. Like hell was I going to say, *nice to meet you.* It probably wasn't even his real name.

Soren wiped his fingers on a paper napkin as he studied me. "You know I had to report seeing your visitor to my superiors. He seemed very protective. I'd even say smitten with you."

"I didn't do anything to encourage that." Like hell I was going to get in trouble over what Laith chose to do.

"I'm not saying you did. But my superiors came to the

conclusion that this...*person's* infatuation with you could be useful."

"Useful?"

"For gathering intelligence. We want to learn about these people, after all."

I waited for him to elaborate further, but he kept digging into his tacos.

"What's that got to do with me?"

Soren finished chewing, swallowed, and wiped his mouth again. "My superiors are permitting you to return to *that* place on our orders. For the sole purpose of gathering information and reporting back to me."

An incredulous huff left my mouth before I could stop it. "And why the hell would I do that?"

"Because you don't have a choice." Soren crumpled his napkin in his fist. "You can be a loose end we need to tie off, or you can serve your country and be useful."

I shoved my to-go container of food further away, the smell of meat and spices making my stomach turn.

"Why me?"

"Again, he seems infatuated with you. It will be much easier for you to collect information than me or any of our other operatives."

I wanted to put my forehead down on the table and not look up until Soren had disappeared for good. Laith might have been a little intense, but he was nice and seemed to have good intentions. It felt wrong to use his feelings for me to feed information to some shadowy operation.

"Why do you look upset?" Soren's smile was slow and calculating. "I know you want to go back there. This way, you can do so with no consequences. Ditch your boring life and your unemployed loser boyfriend for something new and exciting, then tell me all about it. It's easy."

"Wait, stop." I held up a hand. "What are you saying? Justin is not unemployed."

He gave me a pitying look across the table. "It's a shame that I know more about your life than you do."

My heart raced with anxiety. Any attempt to not give him any reaction went out the window. "So you're spying on my boyfriend too?"

"I'm just good at my job, which is being really fucking observant. And persuasive, when necessary."

I lowered my gaze to the table and noticed my hands were shaking. Curling them into fists, I hid them in my lap and tried to take deep breaths.

"What's running through that pretty blonde head of yours?" Soren picked up another taco and took a big bite.

I shook my head, unable to pull my thoughts out of the tangled, panicked spiral. What *didn't* he know about me? He knew where I lived and where I worked. For all I knew, he was spying on me every minute of every day through my phone, computer, or whatever else. And he clearly had no problems with hurting me.

Never before had I felt more trapped. More helpless.

"I just want you to leave me alone," I confessed. "I won't go back there or talk to him ever again if you'd just...stop everything. Stop following me to my house and my job. Stop...*observing* me."

Again, Soren took his sweet time chewing and swallowing his food. "I would honestly love that too. Frankly, you're not all that interesting to follow." He wiped his mouth with a napkin. "But I have my orders. And my superiors are very interested in the information you can gather. So, how about we set a term limit on this job you do for us?"

"Isn't there another option?"

"'Fraid not." Soren's eyes flashed with a type of malice

that made my skin erupt in goosebumps. "I was sent here to make you agree to gather intel, with no limits on how to do so. I don't want to hurt you, Heather. But I can. So here is my offer." He shoved aside his food container and brought his palms together in front of him. "Give me three months' worth of good intel, and I'll be out of your life like I never existed." A smirk pulled at his lips. "This is the best, and only, deal you'll get, so don't bother trying to negotiate. Make this easy on yourself and just say yes."

I felt beyond trapped now. More like I was drowning, and the only way to survive was being allowed a tiny sip of air before my head was shoved underwater again.

Everything in my gut screamed that this was wrong. It would be leading Laith on, and possibly putting the vampires in danger. And that was still saying nothing of the dishonesty and betrayal of my relationship with Justin.

But what other choice did I have?

I just had to endure for three months and then I'd be left in peace.

The answer dragged out of my throat like stones rolling uphill.

"Fine."

# Chapter 9

## *Laith*

I swung a leg off the motorcycle, and craned my neck to look up at the tall, stately home. "Why don't we do all of our meetings at Novak's place?"

"Because we're not of his clan," Thorne grumbled, tossing a spent cigarette. "Can't give him all the power."

"His place is nicer than ours, though. And his chef always has food prepared. Why don't we have a chef?"

"You are more than welcome to hire one," Thorne said irritably. "And knock yourself out with a home remodel. I can't wait to see what you do with that squirrel brain of yours."

Okay, he had a point there. But he didn't have to be so grumpy about it. Actually, who was I kidding? Thorne was always grumpy.

If anyone had an excuse to be grumpy, it was me. I was still starving. Marrow was starting to lose its edge. I needed blood, Heather's blood, really fucking soon or I'd be in big trouble.

Cyan was the third and final person of our merry little band. He'd been the first to park in Novak's courtyard and now waited anxiously for me and Thorne by the front door. His foot jiggled as we approached, then he lifted the knocker to announce our arrival.

I grabbed his shoulder and gave it a friendly little shake in hopes of calming him. "Novak said it was good news. It's gonna be all right."

"Yeah." He didn't sound any more at ease. I could practically hear his teeth clenching.

Cyan was never anxious. Everything rolled off of him like water on a duck's back. Except when it came to Kalix, which was precisely the nature of our visit.

When he was imprisoned by clan Carpe Noctem over twenty years ago, Kalix left a massive hole in Blood 'til Dawn that we all continued to feel. None moreso than Cyan, who Kal had mentored like a father figure.

Quietly, Thorne had been trying for the last decade to break Kal out. But despite having risen to become the ruling clan, it couldn't happen with a single command. Carpe Noctem was powerful and resourceful in their own right. And their imprisonment of Kal was seen as justified, since it was due to the killing of their leader.

The door opened a moment later, with Novak himself grinning from across the threshold. "Hey, everyone. Come in."

He held the door open wide while the three of us shuffled in. The guy was dressed down, but still looked more polished than us in our scuffed leather and jeans. His long, silvery-blonde hair was down, and he wore slacks and a buttoned shirt with the sleeves rolled past his elbows.

I wasn't kidding about Novak's place being nicer than ours; it was swanky as hell. A big foyer with a polished tile floor and tall arching doorways that led to different areas of the house. A grand staircase stood straight ahead, going up to the second level and then splitting off in two directions.

The clan he'd been born into, Rathka's Order, had been a noble warrior's class since their inception centuries ago. They lived well, and usually got the lowlife clans to do most of their fighting for them. In short, no one liked Rathka's Order except for themselves.

They had been so shitty to their fellow vampires that an illness, known as Rathka's Curse, had befallen their clan and nearly wiped everyone out.

Everyone except for Novak.

He'd ended up renouncing Rathka's Order and starting anew as Blood and Truth. Thorne had to approve it, as leader of the ruling clan. At first, I'd wondered if Thorne would make Novak give up the riches and wealth accumulated by Rathka's Order. But it seemed he got to keep his house, which was fine by me.

I let out a low whistle when I caught sight of the chandelier hanging from the ceiling. It was easily bigger than my bike.

"Is that new, Novak?" I asked, pointing straight up.

He looked up. "No, that's been there."

Thorne snorted. "I swear, your eye catches some new shiny thing every time we come here."

"I just cleaned it recently." Novak smirked. "It was really dusty, so it's much shinier now."

"You did? Or you had your housekeeper do it?" Thorne asked.

"I did." To his credit, Novak looked more amused than offended. "Believe it or not, I'm not afraid to get my hands dirty, Thorne. And if my poor housekeeper fell, she'd be in serious trouble. No, I wouldn't let her get up there."

"How noble of you," Thorne drawled.

Even though we were now allied after being bitter enemies with Rathka's Order for centuries, Thorne still didn't seem to like Novak personally. I understood his reservations, with all the bad blood—pun intended—and dark history between our clans, but Novak did seem genuine in wanting our alliance and trust. He was good to Amy and seemed humble for a rich guy, at least.

"Can we focus on what we came here to talk about?" Cyan asked the group.

"Of course." Novak gave his shoulder a brotherly squeeze, similar to the one I'd given him outside. "Let's go up to my office."

The four of us climbed the staircase.

"Where's your mate, Novak?" Thorne asked, his gaze trailing over all the luxury in the home.

"She's with Tavia," Cyan answered for him.

Amy and Tavia were best friends, having grown up like sisters together in Sapien, the only human settlement in Sanguine. If those two weren't with their blood mates, chances were good they were together.

"Bea is with them too," Novak added. "Girl's night, they called it."

"Huh." Cyan rubbed his jaw as we reached the top landing and filed into Novak's office. "Wonder if Bea would've wanted to be here for this."

"Why would that be?" Novak rounded his large wooden desk.

Cyan and I both looked at Thorne. "He doesn't know?"

"Guess not." Thorne dropped into one of the armchairs in front of the desk and said nothing more.

"Know what?" Novak looked between the three of us. "Please, sit." He gestured toward the second chair in front of his desk. "I'll grab another seat."

"No, it's fine. I'll stand," Cyan said.

With a shrug, I took the seat next to Thorne and and Novak settled in his chair across from us. "So what don't I know?" the silver-haired vampire repeated.

Cyan blew out a breath. "Bea is the reason Kalix was taken by Carpe Noctem. Well, her and me, you could say."

Novak's eyes narrowed. "What do you mean? I thought Kalix killed Baros's father."

"Of course you did," Thorne said. "You weren't there. Weren't involved."

"It was me that killed him," Cyan said, eyes burning. "Kal took the fall for me, because I was young and he didn't want me to throw my life away."

Novak's brows lifted in surprise. "Oh. I see."

"Bea worked in the Carpe Noctem household," Cyan continued. "You know how they are. They treat humans like shit. Kal felt bad for her, and I think he was sweet on her too, a little bit. When she came into our meeting to serve us drinks, she dropped a glass. Charos snapped and slashed her throat with no hesitation."

"Fucking Temkra," Novak muttered. "The poor thing."

"She was bleeding out and Kal went to help her. This infuriated Charos even more and he rushed toward them. I didn't think, I just reacted. I grabbed the same letter opener he used on her and stabbed him with it." Cyan closed his eyes and shook his head, as if to dislodge the scene from his mind. "I didn't even realize Kal had given Bea his blood until later. He shoved her body into my arms and said, 'if she wakes up, look after her for me.' And she did. But he was already gone by then."

"Shit." Novak stared at him with an intense expression, one of awe and respect. "That's a lot to carry, Cy."

"Yeah." A sigh deflated Cyan's chest. "Tavia has made it a little easier though."

"I'll say." Thorne looked over at him with a similar expression as Novak. "I haven't heard you say so many words about that day since it happened."

"And did Bea return Kalix's affection?" Novak asked.

"I think so. She doesn't talk about it much, either. But the signs are there. She looks at his photos in the hallway. She hasn't hooked up with anyone for blood or sex in over twenty years. She's just kind of been quietly existing, almost like she's waiting for him to come back."

"Aren't we all," I muttered.

I wasn't as close to Kal as Cyan or Thorne was, but he had been like an older brother figure to many of us in Blood 'til Dawn. Especially those of us who had been orphaned and taken in as juveniles.

"Bea does seem happier since Tavia came along," I pointed out. "I think she needed a friend." I wondered if she and Heather would get along.

"Well, there is hope yet." Novak picked up his cell phone and hesitated, meeting our eyes apprehensively with the device in his hand. "Inessa of Carpe Noctem sent me a video taken by someone on her staff. She claims it's Kalix, but I need you to confirm."

"You should have led with that," Thorne grumbled as all three of us leaned forward.

"It's short but I have to warn you, it's pretty upsetting."

"Play the fucking video," Cyan growled.

Novak turned his phone around to face us, then hit the play button. The video was grainy and low-resolution, clearly shot on an older phone. Whoever had taken the video seemed to be pushing their way through a dense crowd of people, as the camera constantly panned with jerky, hand-held movements. I could make out a low ceiling with long florescent lights, something like a garage or a warehouse.

The camera stilled when the person made it to the front of the crowd, and focused on an elevated platform encased by silver, interlinked chain fencing. A large, muscular figure kneeled in the center of the platform, upper body heaving with ragged, panting breaths. Blood dripped from his mouth, coating his chin, neck and chest.

And there the video ended.

"Can you zoom in?" Cyan asked.

"I can, but it doesn't help the image quality." Novak placed two fingers on the screen and slid them apart until the figure's face took up the screen.

The features looked even more distorted up close, all pixels and light and shadow.

"Fuck." Thorne sucked his teeth and shook his head. "It looks like him but it's hard to tell."

"Where was that taken?" I asked. "It looks like...an arena, maybe? Some kind of fighting ring?"

"Inessa is working on finding that out," Novak said. "She has to tread carefully around her father, as you know, but she'll pass that information directly to you, Thorne, as soon as she has it."

Thorne slumped back in his chair. "How nice of her to come to me directly instead of going through you."

"This concerns your clan, so of course she'll go directly to you." Novak couldn't resist a smirk. "But I am nicer than you and I pick up my phone when she calls with news."

"You're not *nicer* than me," Thorne sneered. "Just richer."

"It's certainly hard to be grumpy all the time when

you're blessed with a blood mate." Novak swiveled in his chair. "Isn't that right, Cyan?"

Cyan had been intently staring at the phone, but then looked up with a wry smile. "Yeah, it's pretty great. Now if only we could get my best friend back."

"We will," Thorne insisted. "But we need to figure out if that's really him."

"When Inessa gets the location to you, a couple of us will check it out," I said. "We'll be low-key, discreet."

"I'll go with," Cyan said. "If it's him, I need to see with my own eyes."

"You got anything else for us?" Thorne asked our host.

Novak shook his head, casting a sympathetic look across the desk. "I knew you'd want to see the video, but it's all I have for now. I wish I had more."

"I'm sure you do." Thorne stood from his chair and abruptly exited the room without another word.

An uncomfortable silence followed, though it didn't last long.

"Thank you for this." Cyan extended his arm out to Novak. "And look, he's coming around. He stayed for the whole meeting this time."

Novak snorted as he clasped forearms with Cyan. "Oh, I know. Trust me, I'm not affronted. It's nice to see Thorne's warm and fuzzy side coming out."

Novak and I said goodbye with another clasping of forearms, then Cyan and I took our leave, heading down the stairs.

"What do you think?" I asked. "Is it him?"

Cyan sighed. "I don't know. It looks just like him. I want to say yes, but I might be deluding myself, you know? If it's not, I don't want to get my hopes up."

I could understand that. And if it was Kalix, the video raised so many other questions. He was supposedly a prisoner of Carpe Noctem for murdering the head of their clan, but the vampire in that video was not in a prison cell.

Cyan bumped his shoulder into mine as we hit the ground floor. "Anyway, how's the search going for your mystery blood mate? Find her yet, Prince Charming?"

"Uh." Our boots echoed across the tiles of the foyer floor. "It's a little complicated."

I hadn't been able to stop yapping about the fact that I'd found my mate purely by the taste of her blood, but since meeting Heather face-to-face, I wasn't sure how to explain the situation to everyone. She was from the human world and had a boyfriend, who she was apparently loyal to.

She had seemed curious about me, since she was a scientist and I was of a different species, but that's where it seemed to end. I didn't get the impression that wanted to *be* with me.

I knew I had to work to earn my blood mate's trust and, eventually, her love. I'd seen what Cyan and Novak went through, but neither of their mates had already been claimed by someone else. How was I supposed to work with that?

Naturally, I continued to watch her after showing up that first night. Something had scared her badly before I'd arrived, and I was determined to keep her safe. Maybe the boyfriend was abusive and she anticipated getting hurt whenever he got home. It was a good thing he wasn't there at the time, but I hated being forced to leave before the sun came up.

Since then, I had followed her to work each night on my motorcycle without incident. Her workplace was secure, with cameras everywhere and an electric fence that scanned an ID card to get in. I hated that I couldn't stay with her longer, but I figured she'd be safe with such measures in place. Watching her drive through the gate was all I could do, because the sun always rose before she left work.

"Complicated, huh?" Cyan scoffed and poked the side of my face. "You're a little gaunt, buddy. Doesn't look like you're feeding."

He wasn't wrong. I was living off of marrow and, without a regular diet of blood, the benefits were dwindling. She would hate me for it, but I was not completely closed off to the idea of removing Heather from her world, and from her boyfriend especially.

Sure, maybe it was *technically* kidnapping, but it would be temporary, of course. I wasn't a monster. I needed her blood to live and she'd need to recover from blood loss. And if she just happened to figure out how good she had it while with me, well that would still be her choice.

"Working on it," I muttered to Cyan as we went out the front door and into the courtyard.

Damn, now I couldn't stop thinking of Heather's blood. We didn't even stay long enough to nibble on any snacks from Novak's chef. It wouldn't satisfy my hunger, but would at least distract my palate for a little while.

"Laith." Thorne leaned against his bike, his eyes meeting mine with his phone to his ear. "I've got Skye from Pulse Point."

"Yeah?" I paused next to my ride.

"He said someone's there waiting for you." Thorne paused, then his brows lifted slightly. "A human woman named Heather?"

I was still for exactly one heart beat, then jumped into action.

"On my way!"

I started my bike and sped down the road toward the club like my ass was on fire.

# Chapter 10

## *Heather*

Laith walked through the door less than five minutes after Skye, the bartender, put down the phone and told me he was on his way.

He spotted me sitting at the bar and started toward me, grinning so broadly that it made my stomach do a little flip. He still looked a little feral and sharp, his cheek bones almost as sharp as his fangs, but I wasn't put off or scared. No one had ever looked so joyful at just *seeing* me. Not even Justin's face had lit up like that when he and I first got together.

"You came back," Laith said when he reached me, his tone softly jubilant.

"I was thinking about what you said last time."

His gaze focused intently. "About being blood mates?"

"That, and what you said about taking it slow. Getting to know each other." I clasped my hands together to stop my fidgeting. "I'd like to talk more about that."

Laith's face lit up and then his features smoothed just as quickly, like he was trying to keep his excitement in check.

"Yeah, sure. Absolutely. Do you want to talk somewhere quieter, maybe?"

He held a hand out toward the loft overlooking the ground floor.

"Yeah, okay." I slid from the barstool and headed for the stairs off the dance floor with Laith at my side. I thought he might touch me, but he kept his hands to himself and a respectful few inches of distance between us.

"Did you order a drink? They'll send it up if you did." He kept pace with me up the steps, even though his long legs could clear three of them easily.

"No, not yet."

"You can order one from up here too, if you want."

I couldn't deny it was tempting. A shot or two of something would be great to take the edge off. I was all swirling nerves and conflicted feelings, but I wanted to keep my head straight and stay sober. The only thing clear to me was Soren's promise.

Three months of gathering intelligence on the vampires and he would leave me alone for good. And, while I felt bad for using Laith in this way, what other choice did I have? Soren didn't seem like a guy who made empty threats, and I didn't want to test that theory.

Now if only I could shove down how much all this secrecy and deception felt intensely, painfully disloyal to Justin.

"I'll just have some water for now, thanks," I said as we reached the loft.

"Of course. Make yourself comfortable, please." Laith gestured to the low couch piled with plush cushions as he crossed the loft to the miniature bar on the far side.

It was surprisingly quieter up here, the music from the lower floor sounding farther away.

I took a seat and he returned with two large glasses—one filled with ice cubes, the other filled with water.

"I wasn't sure if you're one of those humans who likes a glacier's worth of ice in their water," he said a bit sheepishly, placing both down on the coffee table in front of us. "So, I made sure you have options."

"Thank you." It was a small gesture, but I was touched all the same. It made me feel even worse for deceiving him. "I'm a moderate ice person. Not quite a glacier's worth, more like a small hail storm."

He chuckled while I carefully added some ice to my water glass. "So, I take it you're a free woman now?"

I sipped my water while I considered my answer. "No, not exactly. I'm still with my boyfriend."

Laith's face fell and I hated myself for making him look so sad. "So you're still *not* interested in being my blood mate."

"I didn't say that." I set my drink down, angling myself on the couch to face him. "Justin and I aren't over yet but... things have been strained for several months. Almost a year, actually."

The vampire stilled while I swallowed, struggling to get the words out. I'd never talked candidly about my and Justin's issues to anyone. People saw us as a perfectly solid, happy couple, and I carried no small amount of shame that we'd been struggling for a while.

Well, that *I* was struggling. Justin seemed perfectly content with how things were, which often made me wonder if I was the problem.

"Our lives are very intertwined," I said to Laith. "We live together, split rent and bills. If we broke up, we'd have to break our lease and both find somewhere else to live because neither one of us can afford the apartment on our own."

"So you *plan* on leaving him," Laith clarified. "But the logistics are difficult?"

Had I fantasized about leaving Justin? About being single or with some other person who actually put in a modicum of effort and acted like they gave shit about me? Yes. These days, it was almost daily.

Did I actually *want* to end things? To give up on what we once had and prepare for a new life full of unknowns? Those answers weren't so straightforward.

But what I said to Laith was, "Yes," and added, "it is emotionally difficult too. I mean, we've been together for several years. But the relationship hasn't been fulfilling to me for a long time. I've grown...resentful. And I'm not sure I can come back from that."

Laith stared at me for several long seconds without saying anything, and I tried not to squirm under his magenta gaze. I'd said exactly what I felt. Nothing was technically untrue, but could he sense me trying to deceive him anyway?

"Does he hurt you?" the vampire asked abruptly.

"What?" I blinked, taken aback. "Justin? No, he never has."

"I don't just mean physically. Does he threaten you or make you feel unsafe in any way?"

"No." *But someone else definitely does, and I don't know what he's capable of.*

Laith blew out a breath like he was releasing tension from his body. "So, what can I do while you're still *intertwined* with him?"

I reached for my water again, taking a long gulp to cool

my tightening throat. "You need my blood, right? Mine, specifically."

"... Yes." He dragged the word out cautiously. "But it is more than that, as I explained to you last time."

"Right, yes. And I am willing to...feel things out in that regard. Slowly, over time. Getting to know each other."

"Feel things out," he repeated slowly, a lazy smile forming on his lips. "In what way would you like to *feel things out* with me? And don't you dare skimp on the details."

"Not physically," I said firmly. Giving this vampire my blood and leading him on for my own preservation was one thing, but I would not physically cheat on Justin. That was a hard line for me. "No...you know, intimate touching of any kind."

Laith's eyes narrowed with a frown. "Are you and him still fucking?"

The blunt question caught me off-guard. "Uh, no. Not... we haven't for a...while."

"How long's a while?"

"A couple of months. Maybe three, four months."

"You've been turning him down?"

I wanted to curl into a ball and disappear from the shame. "Other way around, actually."

"Temkra's grace." Laith scrubbed a hand over his face, gaze trailing off somewhere distant. "What the fuck's wrong with him?" He refocused on me. "That was a rhetorical question, actually. Don't answer that. I don't need to know."

I bristled with the need to defend Justin. "Nothing's wrong with him. We're just...not connecting."

"That makes it even worse! How could he not want to...*connect* when he gets to see you every day?" Laith pinched his nose bridge, groaning. "Sorry. I've gone a long time without blood and I'm exhausted. I have no filter on a good day, and I feel like a deflated basketball being dribbled by a Marrower."

A laugh burst out of me, the sound unexpected to both of us. "What does that even mean?"

"I don't know." Laith smiled softly, propping his arm on the back of the couch.

He did look tired. Almost haggard, if I was being honest. But there was a brightness about him that was infectious. A warmth emanated from him, not quite like a fire. It was gentler than that. Like the sun on an early spring day.

I had just been spilling my guts about my failing relationship and lack of sex life, and now we were smiling at each other. He made me feel like everything would be okay.

"So, will you let me help with that blood problem?" I said after a prolonged silence.

Laith pushed hair off his forehead, his expression sobering. "Let me make sure I understand this. You want to give me blood without receiving any physical intimacy in return, even though you're not getting any from your partner, who you are still technically with, despite your planning to break up." One eyebrow lifted lazily. "Do I have that correct?"

"Yeah, I guess that's pretty much the gist."

"So what are you getting out of this?" His gaze settled heavily on me. "Because so far, it sounds like an awful lot of giving for nothing in return."

Pulling in a deep breath, I inched closer to him. "Well, getting to know you." My smile was full of nerves for all the wrong reasons. "Learning about you."

Laith did not seem any more moved or charmed than he already was. Justin always said that I sucked at flirting.

"But not physically," Laith said flatly.

"Just until I end things for good." More like until Soren

was satisfied with whatever information I gave and he finally exited my life, but that was for me to know.

He blew out a breath. "I'm not trying to be a dick, Heather, but the blood mate connection is a very physical one. You remember how we both felt in that room at the blood bank? That's the most sterile, unsexy place in Sanguine and I wanted to...well, you can probably imagine, but it's going to be like that every time."

I recalled the deep pulsing between my legs, the sensitivity on my skin, the heat and coiling pleasure within me. At the same time, I furrowed my brow and tried to look confused while my face burned. "I don't know what you mean."

Laith saw right through it. He shook his head and clicked his tongue, chastising. "The dumb blonde act won't work on me, Heather. I can smell when you're aroused. I can hear your heartbeat as clearly as I hear your voice. I took your blood and you were on the edge of an orgasm. I still regret not fighting harder to see you that night, if only to give you the release you needed."

My jaw fell open, which seemed to amuse Laith greatly.

"That long since he tried to make you come, huh? Why don't you call him up and end it right now? I'll take your generous offer of blood and I promise you won't be thinking of him for the next several hours."

I blinked, forcing myself to remember what was at stake, that my relationship was still worth fighting for. But I'd be lying if I said I wasn't a little bit tempted to agree.

Four months without sex sucked. Going longer without *good* sex was even worse.

"No," I said. "I'll give you blood and we can...talk. Have drinks, hang out. But that's it."

"Until you end it with him," Laith said, as if reminding me.

"Until I end it," I agreed. "We'll just have to be adults and behave ourselves."

Laith brought a hand to his chest. "Oh, I am perfectly capable of behaving myself. But if a beautiful human with the most delicious blood on earth begs me to make her come? Well, I have to admit that is a weakness."

I shook my head. "You walked right up to me and *kissed* me. That's behaving yourself?"

"Yes. That was me putting my best foot forward *before* I knew you had someone else and had set your rules with me." He grinned. "Still my favorite kiss. So far."

Holy shit, this was going to be harder than I ever imagined. He was just too easy to like. The smiles he put on my face came too readily. Enjoying myself in his presence would not be an act at all.

I drained the remainder of my water, now wishing I'd added more ice cubes. As I sat back, returning his curious stare, I willed myself to be firm. Resolute.

"So, how do we do this outside of the blood bank?" I rotated my wrist, noting how his eyes went straight to the blood vessels just below my open palm. "Do I just say, here, want some blood?"

"No, thanks. I'm good."

At my stunned expression, Laith's face split into a grin. "Temkra, I'm kidding." He took the back of my palm and gently drew my arm toward him. "Yes, I would love some blood."

I braced myself, waiting for his strike, but Laith gently pushed up the sleeve of my cardigan, examining my forearm tattoo with a curious stare. "What is this?" he asked.

"It's oxytocin. The love chemical." Before he could

comment, I defensively added, "I'm a science nerd and a romantic, okay?"

Laith lifted his eyes to mine, and I was relieved to see that his expression wasn't mocking or disapproving. "That's really cool," he said softly. "So this is what love looks like? Inside your brain or whatever."

"Not exactly, but this illustrates how the compound is structured in a way that scientists can understand."

"I'd like to understand," he said so quietly that I almost didn't hear. And I had a feeling he wasn't referring to how neuropeptides worked.

Laith brought my wrist to his mouth then, his eyes remaining locked on mine as his lips made contact. "It won't hurt. No numbing gel needed."

When he spoke, the heat of his breath and soft friction of his mouth on my skin made my heartbeat jump, but not out of fear. For some reason, I felt a level of trust with this creature that was about to bite into me and drink my blood. Why exactly, I couldn't be sure. Because he was funny and put me at ease? Because he seemed so achingly sweet and sincere, despite being bloodthirsty?

"Okay," I said.

He hesitated one more second before striking, his fangs sinking deep like a knife through butter. A wave of warmth came over me, like sinking into a hot bath. My head leaned back, eyelids falling closed with pure, blissful relaxation. Then when he started to pull, drawing blood from my vein into his mouth, more sensations layered into my awareness. My heartbeat pulsing between my legs. Sensitivity all over my skin, but mostly in my nipples, my lips, and my neck.

*The oxytocin's flowing now,* I thought hazily.

Frustration took over after only a few more draws of Laith's mouth. Each pull was like a caress of every erogenous zone at the same time. With my eyes closed, it was easy to imagine a hand pressing between my legs, my nipples being plucked by firm fingers, and my neck being kissed by a passionate mouth. All of it was driving me into a frenzy, but never increasing in speed or intensity enough to make me reach the peak.

When Laith removed his fangs and the sensations faded, I wanted to sob with agony. Just like the first time he fed from me, I'd been so physically aroused that it felt like torture to not reach release. It felt incredible. And it felt wrong because it wasn't the man I loved making me feel this way.

That man hadn't touched me with any desire for months.

What disturbed me the most was that I had never felt this intensely aroused with Justin, even when things were good. I had been turned on and into it, of course, but this was on a completely different level. I thought the first feeding might have been a fluke. But twice? The scientist in me could not deny the same results twice.

"Fuck, Heather. Your taste..."

My eyes opened to find long fangs, still coated in my blood, hovering near my neck and coming closer.

I startled and leaned away, pressing myself against the arm of the couch. "Laith? What are you doing?"

He blinked, and some quality in his eyes changed like he was emerging from a daze. He drew back, scooting to the opposite end of the couch. "Sorry. I was really hungry and I lost myself for a second. You okay?"

"Uh, yeah." I brought a hand to my heaving chest, urging my heart to calm down. "Are you?"

"Mm-hm," Laith's mouth was closed as he ran his tongue over his teeth. "I'm good. Sorry to scare you."

He already looked better. His cheeks were more filled in and the shadows under his eyes were gone. Even his eyes were brighter, softer. Closer to human than animal.

And it was a good thing he put some distance between us. My body was a confusing mixture of scared and aroused.

"Thank you for your blood," Laith said, a relaxed smile coming to his face. "I feel so much better. Like I just slept for twelve hours."

He turned away from me, discreetly adjusting his jeans. He was avoiding eye contact and breathing deeply, like he too was trying to come back to normal levels after being wound up without a release.

"Do you want some more water? I'll get you some." He grabbed my empty glass and took it to the bar before I could answer.

"Thanks," I called after him while shrugging off my sweater. I felt mostly normal now, except that my skin still felt too hot.

I examined my wrist where he'd bitten me after placing the sweater in my lap. The puncture marks were barely visible and seemed to be healing right in front of my eyes. The redness faded and there was no longer any distinct opening, like my skin had stitched together in seconds with no scabs forming.

I was so entranced by my own wrist that I didn't notice Laith had returned until he touched my arm. I looked up at the contact, surprised to see anger and tension lining his usually happy and carefree expression.

He dropped onto the couch next to me, now very close and invading my space. I could smell him, even sense the heat from his body. It would take no effort at all to touch his face, to curl up into the solid wall of his chest.

But he clearly wasn't in a cuddly mood. His eyes narrowed with menace as he stared at my arm, lightly touching his fingertips to the bruises left by Soren that night outside my apartment.

Laith's voice was low and full of icy rage when he asked, "Who did this?"

# Chapter 11

## *Laith*

The seconds crawled by while I waited for an answer from Heather. When she didn't respond, I said, "Don't you dare protect your boyfriend if he's hurting you."

That seemed to snap her out of whatever trance she was in, and she pulled her arm away from me. "I told you Justin's not hurting me. That's ridiculous."

"Is it?" I challenged.

My gaze fell to the fading purple dots on her upper arm that could only be from fingertips digging into her soft flesh. There were four of them in a vertical line with just over an inch of space between. I'd bet my luckiest pair of boxers that she had one more bruise on the inside of her arm where a thumb would have squeezed. Five marks from the fingers of a strong, aggressive man.

Faster than she could perceive, I reached for her other arm and drew it forward for a closer look. My vision went red at the sight of matching bruises on that side too.

"What the fuck, Heather?" I hissed.

She drew back and started feeding her arms through the

sweater she'd just taken off. "What the fuck, yourself. You can't just grab me, Laith."

"I want to know who hurt you. If not your boyfriend, then who?" I couldn't bring myself to say his name. It would have sounded too familiar, too close to the man who had the woman I needed.

"No one," she insisted.

My pretty little liar. Why would she lie to me about this?

Then again, why wouldn't she? We were complete strangers in her eyes. She didn't know the significance of the blood mate bond. At least, not yet.

"I can keep you safe," I said, forcing my tone to soften. My own anger was making her defensive, and I needed her to realize I was on her side. She didn't need another angry man demanding things from her.

"Whoever is doing this, they're no match against me. I can promise you that. Not only am I a vampire, I'm part of the ruling clan of Sanguine. We're powerful and we protect our people."

Heather hugged around herself, hands rubbing her arms where the bruises hid. "I'm not your people," she said. "I'm not one of you."

"You can be," I said. "We have humans. Well, *a* human. And a couple of brusang, who are human-ish. Let's say we have one and three-quarter humans already. You'll feel right at home."

She let out a soft breath of laughter.

"And if you come with me as my blood mate, the whole clan will go to war for you if need be," I added.

Heather gave me a skeptical look. "Yeah, right."

"They will. We take these types of bonds very seriously."

She sighed deeply, her hands falling to clasp loosely around her elbows. I felt a surge of elation, like this was it. She was finally going to admit that he had done it, express what a piece of shit he was, and that she didn't want to hold on to that farce of a relationship any longer. Not when she could have something real, lasting and satisfying with me.

"It's stupid," she said with a sheepish glance. "They had just mopped the floors at work, and I forgot a document in one of the labs. So I went back and slipped on the floor. My feet just went out from under me. Luckily the janitor was there and he caught me right before I hit the ground. But he had to grab my arms pretty hard. I was dead weight."

*Heather, Heather, Heather. I should spank you for lying straight to my face.*

She started to squirm, her heartbeat quickening in my ears the longer I sat there with no response. It was interesting how she clearly didn't enjoy lying. She wasn't naturally deceptive and seemed uncomfortable with dishonesty. So why do it?

Either she was protecting someone, the stupid boyfriend mostly likely, or she felt like she had to because of some threat or danger. But there was nothing more dangerous to a human than a vampire.

Regardless, she didn't trust me enough to come clean. And forcing the information out of her was not a great way to start a relationship of our own.

"That's unfortunate," I said after a prolonged silence. "You sure there wasn't a banana peel on the ground?"

Heather snorted an adorable little laugh. "I don't know, there might have been. I do feel like a cartoon character sometimes." She straightened, smoothing her hair back. "So, when should we do this again?"

"Again?" I repeated, surprised. "You want to do this again?"

I could smell the arousal from her before and after I had fed. It was even more potent than the first time without the sterile environment of the blood bank. Moving away from her had been the hardest thing I'd ever done in my life. All I'd wanted was to sink in and give her the pleasure and release she so desperately needed.

But I could also sense her distress, the guilt and betrayal she felt. Along with a touch of fear. It all tainted her scent, made it bitter. I hated that she couldn't let go and just enjoy this for what it was. My fangs would never bring her pain. *I* was the one she was supposed to be with. Biology and fate had decided it. Would she even feel any guilt or betrayal over me when she went home to him?

"Yes," she said with a fervent nod. "You do need to feed on a regular basis, right?"

"Yeah, two to three times a week is ideal."

"And it can only be from me."

"That's right, unless I want to feel violently ill and slowly starve to death. Which I don't."

She shrugged as if that answer settled it. "When should I come next?"

*You should come all the time. And you should never leave.*

"How about three nights from now?" I counted on my fingers. "Sunday night."

"Same time and place?"

"Yeah, that'll work."

"Okay." She paused for a moment before shifting around on the couch and then shouldering her purse. "Well, goodnight, Laith."

"Here, I'll walk you out." I stood, letting her go in front of me as we headed for the stairs.

Heather took the steps down slowly, like she didn't really want to go. Or maybe that was just my wishful thinking. I wanted to put my hand on her lower back, to reassure her with a steadying, guiding touch. The impulse was so strong and felt like such the right thing to do, I had to ball my fist at my side to stop myself.

We reached the ground floor and went to the front door together. I saw Thorne and Rhain at the main bar, their eyes following us curiously. But I kept my focus on Heather, pushing the door open for her.

She turned to me on the landing. "I'm good from here, thanks."

"You don't want me to walk you to your car?"

"No, that's okay. I'm good."

I stood in the door, halfway in and out of the building. Another impulse hit me—to kiss her goodbye. It felt so natural, I even started to lean down and had to force myself to stop.

"Goodnight then, Heather," I said. "Be careful."

She nodded, casting a glance at me over her shoulder as she started down the street. "See you Sunday."

I watched her go until she was out of sight, then retreated back into the club. Like a man on a mission I cut across the floor, heading straight for the rear entrance.

"Hey Laith," someone called out, but I ignored them.

With the firm push of another door, I was outside again. I bypassed the dumpsters, stacked pallets, and mountains of crushed cardboard boxes to where several motorcycles were parked together in a small, private lot.

I sat on my bike and fired up the engine, the way to Heather's apartment clear in my mind.

———

I caught up to Heather's car using some old, overgrown forest service roads that straddled the border between her world and mine. The roads probably hadn't been used by humans since the bygone logging boom days of the early twentieth century. But they were getting plenty of use from me lately.

Since Heather had seen my bike when I first showed up at her place, I made sure to stay a few cars behind. In the dark, she wouldn't be able to tell me apart from any other motorcyclist.

When she turned in to her apartment complex, I pulled into a gas station on the corner and loitered in an empty space, pretending to check my phone. After following her from home to work a few times, I knew Heather sometimes parked on the street or a spot far away from her unit due to lack of space. She didn't need to see me while circling her complex. Not until I was sure she'd leap into my arms with joy and leave that boyfriend in the dust.

I gave it a little over five minutes, paying close attention to her distant heartbeat that somehow stood apart from all the others around me. It was getting easier to pinpoint hers, probably because I had more of her blood in my system.

After five minutes passed with no odd spikes in her heartbeat, I drove slowly through the complex's entrance, making my way to Heather's unit. Her car sat dark and empty in a space not far from her front door. She got lucky on parking tonight.

I left my motorcycle in the darkest, shadowy corner I could find and killed the engine, waiting a few more minutes. It was late and, as daytime creatures, humans might investigate a strange noise.

Nothing stirred as I listened, so I walked through the well-lit sidewalks to where my blood mate lived. Rather than go to the front door, I went around the exterior and peeked through the windows.

*It's not stalking if I don't want to harm her, right? It's not wrong if I'm just making sure she's safe.*

*And not sleeping with another guy.*

There were blinds on the windows with the slats partially folded down, but I could still see through the spaces between them. The main large window showed a modest living area with a small nook for a table and a galley kitchen about the size of my bathroom.

Heather was nowhere to be seen, but a human man sat at an impressive PC set up, headphones on, and some kind of co-op dungeon game running on his overly large monitor.

The boyfriend. I narrowed my eyes. *My arch nemesis.*

His current mission in the game seemed to be wrapping up, though I couldn't tell for certain. I was more of a console guy. Nintendo specifically. One of my greatest joys in life was obliterating Des's ass in Mario Kart.

The human world produced only two good things as far as I was concerned. Heather and video games.

I watched him click buttons and chat through his mic for another minute, just to make sure he wasn't going anywhere. Just before I decided to move on, something changed.

The boyfriend minimized his game window and pulled up another. It looked like a livestream, the majority of the window showing the inside of a bedroom with a chat running in the sidebar. A pink-haired woman moved into view in the bedroom, bending over in front of the camera as she smiled. She wore a lingerie set, ensuring that her watchers got an excellent view of those assets.

"You piece of shit," I muttered as the boyfriend typed something excitedly into the chat feed.

His head turned to the right and he leaned back slightly, as if checking to make sure he was alone, before returning his attention to the screen.

Alone to watch a cam girl while turning down a real, actual woman who loved him. Even if Heather wasn't my blood mate, it was still a fucked up thing to do to your live-in partner.

Did she even know? Was this why she was "planning" to leave him? If so, he was a fucking idiot for carrying on instead of groveling on hands and knees for forgiveness.

*But I don't want her to forgive him. I want her to leave him in the dust and be with me.*

Heather was my priority. This guy would get what was coming to him, one way or another. He was so far beneath her, and me, that his slimy ass wasn't even worth confronting right now. No matter how badly I wanted to crash through the window and throttle him.

I moved away from the window just as the cam girl started doing jumping jacks—hey, good on her for getting cardio in while making money—and rounded the apartment corner on my way in search of the bedroom.

At the base of the bedroom window sat a planter box filled with long-petaled flowers. Most were closed, but some remained open. Dark red and orange petals curled back, revealing long stamens in the center. Lilies, I was pretty sure, though I was no flower expert. The flower box was clean and well-tended by someone who obviously cared for them, probably Heather.

This side of the building faced away from all the others, which probably explained why the blinds were completely open, giving me a clear view of Heather lying in bed. I crouched on the far side of the planter box and peered through the foliage.

She was still fully dressed, her phone in hand. Her fingers moved across the touch screen, apparently typing an email or a long text message to someone. I could make out the paragraphs of text filling her screen, but couldn't read the words. Was it a break-up letter to the boyfriend? I could only hope.

Once finished, Heather rolled over to place her phone on the nightstand, then flopped back heavily onto the bed. Her gaze was at the ceiling, arms at her sides.

*Do you know what he's doing just on the other side of that door?* I wondered. *Why waste any more of your energy and love on that when I would never miss a chance to lie in bed beside you?*

She sat up so abruptly that I thought she might have heard me. I ducked under the windowsill, straining to listen through the glass. A muffled sound came like a door closing, and I lifted my head slowly to peek.

Heather was gone, but a door was ajar with warm light spilling through the cracks. My best guess was that it was an adjoining bathroom. She came out a few minutes later and my lips nearly bled from how hard I stifled my groan.

Wearing an oversized t-shirt and panties, she returned to bed and turned off the light. Now *that* was a sight I'd fantasize about for days to come. Only she'd be wearing one of *my* shirts. Jumping jack cam girl had nothing on how hot Heather was.

"You should never be in bed alone," I whispered at the glass pane. "It should be a crime to leave you wanting."

She pulled the bedcovers up to her chest and stilled, her breaths becoming deep and even. I should have left then, should have been satisfied with seeing that she was safe at home, even if her boyfriend was being a fucking dirtbag in the next room. But I selfishly stayed, telling myself I just wanted to make sure she fell asleep. That even if she didn't know it, she wasn't truly alone.

Her legs suddenly moved under the blankets, her knees forming two wide lumps. And then there was a smaller movement a bit higher up, like her hands changing positions. The movement was varied at first, with small lifts and falls of the blanket somewhere on her lower torso. Then the blanket moved faster, the movement becoming a rhythmic pattern.

It didn't fully dawn on me what she was doing until her head pressed back into the pillow with an open-mouthed sigh.

All of the blood in my body went straight to my cock.

It was really happening. Heather was touching herself on the other side of this wall. She was touching herself while *he* was ten feet away, watching someone else on a screen. Fuck, probably touching himself too at this point.

My lids fell shut, and then immediately opened again because I didn't want to miss a single second of her pleasure.

This was the hottest, most fucked up situation I'd ever gotten myself into. I started seriously weighing the pros and cons of knocking on the window and offering her my hand, my mouth, whatever she needed. I'd make sure she got off multiple times, unlike Dipshit out there.

Heather's heartbeat picked up speed, echoing like a drum in all my senses. I swore I could hear her breathing too—the soft, desperate pants as her pleasure ratcheted up.

"Fuck..." I gripped the windowsill hard enough to give myself splinters. My fangs throbbed with my own heartbeat even though I'd had her blood less than an hour ago.

It was like my instincts knew I hadn't cared for her properly.

She had yet to orgasm during our feedings. I would know if she had. Now, I knew just one little bite would get her there. Not that I'd stop at just one.

I unzipped my pants and gripped my hard length before I fully comprehended the action. Her scent was in my nose, her pulse feeling like a soft vibration inside my skin. I was being fucking crazy, stroking myself outside a human woman's window. If anyone came up on me, they'd be traumatized and I'd likely get thrown in a human jail, but I didn't care.

All I cared about was the woman on the other side of this wall. She was mine and I couldn't have her.

"Heather..." I fell to my knees, dragging a punishing grip from base to head. My other hand remained on the window sill, my gazed fixated on the woman in bed.

She was getting close, and had pushed the blankets further down as her body heated up. Her hips lifted off the bed, hand strumming inside her panties with fast, desperate strokes. Those perfect lips were parted, just begging for my mouth to taste all her little gasps and moans.

Then her lips moved as I watched, forming a word. I could barely hear over her rapid pulse, my own heartbeat, and the rough stroking of my flesh. But I *knew*, from the shape her mouth made, and the way her blood seemed to shoot off in sparks inside me.

If I wasn't already sure, she said it again as her orgasm crested.

"*Laith...*"

"Fuck! Heather..."

My release crashed over me and spilled, hitting the exterior wall of her house.

# Chapter 12

## *Heather*

"Explain it to me again."

"I already explained it to you in the message."

"So it shouldn't be hard to repeat it, right?" Soren's expression was all cold arrogance from across the table.

I leaned back and shoved my hands into my lab coat pockets. We were sitting in one of the break rooms at work. He apparently had enough clearance to come and go anywhere on grounds, and even flashed a federal badge when I questioned him. Security was supposed to be tight here, considering we handled crime scene evidence that many people would love to tamper with.

Needless to say, I hated that he could harass me *in* my work place, not just outside at the food truck. Since he obviously watched my apartment, I thought work would be my one safe place away from his creepy surveillance. But no such luck for me.

"He considers me his blood mate," I explained to Soren, my gaze shifting to the large windows looking over one of the labs.

"No one else is listening," Soren said as if reading my mind. "And no one will disturb us. Keep going. What is a blood mate?"

I let out a resigned sigh. "The way he explained it, there's something about my blood that makes it an ideal food source for him. I don't know if it's something about proteins or what, but I guess it makes me taste, um, especially good to him."

"Lucky vampire," Soren remarked.

"And he can only feed from me to feel properly nourished," I went on. "Nothing else will do. Any other blood tastes so bad that he needs me over anyone else. So to me, it sounds like blood mates resemble lifelong pairings, like when certain animals mate for life."

Soren swiveled in his chair. "So there's a sexual component too?"

I swallowed, my face heating with my obvious discomfort. "Well, yes."

He let out a strange little laugh. "Damn, that's sick."

"I didn't have sex with him."

"Oh, no?"

"No!" Anger flared inside me. "I have a boyfriend. You know that."

"A boyfriend isn't a husband. Certainly not a *blood mate*," he added mockingly.

At that moment, I was having a really hard time remembering why punching people was illegal.

"Well, regardless, I'm not a cheater."

"Look, all of that is fascinating and all, but my employers are looking for more...useful information."

I frowned. "Can you be more specific?"

"How long do vampires actually live? Are they impervious to diseases and cancers? Do they have superhuman abilities and, if so, what are they? Do they have advanced weapons or other technology that we don't have?"

I blew out a breath, rubbing my temples. "It's gonna take time for me to build up to that. I can't just grill him about vampire strengths and weaknesses. He'll get suspicious."

"I dunno." Soren's gaze was scrutinizing. "You've got a pretty face and tasty blood, apparently. I'm sure he's willing to tell you all kinds of things. I bet the more you give him, the more he'll talk."

The disgust was clear on my face, but I didn't bother arguing. What was the point? Soren just laughed. He was already the lowest of the low—invading my privacy, putting his hands on me, making me do his dirty work and suggesting I whore myself out for information. God, I couldn't wait until he was out of my life for good.

He rapped his knuckles on the table before standing up. "Break time's over, Heather. Oh, and by the way, my superiors are breathing down my neck for this intel so we've got to move up the deadline. You've got two months now."

"Two months?!"

He slammed his palms down as he leaned over the table, pure menace in his expression. "Keep your fucking voice down."

I shrank back, remembering the painful strength in his fingers from when he grabbed me. And just as quickly, he straightened with a cold smile.

"Better get back to work, Heather."

He left the room and I spent the rest of my shift jumpy and unable to focus. What the hell was I supposed to do? It was uncomfortable enough leading Laith on as much as I was. The last thing I wanted to do was full-on seduce him to make him trust me, but Soren wasn't giving me much of a choice.

While running tests and typing up reports, all I could think about was how to learn all of the vampire's secrets in two months. Without sleeping with Laith and outright agreeing to be his blood mate.

*You could always tell him the truth,* said a voice that sounded suspiciously like my resentment demon.

The memory of Laith's words followed soon after. *Whoever is doing this, they're no match against me. I can promise you that. Not only am I a vampire, I'm part of the ruling clan of Sanguine. We're powerful and we protect our people.*

I had to admit, it was tempting to give in. To let the gorgeous vampire swoop in and rescue me from everything. To *not* fight the pleasure that surged through me every time he fed from me. Would it really be so bad to leave everything behind?

The thought was especially tempting as my shift crawled to its end, knowing home was not the soft landing it had once been.

When I came to work tonight, I had planned on talking to Justin when I got home. I wanted to ask him how work was going, and see what his reaction was. If he tried to dodge the question, I'd straight out ask him if he still had a job. It would most likely lead to a fight and I wanted to be mentally prepared for it.

Then Soren had found me. And now, as I prepared to leave work, I wanted nothing more than to crawl under my bedsheets when I got home and hide.

I swapped out my lab coat for my cardigan at my locker, then checked my phone to see that I had a text from Justin. My breath stopped for a moment when I opened it.

Justin: Hey, I got pastries from the bakery.
Had a late night, so I'll probably be asleep
when you get home. Love you.

My frayed edges softened as I reread the message. It was…sweet. Both the message and the fact that he picked up baked goods. I hadn't used *sweet* to describe Justin in a long time. Maybe home could be a soft place to land after all.

I unlocked the front door twenty minutes later to a quiet, dark apartment. My stomach growled at the faint, lingering scent of sugar and flaky pastry crust. Seeing Soren at work had rattled me so much that I never ate lunch.

I went to the fridge and pulled out the white cardboard box. A whispered, "Fuck yeah," left my mouth when I opened the lid and saw the cherry Danish. My favorite.

After a few seconds of warming in the microwave, that Danish was washed down with a glass of milk, and I felt a little bit better.

I got ready for bed as quietly as I could to not disturb Justin, who was fast asleep. After crawling into bed, I fought the urge to snuggle up against him. He was a light sleeper and if I woke him too early, he'd be a grump the entire day. So I instead sent him a quick text.

Me: Thank you for the Danish. I needed it
today. Love you too, and I miss you.

He really could pull through, sometimes. Lying next to him then, all my previous thoughts about confronting him about his job felt unfair. Of course he was still employed. He wouldn't buy pastries if he wasn't. Plus, he wouldn't keep that from me.

With my mind finally able to relax a bit, I drifted off to sleep.

———

LAITH REMOVED his fangs from my wrist, but kept his lips sealed over my skin while his tongue flicked over the puncture wounds to stop the bleeding. When he let go of my arm, it felt like the end of a kiss. A conclusion to an intensely intimate moment. The two of us were even a little breathless.

"Water?"

Laith's magenta eyes focused on the coffee table in front of us, his whole body turned away from mine.

"Yes," I said. "Thank you."

He sprang up from the couch like it was on fire, hurrying to the bar across the VIP loft. I leaned my head against the back of the couch, fanning myself with my hand as I caught my breath.

This feeding had been intense. I might have even had a mini-orgasm, just a tiny spark of release that was nowhere near enough.

Not for the first time, I wondered what made my blood so special. I was fueled by coffee and late-night takeout food, and *this* vampire was the poor soul who got stuck with me. Should I apologize or something? *Sorry if you got heartburn. My fault for eating birria tacos at three a.m.*

"Here you are." Laith returned with a tall, chilled glass filled with clear water and the perfect amount of ice cubes.

"Thank you." I gulped it down greedily while he sat a generous foot away from me.

"So." He clapped his hands once after I set my water down. "You still want to get to know me in an emotional but not at all physical way?"

I couldn't help but return his smile. "Yeah, if that works for you."

His smile wobbled. "So you're still with him, huh?"

"Well, yeah. It's only been a few days."

I'd thought Justin was finally making an effort to reconnect after surprising me with those pastries, but the next day he'd gone right back to gaming and emotional distance.

After running into Soren at work, I could have really used the support of a partner over the weekend. Instead I'd had Justin's cold shoulder on Saturday, and counted down the minutes until Sunday evening when I could run to Sanguine and bask in the glow of Laith's attention.

Platonically, of course.

And with the ultimate goal of Soren leaving me alone, of course.

"Fine, fine." Laith raked long fingers back through his ash blond hair. "So what would you like to know?"

I pondered what to ask first over another sip of water. "Are any of the human beliefs about vampires true?"

"Most of them are not." Laith tongued one of his fangs. "But you'll have to be more specific."

"Well, are you undead for one thing?"

"No. We're like any other living creature. We're born, then we die. We live a life between those two points. The prevailing belief is that we split off from humans somewhere along the evolutionary line."

How I would love to send a vampire DNA sample to some old friends from grad school. A few were now pioneers in genome sequencing and would be frothing at the mouth for a research project like this.

Soren would probably appreciate such a sample, but I wasn't eager to make things easier for that asshole. Thinking of Soren made me recall what he'd wanted to know in the break room.

"How long do vampires live?"

Laith frowned. "I'm very disappointed you're asking a general question instead of one specifically about me." His smile quickly returned, a sign that he was joking.

"Well, if I'm your blood mate, then how long is this supposed to last? If you live forever, will you find another blood mate after I die?"

"Oh no. No, it doesn't work like that." He chuckled. "Our average lifespan is eight hundred years. Lucky ones can make it to a thousand."

My eyes went wide. "Oh. Holy shit."

"When we have human blood mates, there's a ceremony. It's kind of like a wedding, officially declaring ourselves as life partners. But there's also a ritual that binds our lifespans together. You will age at the same rate as me and only die when I die. So we'll stay together not only in life, but in the afterlife too."

The romantic in me thought that was so beautiful, and melted at the thought. The scientist in me, on the other hand, was highly skeptical.

"How is that possible?"

Laith wiggled his fingers. "Magic."

"Okay, but seriously."

"Seriously. It's a blood magic ritual. Only those from the clan Temkra's Blood can perform it because they come from the same bloodline as our goddess."

"And you know this for a fact?" I pressed. "You've seen a human live to eight hundred years or whatever."

"Well, not personally. The last known human blood mate died when I was a juvenile, maybe eighty years ago."

"Eighty years? How old are you?"

"A hundred and forty." He carried on like he hadn't just dropped an absolute bombshell. "One of my clan mates got mated to a human a few months ago, but obviously neither of them have aged much in that time."

"You're seriously one hundred and forty years old?" I found myself leaning closer, still stuck on his age.

His skin was incredible, with no visible pores and definitely not a wrinkle in sight. I thought at one point he might be younger than me at thirty. No wonder Soren's employer was so desperate for information. Vampires had apparently tapped into the fountain of youth.

"Am I a slide under a microscope or are you just happy to see me?"

I jerked back, my face heating as I realized how close I'd leaned toward Laith's face. Easily within kissing range, not that I would have done that.

"Sorry." I laughed and tried to smooth over my embarrassment by reaching for my water. "Although I would like to see your cells under a microscope. I bet they're fascinating."

"Aw, thanks." His grin broadened, head tilting as he rested an arm along the back of the couch. "You sure know how to compliment a guy."

Trying to stifle my laugh turned into a full-on grin that matched his. "You're ridiculous."

"That and all kinds of other things."

"So, this magic blood ritual," I said after a lull of silence. "Is it the only way for a human's lifespan to match a vampire's?" Soren would absolutely want to know the answer to that.

"As far as I know, yes. And it can only be done when a blood mate pairing is found."

"And you can't perform the ritual yourself?"

Laith's grin turned wry. "Why, looking for a little taste

of forever already? An elopement instead of a full-on ceremony?"

"Me? No."

I protested maybe a little too quickly. Laith's easy, open expression flickered with a touch of hurt.

"I'm just...curious," I added unconvincingly.

"Sure," Laith said with teasing skepticism. "Well, I'm sorry to say the ritual is a closely guarded secret of Temkra's Blood. When you're ready to make it official, we gotta do it in front of them and all of Sanguine. But"—he held up an index finger, eyes bright—"we can do that thing humans do after getting married. What's it called again? A sugar moon?"

"Honeymoon?"

"Yes, that's it! A little of your tradition, a little of mine. It's only fair, right?"

"True." I laughed uneasily. "I'll keep that in mind."

One of the reasons Justin and I hadn't gotten engaged after several years together was that we could never agree on wedding plans. How was this vampire I barely knew already more willing to compromise on ceremony and tradition? Laith's tone was light and joking, but I had a feeling if I gave him the green light, he'd be more than willing to give me the wedding of my dreams.

*There you go again.* My resentment demon announced her presence with that condescending tone. *Comparing your lame boyfriend to the ageless hottie who wants to lock you down and give you endless orgasms. I mean, is it really a comparison?*

I scooted away from Laith and shouldered my purse. "I better get going. Should we do this again in three days?"

He stared at me for a beat with a strange intensity in his eyes. "You know you don't have to leave, right? You're welcome to stay longer than the five minutes it takes for me to feed."

"I just...I—"

"Do you want to dance?"

I stopped short. "What?"

"Dance. The DJ's playing a great set right now." He angled his head toward the stairs, where the heavy bass and electronic beats of some remixed rock song floated up from the floor below. "I'll be appropriate, promise." Laith lifted his hands. "No excessive touching. Just dancing."

Truth be told, I *loved* to dance. In college, hitting dance clubs and raves was my favorite way to unwind after intense exams and long hours in the lab.

Once upon a time I had lived for the warm nights of summer music festivals, dancing until I couldn't feel my feet anymore. Then I'd sleep all day and do it all over again the next night. It was the happiest, most freeing time of my life.

Justin didn't care for the dance scene. It wasn't about the music or unwinding to him. He just saw it as a lifestyle of partying and drugs. While he'd never outright told me to stop, he made it abundantly clear he didn't support the hobby.

"You need to grow up at some point," he'd said. "Do you really think you'll make it through grad school and the professional world hopped up on psychedelics and partying every night?"

That had been our first major fight. He'd made me sound like an immature child even though I always put my responsibilities first. I never missed a class and never received a grade lower than a B. And what little drugs I did partake in were minimal. I studied chemistry for shit's sake,

I knew what those substances could do to me. Did he think I was stupid?

My dancing days had stopped not long after that because it felt more important that Justin wasn't uncomfortable. He was the man I loved, after all. It seemed ludicrous to choose a hobby over him, even though I missed it. Sure I could listen to music anywhere, but dancing in a club or at a festival was a completely different experience. I missed feeling the sound move through my body, and letting the music move me. It had been years since I felt that total freedom, and Laith had no idea what asking me now meant to me.

"You really want to dance with me?"

Laith let out a soft huff like the answer was obvious. "Hell yeah." Then held out his hand.

When I placed my fingers on his, it felt like an act of defiance.

It felt like taking a step toward returning to myself.

A little thrill ran through me as Laith stood up, gently pulling me along with him. He kept me close as we went down the stairs, taking the steps slowly to not rush me. Some other vampires passed us on their way up to the VIP section, giving nods with murmured greetings to him, and curious glances at me.

The dance floor was becoming packed with bodies. Laith kept a firm grip on my hand as he weaved through the crowd. Maybe it was his height or just his presence, but people, vampire and human alike, seemed to instinctively clear a path for him.

When Laith turned around to face me, he lifted our joined hands. I held on and instinctively spun in a little twirl, my body already humming for music and movement, for the pure joy of feeling.

He grinned broadly when I faced him again, fangs on full display. The current song ended and he leaned in to speak in my ear before the next one began.

"I'll let you lead."

I nodded and closed my eyes, weaving on my feet slightly with the gentle opening notes of the next song. For once in a very long time, I wanted to just feel and not think. And with my eyes closed, I'd be less self-conscious of him watching me.

As the music started to build, picking up in speed and intensity, everything that worried me started to melt away. I turned in place, lifting my arms above my head and let my hips follow the beat. I felt the cool, sweat-slicked skin of others on the dance floor, the bass echoing in my chest like a second heartbeat.

My neck and shoulders loosened, my spine rolled and arched as it followed the music. I felt like a snake shedding heavy, constricting skin and finding my new self underneath.

Or, rather, the self I had lost years ago.

Fingertips touched down gently on my sides after I started really loosening up. I knew without looking that it was Laith, following my movements from behind me.

"This okay?" He had to yell the question in my ear.

I answered by reaching up and finding the back of his neck with my hand. Our eyes met for a few seconds, the chemistry between us as palpable as the beat of the song. Laith was smiling gently, like it made him happy to see me this way.

The music swelled into its crescendo and I threw my head back, brushing it against his chest. We moved together, rhythmic and synced to the same moment. His palms rested on my ribs but he still kept a respectful distance behind me.

It wasn't the type of music to grind and simulate sex to anyway.

We danced for three more songs and, like stars caught in each other's orbit, found ourselves coming gradually closer. By the time my unpracticed feet were screaming for a rest, Laith's arms were wrapped loosely around my waist, his chin resting on my shoulder.

I could rationalize it as friendly, platonic affection. My friends and I back in school would be slumped all over each other after hours of dancing all night.

But with my head leaned back on Laith's shoulder, letting him support my weight as my hands rested on top of his, it didn't feel platonic at all.

I realized I never wanted the night to end.

And for him to never let go.

# Chapter 13

## *Laith*

"How does his head not explode with all the blood rushing to it?" Cyan was slumped on the couch next to me, asking the important questions with a darakt cigarette between his teeth.

I stubbed out my own cigarette in the tray on the end table. "His ears release the pressure, I think."

"I would've thought his mouth, the way he's gasping for air."

"True. His nose might start bleeding any second."

"Hey! I don't see either of you assholes trying this!" Des huffed from his inverted position on the stripper pole in the middle of our living room. "No one is tipping me either, which is extremely bad etiquette."

"It has to be a good show to get a tip." Cy slid his palms across each other in the *make it rain* gesture. "What exactly are you trying to do?"

"That hands-free thing Irina did the other night. She dared me to do it next time we came in and I couldn't say no."

"Well, you've been eating shit every time you let go, so..."

"Yeah I know, Laith! I might have underestimated the required leg strength, okay?"

Cyan chuckled dryly. "Never underestimate the squeeze of a woman's thighs."

I fought the urge to punch him. Not hard, just in the shoulder or something. Did he have to be such a smug asshole about being mated? So what if he was getting delicious blood, fulfilling sex, and emotional validation all the time? He didn't have to rub my face in it.

"Speaking of." He nudged my arm. *Aw fuck.* "Where's your blood mate? That was her up in the loft at Pulse the other night, right?"

"Yeah." It had been three days since that night. Since Heather and I danced together. Since I got the sense that she was actually reluctant to leave. I'd never seen her look so happy and in her element as she was on the dance floor. She'd looked beautiful with the lights highlighting her features and the way she moved, so confident and uninhibited. Despite the crowd, she danced like no one was watching. And I couldn't take my eyes off her, couldn't resist being drawn to her. I never wanted the night to end.

"Well? Why isn't she here?" Cyan pressed.

"She's from the human world." I'd said it as an excuse from the moment we'd met, but it was becoming less convincing with each passing day. "This stuff is weird to her. So we meet at the club for feedings. Talk and whatever. We're taking it slow."

Dusk was falling soon and I was meant to see Heather in a few hours. *Maybe this is the time,* I thought. *Maybe she's finally left him and is ready to be with me.*

Before Cy could respond, Thorne cut across the room, his phone in hand.

"Inessa just called," he said. "She found out where some cage fights are happening tonight. Let's go see if Kalix is there."

"Fucking finally." Cyan got to his feet. "But you shouldn't go, Thorne. You're guaranteed to be recognized."

Thorne's eyes narrowed but he didn't argue. "The two of you, then." He nodded at me and Cyan.

"What, not me?" Des asked.

Thorne gave a long, appraising look at the upside-down vampire rotating slowly on the pole, desperately clinging with all his limbs. "You look busy." To us, he said, "I want updates every fifteen minutes. And don't do anything fucking idiotic." He then spoke directly to Cy. "If you see him, don't lose your head and try to be a hero tonight. We've been working on getting him back for years. Don't fuck it up with one stupid action. Be smart."

Cyan nodded. "I got it."

Satisfied, Thorne brought out his phone. "I'm texting you the directions."

Our phones chimed at the same time. "Shit, that's deep." I said, mapping the route in my head. "Is that even still in Sanguine?"

"The furthest possible point from the Heart, and right on our border with Shadowburn," Thorne said.

"Probably also where most of the draitrium comes in now," Cy mused.

Thorne nodded. "Saddle up, you two. It's going to be a long ride."

OUR MOTORCYCLES RACED ACROSS A DRY, dusty landscape and reached our destination in just under three hours. No matter what happened tonight, I'd be late to meet Heather. I wished I had her number. Just one among many wishes. Another being for Kalix to be alive, not too fucked in the head from his imprisonment, and back home with us.

The proximity to the Shadowburn Cliffs was palpable here. All the moisture in the air was replaced with a dry, desert-like heat. The faint outline of mountains in the distance didn't belong to us, but to the dragon shifters.

Cyan and I had left behind our jackets marking us as Blood 'til Dawn and wore nondescript clothes that were now covered in a fine layer of reddish-brown dust.

"At least we'll blend in with the degenerates who live way the fuck out here," Cyan muttered.

"All we need is the yellow eyes," I agreed.

Draitrium was a mineral found only in the dragon shifter territory of Shadowburn. When refined and processed, it allowed vampires to walk in daylight with minimal harm. Most took it as eye drops, with regular use turning the irises a sickly yellow. The shit was highly addictive and had ruined the lives of hundreds of vampires. It also made the dragon shifters rich off of us.

Thorne wanted drae gone for good, but it was also the basis of our longtime alliance with the dragons, who had been our only support against the werewolves and the angels. Untangling ourselves from them would be a long, complicated process, and not without some violence.

"Where are these fights supposed to be happening?" I looked around us before checking my phone again. This was a desolate area with not much to see except some run-down buildings, a dive bar that also appeared to be a strip club, and some rusted-out, abandoned cars.

"There." Cyan pointed to a structure that looked no bigger than a standalone closet and started towards it.

"Are you sure?" It reminded me of those outside toilets that humans used to have. "The directions are so vague."

"The directions say it's under Temkra's bones," he replied, like that explained everything.

"Okay?"

Cyan huffed in impatience. "It's how Marrowers talk about home deep underground. These buildings are entrances to Marrower tunnels."

"Oh! Right, knew that." I wasn't close to many Marrower vampires, but Cyan was. They were not only nocturnal, but also had a strong preference for staying underground. All vampires found comfort in living below the earth's surface. It was the safest place away from the sun, after all, but Marrowers took it to a whole other level.

"Let's go." Cyan swung open the rickety door that looked like it was moments away from falling off the hinges.

I followed him in and, once the door shut behind me, we were thrown into a pitch blackness that was disorienting, despite my eyes being used to low-light environments.

"Are you concerned about any of your Marrower buddies recognizing you?" I shuffled through the downward sloping tunnel, keeping a hand on the dirt wall to ground myself.

"No, I don't think Drace or any of his kin come out this far." Cy's voice came from a few feet ahead of me, and I was slowly able to make out his shape in the darkness. "Wrestling is a big part of Marrower culture, but this sounds a lot more extreme."

"Yeah." My foot hit a rock and I stumbled with a curse. "Shit! Yeah, this has to be crazy to be all the way out here and wrapped in such secrecy."

Cy grunted out an agreement. "They definitely don't want Blood 'til Dawn knowing about it."

Eventually the tunnel widened and a faint glow of light came from ahead. Dozens, maybe a hundred or so, heartbeats and the murmur of a faraway crowd reached my ears. We came to an open area with lanterns and dim incandescent bulbs hung along the dirt walls. A grizzled old Marrower sat on a stool against the far wall, blocking the entrance to another tunnel where the noise was coming from.

"You boys lost?" The Marrower's lower fangs were long enough to scrape past his upper lip as he eyed us suspiciously.

"No, sir." Cyan went toward him, unhurried and confident. I did my best to copy his movements and demeanor. Despite being younger than me and fairly new to adulthood, Cyan knew how to talk his way into, or out of, any situation.

Me? I usually ended up putting my foot in my mouth.

"We're looking for some action on these fights. You got an entry fee?" Cyan asked.

The old Marrower blinked, his pupils tiny in the dim light. "What fights you talking about?"

Cyan chuckled before I could say anything stupid. "All right. That much, huh? Better be worth it." He reached into his pants pocket and pulled out a fat roll of currency. The Marrower and I watched him count out some bills before holding them out. "Will that cover it?"

The Marrower took the colorful stack of money and counted it out himself before stuffing it in his shirt pocket. "Betting tables are immediately on your left. Drinks are fifty a piece. Hope you brought your own drae. We're not responsible for any ill effects if you buy it from someone inside. Hand over your phones." He held out a dinner-plate sized palm.

"Phones?" I blurted. We were already late on our fifteen-minute check-in with Thorne.

"No video, audio, or image recording is allowed."

"Just do it," Cyan muttered, placing his phone in the Marrower's outstretched palm.

I reluctantly did the same and the Marrower moved aside, sweeping his hand toward the tunnel.

"Thanks," Cyan said, his teeth a little gritted.

I gave a nod to the Marrower and followed Cyan through. "Shit," I said over his shoulder.

"Yeah."

The noise at the other end became louder, funneling through the tunnel and echoing all around us. I clasped Cyan's shoulder and squeezed in a show of support. If I wanted to be annoying I would have held his hand, but now was not the time. Tensions were high. We needed to be alert and focused.

The tunnel emptied into a room maybe ten times the size of the one the old Marrower was in. It was carved out into a rough oval shape like an egg. The walls, floor, and ceiling were still packed dirt, but high-powered lights pointed at a large hexagonal cage in the center. The cage was closed at the top, with the intersecting wires pressing into the dirt ceiling above.

Dozens, maybe close to a hundred people crowded around the cage. There were typical vampires, Marrowers, dragon shifters, brusang, and even some humans from what I could tell.

"Let's go to the betting table." Cyan made a sharp left while I was still reeling from the brightness of the lights.

I followed him, deciding to light up some darakt to take

the edge off my nerves. There was plenty of red smoke hanging over the crowd, so I might as well blend in. Cyan was already making friends by the time I caught up to him.

"How's it going?" He grinned at the two yellow-eyed vampires manning the table. They were already high on drae and it wasn't even midnight. "Any chance I can see the odds for each of the fighters?"

The addicts looked at each other before glancing back at him. "What, you don't got a favorite?"

Cyan shrugged. "I like to be strategic about winning a shitload of money."

One of the vampires rifled through some papers before sliding over a single sheet. Cy picked up and leaned toward me as he examined it.

"There's no names," he muttered. "Only numbers. I wonder if they're all prisoners."

"I don't even know how to interpret this," I admitted. It all looked like a bunch of random digits to me.

"These are the fight match-ups." Cyan pointed to the first two columns. "And these are the odds. So for example, number 7079 is favored fifty-two percent over number 9163. They're pretty evenly matched. But number 5406 is favored eighty-nine percent over 8052. Whoever that 5406 guy is, he's a beast. Or at least popular with the betting crowd." He slapped the sheet down on the table and took out his wad of money. "Let me put a thousand on number 8052."

The vampire at the table stared up at him. "Why? You like losing money?"

Cy shrugged. "I like betting on an underdog." He placed his bet and we weaved through the crowd, making our way closer to one of the five sides of the cage.

"How many fights are there going to be?" I wondered.

"There were ten match-ups on the sheet," Cyan said, then nodded at the fresh blood on the cage floor. "Looks like a few have already happened."

A Marrower entered the cage with a metal bucket, which he used to throw water onto the bloodied floor. The half-hearted cleaning attempt barely did anything but spread the blood further out.

"Hey." I nudged another vampire beside me. "How many fights have there been already?"

The guy blinked slowly, his eyes bloodshot and yellowed with draitrium use. Great. He counted on his fingers. "Four, I think."

"Cool, thanks."

He wiped his eyes and sniffed before pulling an amber glass bottle out of pocket. "Want some? Twenty bucks a drop."

"No thanks, I'm good."

"You sure? It's the good shit. Twenty per is a steal."

Judging from the broken capillaries in his eyes and the way he kept rubbing them, I'd bet he got ripped off on a bad batch. Maybe the draitrium was cut with something else to increase the dealer's profits.

"I'm sure. Maybe grab some Visine, buddy. Your eyes don't look too good."

"Fuck off," he growled before disappearing into the crowd.

"Such a fucking waste," Cyan griped at my side. "This group over here's talking about staying up to watch the sunrise after the fights. Can you imagine?"

"I know," I commiserated. Daytime wasn't our world. Watching sunrises was not in a vampire's nature. Even while on drae, it was incredibly risky to be out while the sun was up. Most draitrium-related deaths weren't actually due to overdoses, but misjudging how long the sun protected lasted, then getting burned up while caught outside with no protection.

The surrounding lights shut off and the crowd let out a collective roar. Only the cage remained illuminated. Cyan and I shared a grim look. The next fight was about to start.

About ten feet away from us, the crowd parted to form a lane. I was tall enough to see over most people's heads, and spotted three figures coming through the cleared space toward the cage.

Two vampires entered the cage with a third person, blindfolded with their hands tied behind their back, between them. The bound person looked male, shirtless with tattered shorts, bare feet stumbling up the short steps to the cage door.

He was untied and his blindfold removed, then shoved inside, the chain-linked door shutting and locking firmly behind him.

"Fuck," Cyan bit out at my side.

I agreed but was too dismayed to say anything. The guy in the cage was a brusang. Newly turned by the looks of it. He gazed around at the crowd in stunned horror, then looked down at his hands. Touched his stomach, the bullet hole looking-injuries that had probably killed him, and then touched his face. He looked young, just on the cusp of adulthood.

The crowd laughed as he began to panic, crawling to the edge of the cage and curling his fingers through the gaps in the wires. His mouth formed the word, "Help," but it was impossible to hear him. Impossible to save him.

Another lane formed in the crowd across from where the terrified brusang made his entrance. Spectators turned their attention that way and raised fists in the air as they yelled and cheered.

Much like with the first fighter, two vampires escorted a bound prisoner between them.

"Aw, shit."

"How bad?" Cyan asked.

"Looks like a Marrower."

"Fuck."

"Yeah."

The brusang wasn't scrawny by any means. He was probably of average build for a human. But an average Marrower had twice the heft and muscle of an average human. They were usually at least a foot taller too.

It was almost comical how the escorting vampires brought the Marrower up the steps and untied him. He could have broken their faces with a swat of his hand, but something wasn't right. The Marrower was slow, sluggish. That was, until one of the escorts pulled out a large syringe and stabbed the Marrower in the thigh with it, using a fair amount of strength to push the plunger all the way down.

The Marrower seemed to wake up from a stupor, rolling his massive neck around on his shoulders and snapping his jaws.

"That doesn't look like drae," I observed. The substance in the syringe looked like blood, but it was impossible to tell.

"We need to find out who they are." Cyan jerked his chin at the escorting vampires now hurriedly shutting the cage door behind the prisoner. "They have no clan insignia but these fighters are clearly brought here from somewhere. They don't seem to be here voluntarily."

The Marrower shook his head and clasped his temples with a groan of pain, while the brusang scuttled along the cage wall looking for a way out.

"He hasn't fed in a while," Cyan noted about the Marrower. "He's actually on the thin side for their kind."

I nodded at the brusang. "And he probably hasn't fed since he woke up from dying as a human."

The brusang had apparently just noticed the fangs in his mouth and was touching them with a kind of fascinated horror. Their fangs were smaller than a natural-born vampire's, but had to feel strange if you'd only had blunt teeth your whole life.

Sadly, his distraction was a costly mistake.

Across the cage, the Marrower inhaled deeply and his mouth watered. His pupils went tiny like pinpricks in burgundy irises. Cyan and I both knew the brusang's life had ended the moment he was scented.

The crowd went insane, pressing toward the cage, yelling and cheering at the brutality manufactured for their entertainment.

Cyan and I couldn't watch. We looked at each other instead. His expression matched how I felt—grim, frustrated, and helpless. The brusang's screams at least cut off abruptly early on in the carnage. Hopefully that meant he died quickly.

When I dared to sneak a peak, it was already over. The Marrower knelt with a large, bloodied bone between his hands, using his lower fangs to dig inside and slurp at the marrow within. Around him, others were picking up the pieces of the brusang.

Someone went to pick up another bone near the Marrower and nearly got their head bitten off. The Marrower lunged, snapping his jaws and clutching his prized bone to his chest. It was probably the first meal he'd had in weeks.

While he was distracted, someone else came up and

jabbed him in the neck with another syringe. The Marrower spun around snarling, but whatever drug he'd been injected with was already taking effect. He stumbled, dropped his bone, and shook his head as if to clear a fog. By then, his hands were being retied behind his back, and it took five vampires to heave him to his feet and out of the cage.

Cyan and I shared a long, harrowing look. "I hate it here," he said.

"Same."

No wonder everyone was on drugs. This shit was too brutal to watch while in a normal state of mind.

More fighters were dragged into the cage, all of them death matches. None of them had been Kalix, which I didn't know was a good or bad thing at this point. If that was him in the video, could we have been too late to save him?

"This should be the last fight," Cyan said numbly. "If your buddy counted to four correctly."

"Who the fuck knows." I rubbed my face, feeling disgusting like I'd need to shower for days to clean this place off of me.

The crowd swept into a frenzy that overshadowed all of their excitement from before. Everyone was stamping their feet and chanting. I realized after a while it was a number they were all shouting. 5406.

From the way everyone was acting, this *was* the final fight. The main event everyone had been waiting for. Everything leading up to this had been just an appetizer.

Like all the fights before, the crowd parted to form a corridor leading to the cage. Two escorts led a massive figure between them. I almost thought it was another Marrower. This guy had the height and muscle mass but the fangs and skin tone weren't quite right.

His wrists also weren't tied behind his back like the

others. This vampire was covered in chain restraints that made metallic clinking sounds with every one of his heavy steps. When he stepped into the overhead light, my stomach dropped. And then my heart dropped into the hole where my stomach once was.

"Oh...fuck."

"What?" Cyan demanded. "Is it..."

All words became meaningless as we watch Kalix step into the cage.

# Chapter 14

## *Laith*

**K**alix was unrecognizable.

And yet there was no mistaking him.

He stood at his full, imposing height, like the chains didn't weigh him down at all. There was some kind of metal mask covering his mouth with chains linking from the mask to a metal collar around his throat. Chains wrapped around his arms, connecting his cuffed wrists to his waist, and then his waist to his ankles.

The escorts got to work on the time-consuming task of unlocking him, which allowed us to take in the friend and mentor we hadn't seen in over twenty years.

Kalix was shirtless, and his black hair still reached his shoulders. He still had the muscle of twenty years ago, but was covered in far more scars. His vow to Blood 'til Dawn was gone. The ritual scarification everyone in our clan did to ourselves as a permanent gesture of loyalty was now a puffy mass of scar tissue. It looked like they had literally cut out his vow with silver weapons—the only thing capable of scarring vampires.

"Fucking Temkra, what have they done to him?" Cyan sounded like he was going to cry. "Look at his eyes."

Instead of the warm, dark maroon color they had once been, Kal's irises were a dull yellow.

The collar around his neck came off, and then the mask followed. Kal stretched his jaw and ran his tongue over his teeth.

His flat, fangless teeth.

I swallowed a sound of disgust and disbelief. Filing down a vampire's fangs was not only cruel and painful, it was humiliating. To take away a defining characteristic of our species was reducing him to less than a vampire. Less than a human. The practice had been banned centuries ago, when new clans were forming and fighting between each other was common. And they had done it to him.

The chains dropped at Kal's feet and he...did nothing. The Kal I knew would have acted the moment he had a free hand. Or even started headbutting his captors if his hands were tied. But he just stood there like a statue while one of the escorts stuck a syringe into the side of his leg.

Like with the Marrower in the earlier fight, the injection seemed to shoot life into him. He blinked several times, his eyes sharpening with focus despite the yellow draitrium haze. His fists clenched at his side as his opponent, another Marrower nearly matching him in size, was brought into the opposite side of the cage. This fighter too was unlocked from chains and injected with something.

The fight began with no signal, no preamble. The escorts had barely exited the cage and slammed the doors when the two huge vampires lunged at each other.

Unlike Kalix, the Marrower had two sets of long, prominent fangs, but he couldn't even get close. Kal's long limbs punched and kicked, succeeding at keeping the other vampire out of close range. Cy had mentioned something about Marrowers being into wrestling, so maybe this other guy had a good grappling game and Kal knew that.

Fuck. Did Kal even know who *he* was anymore?

An old memory popped into my head. Des and I had come of age in the same year, and carved our vows to Blood 'til Dawn over our hearts at the same time. I remembered how much the silver blade burned, how hard I'd clenched my teeth in order to not make a single sound of pain.

The whole clan watched us carve our vows. Cyan was still a juvenile, sitting next to Kal who was pointing at me as he whispered in Cyan's ear. I imagined Kal was telling him how brave we were, how we were willing and proud to take silver to our skin for our family. How it was an honor to make this vow and it would be Cyan doing this same ritual when he came of age. Young Cyan had grinned and looked up at Kal, all kinds of admiration in his gaze.

Now Cy looked utterly haunted, his eyes locked on the vampire who'd been a best friend, a brother, and a father figure all rolled into one, now fighting to the death.

Kal was clearly at an advantage in the fight, his long reach working to create distance and tire out his opponent. By the way the crowd hollered every time he landed a punch or a kick, he was heavily favored by them.

After a few minutes, something became clear. Kal wasn't fighting to kill. His blows landed solidly, but without lethal force. Most of his moves were defensive, blocking or dodging the Marrower's attempts to bring him to the ground. He landed strikes of his own only when the Marrower got too close or left a vulnerable spot open.

Cyan and I looked around, sensing the crowd's restlessness as the fight went on. It wasn't the bloodbath they wanted.

"Come on, fuck him up!" yelled the guy who'd tried to sell me drae.

Sweat poured off of the Marrower's gray skin, his breaths heavy and labored as he and Kal continued to circle each other. Kal barely looked gassed at all. He almost looked bored.

I wasn't sure when it exactly happened, but the fighters hit a turning point.

The Marrower got past Kalix's block, grabbed him around the waist, and slammed him to the ground.

Cyan and I both winced at the sound, but the audience let out a roar of outrage. They yelled at Kal, or rather number 5406, to get up and spill some blood. But Kalix remained down, not even bothering to block the onslaught of fists that rained down on him. The Marrower straddled him and, with renewed strength, held Kalix down by the throat as the other hand beat into his face.

Blood sprayed everywhere. Cyan and I were close enough to feel droplets on our faces and clothes.

Eventually Kal bucked off his opponent, but it was with a fraction of the vigor he'd had early on in the fight. He rolled to stand up, made it to his knees, and then was slammed to the ground again. The Marrower had an arm around his throat this time, and got into the perfect position for a chokehold.

Under the blood gushing from his face, Kal's skin turned dark purple. He barely struggled, only holding on to the Marrower's forearm with a weak grip. I stared in disbelief, knowing with my whole being that he could've broken out of that hold if he really wanted to. Was he trying to die?

Cyan made a sudden move forward and I grabbed his arm, hauling him back.

"Get off me, Laith," he snarled.

"No way." I wrapped both arms around his chest, using all my strength to hold him in a bear hug. "You heard what Thorne said. We can't expose ourselves here."

"Fuck what Thorne said," he choked out.

"I know." I held on tighter, locking my hands together. "I know, Cy. I know."

Kal's eyes rolled to the back of his head, his body slumping in unconsciousness. The Marrower grinned as he cradled the top and bottom of Kal's head in both hands, the motion looking like he was going to...

"Oh fuck."

I released Cy and we both started forward, pushing through the crowd like our lives depended on it. More like Kalix's life depended on it. He might have been honorable enough to not fight to the death, but we couldn't expect the same from anyone else here.

Just as we reached the barrier separating the spectators from the cage wall, a flurry of escort vampires rushed inside.

"Fight's over!" one yelled, spreading his arms to the sides. "Stop. Release him!"

The Marrower grimaced, looking thoroughly peeved. He had no intention of releasing Kal's head and every intention of snapping his neck.

But he was distracted just long enough to not notice one another escort injecting something into his neck.

"You won't deny me my...kill..." was all he got out before he slumped to the ground.

"Fights are done!" the first escort yelled, this time to the crowd. "Collect your money and get the hell out."

Cyan and I lingered just long enough to see Kalix rouse, rubbing his neck before the metal collar was snapped back into place.

"Come on." I squeezed Cy's shoulder, urging him toward the exit tunnels.

He followed reluctantly, without saying anything. Neither of us said a word as we collected our phones and made our way back through the tunnels, but my mind was reeling with revelations and questions.

Kalix was alive. And someone — probably his captors, Carpe Noctem — wanted to keep him that way, despite entering him into illegal fights and torturing him. All the chains, filing down his teeth, putting him on drae. Fuck, it was unimaginable. And he'd lived through it for twenty fucking years.

The heaviness of what we'd just witnessed weighed on Cyan and me like an avalanche. Neither of us knew what to say, how to process it. We shuffled over to our bikes while I checked my phone, filled with pissed off calls and texts from Thorne since we hadn't provided updates. Backup was probably already on the way for us.

"I'm calling Thorne back," I said, bringing the phone to my ear.

Cy didn't respond. He just stood and stared as blank as a zombie.

Thorne's ass-chewing over the phone was just as severe as I thought, but I happily took the brunt of it for Cy. That had been his best friend, his father figure, in that cage. Not to mention Kal had willingly agreed to be taken prisoner in Cy's place. That had to be a special kind of painful, knowing he'd be the one in that cage if it weren't for Kal. That Kal had done that, gone through all that, to protect him.

"How's Cy?" Thorne asked once he calmed down from verbally reaming me.

"Not great," I admitted. "I think he's in shock."

"Can he ride?"

"Not sure, but I'll bungee-cord him to me if need be."

Thorne let out a grunt that was probably meant to sound sympathetic. "I'm not getting Tavia involved, but I'll let her know he's going to need her when he gets back."

"Good call. I'll let him know she's waiting. That'll probably snap him out of it."

"Watch out for him. And I want a full rundown as soon as you get here."

"You got it."

We hung up and I went up to Cy, clasping his shoulder and shaking gently. "Hey buddy. You gonna be able to ride home?"

He blinked several times like he was holding back tears. "What did they fucking do to him, Laith?"

"A lot of really fucked up shit. That's why we've got to get home—"

"We can't leave him!"

"We gotta be smart, Cy. We need to do this right. We're gonna tell the others and come up with a plan to get him out. We're gonna make them pay for this, Cy. You know we will."

"It should have been me." He shook his head, his face contorted in anguish. "Fuck, it should have been me."

"No, listen." I clasped the back of his neck and made him face me. "You were too young. You wouldn't have survived a sentence like this. Kal knew that and made his choice, Cy. And you never would have met Tavia. I know it hurts, buddy, but you've got to make it home to your mate. Lean on her and gather your strength so we can get Kal back."

He let out a shaky breath that seemed to deflate his whole chest. "Okay."

"Good." I squeezed his nape once more before letting go. "You ride ahead. I'm watching your back."

The ride home felt too long despite our speed. I had no idea if Heather would still be waiting for me at Pulse Point. A long shower and a hearty draw of her blood was exactly what I needed, but who knew if either of those things were happening tonight. Thorne would want to know everything in precise detail and Cyan was in no shape to relive the event. So reporting back would fall on me.

Again, I was happy to carry the burden so Cyan wouldn't have to. It just sucked that this happened to fall on the same night I was supposed to see Heather.

The moment we got home and off the bikes, I texted Skye to see if Heather was at Pulse Point and if they could pass a message from me. My head was down, thumbs flying over my phone screen as Cyan and I walked into the great room. When I looked up, Tavia was already crossing the room, her arms outstretched and her expression full of love and concern.

Cyan fell into her embrace like a puppet with its strings cut. His head went to her shoulder, arms folding around her waist as he drew her in tightly. I wasn't sure how much Tavia knew, but she seemed to have an idea.

"You're okay," she whispered to Cy, one hand scratching the back of his head while the other rubbed his back. "It's going to be okay, love." Over his shoulder, she caught my gaze and mouthed, "Find him?"

I nodded and mouthed back, "Alive."

She nodded and returned her attention to Cy, holding him protectively. "Hey, let's go to bed and rest, okay?"

I gave them space to head down to the underground apartments, taking the opportunity to wash my hands in the kitchen and splash water on my face. Then I splayed my hands wide on the counter and just let my head hang.

The night was still young, but I felt ragged. Exhausted. Too much horror and evil for one night.

I couldn't imagine Kal living like that for 20 years, day after day. Shit, out of him, Cyan and me, I was probably faring the best out of all of us.

*But at least Cy has a mate to lean on.*

The thought was bitter and selfish and unlike me. My emotions were frayed and uncontrollable, like sparking wires swinging freely. And it was my envy that caught hold of me for the moment.

Tavia was here when Cyan needed her. She was living proof that a mate wasn't just about sex or blood, but supporting each other through highs and lows. Meanwhile, Heather gave me her blood but emotionally kept me at arm's length while she went home to a shitty boyfriend.

She should be coming home to me. And I should be falling into her arms after a rough night. And it was fucked that none of this was happening way it should.

"Fuck! This." My fists came down on the counter and I relished in the pain radiating up my arm. Pain for Kalix, for Cy, and for my own pathetic situation.

"Hey." Thorne came through the double doors, unwrapping a fresh pack of darakt cigarettes. "You done being a juvenile and ready to give me that report?" He took a seat at the island and lit up.

I let out one final self-pitying sigh, then turned around. "Yeah. It's worse than we thought."

# Chapter 15

## *Heather*

The bartender in the VIP loft brought me a spicy margarita and set it down on the coffee table.

"Laith just called. He's on his way over," she said, straightening. "Can I get you anything else?"

"Oh, great! And no thank you, I'm fine. Are you sure I can't start a tab?"

"Absolutely not," she said cheerily before walking to the opposite end of the loft.

I finished the rest of my water before starting on the marg. The bartender up here, Makena, was a dragon shifter and the spices in the drink were a special blend that came from her people's territory, the Shadowburn Cliffs. We'd talked for a while as I had waited on Laith.

He was over three hours past our agreed-upon time, but the truth was, it was a huge relief because I had also been well over an hour late. I was supposed to only do a partial shift at work, but got held over due to a mix-up in the lab. Once cleared to leave, I *ran* to Pulse Point in a panic, only to find out that Laith was also held up doing some work thing. What did he even do for a living? It was embarrassing that I had never asked, when he seemed to admire my field of study.

In any case, I didn't mind waiting for him. I danced on my own to a few songs, chatted with a nice group of brusang and human ladies, and got to know the VIP section's bartender, Makena.

I felt more relaxed and carefree in Sanguine ever since we danced that last time. It felt like I could be myself here and no one would judge me. The days back in my world had crawled by, both with work and looking over my shoulder for Soren all the time.

Nothing in my situation with Justin had changed. Our relationship was on another part of the same old cycle. Currently I was in the phase of not saying a single word to him because I was sick of putting in all the effort. If he wanted to have a live-in girlfriend, the least he could do was say, "Hi, how was your night?"

A flurry of footsteps drew my attention to the stairs, where Laith appeared at the top landing. His pale blonde hair was messy in an unintentional way and still damp like he'd just rubbed a towel over his head. There were a few wet spots on his white T-shirt too, like he'd jumped in the shower and rushed over here with barely any time to dry himself.

"Hey, I'm really fucking sorry." His brow furrowed and his mouth was tight. "I didn't expect work to take so long. I got here as soon as I could."

"It's okay." I leaned back against the couch, my body unfurling with even more relaxation now that he was here. "I was actually held up at work too and was late getting here. And the bartenders told me what was going on."

"Oh, thank fuck." Laith dropped onto the love seat next to me in a heavy sprawl. He rubbed his eyes and then his whole face with a groan. "Thanks for understanding. I felt terrible about making you wait around so long, but I just couldn't get away."

His remorse was touching. I turned to face him, curling my legs underneath me. "It wasn't really that long. I danced for a bit. Talked to some people. Might've made a few friends."

A corner of his mouth pulled up, but it was a shadow of his usual smirk. "Good. I'm glad. Still, I'm sorry. It won't happen again."

"Maybe we should trade numbers? So we can give each other a head's up just in case something does come up again."

I expected him to make some flirty remark, maybe tease me about my boyfriend like he usually did. But he just said, "Sure," and pulled his phone from his pocket. He waited for me to recite my number without another word, let alone a suggestive joke.

After giving him my digits, I decided to dish it out myself. "Wow, I love your enthusiasm about receiving a girl's number. The victorious moment everyone yearns for."

Laith barely gave me a smile. Not even a chuckle. He only made a faintly amused noise as he said, "Texting you now."

I got a vampire emoji from an odd, six-digit number. "Oh good, it works. I wasn't sure if it would."

"Yeah, it should work if we're both in Sanguine. It'll probably be spottier if you're home. Sometimes our signals ping off human-world towers, but it's not consistent."

His voice was flat with hardly any inflection at all. That, along with his lack of humor tonight, was the biggest sign that something wasn't right.

"Hey." I scooted closer, until my knee almost touched

his. "Is everything okay? You don't seem like yourself tonight."

Laith's head tipped back, his gaze on a distant spot in the ceiling. Then only his chest moved with a deep sigh. "It's been a rough night. Sorry I'm not in the best mood."

"Sorry? You have nothing to apologize for." I almost said, *you're human* before remembering that he was in fact, not. "You're a person, not an amusement robot."

That earned me a faint smile as his head turned slightly toward me. "Thanks for saying that. I feel like a court jester sometimes. Like it's my job to always gotta keep the mood happy and light."

I shook my head. "That's not realistic for anybody."

"So true."

He looked so defeated that I couldn't push aside the growing concern in my chest. We'd met up a number of times now, but I didn't really know him. What happened in his life outside of these feedings?

Laith had never been anything but respectful and sweet to me. It suddenly felt wrong to know so little about him personally. He didn't seem to need shallow transactions of blood for information right then. What he needed was a friend.

After a few seconds of hesitation, I reached out and placed my hand on his forearm. "I'm sorry to hear you had a rough night. Do you want to talk about it?"

Laith's throat bobbed as he swallowed. He was quiet for so long, I almost thought he wouldn't say anything.

"Tonight, I saw a friend for the first time in twenty years."

"Oh." I could only infer from his tone that it hadn't been a happy reunion.

"He was imprisoned, and well...it wasn't wrongfully

done, but it was unjust. He turned himself in to protect someone else. Until tonight, none of us have seen or heard from him since he went away."

His voice lost some of the flat affect, tightening with a painful rawness that hurt my heart to listen to. I found myself wanting to soothe those hurts, to comfort him from these pains. On some level, I knew he'd do the same for me.

I held tighter onto his arm as my thumb stroked in a soothing motion over his warm skin. "How did that go?"

Laith sighed deeply again. "Well, he's alive. That's the only positive in this situation."

"Oh God. So he's not being treated well?"

Laith let out a bitter laugh. "No. Not at all. And he's been there, enduring everything they've done to him for so long. He's a different person, putting it mildly."

"I'm sorry. That must be so difficult." I fought the urge to lean my head on his shoulder, to wrap around him in a protective embrace.

"Not as difficult as his life has been over the last two decades." Laith rubbed his face. "I think that's what's mind-fucking me the hardest. Like we've all just been living our normal lives over the past twenty years but he's been in Hell the whole time. He's the most selfless person I know. It's not fair."

"There's a term for that. Survivor's guilt."

"Of course you would know that, Science Barbie." The corners of his mouth inched wider, more of the Laith I knew peeking through.

"That's not a hard science concept. I might have read it in a self-help book, I dunno. But it's a common feeling. I don't know your friend's situation, but I'm pretty sure it's not your fault he's in there."

Laith straightened, his face returning to seriousness.

"No. He made his choice to turn himself in. I had to tell that to another friend tonight. Someone else who's feeling survivor's guilt."

"See? You're not alone."

He nodded, his intense, red gaze locking onto me. "Thanks for listening, Heather."

"Sure." I held his gaze, refusing to stare at his lips. "Thanks for trusting me enough to talk about it."

"We're not sure how yet, but we're trying to get him out." He clenched his hands into fists and then opened them again. "He's our family and he's being tortured in there. But it's...complicated. We're the most powerful clan, but the clan holding him is almost as strong. And ruthless. They're not afraid to spill blood, but we're trying to prevent any unnecessary bloodshed. So we're trying to decide: try to negotiate a release, or go for an old-fashioned prison break. It's delicate, because we need the people of Sanguine to know we're capable of peace. But, if we wait too long, we might be too late for Kalix."

"I'm so sorry." My fingertips stroked lightly down his forearm toward his hand. "That's such a terrible burden."

"Yeah," he sighed. "Still, Kal still has it way worse."

"I can't even imagine. But he's lucky to have family like you, willing to fight for him."

Laith huffed out a mirthless laugh. "You're sweet to say that."

"Just speaking the truth."

An easy silence fell between us. He clasped my hand in his, brought it to his lips and placed a light kiss on my knuckles. My heart picked up speed as his thumbs pressed into my palms. How could a simple hand massage be so sensually charged? The tension was making my chest tight.

Laith's massage traveled to my wrist, his thumbs tracing

the veins he'd begun to know so well. His eyes lifted to mine and his lips brushed the skin of my hand as he asked a question.

"May I drink from you?"

I should have been used to it by now. He'd already taken blood from me three times. But something felt different about tonight. It felt like he was asking for more than blood. Like he was alluding to this intangible, mysterious *something* that crackled in the air between us. I got the sense that he didn't just want to drink from me, but to drink me in. He didn't just want blood, he wanted a connection. With me.

And I wanted to let this sad, beautiful vampire take all that he needed from me. After these brief moments together, I was starting to feel like I could trust him. He had been so open and vulnerable with me tonight, after all.

"Yes." I almost said *please*.

He brought my wrist to his mouth, his lips nuzzling there for a moment as if to find the perfect spot. That was new, like the kiss on my knuckles and the tentative touches when we'd danced.

Like always, there was no pain when his fangs sank in. Just pressure that almost felt good, like his massage. I closed my eyes and gave in to the sensations of his mouth. A pulling draw and then a release. Pull and release. Back and forth. In and out.

My mind turned to the rhythm of sex, of pressing forward and drawing back. Filling and emptying. Connection and then separation.

With pleasure coiling under my heated skin and the heavy thumping of the music, it was easy to imagine the weight of a male body on top of me. Laith's draws on my vein matched the beat of the bass, crashing over me for a stroke of pleasure that left me panting for the next one, and the next.

My thighs squeezed together and then crossed, hating that I couldn't wrap them around Laith's waist. Yes, *his*. Not Justin's, not any generic man in my fantasies. I pictured slender hips with long legs moving in and out of me. I wanted to grip that messy blonde hair and taste fangs with each consuming kiss. He let out a soft moan against my wrist and it felt entirely wrong that his mouth wasn't on mine, on my neck, or between my legs where my pleasure burned hottest.

When Laith removed his fangs, I almost begged him not to stop. Or to at least finish me off another way, but...I couldn't. There was a reason why I couldn't. A reason why I told him this could not be physical. But that reason was becoming more flimsy, my guilt evaporating every time this happened.

My breath sawed in and out of my chest as if I'd run a marathon, and Laith was breathing similarly. He turned away, clearing his throat and subtly adjusting his pants while I went for my water and gulped it down.

"Thank you," Laith said after we'd both managed to compose ourselves. "For your blood."

"You...I don't think you took very much this time." I tried to say it casually. It wasn't like I could get mad at him for not getting me off.

He nodded and glanced at me with a small smile. "I don't need to take as much since we've been seeing—I mean, doing this regularly. I'm not starving like I was in the beginning."

"Oh. I see."

The corner of his mouth ticked up higher. "Do I sense disappointment, Science Barbie?"

"No! I mean, I was just curious." I flipped my hair behind my shoulder. "A Science Barbie should be curious about everything, don't you think?"

Laith let out a genuine chuckle. It didn't carry the same weight as his normal laugh, but I'd take it. "You've taken to the nickname rather well."

"Hey, I *loved* Barbie as a kid. Still do. I don't consider the nickname insulting at all."

"Good," he said seriously. "It's not meant as an insult."

He got that intense look again, the one that made me want to squirm under his gaze. A parade of fully naked women could have strutted up to the VIP loft right then, and I was certain Laith wouldn't glance at any of them. It was flattering to have his full attention like this, especially since I was starting to feel things I'd never expected to feel.

I should have gotten to business and asked more general vampire questions—the type of stuff Soren would grill me about later—but I couldn't bring myself to care at that moment. No one belonged in this moment except me and Laith.

"Hey, did I notice new ink on your arm?" he asked suddenly.

"Oh yeah." I pulled up my sleeve to expose my whole forearm. "My oxytocin molecule was feeling a little plain so I added to it."

He moved closer until his thigh pressed lightly to mine, taking my forearm in both hands. "Oh wow, this is beautiful work."

I couldn't help the giddy grin at his praise. "Thanks. I'm really happy with it."

My oxytocin molecule was now framed by orange and red lilies, my favorite flowers. I'd had the tattoo appointment for months and finally got it done the day after I last saw Laith.

"It's pretty fresh. I hope the ink didn't make my blood taste weird."

Laith licked his lips, his expression turned pensive. "Hmm, I thought I caught some undertones of ballpoint pen in there."

"What?" I laughed. "No, you did not."

"Mm, no, you're right. It was more like the red Sharpie flavor."

"Shut up." I smacked his arm with the back of my hand, already cracking up. "Now I know you're fucking with me."

He grinned. "I'm back, baby. All thanks to you."

The urge to lean in and kiss that sexy grin was so overwhelming, I had to ball my fists at my sides. "Well, I'm glad I could make you feel a bit better after such a shitty night."

"You did," he said softly. "Not just your blood, but you, Heather." One fang dragged over his lip and damn if that didn't make me want to kiss him more. "I'm glad I got to see you tonight."

The worst part about my pulse speeding up right then was knowing he could hear it. "Me too."

"And don't worry. Whatever ink is in your bloodstream did not affect your taste in the slightest."

I swiped a hand across my forehead. "Phew."

He laughed dryly. "What kind of flowers are those?"

"They're lilies. The design is based on the tiger lily, which is probably my favorite variety."

"They're the same kind that grow at your place, right?"

"Yeah, they—" My words stopped abruptly as a sudden thought hit me. "How do you know about the lilies at my place?"

Laith lifted a brow at the abrupt change in my expression and tone. "I've been to your apartment, remember?"

"You stood guard outside my front door." A little nervous laugh escaped me. "The lilies grow outside my bedroom window. In the back of the apartment."

I fully expected him to brush it off with a, "Oh yeah, I did a perimeter sweep," or some similar answer. I'd feel silly for my initial jolt of alarm and we'd carry on having a normal conversation. But that wasn't what happened.

Laith's mouth tightened, his eyes going dark. He didn't say anything for several long seconds. The longer the silence stretched on, the more my alarm grew.

"Laith?"

"I'm sorry."

Another long, uncomfortable silence stretched between us. "What exactly are you apologizing for?"

"I...was at your bedroom window."

"That same night you came to my front door, or...?" I realized I was trying to give him an out, give him an opportunity to lie to me.

"No, a different night."

I didn't know what to feel, physically or emotionally. My body felt numb, disconnected from the words floating out of my mouth. "You came to my house a second time without telling me? And watched me through my window?"

Laith nodded, his expression solemn. I waited for that grin to split his face, for his eyes to light up with amusement as he said, "I'm just messing with you," but it never came.

"I've followed you home several times," he admitted. "And from your apartment to work."

I was reeling. There was no ground beneath my feet. I was in free fall off the side of a cliff with blood rushing in my ears. "You followed me to *work*?"

"To make sure you were safe," he said firmly, as if that justified it. "I only watched you through the window that one time, and make no mistake, that is the *only* thing I'm sorry for. That was a private moment and it was wrong for me to intrude without your knowledge."

My whole body turned to ice. "What did you see?"

He was quiet for a moment, but his gaze was unwavering. "I think you know."

On a dime, my body went from frozen still to heated with shame. If he had seen me doing something mundane like sleeping, playing on my phone, or getting dressed after a shower, he'd say so. But if it was as private as he implied, like the one night in weeks I'd decided to touch myself because Justin turned me down again...

*The night I'd said Laith's name as I made myself come.*

"Don't feel embarrassed because of me." Laith made it sound like he could read my mind. "What I did was an invasion of your privacy and I regret doing it. I want you to be able to trust me, Heather."

My shame boiled over into anger. He was sorry for being a peeping Tom but not for following me? For *stalking* me?

"Fuck. You."

Laith had the gall to look surprised as I stood abruptly, shouldered my purse, and headed for the stairs.

"Heather, stop."

"Don't follow me. If you can fucking manage that, for once."

He didn't listen, because of course he didn't. I heard his footfalls on the steps behind me, heard his mumbled apologies as he slid through the crowd of people on the ground floor. When I burst through the front door, finding myself on the quiet street and cool night air, he killed that moment of peace in an instant.

"Heather, please come back inside."

The slight touch on my arm had me swinging out of his grasp. I wanted to follow through on the swing with my fist and hit him, I was so beyond fucking angry. So fucking betrayed. Just when I felt I could trust him. I was done. The dam had burst and everything I'd be shoving down for weeks was unleashed.

"I said, *stop fucking following me!*" My scream was so loud it echoed off the buildings and Laith actually stopped in his tracks.

"I am *sick* of people, of fucking *men*, walking all over me, feeling entitled to me, and invading my life. Just *FUCK OFF!*"

Laith lifted his palms slowly. "That's not what I want to do, Heather. That's not how I feel about you at all. I'm sorry if I—"

"Stop. I'm done, Laith. I don't want to hear any more." A few ragged breaths sawed out of my chest. The anger continued to surge. "If you follow me again, you will not have my blood anymore, understand? Not a single fucking drop. Just leave me the fuck alone."

His mouth fell open, then closed into a tense line. "So, what? You're going back to him? The guy who doesn't give a single fuck about your safety or your pleasure? Do you want to know what he was doing while you were in the bedroom, alone? Are you ready to face *that* reality, Heather?"

The last thing I wanted to do was defend Justin. He was one-third the source of my current anger, after all. And there was still so much rage flowing through me, I didn't have the words for coherent argument.

I made my voice as calm as I could as I said, "If you follow me, I will never step foot in Sanguine again."

Then I turned, heading for the hill and the woods, leaving Laith to make his own choice.

# Chapter 16

## *Heather*

**H**iking up the hill and trudging through the woods turned out to be a great way to burn off the anger and adrenaline. I felt calmer by the time I reached my car in the parking lot.

When my phone pinged with a voicemail, I thought it could be Laith and considered leaving it until after I got some sleep. But curiosity won out, and I listened to the message while letting my car warm up.

"Hi, Miss Polk. This is Tina from Laurel Canyon Apartments. I'm calling to inform you that we have not received a rent payment for this month. Please call me back as soon as you get this. If we do not receive a payment by the end of the week, we will be forced to give you a notice of eviction. Thank you, goodbye."

I pulled the phone away from my ear and stared at it, confused. Justin was in charge of making the rent payment. I'd sent him my portion last week. Could he have forgotten? But how? It was the first and most important bill that everyone paid.

I dropped the phone in my cup holder with a huff, then

backed out of the parking space and onto the road home. At least my mood had gone from ragingly pissed to simple frustration.

It was about 3 a.m. when I made it home and had to do my usual circle to find parking. This time I didn't have to go too far away, thankfully.

Ever since the night Soren grabbed me, I'd been extra vigilant about any movement or presence in the shadows. He never had popped out of a dark corner since then, but I guess he didn't need to, since he could just waltz up to me at work.

A fresh spark of anger hurried my steps. It never crossed my mind that Laith would also be someone I'd need to watch out for. Someone else trying to control me as they stalked me from the shadows. Creeping in my windows. Following me to *work*, for fuck's sake.

I probably should have figured he'd keep pushing boundaries after that first night. It was obvious in hindsight, which made me feel like an idiot. If he followed me home once, what was to stop him from doing it multiple times? I might have had a Master's degree in chemistry, but I was clearly as dumb as a box of rocks when it came to people's intentions.

My mind kept ruminating on Laith's betrayal, the humiliation of what he had seen me do in the bedroom, as I stuck my key in the front door on autopilot. I hadn't even bothered to glance in the windows to see if the lights were on.

They were on, and Justin was still awake.

I heard a commotion as I opened the door, a sudden smashing of keys at the computer and some frantic mouse clicking. By the time I stepped inside, Justin spun in his computer chair to face me, his face flushed and his breathing a little heavy.

"Hey." He greeted me with a strained smile. "You're home early."

I tried not to sigh too loudly as I closed and locked the door. "I told you, I worked a partial tonight. Went to a bar after to unwind for a bit."

"Oh. Right."

I took in the state of him. His pants zipper was up but the top button was undone and he was sporting an erection.

"What?" he demanded.

"Nothing." Truly, I didn't care if he was watching porn and jerking off late at night. While it used to upset me, especially when he turned me down, I'd become resigned to it. "Hey, I got a voicemail from the apartment manager and they haven't gotten the rent yet. What's that about?"

His flushed face instantly paled. "They called *you*?"

"Yeah. I'm the primary on the lease, remember?"

"Um, shit." He rubbed his face. "Sorry, Heather. It must have slipped my mind. Send me your half and I'll pay it asap."

I stared at him. "Dude, are you losing it? I already sent you my half."

"No, you didn't."

"Jesus Christ, Justin." I whipped out my phone and pulled up my banking app. "Here, see? I sent it to you right after I got paid."

He looked at my screen and frowned. "That's weird. It must not have come through on my end because I never got it."

"How's that possible? It's the same automatic transfer I have set up every month."

"I dunno. Maybe try it again?"

Discomfort prickled at the back of my skull like a warning. "No. The money never got kicked back to me or anything, so I'm not sending you a second payment. Are you sure you didn't get it?"

"Positive."

"Let me see."

"What?" He said it in the same defensive tone as moments earlier.

"Let me see your account. Maybe you didn't see it."

"I definitely didn't get it." He was still in front of his computer, blocking the screen and turning ever so slightly as I moved through the apartment—taking off my shoes, setting my purse down, touching the frame of my family photo, taking out my phone.

"Why are you being so shifty?" I asked.

"What the hell are you talking about?" he shot back. "I'm not shifty. Why are *you* coming home at three in the morning?"

I gave him an incredulous look and in the silence that followed, a tinny, feminine voice piped up from his headphones on the desk.

"Hey, where'd you go, BigJ69? ShadowDaddy is about to overthrow you as the highest tipper for the night. You don't wanna miss my cute little asshole!"

Justin said absolutely nothing, but his expression told me all I needed to know. My nerves were already so frayed about Laith and the rent, that I couldn't react with anything but tired resignation. And deep down, I wasn't even surprised.

"BigJ69, huh? Sounds like I interrupted something."

"No, that's not me," he sputtered. "It's not live or anything. It's a recording. Just a random clip I found."

"Oh yeah? Let me see." I moved toward the computer, reaching for the mouse and he knocked it away.

"Don't touch my shit. I don't need to prove anything to you."

I crossed my arms, stunned as to why he couldn't own up and take accountability for a single thing. And why had I put up with it for so long?

"Are you lying to me about the rent too?"

"I'm not lying!"

"Did you spend the fucking rent money on tipping cam girls?" My eyes narrowed, remembering what Soren had said. "Did you lose your job and not tell me?"

Justin barked out a laugh that sounded forced and fake. "You're fucking crazy. Do you feel high and mighty accusing me of all this shit when *you're* the one coming home at 3 a.m.?"

"You know what? Whatever. I'm done."

I marched to the bedroom and pulled a duffel bag out of the closet. Justin stood in the threshold, watching as I packed clothes.

"Didn't realize you were this dramatic," he muttered.

I ignored him, filling my bag with essential clothing and shoes before heading to the ensuite to gather my toiletries. He came into the bedroom then, still observing me with an air of ridicule.

"You're not *actually* leaving."

I zipped my skincare items and makeup into a travel bag and dumped it in the duffel before I answered.

"I'll call Tina in the morning and tell her I'm off the lease. You work out with her if you want to stay and find a roommate, break the lease, whatever. Not my problem anymore."

"What the fuck, Heather? I can't afford to stay here *or* break the lease!"

"Should have thought of that before you blew all our money, BigJ69. Excuse me." I moved past him, dropped the duffel at the front door, then returned to the bedroom to put my laptop, headphones, all my needed electronics, into my work backpack.

Only then did I hear a soft, "Look, I'm sorry. Please don't leave."

His quiet, sad tone pulled at my heart strings. It almost melted the hard edges of my anger like it had done so many times before. Almost.

But finding out what Laith had done was a breaking point for me. Not just his stalking, but for every single time I let someone steamroll over me. This wasn't the first time I was certain I'd caught Justin in a lie—nor the second or the third—only for him to deny it and accuse me of being unreasonable.

I had to thank Laith in a way. It felt like the wool over my eyes had been thrown back and I could finally see everything clearly. I saw how manipulative Justin was, how he denied any wrongdoing until real consequences slapped him in the face.

And I wasn't going to throw myself under the bus to save him from those consequences anymore.

"I'm sorry I didn't tell you about getting laid off, okay?" Justin said while I packed. "I was gonna figure something out. I still am! I just need a little time, okay? I'll pay you back for the rent."

I sighed, rolled up the cord of my phone charger, and stuck it in one of my backpack compartments. "I know it's embarrassing to not be the provider or whatever, but if you would have just told me the truth, I would have supported you. I would have happily taken over the rent, touched up your resume, if you had just...treated me like a partner instead of an invisible ATM. Did you at least apply for unemployment benefits?"

"Uh, no." Justin shuffled uncomfortably behind me. "I don't qualify because I actually, kind of...quit."

"Oh, wonderful." I shouldered the backpack. "Good luck with everything, Justin."

"Heather, come on! Don't do this."

I started to leave the bedroom, but my momentum rocked backward. I glared over my shoulder. "Let go of me, Justin."

"Look, please don't go." His voice cracked and he blinked quickly, though I saw no tears in his eyes. "I'm sorry about everything, okay? I just didn't want to stress you out. I promise I'm working on something *big* and we won't have to worry about rent or anything soon. If everything goes right, you won't have to work at all!"

"I don't even want to know what kind of crypto scheme or whatever you've fallen for. I'm done, Justin. *We're* done."

I turned and twisted, trying to pull out of his grasp, but he held firm on the backpack's top handle.

"Don't say that. You don't mean it. You're just pissed right now and I get it. When you've cooled off, we can talk about it. Take the bed. I'll sleep on the couch to give you space."

I thought my anger had lowered to a simmer, but those words were like gasoline pouring onto embers. My resentment demon, rather than whispering doubts into my ear, now took possession over my entire body.

My arms slid out of the backpack straps and I whipped around, fists clenched. "You *don't* know what I'm feeling now because you've never bothered to fucking ask," I said in a low, furious growl. "You've *never* cared about how I felt unless my feelings were inconvenient for *you*. You're selfish and immature. You've taken me for granted throughout our entire relationship. I have bent over backwards to make your life comfortable and happy for years, and you're content to just *take* from me. Oh yeah, sometimes you're nice enough to make me think you *could* care, or you *could* be thoughtful, but coffee and pastries don't win you any boyfriend awards. You've never *really* listened. You've never *once* put me first while I have diminished myself for you over and over again. So listen carefully because this is the last time I'm saying it: I. Am fucking. Done."

I turned and headed straight for my purse I left on the living room side table, grabbed it, and then the duffel bag I left by the front door. The photo of me and my parents passed in my periphery, but I couldn't risk crossing the room to grab it. I didn't think Justin would physically prevent me from leaving, but I didn't want to take that chance. If I was leaving, it had to happen right now.

With a hard yank, I pulled the front door open. "You hear that, Soren?" I yelled into the empty living room. "I'm fucking done with you too, you piece of shit!"

From Justin's view, I must have looked actually crazy, but what did I care? I took my luggage and walked away from the last five years of my life.

# Chapter 17

## *Heather*

Leaving was both exhilarating and terrifying.

As soon as I got in my car and left the complex, I didn't know where to go or what to do. So I just drove. I rolled down my windows, opened my moonroof, and hit the freeway.

The cold night air rushed in and washed over me, stinging my skin and making my hair blow around wildly. The wind tempered my anger and brought my mind into sharp clarity.

I had done it. Actually done the thing that had been buried under excuses, fears, and justifications for months. I was free. I was also alone and without a place to stay.

As the sky began to lighten with oncoming daytime, I realized I was approaching the same park I hiked through to reach Sanguine. How funny that my internal autopilot would bring me back here.

I entered the park but took a different route, choosing to stop at a lookout spot to watch the sun rise and figure out my next moves. I kept the windows open as I turned the car off, letting the fresh air and sounds of birds and animal calls fill my senses.

Tonight I had to work. When I got off, I needed a place to stay. A hotel room would work for a little while, but I'd have to figure out long term housing soon. Maybe someone at work could use a roommate. It would be a good place to start.

At some point I would have to go back to the apartment to retrieve my backpack, since I slid out of it to escape Justin. Hopefully he wouldn't be too quick to sell my laptop and headphones that were in there.

I pulled out my phone and cursed. "Shit." The battery was running out and my only charger was in the backpack too.

The phone vibrated to life in my hand, startling me. Justin was calling. I swiped the red button to end the call, but then the texts started flooding in.

> Justin: Heather, please answer the phone. I just want to know you're okay.

I rolled my eyes at that and stuck the phone back in the cup holder.

> Justin: I will be patient and wait for you to come home. This is not the end of us.

> Justin: We have a life together. I made mistakes, but don't throw us away like this.

> Justin: Just let me know you're alive and I'll give you the space you need.

He called a second time. I ended it without answering again, then turned my phone off to save the battery.

Motion flashed in my rearview mirror and I froze, wondering if it could be Soren or even Laith, following me from home and stomping all over my boundaries as usual. I reached for my keys, ready to stick them in the ignition and stomp on the gas pedal to get away from all prying eyes.

But it was only a flock of wild turkeys emerging from the brush and I sighed out my relief, sagging into the seat.

The sun rose slowly through the trees, casting long, orange shadows and I huffed out a laugh at my stupidity. Laith wouldn't be out here in daylight. But Soren? Who knew. He might have a GPS tracker, cameras and microphones in my car. Shaking him wouldn't be easy.

*Unless you stayed in Sanguine.*

The voice in my head now sounded less like resentment and more like a bolder version of me with dangerous, wild ideas. Where would I even stay in Sanguine? With the vampire who admitted to stalking and spying on me?

A thought came to me then, one that might have been pure coincidence but it held enough weight that I sat with it a while. Soren had never bothered me at home after that first night. He came up to me at work because he could get past the gate. Laith couldn't.

Could Soren have been keeping his distance because of Laith? Was there actually a kernel of truth to Laith's claim that he was protecting me?

I drummed my fingers on the steering wheel, glancing at my blank, silent phone. It was too early to call my apartment manager or check in to a hotel. I had hours to kill, needed sleep, and wasn't too keen on napping in my car. Even if I closed all my windows and locked the car, I felt too vulnerable, too exposed.

There were a few coworkers I could call and ask to crash on their couches, but the idea was...off-putting. No one had any idea that Justin and I were rocky, plus they were just now getting off the night shift and had their own families and lives to manage. And if Soren had bugged my car, I didn't want any more innocent people getting caught in his crosshairs.

Where else could I go?

The more my thoughts tumbled around, the more Sanguine and Laith seemed like the best of my shitty options. Despite what he'd done, I got the sense that his intentions had been pure. There was almost an innocence about him, a genuine earnestness that I wanted to believe in. But then again, I was clearly a shitty judge of character.

He'd at least come clean about following me, and didn't try to deny it or twist my words into a situation that made me sound crazy.

I absently watched the family of turkeys cross the road, unable to believe I was making excuses for a guy who literally stalked me. But of the three men I was fed up with, Laith seemed the least likely to be using me for his own gain.

Well, aside from taking my blood. But at least he was honest about that.

After a few more minutes of hemming and hawing, I turned my phone back on. It buzzed and lit up with notifications, all texts and voicemails from Justin, of course.

"Motherfucker," I hissed. My battery dropped to three percent.

I swiped away all the messages from Justin and paused when I saw one from Soren.

> S: You missed our check-in. Message me
> ASAP. Better have info for me or I'll come
> find you. :)

My stomach knotted with anxiety as I remembered his threat that night he grabbed me. How in the world would I get him to leave me alone? Would the cops even be able to do anything?

*Laith can help. He told you as much.*

I scrolled to the end of my notifications. There was nothing from Laith except that message with the vampire emoji. God, was that just a few hours ago? How had my whole life flipped on its head between then and now?

It had to be a good sign that he never texted or called, right? That meant he was honoring my wishes about being left alone. I didn't know for sure if he'd followed me home or not, but if he had, would he have appeared if he heard me and Justin fighting? If he saw me leaving the apartment with a packed bag, would he have checked on me?

All my instincts said yes, he would have. In every interaction we had, Laith did seem to care about me. Maybe even a little *too* much for someone he barely knew.

He was...a lot. But I was exhausted, raw, and wrung out. And being around someone who cared and knew how to make me feel like myself seemed like exactly what I needed right then.

My battery dropped to two percent and I called his number before I could second guess any longer.

It took a while before I heard the line ring, accompanied by soft static. The ringing went on until I got his voicemail.

"What's up? This is Des. You've reached Laith's phone. Laith is busy trying to balance a teacup on his ass, but if you ask me, he does *not* have enough junk in the trunk to compete with a Kardashian."

In the background, I heard Laith's voice call out, "Hey, what are you doing with my phone? Give me that!"

Even with my raw, frayed feelings, I managed to smile

at the scuffling noises that followed. Then too soon, I heard the beep that signaled me to record a message and I had to remember why I was mad at him.

"Hey, it's me. It's Heather, I mean." I paused to chew my lip. My impulse was to apologize for my outburst last night, but was I really sorry? No. Getting chewed out was a light punishment for stalking. But, unlike with Justin, I wasn't completely ready to close the door on Laith yet.

"I was wondering if we could talk," I said. "I'm still upset about what you told me, but...some stuff has happened and I could use a friendly ear right now. It's morning now, so you're probably asleep but maybe we can meet at our usual spot tonight? I have to go into work so it'll have to be earlier. Maybe 8? My phone's about to die so you might not hear from me until—shit!"

A series of warning beeps sounded in my ear and I pulled the phone away to see a dead, blank screen. "God-damn it." I pressed on the power button, but my phone was well and truly dead.

I thought of returning to the apartment right then for my charger, but quickly nixed that idea. It was too soon to face Justin again. I'd be better off buying a new one, but again it was too early for any stores to be open.

"Well." I turned on the car and started backing out of the parking space. "Might as well explore a vampire city in the daytime, I guess."

There were humans in Sanguine, after all. Some places had to be open during the day, right? Maybe I could borrow a charger while grabbing breakfast in a cafe or something. Hopefully no one would mind if I put my head down for a nap. I was so accustomed to being a night owl at this point, it was a wonder how I wasn't a vampire myself.

I drove to the parking lot at my usual trail head. After

making sure my duffel bag was locked up and secure, I shouldered my purse and headed off into the woods.

Before, I had only seen the fringes of Sanguine by the light of day. That felt so long ago—back when I'd been too afraid to actually set foot in the city. Now, I walked through what truly felt like a ghost town.

Not a soul was out on the streets. The rising sun illuminated wooden and metal shutters sealed tightly over the windows of businesses and homes. Nothing stirred. There wasn't even a breeze.

I came to Pulse Point, the club I'd become so familiar with in the last couple of weeks. All the lights were off, windows and doors shuttered tight enough so that not even a crack of sunlight could get in. It looked abandoned, desolate. If I were seeing it for the first time now, I wouldn't have believed that it was a lively, busy club only a few hours ago. It looked like it had been closed down for years.

I turned in a circle, considering my options. A couple of blocks away was the blood bank. The white square building looked yellowed and aged in the morning sun. All of its lights and signage were turned off. Not a sign of life there either.

"Hmm." I kept walking deeper in to the city, figuring I'd go a couple more blocks before hiking back to my car and driving to the nearest Starbucks.

The streets and buildings looked older as I headed into the heart of the town. Most homes were modest, single-story attached buildings, but there were a few grander looking structures that were two or three stories tall with steep roofs, aged brick walls, and ivy climbing up the sides. They reminded me of those classic brownstones on the east coast.

It occurred to me that I didn't know anything about

where Laith lived. He had said he was part of the ruling clan, so did he have one of these bigger, fancier homes?

I came to a small open square and scanned the surrounding buildings, wondering if Laith was inside any of them. Did he sleep in a coffin, forearms crossed over his chest? I snickered, picturing the likely offense and horror on his face if I were to ask him that.

Everything had been so still since I arrived in the vampire city that the movement in the corner of my eye nearly made me jump out of my skin.

"Oh fuck!" I gasped, my hand slapping to my chest. "You scared the hell out of me."

A man walked through the shadows of a narrow alley-way. His gait was odd, feet dragging heavily like he was bone-tired or maybe injured.

I lowered my hand, squinting as I tried to get a better look at him. "Are you okay? Do you need help?"

He was muttering something under his breath as he shuffled closer, and I felt the first pinpricks of danger at the back of my skull.

"Wait, stop." I stretched out my hand. "The sun's out. Don't come any closer! You'll get hurt, right?"

The man emerged from the alley into the square, straight into direct sunlight.

He didn't burst into flame, but he did look badly sunburned with red skin and blisters covering his face. His eyes were yellow and bloodshot with thick tear tracks running down his face. So maybe he wasn't a vampire? But his mouth hung partially open and I could see the tips of fangs.

He looked dazed, unfocused. Possibly on drugs. What kind of drugs did vampires even have?

"Hey. You shouldn't be out in the sun, right?" I injected

every ounce of friendly and pleasant I could muster into my voice. Who knew what would set him off?

"The sun." He looked toward the sky, a jubilant smile breaking out across his cracked lips. "The sun is out! It's beautiful."

"Yes, but you look a little burned. Maybe you should keep to the shade for a while? I can find you some help." I felt like I was trying to convince a tiger to go back into its cage.

"My kind, we never get to see the sun. Never get to see the world like this." Thick tears ran down his face as he turned, taking in his surroundings. "The light! The shadows! We never get to see this. Fuck, it's so beautiful."

He had apparently forgotten about me, which was a relief. I started edging toward another alley across the square, as far away from him as possible. He continued to spin around in circles, marveling at the sunlight. I waited until his back was turned before speedwalking into the alley. But my relief was short-lived when my foot caught a loose cobble stone and kicked it across the ground.

The vampire whipped around, his fangs bared and saliva dripping from his mouth. There was no time to reason with him, no space between breaths that allowed me to think. My instincts recognized a predator at the first sight of those fangs and I ran.

It felt like I barely got anywhere, barely crossed any distance when he caught up to me.

He tackled me from behind and I landed hard with a pained cry on my hands and knees. Then a sharp, ripping pain at my neck had me screaming. It hurt so bad that it stole my breath. Warm blood ran over my chest and coated my hands.

Fangs withdrew from my flesh and I scrambled to get

away, but my own blood made the ground slick and I couldn't gain any leverage. The vampire pulled me back by my arm, and this time he bit roughly into my tricep.

"Stop!" I cried. "Stop! Somebody help!"

Blood continued to pour down my neck and he removed his fangs to lick a trail from my collarbone to my ear with a savoring moan. It would have turned my stomach if I wasn't so concerned with escaping.

"Please stop," I whimpered. "Please, you're hurting me."

He said nothing, just licked and bit me like I was some kind of living buffet. Every time I tried to pull away, he drew me back. My strength was quickly depleting as more blood left my body, while his strength seemed to be growing. He was rough, jerking and pulling me in various ways to bite different parts of me with no reactions to my cries of pain or pleas to stop.

My vision began to darken and my brain grew sluggish. *I'm losing a lot of blood. Oh god, I'm going to die out here.*

The vampire dragged his tongue down my forearm to my wrist, chasing a trail of blood from my upper arm. His fangs scraped my wrist, the same place Laith had fed from me so many times.

My last conscious thought was of Laith holding my wrist to his lips, kissing my knuckles, and how much care he always took to not hurt me.

# Chapter 18

## *Laith*

I woke up with a start, shooting straight up in bed with ragged breaths and my heart racing. "What the hell?"

I scrubbed my face, trying to remember if I'd had a dream that was slipping away or heard some noise that startled me.

But there was nothing. I had been dead asleep and my bedroom was silent.

Falling back on the pillow, I reached for my phone. And just as quickly, my heart started racing again. There was a missed call and voicemail from Heather.

I frowned at the time of the message. Nearly 6 a.m. this morning. Why would she call so early? She *knew* I couldn't be out in the daytime, right?

In any case, it was just past dusk now. Well over twelve hours since she called.

I listened to her message, confusion knitting my brow. She wanted to meet? Did she have a change of heart so soon after walking out all pissed off? And what did she mean by *some stuff happened*?

I called her back and immediately got her voicemail.

Unsurprising, since her message had cut off just as she mentioned her battery dying. I let the phone drop to my chest, and noticed this sense of unease, of distress and alarm, hadn't stopped coursing through my body since I woke up.

The last time I'd felt this had been the first night I'd showed up at Heather's apartment, when I'd just missed whoever spooked the hell out of her.

I got out of bed and quickly dressed, then left my apartment to head up to the main floor of the Blood 'til Dawn compound. A few clan members were already up and around the great room. Thorne and Rhain looked like two dark clouds, their heads bent together over the island counter.

"What's going on?" I asked by way of greeting.

"Pyke most likely attacked someone," Thorne grumbled. "A couple of brusang reported seeing him before sunset, clothes and skin drenched in blood. Looked like a butcher, they said. The blood bank hasn't reported any stolen blood from their storage, so he's probably hurt someone. Or worse."

"Fuck." My hand came to my chest. The sense of unease was getting worse, like a fist trying to squeeze the life out of my beating heart. "But that's...he's never harmed anyone before, has he?"

"No, which is the only reason we've let him be. He just wanders around all day, high on drae and staring at the sun." Rhain closed and opened a fist on the marble counter. "But who knows how long he's gone without feeding? He probably got desperate. And if he attacked someone during the day, it was probably a human. They're gonna be freaked out."

"Even though we've told them, time and time again, not

to go out during daylight hours." Thorne rolled his eyes before he stuck a darakt cigarette in his mouth and lit up.

The unease in my chest turned to straight-up dread. "Where is Pyke? Do we have him?"

"Not yet. We're about to hit the streets now, to find him and his possible victim." Thorne lifted a brow at me. "You coming?"

"Yeah, let's go! What are we waiting for?"

Rhain gave me a curious look over his shoulder. "What's got you so riled up?"

The words didn't want to come out. To speak them would make the possibility even more real.

"I got this bad feeling, guys." My hand returned to my chest, as if I could massage away the suffocating sensations of dread and panic. "I think he might've hurt Heather. My blood mate."

———

EVERYONE RALLIED to help me find Heather, even those who were off their patrol shifts that night. My gratitude couldn't be put into words, but the guys understood. Even Cyan, haunted and depressed from seeing Kalix, dragged himself out of bed and Tavia's arms to join the search.

"You'd do it for me," he said with a slap on my shoulder when I told him he didn't have to come. "I need fresh air and something else on my mind, anyway."

Dusk fell to night and Sanguine came to life as Blood 'til Dawn spread out in search of one of our own. Heather didn't know it yet, but she was part of us. The ruling clan of vampires would make sure she was safe and unharmed.

Best case scenario, she wasn't in the territory at all. She was in the human world, still pissed off and avoiding me, and this feeling in my chest was just gas or something. And whoever Pyke had fed on was minimally injured.

The first place I went to was Pulse Point, since that was where she'd mentioned meeting in her message. None of the staff had seen her, so it was a quick dead end. Regardless, I checked every room, storage closet, and circled the perimeter of the building. All the while, I kept calling her phone, even though I knew it was a long shot.

There was no sign of her, not even a trace of her scent. If she had been to the club, too much time had passed. Too many other bodies had occupied the same space and contaminated it with their own scents.

I left the club and started walking up the next block, senses alert like a bloodhound. If the slightest breeze carried that sweet, lily fragrance my way, I did not want to miss it. I checked every dark corner, under every stoop, and even in dumpsters. Finding nothing time and time again was both a relief and a disappointment.

A call came through as I was re-listening to Heather's voice message for the tenth time, trying to figure out if she mentioned anything I had missed. I answered it, dread and desperation tightening my throat.

"Hey, Cy. Got anything?"

"Not yet," he said. "Just updating you. We finished one sweep and are moving on to the next block." He rattled off the streets he and the others already covered.

"Thanks. I'm a bit north of the Heart, heading toward Novak's place."

"Sounds good. Rhain's headed that way, you two will probably overlap soon. We'll keep you posted."

I rubbed my chest after ending the call. It was getting harder to breathe and more painful by the minute. My heart and lungs felt like they were being squeezed in a vice.

"This better not be you, Heather," I muttered, sweeping my gaze down all over the alley. "You better be snuggled up in a blanket or something. Watching TV. Petting a dog. Whatever humans do when they're cozy and safe. Temkra, please keep her safe." I didn't know if our goddess could watch over blood mates in the human world, but it didn't hurt to ask.

The minutes crawled by and the sensation in my chest became crushing. I had to keep looking down to make sure my sternum wasn't caving in. My instinct was to move faster. There was a pressing sense of *running out of time* that scared the hell out of me. But I focused on each breath and made sure to do thorough sweeps. The last thing I wanted to do was hurry and miss something important in my rush.

My phone rang and I brought it up to my ear without checking who it was. "Yeah?" I rasped.

"Found him," Rhain said over background noise that sounded like a struggle. "He's covered in blood like they said. Want to come over here and take a whiff?"

"Where are you?"

He named a street that was two blocks over. I ran over there, the chest pain easing up slightly. Hopefully that was a good sign.

Rhain stood under a street lamp with his arms crossed. His stillness and the heavy shadows on his huge, hulking form made him look like a gargoyle. At his feet, Pyke sat on the ground. He was fidgeting and rocking slightly back and forth, muttering to himself.

I was across the street, heading their way when the scent of her blood hit me. Velvety petals, floral and sweet.

Fucking hell. My worst fear was true.

"Where is she?" I demanded, coming to a stop in front of the addict. "What the fuck did you do with her?"

Pyke took his sweet ass time looking up to meet my eyes. He had the yellow gaze and tear tracks of long-term draitrium use. Dried blood coated his mouth, chin, neck, and stained the front of his already-stained shirt. Heather's blood.

"Huh?"

The pain in my chest spread to my limbs like kindling catching fire. All my restraint focused on not swinging at him. It wasn't that I didn't want to hurt him, I just didn't trust myself to hold back. He couldn't tell me where Heather was if I killed him.

"Your last meal," I said through clenched teeth. "The source of all the blood covering you right now. Where is she?"

He brought a hand to his lips, rubbing off some of the dried blood flaking there, then touched his fingertip to his tongue.

That was when I fucking lost my shit.

I grabbed his shirt and hauled him upwards. He was thin and light, thanks to too many drugs and not enough actual sustenance. Using Rhain's torso as a wall, I held up the junkie while unleashing all of my fury into his face.

"You had no fucking right to take from her!" I roared. "Her blood is all over you like yesterday's vomit and you don't have enough fucking brain cells left to tell me where you left her?"

Pyke struggled in my hold to the best of his ability, which was not much. "I don't know what you're talking about," he whined, legs kicking in the air. "I was high, I don't remember the last blood meal I had."

I released one fist from his shirt and clamped it around

his throat. His eyes bugged out in fear, and then the real struggle for his life began.

"Laith," Rhain said with a note of warning. It was the *don't-kill-him-or-you'll-be-in-deep-shit-with-Thorne* warning.

Thorne hated the drae junkies probably more than anyone, but killing one without cause was still a serious offense.

"I'm good," I assured Rhain. "I'm not going to kill him. Yet." I cocked my head, my only movement except for the flailing vampire at the end of my arm. "But depending on what he tells me about my blood mate, he might enjoy a cold turkey detox for the rest of his pathetic life."

That got Pyke to stop fighting me, the fear on his reddening face kicking up another notch. If there was one thing addicts feared more than death, it was going without drugs.

"I didn't know she was your blood mate," he wheezed. "I was just so hungry. The blood bank blacklisted me so it's been weeks since I fed."

"That's interesting. I don't recall asking. Can you rub those last few brain cells together and tell me what I actually asked you?"

"I can't...can't breathe..."

"Laith," Rhain said again.

I opened my hand and let the addict fall in a heap of dead weight. He lay on his side, coughing and wheezing while I paced the ground in front of him, eyes up. I'd be too tempted to kick him in the ribs if I looked down at him.

As soon as his breathing started to normalize, I paused to stare down at him. "Better tell me what I want to know or you're going up in the air again."

"No. No up in the air." He pushed himself to sitting, his

hands raised in surrender with his head lowered. "I—uh, my memory's hazy but uh—"

"Did I fucking ask you for excuses?"

"Sorry! I, um, I'm pretty sure I saw her in the square. The sun was shining on her hair, it was really bright. Like gold. Or honey."

Rhain was already getting his phone out. "Check the square and all the surrounding alleyways," he barked into it before ending the call. "You go ahead," he said to me. "I'll get him to the detox center."

"Thanks, bro. Love you!" I took off running but didn't miss his answering grunt.

The urgent feeling in my chest grew as I neared the square in the center of the Heart. The open, flat space was where we held many festivals and events, including Cyan and Tavia's mating ceremony a few months ago.

I turned into an alley and spotted Des at the far end, closest to the square. "Hey, find anything?"

He shook his head as I approached. "Plenty of suspicious stains in this one, but if you didn't pick up her scent in there, we're crossing off."

"No, I didn't scent anything." I rubbed my chest again, which Des noticed right away.

"You keep doing that. On the verge of a heart attack or what?"

"I dunno. I think it's got to do with her, though. Almost feels like...like she's dying or something. Like her life force is trying desperately to hold on but it's losing grip. I just feel this...clawing, squeezing pain on my heart and lungs."

"Well, tell her to hold the fuck on. We're not stopping 'til we find her. And if the sun comes up first, we'll send humans out to search."

Des strode confidently toward the center of the square,

heading for the alley directly across from the one he just checked.

"What if we're in the completely wrong area?" Panic started settling in as I followed him. "He's so blitzed out of his mind, he could have thought someone's courtyard was the square. She's in bad shape, Des, and if we're too late..."

I paused, all my nerves lighting up at the distinct floral scent in the air. My head whipped around, looking down one of the other nondescript alleyways. The fist around my heart made a crushing, desperate squeeze.

"Laith?"

I made a beeline for the alley without answering, trusting Des to connect the dots. Heather's scent grew stronger and there was a dark, bitter undertone to it. It was her blood, lots of it, that had been dried for *hours*.

"Heather!" I called. "Heather, I'm here. Can you hear me?"

There was no movement or sound answering. I moved aside debris, stacked crates, flattened cardboard, garbage bags, and found nothing. The scent of her dried blood was so overpowering, I was nearly choking on it. It surrounded me and I was panicking too fucking much to follow it like a trail. Where the fuck was she?

I got on my hands and knees, desperately looking under dumpsters and shallow porch stairs. The ground was fucking filthy, but her dried blood was under my palms. There was no surface I wouldn't crawl on to reach her.

And then...there she was.

I saw her hair first. Honey-golden waves matted with filth and blood.

She was pale and unmoving, curled up in a fetal position against the wall and the dumpster. A flattened cardboard box covered her torso, like it was supposed to be a blanket or the only protection she could find against her attacker.

Protection that *I* should have provided.

"Heather! Oh fuck. Oh, sweet Temkra."

I moved the box away gingerly, and a rage I'd never felt before filled my veins at the sight of her injuries. She hadn't just been bitten. Her whole body had been mauled.

Ragged flesh wounds covered her neck and her arm, and that was just what I could see. My heart that had felt like it was going to stop at any moment, now beat at a furious pace.

"Heather?" I sounded like a child, small and afraid. "Time to wake up, Science Barbie. We've got to get you out of here."

She was *so* still. I feared the worst but my brain refused to acknowledge the possibility. Her cheek was cold when I touched the backs of my fingers to it. I tried to move her hair away from her neck, but it stuck to the wound due to all the dried blood.

"Heather, please."

I didn't know what I was asking for. I was unraveling.

She couldn't be gone. She just couldn't.

And if she was...

There was only one way to bring her back.

I brought my own wrist to my fangs just as a hand clamped down on my shoulder.

"Hold on, Laith." It was Cyan.

"Get off me." I rolled my shoulder out of his grip. "I have to save her."

"Her heart's beating. Take a breath and listen. She's still here."

I listened intently, hoping against hope that he was right. My own heartbeat was so loud and erratic, her injuries so awful and gut-churning, that I couldn't focus on anything else.

My ears strained, but I heard it. Fuck, her poor heart was sluggish, weak, and not moving enough blood.

"Let's take her to the blood bank," Cyan said. "She needs a transfusion and they have blood in storage."

His words were reaching me. They made sense. Heather was alive and she could be saved if I hurried. I was terrified to move her and possibly injure her further, but there was no fucking way I was letting anyone else touch her.

I slid my arms under her legs and back as gently as I could. She weighed practically nothing and felt like a block of ice. Des, my best fucking friend, was ready, covering her with his jacket as soon as I secured her against my chest.

"Come on, Science Barbie." I tried to walk smoothly so as to not jostle her. "I know it's gonna piss you off, but I'm not letting you out of my sight again. Forget your boyfriend. I'm done sharing you with him." My mouth brushed her cool forehead. "If you want to fight me about it, fine. But you've got to get better and wake up first. That's the deal."

# Chapter 19

## *Laith*

Heather ended up needing four pints of blood before she was considered in stable condition. It was touch and go for a while. The blood bank staff weren't emergency surgeons, so they had to call in a human doctor who'd driven across the territory, because he only served one of the more densely human populated areas of Sanguine.

They kept her all night and promised to monitor her during the following day. I refused to leave, naturally, so I spent the day sleeping fitfully in one of their tiny sun-proofed rooms.

By dusk the following night, Heather was cleared to leave. Thorne arranged for her to be transported in an ambulance, since she was still unconscious and we didn't have vehicles that could move her safely.

I insisted on riding along, naturally.

Rebecca was giving me discharge instructions while other staff loaded Heather into the van, but I was so exhausted and wrung out, I was only half-listening.

"Heather needs rest and good nutrition, most of all," she said. "I know it's difficult, but I don't recommend feeding from her for about a week. Nor any...strenuous physical activity," she added with a lifted brow.

"What the fuck?" I stared at her, unblinking. "You've known me for how long, and you think I'd make demands of my blood mate while she's recovering?"

"I just—I'm sorry," she stammered. "Forget I said anything. I wasn't trying to be disrespectful."

"No, Becks. I'm sorry." I scrubbed my face. "I'm running on fumes and not in a jokey mood. Sorry I snapped."

Rebecca gave me a sympathetic look. "Here." She handed me a couple sheets of paper stapled together. "In case you forget anything."

"Thanks." I scanned the discharge instructions and nearly went cross-eyed at the second page. It was a list of things, some of which I vaguely recognized as human foods. "Uh, what's this?" I showed it to Rebecca.

"That's a chicken noodle soup recipe. It will be excellent for Heather's recovery." She smirked. "Show it to Tavia. She'll help you out."

"She better." The amounts next to each item didn't make any sense to me. A cup of chopped carrots? What kind of cup, like a coffee mug? "Looks like witchcraft to me."

"The best recipes always are." Rebecca's smiled softened. "I know you'll take good care of her. Call us if you need anything."

Even though the fist around my heart had loosened since Heather was deemed stable, I knew she wasn't completely out of the woods yet. I wouldn't be able to take a full breath until she was awake and talking. Her coloring looked better at least, and her heartbeat sounded much stronger.

I held her hand in the ambulance just so I could feel the delicate pulse in her wrist the whole time.

Once home, I carried her straight to my room, bypassing Amy and Tavia in the kitchen with a couple glasses of wine. The two of them immediately stopped talking and openly stared, mouths agape at Heather in my arms.

"Oh my God, is that—" Tavia started.

"Heather?!" Amy finished.

"Keep your voices down," I groused. "Wait, you both know her?"

"She was in Sapien for a few days. She stumbled in from the human world." Amy followed me first, with Tavia on her heels.

"When was this?" I pushed open the door with my shoulder, then Tavia darted around and slipped past us to hold it open. "Thanks."

"Sure. And this was months ago." She looked at her friend. "Before Amy became a brusang. Me and Cy weren't even officially mated yet. I met her when he took me back to visit."

"Huh." I took each step down the stairs slowly, wishing for the first time that we had an elevator to the basement level. "I had no idea she was in Sapien."

"She was totally in the dark about vampires existing," Amy said, still behind me.

"'Til she saw Cy with her own eyes," Tavia added wryly, a few steps ahead of me on the stairs. "Pretty hard to deny at that point."

"Of course Cy would be the first vampire she encounters and not me," I huffed.

Tavia whipped around once she hit the floor, her gray eyes wide. "Oh my God, it just hit me. *Heather* is the blood mate everyone's talking about? The one you tasted before knowing anything about her?"

"Yes, Tav. It's very exciting. Can you *please* keep your voice down?"

"Shit, sorry," she whispered. "It's just...wow. So uncanny that we're all getting mated to you guys, right?"

"Straight out of a romance novel," Amy teased in a singsong voice, skipping past me to join Tavia.

"Oh hush, you." Tavia smacked her best friend playfully, then twirled around to face me. "Want me to get the door, Laith? So you don't have to let go of her."

"Yeah, thanks. Keys are in my left pocket."

"Do you have stuff in your place for her?" Amy asked. "She'll need water and juice for sure. Plus snacks and blankets."

"Toiletries too," added Tavia, maneuvering around Heather's feet to fish my keys out of my jacket pocket. "And spare clothes. Me and Bea will loan some of our stuff, but she'll probably want some of her own soap, moisturizer, shampoo, and conditioner at very least. Oh, and a hairbrush, and scrunchies, just in case she wants her hair out of the way. And a toothbrush."

My shoulders sagged, which had nothing to do with Heather's slight weight in my arms. "I don't have any of that stuff," I admitted. "I didn't expect to bring her home until..." *Until she finally ditched her boyfriend and fell in love with me.*

"Leave it to me," Amy said. "I can get everything she needs right now. You good, Tav?"

"Yep." Tavia unlocked my door and held it open, standing aside to let me and Heather through.

"Here we go, Science Barbie." The lights turned on automatically as I entered my bedroom, thankfully staying low and dimmed.

"Here." Tavia followed us in and pulled down my sheets and comforter, then fluffed up my pillows.

"Thanks." I lowered Heather down carefully and pulled the covers up to her chest. Then and only then, did I step back and allow myself to take a huge sighing breath.

"She'll be alright." Tavia pinned me with a hard look as she headed for the bedroom door. "Don't pull a Cy and blame yourself for this. You didn't hurt her, Laith."

"I know, but I just...I don't get why she would come here during the day. She even works the night shift. She's nocturnal already."

"She made a mistake, and she's lucky that you found her."

"If I had just warned her against—"

"Nope, don't go there."

I could see why Tavia had no problem standing up to Amy's bullies when they were growing up. She stared me down from the doorway and I knew she would not give me any room to argue.

"You need to sleep too," she informed me. "Gonna get in next to your girl or should I make you a bed on the couch?"

"Neither." I smoothed the covers over Heather one last time. "I'll sleep on the floor in here."

"The floor?"

"Yeah, but not yet. You've been amazing and I appreciate you, but I've got one more favor to ask."

"Okay." Tavia cocked her head, waiting.

I pulled the discharge instructions out of my pocket. "Will you help me make chicken noodle soup?"

"Cy, Cy! Come here, you've got to take a picture." Des stuck his obnoxious finger in my face. "He's crying! I see actual tears."

"You want to lose that finger, Des?" I lifted the knife and waved it in his direction.

"Don't! That's dangerous." Tavia grabbed my wrist and brought it back to the cutting board. "But yeah, that is a *potent* onion. Geez." She sniffled and used her upper arm to wipe the tears from her own eyes.

"I don't understand how humans can eat these things." I blinked, trying to clear my eyes of the stinging. It felt like the air was biting me.

At least I didn't wipe my eyes with my hands this time. I'd already made that mistake once.

"Well, we don't usually eat them raw. Once they're cooked, they don't taste as strongly." Tavia, to her credit, was making a valiant effort to teach me without making fun of me too harshly.

"Are the other ingredients like this?"

"No, this is the worst one. Everything else is easy."

"Thank fuck."

"You're doing great, Laith." Tavia's smile and praise seemed genuine, but she was probably on the verge of bursting out laughing.

"Are you sure this is going to make Heather's soup taste good?"

"Yes. Onions, carrots, celery." Tavia counted them on her fingers. "Those three are the backbone and base of almost all great soup recipes. I'm not even much of a cook, but Amy's a pro. She'll vouch for me."

"Okay." I was skeptical, but continued my chopping as Tavia had shown me.

She claimed chicken noodle soup was a staple in many human households and was often made when someone was feeling ill, which backed up what Rebecca had said. I just didn't understand how a staple food could be *so* much work. There were no less than twelve ingredients on the list and they all had to be added in a particular order. The pot in which everything cooked also had to be at a certain temperature.

How had humans survived this long when they needed to eat so many different things? Vampires *only* needed blood. Sometimes we supplemented with bone marrow and raw or lightly cooked meat, but that was it.

"Okay, done with onions," I announced.

"Carrots and celery are next. Same thing, just dice them up into roughly uniform pieces." Tavia hovered at my elbow. "You sure you don't want help with chopping?"

"No. I want to be the one to make this for her. I just need to make sure I'm not fucking it up."

"I could start the chicken broth and save you some time. It's just putting bouillon cubes in hot water."

"Nope. Thank you, but I will do every step of this recipe myself."

"All right, suit yourself."

Amy returned not long after I finished dropping my first ingredients in the pot. Her arms were full of shopping bags and Tavia rushed over to help her unload.

"I got all of Heather's essentials. Smells amazing in here. Whatcha cookin', Tav?"

"Me, nothing." Tavia grinned and angled her head toward me. "Laith is making soup for Heather."

"Oh, really?" Amy's black eyes, surrounding her blue irises, widened with interest. "What kind of soup?"

"Chicken noodle." I peered into the pot on the stove with zero idea of what I should be looking for.

"Aw, one of the classics," Amy cooed. "Have you made it before?"

"I've never cooked anything before."

Amy made an odd little squeak of noise, then pressed her palms to her heart, looking at Tavia with an odd expression.

Tavia snorted. "Please don't swoon."

"I can't help it. He's being *sooo* sweet."

"I just want her to feel better. How do I know when it's ready for the next stuff?"

"Oh, let me help!" Amy ran to my side, standing on tiptoes to look inside the pot. "You've got the aromatics, good. Grab a spoon and give that a stir. Then we need to add some salt."

Amy gave me no-nonsense instructions for the rest of the dish, which I appreciated. A half hour later, I dumped dry noodles into the pot and stirred them in.

"Let that simmer for about fifteen minutes, and you'll be done." She flicked a dishtowel over her shoulder and crossed her arms, beaming at me. The tips of her diminutive fangs showed through her smile. "Congratulations on cooking your first dish, Laith."

"Will you taste it when it's done?" I asked. "I've never had it so I won't be able to judge if it's good or not."

"Sure, but I know it'll taste great. Everything I told you to do was exactly how I've made soup in Sapien for years. It was always a hit." Her expression shifted slightly. "You're already taking great care of her, Laith. She's lucky to have you."

"Thanks for saying that, but it doesn't feel like it." I turned back to the soup, watching the condensation form on the pot lid. "She could have died. I know I wasn't directly responsible for that, but I keep wondering what more I could have done to keep her safe."

All the chicken noodle soup in the world couldn't make up for what she had been through.

# Chapter 20

# *Heather*

Inever realized how much my entire body could hurt until I started waking up right then. It hurt to breathe, hurt to move my eyelids. It hurt to moan in pain because my throat and mouth were so dried out and sore.

"Hey," a soft male voice said. "Welcome back. Take it slow. I've got water here when you're ready."

It didn't sound like Justin. A doctor, maybe? Was I in a hospital? It sure felt like I'd been hit by a semi truck.

There was something about the warmth in that voice that soothed me.

"Where..." That one word was all I could croak out. I still didn't have the strength to lift my eyelids yet.

"You're safe, Science Barbie. That's all that matters."

That nickname sparked connections in my mind, a verbal trigger waking up memories, feelings, and lighting up the threads between all of them.

"...Laith?"

"No need to sound so disappointed."

I didn't have the strength to laugh, but a rush of joy and relief coursed through me at the dry wit in his voice. My instincts knew this person was safe, even if my head was still a little fuzzy at connecting the dots.

"Can you sit up just a little? You must be thirsty and I don't want to waterboard you."

"Give me...a sec."

"Yup. Go as slow as you need."

It took an agonizingly long time to lift my head and my eyelids still weighed a million pounds each.

"Here, how about I do this?"

A large hand gently cradled the back of my skull, prompting my head to tilt forward. Moments later I felt a glass rim against my cracked lips, and then the cool, sweet kiss of water.

"Easy. Not too fast."

I took a few eager sips. The angle of the glass made the water flow slowly and didn't allow for me to take big gulps. Probably to keep me from choking, which was a sound idea.

"There we go. Good job."

The glass pulled away, and the hand gently slid from the back of my head. I missed the contact of that hand before it was fully gone. I couldn't be sure, but it felt like fingers trailed through my hair as it pulled away. An intimate, loving touch.

Everything about this was intimate, I realized. The soft way he spoke to me and the way he'd been waiting for me to wake up, water at the ready.

Those tiny sips of water were everything. I already felt stronger, despite still feeling like a piece of flattened hamburger meat.

"Gonna try sitting up again." My voice sounded clearer, which spurred me on even more.

"Go for it. I'm right here. And so is the bed beneath you in case you fall, like, six inches."

I braced my arms at my sides. "Hell of a drop that would be."

"Yeah, but you've got this."

It took a few false starts, but I managed to press myself up at the same time I finally opened my eyes. Laith sat on the bed next to me, his magenta eyes exhausted and full of concern. His blond hair was mussed and not in that sexy-on-purpose way. He looked like he hadn't slept in days.

Our eyes met and he cocked his head with a smirk. "I knew you could do it, Science Barbie."

I was only upright for a few seconds before everything came back to me in a rush. Fighting with Justin. The break up and leaving the apartment. Watching the sunrise in my car before deciding to come to Sanguine. The strange man in the square, and then...

"Fuck, fuck! Oh my God—" The room and comfy bed were gone and I was back in that filthy alley with the cold ground underneath me. Hot blood poured over my skin, *my* blood, from jagged wounds left by sawing fangs.

"Hey, Heather. Look at me. You're okay. Shhh, it's over. We got you out of there."

I blinked and saw red eyes, not yellow ones. I felt the weight of two hands holding the sides of my face, the same hands that had brought my head up to drink water.

Thumbs stroked my cheekbones while I hyperventilated. My shaking hands flew up to my neck, where I now felt a large bandage over my ragged wounds. More bandages covered my hands and arms. I held my hands out in front of me and saw scraped palms and broken fingernails.

"What...happened?"

Laith made a groaning noise like he didn't really want to tell me. "A draitrium junkie got you. They're vampires addicted to a drug that lets them walk in the daylight. They get so obsessed with feeling the sun that they forget to feed. It was probably weeks since he'd last had blood." His hand lowered, resting lightly on top of mine. "You never could have known, but Sanguine isn't safe during the day because of the likes of him. I didn't get your voicemail until I woke up at dusk. But if I'd known you were coming right after you called, I would have told you to stay in your world until the sun went down."

"How..." I swallowed and coughed, which prompted Laith to hand me my water glass. I took a few large gulps this time and tried again. "How long until you found me?"

He closed his eyes and gave a sad little shake of his head. "Too long. I just...I'm glad we weren't too late."

I tried to set the water glass aside and he took it from me, placing it on a nightstand next to a steaming bowl that smelled absolutely incredible.

"You hungry?" he asked.

My stomach was still knotted from the lingering terror of being in that alley, but food would probably go a long way towards regaining strength. So I nodded and sat up a little straighter. "What is it?"

"Chicken noodle soup."

"Oh my God, that sounds amazing."

"Really?" Laith laughed as he stirred the soup. "Tavia, Amy, and Rebecca from the blood bank all said the same thing, but I can't wrap my head around it."

*Amy and Tavia?* Those names sounded familiar, but my brain couldn't quite connect them to anyone yet.

"Our food is probably so strange to you," I remarked.

"It is strange. And overly complicated."

He brought a spoonful to my mouth. Truthfully, I wasn't sure if I could feed myself without making a mess, so I was grateful to be babied. No one had ever fussed over me when I wasn't feeling well, so this was quite the silver lining to almost dying in the street.

And when that soup hit my tongue in an explosion of rich, hearty flavors, I closed my eyes and let out an audible, "Mmmm," that bordered on sexual. "Holy shit, that is the best chicken noodle I've ever tasted."

Laith paused in his stirring of a second spoonful for me. "Are you being serious?"

"Yes! More, please." I couldn't remember the last time I had eaten anything and was probably starving, but I had meant every word. "It tastes homemade, like something a grandma would make from scratch for the people she loved."

"You mean that? Like, actually?"

"Hurry up and feed me some more." I actually managed to laugh through the ache in my throat. The water, the soup, just Laith being here, all of it was making me better in a matter of minutes.

Laith fed me spoonful after spoonful until the silverware clattered in an empty bowl and my belly felt delightfully full.

"There's more if you want some," he said. "I made a pretty big batch."

I stared at him, not fully comprehending the words. "*You* made the soup?"

He shrugged. "I had help."

"You made it for *me*?"

He nodded. "I was told it would make you feel better, so it was a no-brainer. And you definitely look better than when you first woke up."

This vampire, who probably barely knew what a noodle was, had made me soup. Really good soup. And then fed it to me.

The kindness of that entire gesture felt like too much to face at the moment. So I deflected with some good old-fashioned self-deprecation.

"Oh yeah? I went from day-old garbage to slightly fresher garbage?" I glanced down at my cut-up, bandaged hands again, feeling self-conscious in front of Laith for the first time since waking up. Fuck, I probably looked just as road-killish as I felt. He still looked gorgeous, despite the messy hair and fatigue.

"No," he said softly. "From a survivor to a fighter."

My eyelids drooped and I stifled a yawn. "Well, I'm about to go from fighter to sleeper."

"Good. Rest. You still need plenty of it."

He gathered up the dishes while I scooted down in the bed, pulling the covers up to my chest. The sheets smelled faintly of him. Was this his bed? His house?

My thoughts trailed off into the emptiness of sleep before Laith even closed the bedroom door behind him.

———

Waking up the second time was much easier and far less traumatic. I stretched out stiff, sore limbs and let my eyelids flutter open. The aches and pains were still deep and ever present, but I definitely had more energy than before.

*I would kill for a hot shower right now.* Nothing sounded better than scrubbing myself clean from what had happened in the alley, at least physically.

But first I had to find my way to a bathroom. The room was completely dark except for a small, plug-in night light in an outlet. It illuminated a dark shape on the floor I couldn't make out. My best guess was a pile of laundry.

After letting my eyes adjust, I saw an outline of a lamp

on the bedside table and fumbled for a switch. The light that clicked on was so soft, I hardly needed to blink. What came into focus next to the lamp, however, shocked me into blinking several times.

A vase full of lilies greeted me with their bright, beautiful colors, long stamens, and curling petals. Red and orange tiger lilies filled most of the vase, with a few pink and white varieties adding their own pops of color.

The sound of rustling tore my attention away from the flowers and a jolt of fear had me scrambling across the bed, curling up and looking for a place to hide.

"Hey, you're awake," said the laundry pile on the floor, which turned out to be Laith on a messy pile of blankets and pillows. "How are you feeling?" he asked with a yawn.

"Um, better." I settled back against the headboard, willing my racing heart to calm down.

After a moment of thought, I slid further down the bed, feeling a little faint. My body was stiff and aching from lack of movement, and I was probably still dangerously low on blood.

"Good. You hungry? There's more soup, although I'm told that's not what you eat when you first wake up, so I got some breakfast things too."

Homemade soup, my favorite flowers next to my bed, and now breakfast? His care was...overwhelming. Not in a bad way, but I wasn't sure how to receive it.

"I'm okay right now," I said. "Why are you sleeping on the floor?"

Laith rolled up to a seat, the hair on the back of his head adorably cowlicked and messy. "I wanted to be close by if you needed anything but I also didn't want to freak you out by sleeping in the bed next to you. Hence the floor." His arm swept out as if showing me something grand.

"This is your bed?" I had already suspected as much, but it was another thing to have it confirmed by him.

"Uh-huh. Comfy, isn't it?"

"Well, yeah. But you didn't have to put me here. I mean…" I rubbed my face like trying to clear cobwebs from my mind. "A couch or something would have been fine. I didn't need to take over your bed."

"Nonsense. You're injured and should be comfortable." He flopped back down, hands behind his head. "I don't mind the floor, anyway. Vampires can sleep almost anywhere. We're heavily controlled by our circadian rhythms. Back in the day, our ancestors used to bury themselves alive to sleep and escape sunlight."

"Or they'd sneak into empty coffins?"

Laith laughed and the sound warmed me almost as much as the chicken soup had. "Not really. I'm sure it's happened once or twice, but those old pine boxes weren't exactly light-proof. To be honest, I'm not sure how we came to be associated with sleeping in coffins. Maybe they used to jump into open graves and pull dirt over themselves."

"That saves the hard work of digging the hole themselves."

"Exactly. I bet you're on the right track, Science Barbie."

Even now, talking to him was easy. I wanted to curl up in the nest of his bed and just listen to his voice. Then I remembered how filthy I was, and how that filth was now all over his sheets.

Guilt pierced my chest. "Do you think I could take a shower? And maybe borrow a change of clothes? I'll wash everything, including your bedding. I've probably made your whole room stink like that alley. I'm really sorr—"

"I have one rule." Laith cut me off with a raised finger.

"No apologizing. None of what happened is your fault, Heather. Of course you can shower. The girls have already lent you a few changes of clothes. And don't worry about washing my stuff." He rolled and sprang to his feet, approaching the bedside with a cheeky grin. "Any other questions?"

I glanced at the bouquet of lilies. "What's with the flowers?"

He looked at the vase and then back at me. "They're your favorite, right? I just thought you might like them." His tone was casual, but I detected a note of hurt in his voice. "I didn't go by your apartment again, if that's what you're worried about. We actually have an excellent plant nursery here with an attached florist. They didn't have a huge lily selection, but I bought what they had."

It hadn't even occurred to me to wonder if Laith went back to the apartment. He was always so earnest, so genuine and open that it was easy to take him at his word. So unlike Justin, who I always had to wonder if he was telling me the full truth about anything. Who also *never* brought me flowers just to make me happy.

"I love them. They're beautiful." The relief was palpable on Laith's face. "I didn't think you went back to the apartment. They're just unexpected. Thank you."

"Of course," he said easily before holding out his hands. "Here, I'll show you where the shower is."

With some effort, I swung my legs down to the side of the bed and placed my hands in his. I allowed him to pull me to my feet and quickly realized I could barely support my own weight. He didn't yank me up hard and yet the momentum sent me crashing against his chest.

"Whoa, I've got you." Laith held me upright, supporting my upper arms.

"I guess a shower's a little ambitious." Already I felt out of breath, my heart straining to distribute blood to all the necessary places. "Should've tried getting out of bed first."

"Give it a minute," Laith said. "Take it slow. It's not the end of the world if you don't shower today."

Eventually, I could stand on my own but walking was a little more dicey. With every attempt, I only took a few steps before the world seemed to tilt from under me and I had to grab Laith for support. We'd barely crossed the bedroom before I was out of breath and trembling with effort.

"What the hell?" I wheezed. My forehead leaned against Laith's chest because just standing took that much out of me.

"You were badly hurt. You're still healing." His arm was slung around my waist in an easy, casual hold that felt supportive and maybe even affectionate. Like he was built for me to lean on and be held by, and he was one-hundred percent on board with that.

"Do you want to go back to bed?" he asked after a few moments of my labored breathing. "We can try again after a nap."

A nap sounded excellent but I *needed* to scrub that alley off of my skin. Maybe it was just psychological, but I felt like I couldn't begin to distance the attack in my mind until every physical trace was gone from my body.

"Is that the bathroom?" I nodded at the door a few feet away.

"Yeah."

If the nearest bathroom was halfway across the house, I might have rethought it. But an ensuite was doable.

"No, I want to keep going."

I braced myself for an argument, for Laith insisting that I rest some more, and he wouldn't have even been wrong.

But his fingers gently drummed on my waist and he said, "Ready to move when you are, Science Barbie."

I took a few more breaths and made sure my feet were solid under me. "Let's go, Vampire Ken."

He barked out a laugh. "That's great. I love it. When you're better, we'll get matching T-shirts."

With slow, shuffling steps, and one hand on Laith's arm, I made it to the wall. Using him and the wall for support, I made my way slowly over the threshold.

Laith flicked on the light, revealing a clean and somewhat bare bathroom with a small vanity, toilet, and a standing shower with a simple blue curtain.

"Take a rest and I'll start the shower," he said, helping me to the toilet.

"Clean bathroom *and* you even have the seat down." I was already dizzy and out of breath by the time I lowered myself down to the closed lid.

He laughed and pushed the shower curtain aside to turn on the taps. "I've been single for a while but I'm not *that* terrible of a bachelor."

"Why?"

"Well, I'm not a neat freak or anything but a clean bathroom's essential. What's the point of taking a shower when the rest of the room is all nasty?"

"No, I mean..." I started to laugh and had to catch my breath again. He was so damn...adorable. "Why have you been single for a while?"

"Oh." He paused, looking away while he tested the water temperature with his fingers. "I don't know. Just never met someone I was that interested in, I guess."

"Sorry." I rubbed my eyes until colored dots swam in my vision. "I don't know why I asked that."

"It's okay. You can ask me anything you want." He tested the water again, then dropped his hand and stepped away. "Water's ready. All that stuff is yours." He pointed at the soap, shampoo, and conditioner in the shower wall cubbie, and then at the stack of towels and clothes neatly folded on the back of the toilet.

The room was already humid and warm, and I couldn't wait to feel the hot water pelt my skin. I placed one hand on the vanity counter, preparing to stand up.

"Thank you, Laith."

"Of course." He started backing toward the door and hesitated. "Are you sure you'll be okay to..."

I pushed down on the counter, using all my strength to propel myself up from the toilet lid, and immediately began to wobble.

"Easy." Laith was there in an instant, holding me to soften the hard landing of my butt back on the toilet lid. "You're good. I got you."

"God damn it," I groaned, dropping my forehead on his shoulder. "This is so annoying. I hate being helpless."

"I know, Heather." He rubbed my back in sympathy. "You're so strong and capable. I know this is hard for you."

There was no teasing and not an ounce of malice in his voice. It was almost a shock that he was being genuine and not making fun of me for being less coordinated than a toddler. But that was who he was.

I squeezed my eyes shut against the hot prick of frustrated tears. I had gotten so close. I could *feel* the water. I was sitting on the toilet for shit's sake! But I had too much pride to ask Laith to carry me into the shower, even though I knew he'd do it without a second thought.

"It's okay to accept help, you know," he said gently, as if reading my thoughts. "It doesn't make you weak."

"You're not helping me shower," I said through clenched teeth. "I just...I can't. I know you wouldn't *do* anything, but I need privacy, okay? I need to be in here alone."

Laith sighed and leaned back, leveling me with a hard look. "If I was confident you wouldn't fall and crack your head on the tile, I'd be happy to leave you alone in here. But as you are right now Heather, I'm not confident in that at all."

He angled his head toward the steaming water. "If you want this shower right now, you're going to have to let me help you. So what's it going to be?"

# Chapter 21

---

*Heather*

I couldn't say how long I thought about it, sitting on the toilet lid while the shower ran. As the small room filled with steam and heat, Laith never rushed me for an answer. He just waited patiently for me to make the call.

"Here's the thing," I said after a long silence. "I know you're trustworthy and not a bad person. I'm really grateful that you found me and you're taking care of me."

"Okay." He sounded tentative.

"But if you're going to help me take a shower, I don't want you to look at me. To watch me like you did through my window that night."

There it was. His mouth tightened and his Adam's apple bobbed in a hard swallow. "I won't. I promise."

Hearing him say those words was sufficient, but he went on.

"It won't happen again, okay? Whatever the future holds for you and me, I'll never look at you in such a gratuitous way again. That was wrong of me to do. It was violating and I understand if you don't trust me. I mean it when I say I just want to help you right now. That's all. I'm not trying to sneak peeks of you or anything."

His magenta gaze flicked up mine, looking almost as raw and vulnerable as I felt, before dropping. "I'm sorry for spying on you."

He'd already apologized right after he told me about it, but I felt a new sense of calm and acceptance in hearing it again. Unlike the first time, my thoughts weren't clouded by anger. Now I was ready to hear him, to believe him.

The regret was painstakingly clear in his body language, and the remorse genuine in every word he said.

"I do trust you, Laith," I said. "And I believe that it won't happen again. I just..." I waved a hand toward the shower. "I'm nervous about this, I guess."

"Of course you are." He looked at the shower stall and then at me, chewing his lip as if trying to work something out in his head. "I could just stand nearby. You can grab me if you need support, but maybe do all the important stuff on your own?"

"Okay." I nodded, trying to muster confidence about undressing and bathing in front of this vampire that I was definitely attracted to. "Sure. Let's try it."

Laith helped me stand up and together, we peeled all the bandages off my wounds. Nothing was open and actively bleeding, so I figured it was safe to wash my injuries, albeit carefully.

I watched Laith's face as he carefully lifted the largest bandage from my neck. His brows furrowed slightly in concentration and concern. He knew what my blood tasted like, what it smelled like. It was the thing that drove him to pursue me, after all. But he never looked lustful or hungry as any of my wounds were exposed.

When it came time to undress, he dutifully looked

away. Then with one hand on his shoulder, I made my way into the shower stall. Thank God there wasn't a tub to step into. Laith shuffled forward, looking only as far as seeing where he needed to be to support me.

"Oh my God…" I moaned when the hot water hit me, closing my eyes to relish in the sensation.

"Bet that feels amazing." I could hear the smile in Laith's voice.

"So fucking good." I released his shoulder to scrub a hand over my hair and face, using my opposite hand against the shower wall to support my weight.

"You okay?"

"Yeah." I wiped the water from my eyes and almost laughed. Laith was standing halfway in and out of the shower, his face on the outer side of the curtain. "Your clothes are going to get soaked." His lounge pants and T-shirt were already getting dotted with water.

"It's fine. I'll change out of them later. Am I in a good spot?"

"Yeah, I think so."

I let the water saturate my hair and skin for another minute, then reached for shampoo and conditioner, which was where I ran into a problem. I needed both hands to pour the hair products.

Stubbornly, I tried bracing my elbow against the wall for balance, but my stupid body wasn't strong or coordinated enough to do that while pouring shampoo into my palm. I listed sideways, letting out a little squeak of alarm as I started sliding down the wall.

Before I could even say his name, Laith was there. His hand wrapped around my arm and he gently righted me. He took the full force of the spray, becoming completely soaked. In the next moment, he slipped behind me and brought both hands to my waist. Holding me steady.

"Go ahead," he said. "I got you."

I hesitated, glancing at him over my shoulder. Water plastered his hair to his skull and dripped down his face like tears. His gaze was down and to the side, keeping me in his periphery without looking full-on.

Between the support of his hands, I managed to shampoo and rinse my hair twice then rub in an obscene amount of conditioner. My arms were fatigued from the effort but I felt a thousand times better.

With my hair done, a new challenge emerged.

"Laith?"

"Yup?"

"Can you move the shower head? I need to use body wash."

One hand lifted away from my waist and the water overhead began spraying the shower wall instead of us. And then his firm, secure hold returned to my waist without any comment.

"Thank you."

"Of course."

Washing my body was far more nerve-wracking than washing my hair. I knew he wasn't looking, knew he was being steadfast and silent to keep me comfortable, but his presence was overpowering as I soaped and scrubbed my most intimate areas.

With my limited balance and mobility, there was also one place I couldn't easily reach.

"Um, do you think you could wash my back?"

Laith said nothing, but his open hand appeared in front of me. I placed the loofah in his palm, and his other hand gently transferred from my waist to my upper arm. The sponge swept across my upper back and shoulder blades in firm, circular strokes.

My eyes fell closed and my lips parted in utter bliss. God, what would a massage from him feel like? Every touch between us until this point had always been fleeting, which felt like a damn crime. His hands on me in this shower had to be the longest time he'd touched me continuously since we'd first met.

His steadying, solid contact, plus the simple intimacy of washing my back, made me want this shower to never end.

I wanted more of his touch, in fact. And I wanted him to look at me. *Really* look at me like he used to. With desire.

Too quickly, his scrubbing reached my lower back and lifted away just above my butt. "All done. You ready to rinse?"

"Yeah."

The stream of water returned, cascading over my hair and body. Washing away the alley, the dried blood, the terror of that moment. I knew, every once in a while, all the memories and intense fear would pop up to haunt me. But for now, I felt a quiet calmness settle in to my bones.

"Okay," I said to Laith once all the soap and conditioner ran down the drain. "I'm ready to get out."

He reached forward and shut off the water. "You good with the wall for a sec while I grab you a towel?"

I planted my palm and forearms against the wall, making sure I was secure before giving him the go ahead. He left the shower, then stuck his arm back inside the curtain, holding a folded, dry towel.

"Thanks." I pressed soft fabric to my face, neck, and chest with my free hand.

"Do you need help with, um..."

"Uh, yeah. Maybe."

Laith was back in the shower a second later, helping me unfold the towel so I could wrap it around my body. The whole time, his eyes were downcast, and I started to think he was taking the not-looking thing a little *too* seriously.

"I'm going to let you sit on the toilet again for a second," he said, leading me out of the shower. "I'm going to change into dry clothes. Things are getting wrinkled that I'm pretty sure aren't supposed to."

"Do I even want to know?" I snorted, dropping onto the toilet lid.

"The inside of my bellybutton. Feels really weird." He grinned at my befuddled look. "I'll be right back."

He was gone long enough that I managed to re-bandage the worst of my injuries, then pull on a borrowed T-shirt and soft cotton shorts from the stack of loaner clothes. By the time he returned, I was mostly dressed and completely exhausted.

"Hey now, don't fall asleep in here."

My impossibly heavy eyelids lifted just enough to see Laith kneeling in front of me, his hands out and hovering as if to catch me if I fell.

"You're so cute." In my half-asleep state, I wasn't sure if I thought the words or said them out loud.

"Well, thanks." Laith laughed softly. "Since I'm so cute, will you let me carry you to bed?"

"Mmkay." I was too tired to be mortified that he'd heard me. That was an awake-Heather problem.

I felt him scoop under my legs and back, and let myself fall limp against him.

"I put fresh sheets on for you," he said, breath soft against my hairline.

"You're the fucking best, you know that?" I mumbled into his shirt.

His chest shook with his soft chuckle. "Nah, you are."

The clean sheets felt like the greatest luxury on earth when he lay me down. With the last of my flagging strength, I grabbed his hand before he could move away. "One last favor to ask."

"Name it." Laith's thumb stroked over my knuckles.

I steeled myself with a breath. "Will you sleep next to me?"

He went completely still. "Are you sure?"

"Yes. I mean, you don't have to right *now*. I have no idea what time it is, but whenever you go to sleep—"

He jumped over me, sailing over my legs to land with a soft bounce on the other side of the bed. "Thought you'd never ask." He grinned while tucking himself under the top blanket.

I drifted off to sleep with a grin that matched his, and a sense of contentment that I hadn't felt in a long time.

# Chapter 22

## *Laith*

I woke up with the scent of lilies in my nose. Instinctively, I drew closer and realized my arm was draped around something soft but solid. A pillow?

My eyes drifted open to find honey blonde hair filling my vision. It was funny how dreams filtered over to reality upon waking sometimes. Any second now, I'd snap out of it and wake up alone like I usually did.

But that didn't happen.

With every blink I returned more solidly to the waking world and the memories of last night came rushing back. Helping Heather in the shower and her request to sleep next to her.

Next to her. *Not* spooning her, which was what I was currently doing.

I swallowed a curse, not wanting to wake her. How did this happen? I was firmly on my side of the bed and always, without fail, slept like a corpse.

But at some point during the day, I'd crossed the invisible barrier in the middle of the bed and buried my nose in her hair. Wrapped an arm around her waist and drew her into me.

I should have released her and scooted away the moment I figured it out. I knew, if I was going to stare at the side of her face, at her eyelashes low over her cheekbone and the adorably biteable curve of her exposed ear, I should do it at a distance.

But how could I when the dip of her waist fit my arm so perfectly? How could I be expected to pull away when her silky hair brushed over my lips and nose and her neck was right *there?*

My fangs pulsed with a dull ache in my mouth. It had been nearly a week since I'd fed from her and the hunger was starting to gnaw at me. But there was no way I'd take from her until she was fully recovered.

That thought was what made me scoot away. I'd always been good about my self-control, but with her, I wouldn't take chances. Being too close while she continued to heal was too much of a risk. I'd have to get ahold of some marrow to hold me over.

As soon as I severed the contact between our bodies, Heather stirred. She looked at me over her shoulder, and I was already a good two feet away on my side of the bed.

"Evening." I gave a little wave. "Or do humans say 'morning' even when they're waking up at night?"

"Mmm," was her only response as she rolled to her back, rubbing her eyes.

"Sleep well?"

She stretched and I couldn't keep myself from staring at the long, arching line of her back. Only when she opened her eyes again did I snap my gaze away. She didn't want me looking at her too closely. It probably went without saying that she didn't want me spooning her or smelling her hair either.

"Yeah. Amazing, actually." Heather pushed herself up to sit against the headboard. "I feel like a whole new woman."

"I'm glad to hear it." She looked much better too. Color had returned to her skin and her eyes were bright and clear. Her strength had also returned, as she'd sat up with no struggle.

"Fuck." She rubbed her face with both hands. "What day is it? How long have I been here?"

"This is the third day you've been here," I said. "It's been about five days since you came to Sanguine."

"Shit, I need to call my job."

My ears perked with interest that her first thought went to her workplace and not her boyfriend. "Your phone's a bit battered, but we found it in the alley and it's charging on the nightstand."

"Oh my God, thank you, Laith."

She turned toward the nightstand, pausing at the bouquet of lilies taking up most of the space. A surge of superficial pride filled me when she leaned in to smell them and lightly touched one of the soft petals.

I kept silent but watchful as she reached across for her phone, unplugged it from the charger and turned it on. Immediately, the device lit up and pinged with multiple notifications. Heather frowned at the screen and swiped with her finger but didn't comment on what she saw.

Was her boyfriend concerned about her being missing? Was he angry that his emotional—possibly physical— punching bag wasn't around for him to unleash his rage? Did he even care at all, or was he too busy jerking off to cam girls to notice Heather gone?

Heather tossed her phone down on the bed and sighed, then started pushing the covers back.

"Going somewhere?" I asked.

"Yeah, I gotta get back. Everything's a mess right now. My boss is probably pissed at me. My car probably has a dozen parking tickets on it. It's the middle of the week, so people must be wondering where I am."

"And let me guess. You've got to get back to *him*." The statement came out laced with all the pent-up bitterness I'd been feeling for weeks.

Heather cast me a surprised look, but the top had blown off everything I'd been holding back and it all came rushing out.

"I can't do this with you anymore, Heather. You're my blood mate. You should be with me. End of story." My fist curled around a piece of the blanket. "I have been patient with you. I've never pushed you. I've been trying to protect you from a distance since your boyfriend is so fucking useless at it. I will never treat you like a captive, but I can't even *begin* to tell you how wrong it always felt, letting you go home to him after I had your blood. I needed to have you every time, and I could smell that you wanted me. But still, I let you go because I respected that you didn't want to be unfaithful. I believed that you would choose me in the end. And now..." My fist tightened so hard that my palm ached. "I feel like an idiot for believing that."

"Laith, no." Heather started crawling across the bed toward me, but I held up a palm.

"Let me finish. Choosing me is asking for a lot, I know. I'm not gonna sit and try to convince you anymore. You know me now. You know vampires well enough. And I don't want to be an asshole, but I have to look out for myself here too." I brought my palm to my chest, meeting her gaze firmly. "If you go back to him tonight, do not come back to me."

Heather let out a soft gasp. "Laith—"

"I'm done waiting around, Heather. You're either mine or you're not. If you're not going to choose me, I'd rather know now than after weeks or months of false hope."

Silence ticked by, and Heather's blank face unnerved me with each passing second.

"Is that all?" she said with a surprisingly dry tone. "Have you said everything you wanted to say?"

A huge sigh deflated my chest. "Yeah, that's it."

She scooted closer, a weird smile playing at her lips.

I frowned. "What?"

Her hand slid over my fist, gently unclenched it from the blanket and threaded her fingers through mine. "I already broke up with him."

I stared at our joined hands and then at her face. "What?"

"After I saw you at the club, I went home and we... fought. It wasn't anything out of the ordinary, just the straw that broke the camel's back, I guess. I packed a bag and left. Then I called you because...I couldn't think of anywhere I'd rather be than with you."

Despite the elation spreading throughout my chest, I hadn't seen the fight for myself and couldn't tamp down my concern. "Did he hurt you?"

"No." She shook her head. "He tried to stop me from leaving, but I slipped out of the backpack he was holding onto. So I do have to go back eventually for my stuff, but not for him. Never for him." She looked up at me, her expression relaxed and open. "Because I'm yours."

I traced her cheekbone with my knuckle, marveling at the mere fact that I could touch her.

"Why didn't you say anything before I went off on my embarrassingly long and vulnerable monologue, Science Barbie?"

She snorted. "I tried, Vampire Ken, but you wouldn't let me."

"Oh, right."

"It was a very sweet monologue, though. Lots of passion. I could feel every word."

"You're going to rub it in at every opportunity now, aren't you?"

"Definitely."

Her smile lifted and mine lowered until we met in the middle. I fell into the kiss just as fast as I'd fallen for her. She opened for me at the slightest flick of my tongue and I surged inside greedily. I captured her little gasp of air as delicately as holding a bird between my palms. Her wings would never be crushed because she was wholly and completely mine.

My hand found its way to the back of her head, fingers luxuriating in the softness of her hair as I pulled her closer. Her hands on me were tentative at first, light touches of her fingertips on my neck and jaw, then grasping and holding just as desperately as I was.

Each kiss was a perfectly synchronized beat, growing braver and deeper, hungrier with each taste.

"Are you really mine?" The thought escaped in an awed whisper against her mouth.

"Yes." Heather's tongue darted out to meet mine, playful and teasing, before drawing away abruptly. "Are you mine?"

"Yes." I pressed her palm to the left side of my chest where my heart felt alive and beating for the first time in my life. "This is yours. Completely yours."

Heather smiled, then her expression shifted, becoming coy. "What else is mine?"

"Everything you want." I brought her hands to my lips and kissed her knuckles.

Her fingers uncurled and one slid under my top lip to graze the tip of my fang. I pulled her hand away, my hunger raging at the close proximity of her incredible blood. "Except for that."

She looked confused and even a bit rejected. "Don't you need my blood?"

"You need it more." I dared another kiss to the center of her palm. "To heal."

Heather pulled her hand from my grasp and let it drop to the bed between us. "Why are you like this?"

The question was abrupt, and a complete 180 from the light, happy mood of a moment ago.

I watched her expression carefully. "Like what?"

"Why are you so...caring?" She sounded genuinely frustrated, which confused me even more. "The flowers, the way you kiss, the way you make me laugh. You helped me take a shower without sneaking a single peek. You saved my life and made me fucking *soup*!"

Her explanation did not help with my confusion one bit. "Because I do care. About you. It's just what I'm supposed to do."

"You..." She trailed off, shook her head, then laughed quietly to herself. "You have done more for me in the few weeks I've known you than every boyfriend I've ever had, combined."

"And it still doesn't feel like enough." I reached for her hand, already hating any absence of touch from her.

She didn't pull away, but didn't return my hold either. "What if *I'm* not enough?" she said in a small voice.

The idea was impossible for me to comprehend. "What are you talking about? You're brilliant and beautiful, Science Barbie. You take my stupid sense of humor and dish it back twice as good. I can't imagine anyone better for me." I leaned forward until my forehead gently nudged against hers. "What have I done to give you the impression that you're not enough? Tell me and I'll fix it."

Heather's hairline brushed mine as she shook her head. "Not you. You've been amazing to me from the beginning."

"But your ex-boyfriend made you feel that way." It was damn satisfying to put the *ex* in front of that word.

She nodded. And despite the satisfaction of knowing she was no longer his, my chest felt heavy with sadness that she was ever made to feel less than.

"I bent over backwards for him," she admitted. "Did everything in my power to make his life easier and I wanted nothing in return except to just feel appreciated. Desired. Loved. All those things that are supposed to be normal, right?" Her fingers finally clasped around mine. "Then, with you, I did nothing but give you blood and you treat me like...like I'm worth keeping."

"You are worth that and so much more," I said. "And I'll tell you right now, Science Barbie, I don't intend on letting you go."

Another coy smile broke out on her face. "I feel like hearing that should be a red flag, but I just love that you want to keep me."

"I'll never hold you against your will. I'll just make you so incredibly happy and satisfied that you'll never want to leave."

"How do you intend to do that?" The note of playfulness returned to her voice and my senses lit up with desire.

"Come here."

I cupped a hand around her nape and closed the short distance for another kiss, this one harder and hungrier than before.

We fell to the bed together, one hand supporting the back of her head while my other hand roamed. She'd never been properly appreciated? Desired? Loved? I would show her, again and again.

Our tongues tangled while hands explored. Heather's legs slid apart and I took the space between them. Her hands never stopped moving, running up my arms and back like she couldn't get enough of me. The quickening beat of her heart was music in my ears. I loved hearing the anticipation from her body while she melted in my arms.

Then, all too quickly, she stiffened. I paused my next kiss, noting her heartbeat going a bit *too* fast.

"Heather?" I lifted away, finding her panting and her face flushed.

"Give me a sec. I'm just a little dizzy," she said between quick breaths.

I rolled to my side. "Guess it's too soon for any real heart-pounding fun. You're probably still low on blood."

She let out a frustrated groan, which made me laugh.

"There's no rush, Science Barbie. Your wellbeing comes first."

"Don't orgasms count toward well-being?"

"Well, yes. But probably not if they make your heart stop."

"Fine." She made a loud, exasperated sigh. "What else can we do?"

I lowered over her until our lips hovered inches apart. "I could kiss you breathless some more."

I stayed there long enough to see her answering smile before lowering all the way down. Our mouths fused together with practiced eased like we'd been doing this for decades already. My hand slid between her back and the bed, rolling her toward me. Her leg slid over my hip and I resisted the urge to press into the open space again. Kissing was plenty for now. We could have been counting cobwebs on the ceiling for all I cared. She was here and she was mine.

Heather's kisses deepened, pulling and nipping at my lips with an urgency that I also felt. Her leg wrapped around mine and drew me closer until we were flush against each other.

"Don't make this hard," I groaned.

I felt her grin against my neck. "Feels like it already is."

"Heather."

"Laith."

"Trust me, Science Barbie, I want to give you all the pleasure you've missed with human men." I brushed hair away from her face, entranced by her sparkling blue eyes. "But I want to take care of you properly first."

She tilted her hips, increasing the friction on my very hopeful erection. "So what are you waiting for?"

My fangs nearly stabbed into my lip. "Fucking Temkra, you're wicked."

"I want you." She kissed the racing pulse in my neck with eerie accuracy for a human. "I want to do more than just kiss."

"So do I. Just, hmm..." I couldn't think straight. The way she wrapped around me, the needy little whine in her voice, and her kisses peppering my neck were too much. Too distracting. Fuck me, how could I say no to her anyway?

Out of nowhere, she abruptly jerked back. "Wait. I have an idea."

I was instantly suspicious. "What?"

Her expression was a mixture of shyness and coy suggestion as she untangled from me, putting a foot of distance between us.

"What if I watched you like how you watched me?"

An image popped into my head; one I wasn't supposed to see. Heather in her bed, her head thrown back and back arched, hands working between her legs.

My body became doused in heat at the realization, erection aching in my pants. "You want to watch me...?" I stared at Heather, needing her confirmation.

"Yes." Her teeth sank into her bottom lip. "I want to watch you touch yourself."

## Chapter 23

---

### *Heather*

I didn't know how Laith would react. He became eerily still but didn't look shocked. He seemed more curious.

"You'd like that?" His voice took on a low huskiness, a smirk playing at his lips. "Or is this about getting even for when I saw you?"

My chest felt tight, my breaths coming in short. "It's not. I accept your apology for that and I'm ready to put it behind me."

Laith moved slowly, lithe like a panther as he sat up against the headboard. "So you just want to see me?" His hand moved over the front of his sweat pants, palming the thick ridge there. "You want to see how hard you make me?"

He'd barely done anything and my breath was already stuttering. I could partially blame it on my blood loss, but I knew that wasn't the real reason.

"Will you take off your shirt first?"

An eyebrow lifted. "Oh, you're going to be bossy about this, are you?" He leaned forward, reaching behind him to pull his T-shirt over his head.

Oh, he was into this. And so was I. A lot more than I thought I would be.

As the T-shirt lifted away, I saw wisps of dark golden hair on his stomach. Inch by inch, he slowly revealed pale skin and taut muscles. Long arms with rounded shoulders. Well-defined pectorals, obliques, and a flat stomach. There was scarring on the left side of his chest, raised tissue that looked intentionally done. That was interesting, but my attention seemed unable to focus on just one singular thing.

"Do you like being told what to do?" I asked, drinking in the long lines of his bare torso.

"Only when it's you." Laith inched his pants lower, exposing more of his hips and lower stomach. "I want to please you above all else, even if I'm touching myself. So tell me exactly what you want, Heather, and I'll give you something worth watching."

How could my heart be beating so fast if I was sitting still? The tension in the room felt solid, like a tightly wound string between us. Laith waited patiently, his eyes on me while his hands smoothed up and down his thighs. He seemed almost...nervous. A little self-conscious maybe, despite being objectively gorgeous and clearly experienced.

Laith had proven that I could trust him. Now it was my turn to show that he could trust me.

"Take your pants off slowly," I said. "And don't stop looking at me."

He inched the sweatpants lower down his thighs, his gaze warm and appreciating. "As if I could ever take my eyes off of you."

"You did a pretty good job of that in the shower."

"Because I promised you that I would." His pants were nearly to his knees, revealing red boxer shorts underneath.

"Now those, slowly."

Laith pulled in a sharp breath and did as he was told, eyes on me. The silky red fabric reminded me of a stage curtain lifting away for a tantalizing reveal. And what a reveal it was. His erection stretched up to his navel and the girth of him was almost more impressive than his length.

"What next, Heather?" He'd kicked the boxers all the way off and now sat fully naked, legs outstretched in front of him.

My mouth felt entirely too dry. He didn't have to do anything to be incredible to look at. "Go ahead and touch yourself how you usually would."

"You mean when I'm thinking of you?" He slid both palms over his inner thighs, then lightly gripped his balls and the base of his cock.

"You don't have to flatter me." Sure, I was cute. Even pretty when I put effort into my appearance. But I was no one's masturbation fantasy.

"I'm not." Laith began long, lazy strokes up and down his length, bringing himself to fully hard in mere seconds. "One taste of you and I was ruined for anyone else."

"Slow your hand down."

He groaned, eyes half shutting with the effort, but his hand slowed, his grip on himself loosening.

"What do you think about?"

"Fuck." His head fell back, connecting with the headboard with a thunk.

"I figured. But tell me how."

His chest heaved with a few ragged breaths before speaking. "I've thought about fucking you in front of him. Your ex."

That was not what I expected to hear. Heat radiated from my core outward. "You have?" I stuttered out.

"So many times. It's my biggest fantasy, actually." Laith

released his cock for a few rough breaths, his erection bobbing stiffly before coming to rest on his stomach. "I want to show him how you should have been treated the whole time. Fucked into oblivion every night. I want your screams of pleasure from another man to haunt him until his dying days." Laith thumbed the head of his cock and spread the bead of precum down his length. "In my mind, he's jealous and pissing himself in fear."

"Fear?" I choked out. "Fear of what?"

Laith grinned, his eyes flashing as he dragged his tongue along his fangs. For a moment, I saw the same predator I first noticed in the club.

"Because you're a bloodied, beautiful mess and he doesn't know how to handle it. He's freaking out over watching you come as I bite you and fuck you and drink your blood. Every bite is a claim on you that he was never man enough to take. You don't even realize he's there because I'm fucking you so well and making you delirious with pleasure. You're begging me for more, harder, and I'm giving it all to you. All the sad little human can do is watch and listen. It's my heaven and his personal hell."

At some point while listening to Laith's fantasy, I realized I was soaking wet. My thighs pressed together and I squirmed. My vampire's nostrils flared, inhaling deeply as he gripped the headboard, arm flexing as he anchored himself. His other hand jerked roughly at his cock.

"Why do you fantasize about that?" Maybe a better question was why did *I* find it so hot.

Laith made a sound somewhere between a laugh and a groan. "Because he should know what he lost and I won." His heavily lidded eyes met mine. "I don't have to fantasize to know he'll figure out that first part soon enough."

"Are you sure about that?" Before he could answer, I added, "Stop stroking."

"Fuck..." Laith slapped his hand down on the bed next to him, balling it into a fist. Then he quickly abandoned that idea to grip the headboard with both hands, as if bracing himself.

"Feels like you're gonna kill me," he panted, grinning. "And yes, I'm certain he'll be full of regret soon if he isn't already. I see you squirming. I can smell how turned on you are, and it's fucking delicious. You can edge me until my balls are as blue as a daytime sky. You're a prize, Science Barbie. And you're mine." His grin broadened through his heavy breaths. "I. Won."

My original idea was to be purely a viewer from beginning to end. It wasn't a hard and fast rule, but I'd never intended to touch him while he pleasured himself. But I couldn't stop myself from crawling across the bed. I planted my hands on either side of Laith's hips and kissed him with all the torrential emotions I didn't know how to put into words.

He kissed me back with equal force, a rough scraping of lips and fangs and tongues. The wooden slats in the headboard creaked under his punishing grip.

"You can let go," I whispered in the breath between one kiss and the next.

"Never." He tugged on my lip with his fangs, just enough for a nip of pain without drawing blood. "This is forever."

"I think we're talking about different things."

"Are we?"

I removed one of his hands from the headboard and wrapped it around the base of his cock. "Now show me how you make yourself come."

He kissed me again, swallowing my gasp as he wrapped my hand around his thick shaft, holding my fist closed around him. "Like this." Another nip of his fangs as he stroked my hand upward. "This is the only way I come from now on. By what you do to me."

Our hands moved together, his skin burning hot and velvety under my palm. Meanwhile his tongue surged across mine. He dominated the kiss, making my pulse fire rapidly until my lips tingled.

"Your taste," he groaned between one kiss and another. "Your scent. Your touch. Your *existence*. All my pleasure comes from you."

He swelled in my hand, hard as iron and slick with precome. Our hands became a blur and his breaths grew shorter, panting through his kisses.

"If you edge me again, I might actually die," he warned with a tight smile.

"No. I want to see you explode." My own breath came in short bursts as if I were the one on the edge. "I want to see how good I really make you feel."

"Fuck, Heather…" His forehead leaned on mine, his entire body wrought with coiled tension.

His release came with an animalistic growl and a spray of come that coated his chest and stomach. I heard a crack and wondered distantly if he'd broken the headboard, but my main focus was stroking him to completion, watching the utter bliss on his face as he reached the peak and came back down. Feeling the rough jerks and twitches as the aftershocks hit him.

Laith slid down until he was fully reclined on the bed. One hand remained stretched above him on the headboard, which he just now seemed to notice. "Yeah, I definitely broke that."

The busted slat was a hair's breadth from being completely ripped in two.

"Oh shit. I'm sorry."

He snorted. "For what? Making me come within an inch of my life?"

"Hey, you did most of the work. I just feel bad that your stuff got broken."

"It's nothing a few nails can't fix." He panted through a lopsided grin. "Can you get me a towel?"

I grabbed him one from the bathroom. Once cleaned up, Laith propped up some pillows and held his arms out. "Come here."

There were truly no words to describe the sensation of laying my head on his chest, feeling his arms fold around me while his heart beat under my ear. Especially after what we'd just done. It was everything I hoped for in a post-sex cuddle. Every part of me melted, and I felt completely at ease.

We didn't speak for several minutes, but the silence was relaxed. Intimate. Laith's fingers drifted through my hair. I felt his breaths slow and deepen. My own fingers started to explore, tracing across his chest.

"What's this?" I asked when my fingers found the raised texture of scar tissue directly across from where my head rested.

"My vow to Blood 'til Dawn." Laith's head turned, his lips brushing softly across my forehead. "We take vows and loyalty very seriously. Silver is the only substance that can scar a vampire, so we carve our vows into our skin as a permanent reminder."

"What vow did you make?"

"It's a coming-of-age ritual we do. When we turn one hundred, we're considered adults. The vow to the clan is part of the ceremony." He moved my finger over the characters, speaking each one in a language with rough, but beautifully rolling consonants. "My life belongs to my family, whether found or by blood. I am shelter to my kin and the vulnerable."

"That's really beautiful." I let my palm cover the markings. "Sounds painful, though."

"It was." I heard the smirk in his voice. "That's how you know I take my vows seriously. We are willing to endure anything to protect our people." His hand came over mine, fingers lacing together. "You know I'll be carving a vow to you during our mating ceremony, right?"

"Jesus." My fingers lifted, running over the raised tissue again. "And if I say you don't have to do that?"

"Doesn't matter. It will be looked down upon if I don't. People will question how committed I am to you if I'm not willing to put a little silver to my skin."

"*I* won't question it."

"Mm, maybe you should," he teased. "Maybe there wouldn't be so many human divorces if you had to sacrifice a little more."

"Do not go there, sir." I brought a finger up to his lips, which he promptly took into his mouth. "We already argued about human marriages. We don't need to hash it out again."

Laith chuckled while chewing affectionately on my finger like a teething puppy. "I'll be proud to carve my vow to you into my skin," he said. "Besides, I can't let Cyan show me up. His vow to Tavia goes from like nipple to bellybutton."

"Oh my god, that sounds terrible."

"I am kind of surprised that he didn't pass out."

"Do I have to carve vows into my skin too?"

"No, of course not." Laith removed my finger from his mouth and kissed my brow. "Your sacrifice will be your human lifespan. You'll be giving up what is natural to your kind to spend forever with me." His face drew back, his expression suddenly apprehensive. "I guess I never actually asked you. Is that something you're willing to do?"

Honestly? I couldn't comprehend living hundreds of years. It would probably be amazing in some ways, detrimental in others. But it seemed I wasn't the only human living past my natural lifespan, and all I really cared about right then was that I had Laith, and that he would be with me throughout those years too.

We were already off to a hell of a start. So why not see it through?

I leaned in, closing the distance again as I grabbed his lower lip with my teeth. "What do you think? There's no Science Barbie without her Vampire Ken."

His grin lit up his whole beautiful face. And the joy and lightness in my chest as we melted into more kisses felt like a sure sign that I made the right decision.

# Chapter 24

## *Heather*

"Laith."

"Mm." His voice was a gentle rumble and a puff of air on the back of my neck.

I tried to slide out from under the heavy arm around my waist, but he clamped down tighter.

An easy smile pulled at my lips as I looked over my shoulder and brushed a kiss over his cheek and the bridge of his nose.

"Let me go just for a minute."

"Never." His arm locked around me tighter and he even threw a leg over mine.

It would have been annoying if it wasn't so sweet.

"Laith, I really need to pee."

"Just pee on me. It's fine."

"Eww!" The sound of disgust became laughter as I smacked his arm, which finally loosened its hold around my waist.

"Hurry back." Laith's fingers trailed along my skin until the last possible moment as I climbed out of bed. "I miss you already."

I couldn't stop grinning as I did my business in the bathroom and washed my hands. How had I upgraded from a guy like Justin to a gorgeous vampire who was obsessed with me?

When I returned to the bedroom, Laith was a sight that stopped me in my tracks. He was stretched out, lithe muscles relaxed and pale skin unmarred, except for the scarification on his chest. His magenta eyes were hooded with sleep. He smiled when he saw me, and a fang glinted in the dim bedroom light.

"Come back here." He reached an arm out, inviting me back to the cocoon of warmth and sleep we'd made.

Tempting as it was, I was starving and getting a little cabin fever after days in this room.

"You got any more of that chicken soup left?"

Laith's hand dropped to the mattress as he sat up, feet swinging to the floor. "Yes, plenty. I'll bring you some."

"Let me come up with you," I suggested. "I'd love to stretch my legs, see the rest of where you live. Maybe meet some of your clan if they're around."

Laith looked surprised and then pleased. "I would love that. But are you sure you're up for it?"

"I'm hungry enough to eat a horse, but I feel great besides that." I raised my arms and did a little spin on the balls of my feet. "See? Balance is back and I've been standing on my own for a whole minute."

"You sure have." Laith's grin widened after I completed my twirl. "We should go dancing again when you're feeling a hundred percent."

Joy sparked in me like fireworks. "That would be amazing. I can't wait."

"Soon enough, Science Barbie." He rose from bed and started to get dressed.

"Speaking of hunger," I said, my pulse elevating slightly. "How are you doing? Do you need to feed from me?"

Laith's gaze immediately went to my neck while he secured his jeans with a belt. The raw want in his eyes made my heart beat faster. It would be different from now on. We no longer had to fight any urges. When the desire came, we could just let those feelings take over us. I couldn't wait to feel him drink from me with no reservations.

"Not yet." Laith jerked his gaze away, searching for a T-shirt. "You should eat another meal. Maybe have another day of rest to be safe. I know you feel fine, but I don't want to cause your body any undue stress."

"Are you sure?" I moved closer, taking advantage of his temporary blindness as he pulled a T-shirt over his head. "Maybe just a little taste?"

His smile grew vicious, fangs raking over his bottom lip as he drew me against his chest. "As if I could stop at just a little taste of you." He kissed me, sharp enough for his fangs to poke me without piercing. "When I have you, I'm taking my fill. So I need my blood mate in prime health." He swatted my ass. "Now, let me feed you and introduce you to the assholes I live with."

The apartment outside his bedroom was modest and simple. It was mostly an open living area with couches and a small table. A TV took over nearly one entire wall with gaming consoles and controllers set neatly in the cubbies of the TV stand. The kitchenette was little more than a small refrigerator, a counter and a sink.

"You didn't make that soup in here, did you?"

"Nah, I don't think that fridge is even plugged in." Laith grabbed my hand, leading me toward the front door. "The main kitchen upstairs is a shared space. Only Tavia and Bea actually use it to make food. We mostly use the island for meetings."

There was that name again, Tavia. Where had I heard it before?

Outside Laith's front door was a industrial-looking hallway with concrete floors and a tall ceiling stretching at least two stories up. More doors lined the hall, with some hanging framed photos and console tables lining the walls between doors. The air was cool and dry, reminding me of a wine cellar.

"Are those other apartments?" I nodded at the doors. "For your clan members?"

"Yeah, everyone's got their own place. Mated couples live together, obviously."

"How many couples are there?"

"Aside from you and me?" He kissed my temple. "One. Cyan and Tavia live there." He pointed at one door, then led me toward the end of the hall, where a metal staircase rose up to meet a set of two carved wooden doors. "The greatroom is up there. Where everyone gathers."

"Are we underground?" I asked as we started to climb.

"The apartments are, yes. It's an instinctual thing for vampires. We're better able to rest the further away from sunlight we are. That tends to be below the surface."

"Makes sense."

We reached the top landing and Laith pushed open one of the doors to reveal an open, brightly lit space. A luxurious kitchen with marbled counters and a massive center island took up nearly half the space. The other half looked to be a living area with couches arranged around a...

"Is that a stripper pole?" I blurted out.

"Sure is," answered a vampire lounging on one of the

couches with his legs dangling over the arm. "You should see your mate turning tricks on it."

"Oh, really?" I looked at Laith behind me.

"I'm out of practice but I know you've been putting in work, Des. Did you win your bet with Irina?"

"Ugh, no." The other vampire's head flopped back in disappointment. "Couldn't get the leg squeeze right. Just about landed on my face and had to buy drinks for all the dancers."

"Well, maybe don't quit your night job." Laith cupped my nape and massaged. "Des, this is Heather. Heather, Des."

"Hi." I waved, which Des returned.

"You're looking way better than when we pulled you out of that alley." Des's grin was friendly, with one blunt fang adding some rogueish charm. His eyes were a darker red closer to brown, the color of aged bricks.

"Thanks. I would hope so."

"Have a seat." Laith steered me to the island. "I'll heat up your soup."

I just settled into a stool when more people came through the same doors we had. A huge, musclebound vampire so tall that he had to duck through the doorway scowled at me as he entered the room. Or maybe that was just his normal face.

He was followed by a more slender vampire. He was closer to Laith's build, but that was where the similarities ended. This vampire had dark hair and there was a coldness to his blood-red eyes. Something about him seemed aged, a kind of jaded weariness. He also had neck tattoos, which was surprising to see. How was that possible when vampires healed so quickly? Silver ink?

Behind him came one more vampire, one with his dark

hair buzzed close to his scalp and more youthfulness and energy behind his red eyes. He also looked familiar. Our gazes met as he closed the door behind him and a smile of recognition lit up his face.

"So, she lives," he declared, coming toward me. "Hi, Heather. I'm Cyan. I don't know if you remember me."

"Were you also there when I was pulled out of the alley?" Maybe I was semi-conscious then but had forgotten.

"Yes, but we also met before then. I'm Tavia's mate. She's from Sapien, the human settlement."

"The human settlement," I repeated. "You mean the weird prepper village?"

"That's the one," he said with a laugh before glancing at his phone. "The girls are on their way up. Tavia and Amy will be glad to see you."

A memory hit me, one that had gotten lost in the chaotic mess of events since. During my first accidental stumble into Sanguine, when I was held at the human village for a couple of days, they had been trying to convince me that vampires were real. That this was a vampire territory and they were only all-human settlement left. I didn't believe them back then, because why would I? Two of the women I'd talked to had been Tavia and Amy.

Tavia had been visiting her old home and Cyan was due to pick her up that night. I waited with them, ready to debunk this so-called vampire that rolled up on a motorcycle. But, as Cyan pulled up, every one of my instincts of *danger* and *predator* had fired warning signs. He was clearly not some guy with red contacts and fake fangs. My central nervous system knew before my eyes did that he was definitely not human.

"That's right," I said, the clarity dawning on me. "You were the first real vampire I saw with my own eyes."

"Should've been me," Laith muttered irritably from the stove.

"Oh, relax. You're the only one who's fed from me."

*Consensually, anyway.* I forced back the shudder at the thought of that monster in the alley. That was the last thing I needed occupying my mind right now.

"Welcome to vampire jealousy." Cyan leaned one hip against the counter. "We're ridiculous when it comes to our mates. I hope you know what you're getting into."

I returned his grin. "I have some idea."

"Stop smiling at her." Laith placed a steaming bowl of soup, spoon, napkin, and glass of water in front of me, then made a shooing motion at Cyan. "Go away. She needs to eat."

Cyan gave me a pointed look, fangs digging into his lower lip to suppress his laugh, then pushed away from the counter to join the others across the room.

I turned to Laith, tilting my face up for a kiss. "Thank you. I still can't believe you learned to make this just for me."

He leaned down, his kiss brief but firm. "I know you're trying to soothe my jealousy. We're...possessive, but I would never get angry at you because of it. Cyan, Des, and I especially like to mess with each other. I want you to know it's just friends giving each other shit."

"I wasn't worried about that." I picked up my spoon and stirred the soup. "I think your jealousy is sweet, actually."

As if he couldn't get any cuter, Laith made a grumpy, "hmph" sound. "Let's see if you feel that way a decade from now."

"I will absolutely let you know if there is shit I can't deal with." I blew on my spoon and took a tentative sip. *Oh yeah. This homemade gesture of love I can definitely deal with.*

Laith cupped my nape again, his thumb massaging the crook of my neck as he brought his lips to my ear. "The other two that just walked in are Thorne, head of Blood 'til Dawn," he nodded at the tattooed, older-looking vampire, "and the gigantosaurus with the long hair is Rhain. They are actually nicer than they look."

"Noted." I chuckled around a mouthful of soup.

"Laith." Thorne barked his name with a jerk of his head.

My vampire made an annoyed sound and kissed my neck. "Be right back."

"Sure." I watched him cross the room, inhaling my soup.

Female voices then floated from the other side of the large double doors before they were pulled open. Three more people entered the greatroom, led by a tall woman with reddish-brown hair, gray eyes, and a self-assuredness in her stride. Our gazes locked and my brain clicked two puzzle pieces together.

I had been hearing her name and finally could put it to a face I recognized.

"Tavia," I said, blinking with surprise.

"Hey, Heather." She approached me with a warm, sisterly smile. "It's great to see you again. You look better."

"Thanks." She had definitely been one of the women at Sapien trying to convince me that vampires were real.

"Do you remember Amy?" Tavia stepped aside, and a smaller woman with darker hair grinned at me.

My breath caught in my chest with shock. Amy had been an adorable, diminutive woman with an innate sweetness I couldn't help but like. Now, she had small fangs and her blue irises were set in black. She definitely hadn't had those features when I'd last seen her.

I recalled the blood bank employee who had walked me

through the donating process. He'd had those same features and called himself a brusang, a human who had died and been given vampire blood.

"Yes. Amy, hi." I cast my eyes away, realizing I'd been staring at her. "Good to see you. I'm...uh, sorry about...sorry for..."

Embarrassment swept through me as I glanced around for help. I probably shouldn't have said anything, but it also felt wrong to not acknowledge the change.

"My death? Don't worry about it, Heather." Amy's smile was sweet, though the fangs made it sharper. "I got a second chance as a brusang and life is good. No need to be sorry."

"We'll have to catch you up on what you missed." Tavia rested her elbow on Amy's shoulder. "I just couldn't let my bestie go."

"She's everyone's bestie now," said the third woman, another brusang, coming up to squeeze Amy's opposite shoulder.

She had straight black hair, blunt bangs across her forehead, and bright bluish-green irises that looked like jewels in black settings. "Hi, I'm Bea." She extended a hand with a fanged smile that mirrored Amy's. "No need to be sorry for me, either. I became a brusang twenty years ago."

An awkward laugh escaped me as I shook her hand. "Well, that's good to know. It's nice to meet you."

"Welcome to the best family in Sanguine." Bea spread her arms and wiggled her fingers. "Where the men are annoying as shit, but at least they're hot."

"Hey, that's mean!" Des called from the couch, then immediately straightened. "Wait, you think I'm hot?"

The women laughed as they settled around the island counter. Tavia took wine glasses and a corked bottle down from an upper cabinet. "You want some, Heather? We're not getting smashed, just doing a little taste test."

"You want to say yes." Amy took a seat next to me. "Tav's wine is the best. She's going to create a monopoly in Sanguine."

"Shut up with that nonsense." Despite the protest, Tavia grinned to herself as she poured.

"Sure, why not?" I pushed away my finished bowl of soup and accepted the small pour from Tavia. "So, do you ladies have vampire mates too?"

"Technically, no." Bea placed her chin in her palm as she swirled her wine. "I'm not attached to anyone at the moment, but I'm not exactly available either. My situation's a bit complicated."

"Sorry to hear that. I can definitely sympathize." I copied her movement, creating a tiny, swirling tempest in my glass. "My situation until recently was kind of complicated too."

"Because you didn't believe in vampires?" Tavia teased.

I chuckled. "Never gonna let that go, are you?"

"Oh, I'm sure I'll move on to something else eventually." Tavia touched her glass to mine. "But once you do the mating ceremony, you're going to live much, much longer. So *eventually* might be longer than you expect."

"Great," I deadpanned, earning soft laughter from the women.

"Amy was mated a couple months ago." Tavia grinned at her bestie over her glass and swayed her hips. "She's in that honeymoon phase."

A blush rose in Amy's cheekbones. "You say that like *your* honeymoon phase is over."

"I made no such claims."

"These two got mated like a month apart." Bea pointed

to both of them. "And it's sickening how happy and lovey-dovey they are. Just gross."

"You're exaggerating. It was closer to two months," Tavia protested.

"Whatever. You're both glowing and beautiful enough to make a bitch jealous."

"Well, congrats to you both," I said, raising my glass.

"And to you!" Amy touched her glass to mine. "I'm glad Laith found someone. He's really sweet and funny."

"Thanks." I nodded at Bea. "And I bet some of our mojo will rub off on you soon, Bea. You'll find your person."

She waved a hand through the air. "I might have already, but again, complicated."

Well, that was interesting. What could be preventing them from being together? Laith had been determined to find me and start a life together, at any cost. Laith said the guys were possessive. Did Bea's mate just not have that same drive to be with her? Or was it something out of both of their control? I didn't want to pry, but I was definitely curious.

"So, which one's yours, Amy?" I asked with a thumb over my shoulder, pointing at the couches where the men were gathered.

"Oh, none of them. My mate is Novak of Blood and Truth. You'll probably meet him soon." She rolled her eyes toward Tavia. "I just spend half my time here, with my sister from another mister."

Tavia let out a fake, dramatic sigh. "And you're about to leave me for him, *again*."

"Yeah, yeah. I'll be back tomorrow night." Amy threw back the remaining sip in her wine glass. "That's really good, Tav. You don't need to change anything."

"Mm, I dunno." Tavia stuck her nose in her glass. "Might be a little on the tart side."

"Amy," a raspy voice called from the far side of the room. "You're heading home soon?" Did Thorne ever sound like he wasn't barking out orders?

Amy stiffened a little, but she otherwise didn't seem distressed. "Yes, that's right."

"We're all heading that way too. We have some clan matters to discuss with your mate, so we'll escort you home."

"Okay, I'm heading out now." Amy slid from her stool, and nodded once at me. "Nice to see you again, Heather." Then to Tavia and Bea, "See you around, ladies."

Laith came to stand beside me, his palm smoothing around my waist and back. "We shouldn't be too long. The girls will take care of you. Rest, relax."

"Everything okay?" He and the guys seemed tense. They'd been talking to each other in low voices out of earshot of the women.

"Yeah." He leaned in closer to me. "You remember my friend I told you about? The one who's been locked up for twenty years? Well, Novak's gonna go over some test results that can hopefully give us more info on his situation."

"Test results?" I narrowed my eyes. "Like what, drugs? Blood tests?"

Laith's mouth pressed into a firm line. "I probably said too much. Don't worry about it."

"No, Laith." I turned on my stool to face him directly. "Did you forget I work in a crime lab? I test things like that all day. I can help."

"I'm sure you can." Laith cupped the back of my neck, his thumb stroking my cheek. "But you still need to rest. You'll be safest here."

"Honestly? I need a change of environment and something stimulating my brain. I've already rested and eaten, Laith. Let me come with you."

He sighed, dropping his forehead to mine. Just behind him, I caught a glimpse of Thorne watching our exchange with mild curiosity.

"Why not? Let's bring her." Thorne stuck a cigarette in his mouth. "The humans you all bring always seem to surprise me."

With that, the Blood 'til Dawn leader headed out another door and Laith's sigh hit my lips.

"Fine," he groaned.

It was a fairly short walk to Novak's place. I was grateful for the crisp night air and the opportunity to stretch my legs. Amy hooked her arm around mine and pointed out the various businesses and fixtures of the vampire territory.

"This area, including the square, is called the Heart of Sanguine," she explained, gesturing around us. "Rather than divide the territory into cities or towns, they use body parts or organs to refer to different regions. Novak's family is from the northernmost region called the Crown. Sapien, the human settlement, is further south in the Ribs."

"That's fascinating. What's the reason for that?"

"Because Sanguine was born from the body of our goddess, Temkra." The answer came from Rhain, the huge, long-haired vampire with a permanent scowl, who walked in front of us. "She laid down to die so that vampires, her children, could have a home."

Rhain didn't look back at us as he spoke. An awkward silence followed, like I'd committed some social faux paus by asking the question. Cyan, who walked beside him, gave a little nudge to Rhain's elbow and mouthed something that I couldn't make out.

"I didn't mean any disrespect," I said. "I was just curious."

The hulking vampire glanced over his broad shoulder at me briefly before muttering, "Never said you did."

A moment later, I felt Laith's reassuring squeeze on the back of my neck. "Ignore him. He's always in a bad mood. Probably needs to get laid."

"I can hear you," Rhain groused.

"Good. Take the advice then." Laith hugged around my chest from behind, dropping his chin to my shoulder. "You never know. You might find your blood mate in the process."

Rhain grumbled something I couldn't hear, which made Cyan chuckle.

A few minutes later, we gathered around the front steps of an expensive-looking townhouse. Amy cut through to the front of our group. "No need to ring the bell, guys. Come on in."

She opened the doors with a key and ushered us into a beautiful, spacious foyer. The wood accents were dark and polished to a high shine. The wall colors were deep greens with a subtle damask pattern. Furnishings were more dark wood with pops of red.

A grand staircase stood directly ahead of the foyer, and Amy called up from the bottom step, "Honey, I'm home!"

"Be right down, akra!" called a warm male voice from the upper level.

I was very curious to know what the owner of this house looked like because *goddamn.* I couldn't stop looking at everything.

"Welcome home, Amy. Hungry?"

I turned in the direction of the voice to see a woman in a

luxurious open kitchen whisking something in a metal bowl. She looked to be human, in her 40s, and wore the signature white-buttoned coat of a chef.

"No thanks, Jo. Tavia and Bea spoiled me." Amy rubbed her stomach.

"How about your guests?" The woman looked over her glasses at us. Those were definitely human eyes, a deep brown set in white sclera.

"Thank you for the offer, but we are fine." Thorne placed a hand on his chest and made a little bow toward the chef.

"I'll have some cold bites available just in case. Looks like the boss is about to have a meeting."

My mind was spinning. A rich vampire with a human chef? Was this...normal?

Movement drew my gaze to the figure coming down the stairs. The vampire had hair paler than Laith's, practically silver, falling past his collarbones. His eyes were the typical blood red, but his skin was darker, a medium brown.

He wore dark slacks that fit him like a glove, and a white buttoned shirt that was slightly rumpled with the sleeves rolled to his elbows. The casualness of the shirt didn't make him look sloppy or any less polished. And, as expected, he was handsome. Especially when his face lit up at the sight of Amy.

"Hi, akra." He said the foreign word with a flawless rolling r and unique inflection, like it was his native language. "Did you have fun with Bea and Tavia?"

The rest of us might as well have not existed as the couple met in the middle of the stairs with a kiss and embrace.

"I did, but I still missed you." Amy turned back to our group gathered at the bottom of the stairs, her face flushed and glowing. "Thorne and the others said they had business with you, so they escorted me home."

"Thank you, Blood 'til Dawn, for keeping her safe." Novak made his way down the stairs, his hand clasped around Amy's.

"It's an honor." For once, Thorne's voice didn't sound like it was dripping with sarcasm. "She is of our clan as well."

Hearing that surprised me at first, but it actually made sense. Amy and Tavia seemed as close as sisters, so it seemed natural that Blood 'til Dawn considered Amy one of their own. That sense of belonging must have felt wonderful.

Novak's eyes landed on me and gleamed with curiosity. "Hello. I don't believe we've met." He came forward, his movements lithe as a cat's. "I'm Novak, head of Blood and Truth."

All at once, I felt very overwhelmed. It felt like I was being perceived by a prince of foreign nation.

"Ah, hello." My voice shook slightly, and I didn't know what to do with my hands, so I kept them flat at my sides. "I'm Heather."

Laith stepped up to my rescue, chin raised proudly. "Heather is my blood mate."

Novak's face broke into a smile that crinkled the corners of his eyes. "Really? That's wonderful." He slapped Laith's arm with brotherly affection. "I'm so happy for you both. Please let me know if you'd like to use Jo, my chef, for your mating ceremony. She's incredible. I'll take care of all the food. It'll be my gift."

"Another mating ceremony?" Jo called from the kitchen. "Whether you hire me or not, count me in!"

"Thanks, Novak. That's really kind." Laith's hands

came to my shoulders and squeezed. "We'll keep you posted. It's pretty new, so we're figuring things out. Heather is from the human world, you see."

"Oh, fascinating." Novak's eyes returned to me. "Well, welcome to my home and to Sanguine. I hope everything hasn't been too overwhelming."

"Thank you," I said, a bit floored by his graciousness. "Your home is beautiful."

"I can't take credit for it." He chuckled. "My ancestors knew how to make themselves very wealthy. I'm just a nerd with a big house and very tolerant staff." He drew Amy toward him and put his arm around her shoulders. "And a stunning blood mate."

Amy rolled her eyes but her grin was entirely smug. "Heather is a scientist in the human world. She came along to offer help on the test results."

"Really?" Novak's interest returned to me. "What do you do?"

"My degree is in forensic chemistry," I said. "I work in a lab that tests evidence from crime scenes."

"Wow." Novak crossed his arms and leaned toward me slightly. "One of my degrees is in chemistry as well, but I went the organic route."

"Ah, that's the smart-people chem degree," I said. "I couldn't get that far into the weeds. Not my bag. I just wanted to run tests and catch bad guys."

Novak laughed, his eyes twinkling. "I don't know about smart. I just had a lot of time on my hands. But I'm glad you're here. We could definitely use a second opinion because some of the results have honestly stumped me."

"Sure. I'll do what I can." I immediately began to relax. In contrast to the grandness of his home, Novak seemed genuine and humble.

I also couldn't ignore the excited little thrill that lit me up. Puzzling out a scientific problem with a fellow nerd was one of my favorite pastimes. I loved the challenge and collaboration of it.

"Wonderful, thank you." His gaze lifted to the surrounding vampires. Let's get started, shall we? If you would all follow me."

Amy slowly unwound herself from her mate. "I'll be in the library."

"Sounds good." He beamed. "I'll come down when we're all done."

Laith grabbed my hand as we all trailed Novak up the stairs. I glanced at his face and tried to gauge his mood. He'd been pretty quiet during the whole exchange. He met my gaze with a lopsided grin and kissed my temple.

"I can't wait to see you do your super smart science stuff," he said, affection and pride in his voice.

"Really?" I didn't mean to sound so surprised, but it took me aback. Justin always got annoyed when I talked about anything work-related, either to him or others in front of him. He'd said I made him look stupid.

"Hell yeah. It's awesome that you know this stuff already, but if your knowledge helps us free Kalix?" Laith tucked me into his side, my shoulders fitting comfortable under his arm, and kissed the top of my head. "Blood 'til Dawn will be in your debt. Forever."

I hugged around his waist, my cheek finding a comfortable resting spot on his chest. "I'm not a miracle worker. Novak probably knows more than me, but I'll do my best."

We filed into a luxurious study filled with more dark, polished wood. A large desk sat in the center of the room. Directly behind it were French doors leading out to a cozy balcony.

"Please, make yourselves comfortable." Novak gestured to armchairs and couches placed around the study.

Laith sat, so I followed his lead. Cyan, Thorne, and Rhain remained standing.

"All right, so I tested the blood samples from Laith and Cyan's clothes from the night of the fight." Novak leaned against his desk and plucked a single sheet of paper from its surface, looking every bit the posh-but-casual Oxford professor. If they hired vampires, that is. "Do you want the bad news, good news, or the confusing news first?"

"Bad. Just spit it out." Thorne held a cigarette between his teeth and lit it, his cheeks hollowing out as he inhaled.

Novak didn't hesitate. "Kalix has definitely been given draitrium, I'm sorry to say."

The vampires around me made lots of angry groaning and "*Fuck*"s.

"How bad?" Cyan asked.

"Pretty bad." Novak scanned the sheet in front of him, which I assumed was some kind of toxicology report. "I don't have a lot to compare to, but the concentration in his blood was the highest I've ever seen. Three times higher than from the Marrower blood samples you sent me. Which brings me to the relatively good news."

Novak set the paper on his desk and shoved his hands in the pockets in his slacks. "The draitrium molecules bonded to a foreign blood source in both Kalix's and the Marrowers' systems. So they most likely came from the same source. Or at least, were dispensed using the same process."

"Carpe Noctem." Cyan's lip curled with a snarl. "It has to be. Kal is their prisoner, and they stood only to benefit by drugging those Marrowers."

Novak lifted a brow. "When Baros was trying to ally with me, he made it seem like he had no idea who was behind the Marrower attack. Doesn't surprise me if he was lying."

"Sorry." I raised my hand like I was in school. "By foreign blood source, you mean blood that was ingested, correct?" As the only non-blood drinker in the room, I had to make sure my facts were straight.

"Yes, that's correct." Novak nodded.

"What's the blood source?" Des asked.

"That's what I'm hoping Heather can help with." Novak's eyes shifted toward me. "Because I've never seen red blood cells like that in my life. They're not human, vampire, or brusang."

I perked up, intrigued. "Do you have slides I can look at?"

"I certainly do. Over here." Novak showed me to a corner of his study that was sort of a tucked away cubicle with a large microscope. It was an older model, but had definitely been state of the art during its time.

"What are you thinking the blood is, some kind of animal?" I watched while he switched on and adjusted the machine.

"Possibly that, or one of the other sentient species of Shyftworld." Novak frowned. "I did eliminate dragon shifter, but that leaves werewolves or angels, both of which are forbidden to feed from."

"Why is that?"

Novak laughed awkwardly as he stepped back from the machine. "There's a long, ugly history between them and us. We don't exactly get along."

"I see." I stepped up to the machine and adjusted the focus and magnification. "It's not that different in the human world. A lot of nations have been fighting each other for years and years."

"It's sad to hear that war isn't unique to supernatural species," Novak said.

"It is." I peered through the microscope. "Okay. What am I looking at?"

"Kalix's foreign blood source."

"Huh. Those blood cells definitely aren't human." They did look familiar, though. I thought back to my undergrad days, all the way to freshman year where I had to identify dozens of different samples under a microscope.

"You don't happen to have a Raman spectrometer, do you?"

Novak cocked his head. "I don't. What is that?"

"Oh, it's a great tool for identifying all kinds of substances. Most government labs have them now. They're very pricey, but I highly recommend one if you're going to be trying to ID blood samples of different species."

"I'll see what I can do." Novak grinned, his eyes lighting up with the prospect of a new toy. "Do you need one for this sample?"

"I *might* be able to ID it by sight. Is that connected to the internet?" I nodded at the laptop on a small desk, the only other piece of equipment in this little cubicle.

"It is. Help yourself."

"Thanks."

I pulled up the best images of red blood cells I could find and started comparing, going back and forth from the computer to the microscope and mentally eliminating the ones that didn't match.

Someone without a biology background but a keen sense for matching details could probably do a visual comparison successfully, but I wanted to be absolutely sure. I thought back to the thousands of blood samples I'd tested, all the identifying characteristics of cells unique to certain species.

I wasn't sure how much time had passed, but a headache began to throb at my temples and my eyes felt strained from looking through the microscope over and over. Black dots danced in my vision when I switched it off and turned around. Laith had joined Novak waiting patiently outside the cubicle. If the two of them had been talking, I'd been too focused on my task to hear them.

"Okay," I said, rubbing my eyes. "From a visual comparison, the best I can tell you is the blood comes from some sort of canine. A dog or a wolf, most likely."

Laith looked at Novak. "It's gotta be a werewolf, then."

The longer-haired vampire chewed his lip with a fang, brows knitting together. "So the werewolf blood bonds with the draitrium molecule and creates side effects of extreme strength and aggression. I wonder how they discovered that."

"Someone who profits from draitrium probably also deals in illegal blood." Thorne stood by a cracked window, exhaling red smoke to the outside air. "It's not a huge stretch by any means."

Rhain went to stand by the same window, lighting up his own cigarette. "They probably started mixing to dilute each product while keeping profit high. Once they saw what it did, I bet they started using it on their fighters to gain an edge."

"The Marrower attack may have been a test," Cyan suggested, wandering closer to join Laith and Novak. "To see what would happen if they started dealing this mixture to the public."

"Wait, there was an attack?" My voice raised with alarm. "Where? When?"

Cyan turned toward me. "It was a few months ago. A group of Marrower vampires, high on draitrium, attacked Sapien, the all-human settlement."

"It was how Amy became a brusang," Novak added softly. "She lost her human life in the attack, but Cyan and Tavia managed to bring her back with his blood."

Cyan waved off the heavy look of gratitude Novak leveled at him. "You must have missed it by a few days," he said to me.

"Yeah, I definitely had no idea." Now that I knew that my capture in Sapien had been for my own safety, from the citizens' perspective, I felt a lot more sympathy for those people.

"Regardless, we are not letting another attack happen." Red smoke curled around Thorne's lips as he snarled.

"I mean, the damage has already begun." Des shrugged at the glares everyone sent his way. "Those Marrowers hurt the human settlement and our credibility as the ruling clan who protects everyone. Carpe Noctem sees that as a win, I'm sure. What's to stop them from doing it again?"

I lifted my hand as if I were in class. "Would someone mind giving me a brief rundown of what Carpe Noctem is?"

The vampires all exchanged a brief glance, and I got the sense that humans, blood mate or not, were not usually privy to these discussions.

"Carpe Noctem is one of the oldest, richest, and most powerful clans in Sanguine," Laith explained. No one tried to stop him from talking, so he continued. "They're extremely archaic in their views. To them, humans, female vampires, and anyone below an aristocratic class are meant to be subservient. Their few stints at being ruling clan in the past have been extremely oppressive. They've been overthrown by a rebellion every single time, but their wealth and resources run deep. And they're obsessed with sitting at the top, no matter who they step on to get there."

"Blood til Dawn is a clan of working class vampires," Rhain supplied. "We've always been mechanics and builders. So Carpe Noctem is especially pissed off that we've been the ruling clan, peacefully I might add, for the last fifteen years."

"They're also the ones who took Kalix prisoner," Cyan added. "They were the ruling clan at the time, about five years before we took power."

"Whoa," I said when the guys fell silent. "Yeah, fuck those guys."

A frustrated growl of agreement came from Thorne as he stabbed his cigarette out violently in an ashtray on the windowsill. "Carpe Noctem needs to be dismantled. They'll destroy vampires as a whole and thousands of humans along the way if they're not stopped."

"Or," Novak piped up. "We can try to make Inessa the head of Carpe Noctem. She'll steer the ship in a much better direction."

Thorne paused like he was considering that. "That'll be difficult and dangerous in a whole host of ways. Carpe Noctem won't support a woman as their head."

"Not without reason. She'll have to prove herself."

The room fell into plans and discussion of vampire politics and things that went way over my head. My headache was increasing in intensity and I was becoming fatigued. I plopped down in a chair at the laptop desk, rubbing my temples.

Laith immediately came over and kneeled in front of me. "Are you okay?"

I offered him a smile. "Yeah, just a little tired and dealing with some eye strain."

"Do you want to go home?" He squeezed my knee, concern and affection in his eyes.

"I can find a couch to lie on or something. It seems you guys have important things to discuss."

"Go ahead, you two." Thorne's hearing was apparently sharp enough to hear our murmured conversation. "We'll catch you up to speed, Laith."

Laith rose to his feet and held out his hand. "You heard the boss."

I glanced at Thorne. "Are you sure? If you need him to stay, I can just—"

"Go." Thorne made shooing motions with his hands. "Blood mates go apeshit if they're separated and I don't want to deal with his whining."

Laith grinned. "Dad knows me so well."

Thorne groaned and muttered under his breath, "For fuck's sake, I'm not your fucking dad."

After accepting his hand and letting him pull me to my feet, Laith led me toward the office door. At the threshold, I heard Thorne's raspy voice once more. "Heather?"

I turned back. "Yes?"

The head of the ruling vampire clan dipped his chin in my direction. "Thank you for your help. Because of you, we'll be able to move forward with a plan."

My instinct was to deny and minimize what I'd done. I'd just compared images and tried to match them. Novak could have done it himself if he knew what to look for.

But he hadn't. All the vampires in the room were looking in my direction now, giving nods and murmurs of thanks. And Laith was squeezing my hand. I could feel his gaze on my profile, feel the pride coming from him like the warmth of a banked fire.

I waited for the voice of my resentment demon to pop up with a disparaging little quip, but none came. I glanced at Laith and his genuine expression of adoration made my heart swell. What did he see in me to look at me like that?

*He sees the real you.* That wasn't the resentment demon's voice, but my own.

Of course. Because now that I'd found someone who didn't see my personality, quirks, and accomplishments as a threat to his ego, my resentment had withered and died. What replaced it was bright, shining, and warm. A feeling I could wrap myself in like a blanket. A feeling I could certainly get used to.

So I swallowed the impulse to reject the compliment and smiled at the room of vampires.

"You're very welcome," I said. "I'm happy I could help."

With that, I followed Laith out of the study, and we took the stairs side by side. Our hands never disconnected and his gaze rarely left me. Once we left the house and spilled out into the street, he tucked me into his side. His arm went around my shoulders, our fingers still locked together.

A thought hit me as he kissed my temple.

*Is this what it feels like when someone loves me?*

# Chapter 26

## *Laith*

"You were incredible back there." I kissed Heather's hairline again, my fingers curling around hers.

"Thanks. It's sweet of you to say that." The smile she gave was bashful, but I didn't miss the pride shining through. She was glowing with it and about fucking time. She deserved to feel pride in her accomplishments.

I brought our joined hands to my lips and kissed her palm. "You heard Thorne. You've done a great service to our clan. Blood 'til Dawn is grateful. *I'm* grateful."

Moving Heather in front of me, I wrapped my arms around her from behind. It made walking a little awkward, but I didn't care. I couldn't stop myself from touching her.

"It was...very nice of him to say that." Heather held on to my forearm and let her head rest on my shoulder. "I get the feeling he doesn't say thank you very often."

"He's got a thankless job. On the rare occasion he gets help that's actually useful, he's very appreciative of it. The clan will protect you for life now." I kissed the side of her neck and smiled at the resulting shiver passing over her skin. "And I just loved seeing you in your element, Science Barbie. You're sexy as hell when you're doing science. Will you tell me more about it?"

Her steps faltered and made the front of my body press deliciously against her backside.

"You really want to know more about what I do?"

"Hell yes I do. I want to know all about your passions and interests." My arms tightened around her. "Everything that goes on in that sexy big brain of yours."

A laugh bubbled out of her as she resumed walking. "Well, you might not find forensics all that interesting. And it's definitely not sexy."

"Oh I can definitely prove that wrong, scientifically." I kissed her neck again as we approached the Blood 'til Dawn compound. "Everything you do is sexy."

"Laith..." My name left her mouth in a soft, breathy sigh that hardened me into iron. Her pulse also fluttered beneath her skin in the most tantalizing way. My fangs ached with a dull throb. I hadn't fed in days and my self-control was unraveling.

"Heather?" It was both a question and a plea, and she seemed to understand instinctively.

"Yes." Her head turned, mouth brushing against mine in a soft kiss. "Yes, Laith. I want to."

Those words were gasoline on the embers I'd purposely kept low and calm while she recovered. Now my desire roared for her in every way, as a mate and a blood source. Even so, as we entered the compound and bypassed the main kitchen, I hesitated.

"Are you sure?" My question was low and husky. "Do you want to eat something first? Or rest?"

She turned to me, arms encircling my neck. Her eyes were alert and just as hungry as I felt, though not for food.

A rosy blush darkened her cheeks. There was plenty of blood in her now, but I wanted to hear her say it.

"I don't want anything but you right now, Laith."

"Fuck." I took her hand and made a beeline for the basement level. I wasn't opposed to having her right there on the counter, but there was no telling when the others would show up. She was a feast for my eyes only.

We made it to my apartment and she paused at the threshold to my bedroom. My fangs were full-on stabbing my lower lip and aching painfully, but if she was having second thoughts, I would endure it. A blood mate relationship was only as good as the blood source was satisfied.

"Something wrong?" I tried to stay lighthearted, but my voice had gone low with a needy rasp. I felt like I would die if I didn't have a taste of her soon.

Heather was looking at the bed, the covers still messy and unmade from when we'd gotten up at dusk. "Can I... request something?"

"Anything." I pushed her hair behind her ear and stared at the curve of her neck. "Anything you desire is yours, Heather."

Her eyes fell half-closed, head tilting slightly as if to extend her neck for me. "What if I asked you to...to act out the fantasy you told me about?"

I didn't think my desire for her could rise any more, but it surged in me like a tidal wave. "You want me to take you as if *he* were watching us?"

She nodded, her eyes shifting to mine. "Show him and me what it's like to be yours. What it means to win me."

I was painfully hard and nearly panting with anticipation. My imagination ran wild at everything I could do, all the ways I could claim her. I ached to toss her on the bed right then, sink into her with my cock and fangs until exhaustion claimed us both at dawn. But clarifications had to be made first.

"Heather, I am...beyond grateful that you would want to act out this fantasy with me." I cupped her face, fingers stroking both sides of her neck. "But you need to be aware that it's not gentle. Claiming you is taking you roughly. I'd be biting you in various places. Intimate places. It may get messy. Your pleasure is my priority, always, but there might be some pain along with it. If you want me gentle, I will absolutely treasure and worship you in bed. But that's not what this particular fantasy is. We don't have to act it out. You're already mine."

I kissed her forehead and drew her into my chest. "If you like it rough, it'll be enjoyable and maybe cathartic. I don't need to prove a fucking thing to some loser human male. I won already. So I'll leave it up to you. As long as you're mine, I'll always be satisfied."

Heather melted into me as I spoke. Her cheek had rested on my chest and her arms held loosely around my waist. Now, she pulled back and gave me a challenging look.

"What are you waiting for, vampire? Claim your blood mate."

My hesitation lasted only a moment longer before I yanked her forward. She crashed into my chest and I captured her lips with my teeth—not hard enough to draw blood, just enough to keep her in place. Heather softened, mouth parting with a little moan that threatened to undo me.

I released her lip and kissed her deeply, teeth scraping and tongue surging. My palms wrapped around her upper arms, holding her exactly where I wanted her. I fought to stay rational, constantly reminding myself to slowly increase the intensity, despite her consent. She still didn't know what she was fully getting into because she had never been truly taken by a vampire before. All of our previous feedings had been child's play in comparison.

This would be on another level, and if she wasn't prepared, it could become too much.

After a few minutes of bruising kisses I angled my mouth just enough to let a fang prick her lip. Heather startled with a soft gasp, but she was not deterred. She reached her tiptoes to kiss me again, and the flavor of her blood mixed with the natural taste of her was the final snap of my control.

With a groan I lowered, wrapped my arms around her thighs, and lifted. Her legs went around my waist in a snug hold as I turned us toward the bed. I dropped forward, letting her back hit the soft mattress. I slapped one hand down to not crush her under my weight as I followed. The impact broke apart our kiss and when I dove again, it was for her neck.

Heather's moan of surprise and pleasure filled the room, her arms and legs tightening around me as my fangs sank in. My lips sealed to her skin as I drank, relishing in her taste as it quenched me, fulfilled me. She was heady and potent, pure magic pouring down my throat. Still, I forced myself to break away before I felt full. There were many, many more places I wanted to drink from and we were just getting started.

"No, don't stop." Heather writhed underneath me, her lush body pressing into me as I licked the puncture wounds to seal them closed.

"I'm not stopping." I grabbed her hands from around my back and pinned her wrists above her head with one hand. Her forearm tattoo was visible in the dim light. I'd have to remember to refresh the lilies next to the bed when we were done.

In the meantime, I used my fangs to make a small tear in the neckline of her shirt. Then I used my free hand to rip the shirt completely down the middle. Heather gasped but there was no fear in her eyes. Her breasts were barely contained in the simple cotton bra and they hypnotized me like a swinging pendulum.

"Fuck, look at you."

My free hand took all the liberties, running over her with reverence. The bra cups were thin, her nipples poking through and making my mouth water.

"Hottest fucking woman I've ever seen," I groaned, palming and pinching over the fabric while she made sexy little moans and squeaks. "And you were stupid enough to let her slip through your fingers, Justin."

I didn't intend to say his name, but it felt natural. It didn't fill me with rage. On the contrary, I felt utterly calm and in control. This scenario was my fantasy, my little universe. And damn, did it feel good to imagine him sitting in the corner, stewing in his humiliation while I touched the woman that used to be his.

Heather barely reacted to hearing his name. She focused fully on me, back arching, plush lips parted and eyes pleading for me to do more, to touch her again. I gripped her waist and leaned down again, nuzzling her soft skin before tearing my fangs through the straining fabric holding the bra cups together.

The ruined bra fell away with one jerk of my head, releasing the most gorgeous, luscious breasts I'd ever seen. I forgot all about restraining Heather's wrists and swept both hands over her chest, bringing her dark nipples to stiff points. Perfect for my mouth.

My tongue and fangs dragged over her flesh, eliciting shivers and more soft sounds from her. I touched the tip of one fang to her nipple and earned a soft gasp. But a bite right there would be far more pain than pleasure, so I pulled the sensitive tip with my fingers while my mouth sucked and licked, on the hunt for a perfect spot.

The inside curve of her left breast called to me, her heartbeat like a drum summoning my bite. I didn't warn her, I just struck. Heather's short scream became a low moan, hips rolling against me as her nails dug into the back of my neck.

I made sure to keep the bite shallow and again, fed only briefly. But this time, I didn't seal the puncture wounds when I pulled away. Blood welled at the two points before traveling down her chest to stomach in two thin rivulets. I was ready, tongue flat to her skin as I licked up one trail and then the other.

"I could cover you in your own blood just to taste every inch of your skin," I groaned, kissing her sternum.

"Fuck." Heather's head pressed back, her throat column long and sexy.

"Do you like me drinking from you?" I rolled both of her breasts in my hands, fingers closing at the tips and pulling.

"Yes," she cried. "But you're doing it so quickly that I can't come."

I grinned against her stomach. "You'll earn your orgasm soon, blood mate."

More blood made a lazy trail down her body and I lapped it up, dragging my lips and tongue indulgently over her skin like she was a decadent piece of fruit. The wounds on her chest were already clotting, so I made my way further down her body.

I kissed her bellybutton and lower stomach while positioning her thighs over my shoulders. Heather's hands were in my hair, scratching my scalp and tugging at the strands. With my fangs and hands I made quick work of her soft lounge pants, tearing apart the seam down the middle. Her panties were a simple cotton like her bra, and they were already soaked.

"Fucking Temkra, this is everything." The scent of her arousal hit me like a drug, every bit as potent and luscious as her blood.

I pressed my mouth against her pussy and sucked at the damp fabric of her underwear. A jolt rolled through Heather, her hips bucking into my face.

"Laith!" she cried out, fingers curling in my hair.

"Heather," I moaned against her flesh. "I want to die right here. Fucking face down and drowning in you."

Every fiber of my being wanted to move that scrap of fabric to the side and taste her properly, but there was more I wanted to do here. I had to pace myself.

I turned my head and kissed her inner thigh, then did the same to her opposite leg. Alternating between each leg, I ramped up the intensity with every kiss—sucking harder and scraping my fangs against her sensitive flesh until she was shivering and squirming.

"Such a good, beautiful blood mate," I murmured before my next pair of kisses. "Letting me feast on her body like this. I think she's earned an orgasm."

"Yes," Heather panted. "Please!"

"Watch and learn, Justin. Maybe you'll learn something about pleasing a woman." I grinned, nuzzling the erotic pulse in her femoral artery. "Not that you'll ever be in the same league as a vampire."

I struck and Heather's flesh yielded like butter to my

fangs. Her blood filling my mouth on that first pull was the best-tasting yet. It was rich with oxygen and the essence of *her*. Heather's body shook while I held her leg firm to my mouth. Her back arched off the bed with the force of her release, her other thigh clamping like a vice around my head. Her fingers may have drawn blood from my scalp, but fuck if I cared.

I released her and sealed the wound with my tongue as she started to come down, but I was far from done. Her legs fell open, body limp as she panted. She only got a few seconds of reprieve before I couldn't fight it any longer. I pulled her panties aside and licked a long stripe through her cunt.

"Laith." Her voice was breathless, surprised.

"Heather." I tongued her opening and sucked her lips into my mouth. "You think you can come so beautifully and I won't need a taste of that too?"

"Oh, God..."

Her moan was long and wanton as I pressed two fingers inside her and spread them to stroke her inner walls.

"So tight. You're squeezing around me already." I teased her clit with my tongue while my fingers built up to a steady rhythm. "Such a sweet pussy should never go neglected. You've been dying for good cock, haven't you?"

"Yes!" Heather was so turned on that her wetness began dripping down my wrist.

"You need to be properly fucked, don't you?" My slick-ened thumb rolled over her clit, massaging the firm little mound in lazy circles. "You need someone that can actually give you what you need. Make you come and scream until you crash out, don't you?"

"Yes!" Heather planted her heels in the mattress and

thrust her hips against my hand, matching my rhythm and seeking more. "Yes. Please, Laith."

"You don't need some fucking loser who will never touch you, who will never anticipate your needs or even try to meet them." My gaze was riveted on her, watching her breasts bounce with each thrust, her beautiful face in agonized bliss, but I could almost see Justin in my periphery. I could feel the weight of his shame and it was fucking delicious.

"No, I only need you, Laith," Heather whimpered. "Please, I'm so close."

"So fucking sweet when you beg." I added a third finger and drove into her with more force, my hand making wet sloppy sounds with each impact.

"Oh, fuck!" Heather stretched around my fingers and she fisted the sheets at her side.

"You're taking me so well." I sped up my ministrations on her clit, sending her toward that peak that she so desperately needed. "My beautiful blood mate was made to take everything I give her."

Heather's mouth opened like she was about to agree, then she let out a choked cry as her eyes rolled back, her whole body stiffening. She jolted and shook like she'd been electrocuted, the tremors shaking her from head to toe as she squeezed around my fingers.

From the build-up to the aftershocks, she was a fucking vision. I withdrew my hand from her and made sure those hooded doll eyes watched as I sucked her taste off my fingers.

"Delicious."

She laughed breathlessly. "You're crazy."

"If wishing I could bottle your taste to drink you at all times is crazy, I don't ever want to be sane."

Heather smiled lazily, stretched out and exquisite in my bed. Her skin was flushed and glossy with a light sheen of sweat. I bent lower, brushing a soft kiss against her lips. Her mouth pressed harder to mine, which made me grin. My woman wanted more.

"Do you want something in that pretty mouth?" I dragged a thumb across her plump lower lip.

Her eyes widened. "Yes." She was already reaching for my pants.

I pressed back, kneeling on the bed as she rolled forward. Heather took off the remains of her torn clothing while I pulled my shirt over my head. The sight of her drew a deep groan from my chest.

On her hands and knees. Her dark honey hair spilling over her back. The dip of her waist and flare of her hips. The round curves of her ass that begged me to grab them. But what captured me most were her eyes, glancing up with a trusting but shy vulnerability as she pulled apart my belt.

"You're so fucking beautiful." I stroked her cheek, pushing hair out of her face while helping with my button and zipper.

"I don't know why I'm nervous." Heather laughed lightly, shoving my jeans down my thighs.

"Maybe because my attention is entirely on you, as it should be." I caressed her upper back and shoulders. "But you have nothing to be nervous about. You've already got me like putty in your hands."

She peeled down my boxers, releasing my cock in a slow, torturous reveal. "I don't know about that. Looks pretty hard to me."

Her lips slid tentatively around my head and I forgot any witty retort that might have been on my tongue. "Won't take very much," I choked out.

She made a soft humming noise, her tongue swirling around my shaft as she slowly took me deeper into her mouth.

"Holy...fuck." My fists closed in her hair, head tipping back in bliss. "Okay. I'll admit I should have let you suck me the other day."

Heather chuckled, the vibrations running down my length straight into my nerves, my brain, my blood. I realized she was approaching it like an experiment, trying different things with her tongue, testing my reactions and her own limits. She took as much as she could without forcing me down her throat.

"I should have known my Science Barbie would give the best brain I've ever had."

Heather pulled away laughing while she continued to stroke my length with her hand. "That was terrible."

"What are you talking about?" I rubbed her neck, already missing the taste of her blood on my tongue. "That was a good one."

"Mm-hm." She didn't sound convinced but her tongue swirled my head again, so she must have been a little impressed.

"Fuck, you're amazing," I groaned, head toward the ceiling again. "I thought my mouth was pretty good, but yours...damn."

My gaze returned to her with an imaginary Justin sitting in a dark corner of the room, and a wicked vindication filled me as I slid back into the fantasy.

"Look at the girl you lost, Justin, on her knees and sucking my cock so well. Can you hear how wet her mouth is? How deep and greedily she takes me?"

Heather let out a little moan, her throat relaxing and taking more of my length.

"You fucked up losing a mouth as talented and gorgeous as this." I twisted Heather's hair in my fist, pulling just tightly enough for her to feel. "You probably never got many blowjobs anyway, and I bet you blame her for that. But guess what, Justin?" I started thrusting into Heather's mouth. "That's on you, buddy. You didn't earn them because you're a piece-of-shit boyfriend. You want a woman on hands and knees for you, happily taking your cock in her mouth? You need to take care of her first."

Heather drew back and released me with a pop of her lips, a wicked gleam in her eye as she stroked me from base to tip.

"What's on your mind?" I ran my knuckles over her cheek, endlessly awed by her beauty.

"Is it okay if I..." she chewed her lip. "Touch myself?"

Fuck.

Me.

"Of course you can touch yourself. Your pleasure comes first, always." I smirked down at her. "Does sucking me turn you on?"

"Maybe." She said the word shyly, but her eyes sparkled.

"I'm the luckiest vampire who ever lived."

Heather slid one hand down her body to strum between her legs. I could barely see anything from my vantage point but it was still the hottest thing I'd ever seen.

"We should get some toys," I said, running my hands down her back. "Make your multitasking a little easier."

Her expression was one of surprise. "I've never used toys before."

I let out an exasperated sigh, narrowing my eyes at the dark corner of the room. "Intimidated by *toys*, Justin? Your insecurity knows no bounds, does it?"

Heather smiled before her lips took me in again, gliding over me with exquisite heat, pressure, and softness.

"Make yourself come." I gathered her hair away from her face, watching her whole body rock forward and back. "Forget about him. I only want to watch you. Show me how much you like this."

Heather's moans increased in volume and intensity, her hand between her legs picking up speed with each greedy gulp of my cock down her throat. Watching her come undone was almost too much for me. Combined with her mouth, it took every last thread of control to hold my own pleasure back.

"You're doing so good...so good..." I wanted to tip my head back and let go, but my determination to watch her would not be deterred. "Fuck, that's the best thing ever."

Heather's body quaked with her orgasm, the shaking release forcing a long keening from her throat, her toes and fingers curling. She was so overwrought with pleasure that she could barely hold herself up on hands and knees. And yet she kept me in her mouth the whole time.

That was what finally did me in. A choked cry of her name was her only warning before my pleasure crested and spilled onto her tongue. My fists curled tightly, pulling on her hair. It had to be painful, but she took my release eagerly. Her throat bobbed with a swallow, and that sexy motion sparked a fresh wave of blood lust. Through my own heartbeat and ragged breaths, her pulse pounded like music in my ears.

I backed up until I stood at the edge of the bed, grabbed Heather's ankles and yanked her down toward me.

"I'm not anywhere near done with you."

# Chapter 27

## *Heather*

Laith looked monstrous in the hottest way possible. He was breathing hard, mouth open and fangs longer than I'd ever seen them before. His eyes were dilated, a much darker red than usual, his gaze ravenous and fixated on me. The dim light accentuated the contours of his body, muscles tense like he was moments from capturing prey.

Even though he didn't need to capture me. I was already his.

He dragged me to the edge of the bed by my ankles and pulled my legs apart. The move was possessive, even a little aggressive, and if my orgasm hadn't already turned me into a limp puddle, I would have become one right then.

Laith wrapped a hand around the back of my head, lifting me only a few inches to kiss me roughly. My thighs immediately pressed into the sides of his waist. With a possessive hand, he kneaded my hip, my ass, and my leg all the way down to my ankle. It felt like he was luxuriating in a prized possession—me. Like he would touch priceless jewels or the rarest, most expensive silk with the same reverence. And I could not get enough.

I came up on my elbows to return his kiss. His hand came around my neck, thumb stroking over where he bit me before. I shivered in anticipation; the skin in that spot was extra sensitive despite being healed.

Something hot, heavy, and slick rubbed over my swollen clit, and my head fell on a moan. "You're still hard?"

"Of course I am. Look at you." He straightened, eyes drinking me in while his hips made small, lazy thrusts.

"But...you came in my mouth." It was extremely hard to form a coherent sentence, let alone a thought while that thick cock dragged back and forth over my clit hood.

"So?" Laith's smirk was cocky. "I still need to be inside you. I need you more than I need to fucking breathe."

"Stop teasing me, then." My hips shifted, trying to find an angle that would bring him inside. I needed him just as badly.

"I'm just savoring this." Laith's gaze roamed over me like he was taking in a work of art. "You're just so fucking breathtaking."

He bent to kiss me again, and the moment our mouths locked together, he pressed inside me to the hilt.

My scream was swallowed by his mouth. My legs clamped tighter around him, like I never wanted to leave. The sensation of him was intense, but not painful. I didn't know a man could fill me this much. The size of him stretched me to my limit, and every tiny movement sent such delicious friction through me that sparks lit up my vision.

Laith gripped my waist with both hands, holding me in place while he moved through me. He pressed inside slowly, and deeply enough to push the air from my lungs.

When our lips broke away from a kiss, he went to my neck. I closed my eyes, savoring the drags of his cock along my inner walls as I waited for his bite.

He spent time kissing my neck first, sucking and nipping the sensitive skin in a way that drove me into a frenzy. His thrusts picked up speed, hips driving into me with more force and building my pleasure to yet another peak.

Only when I was on the knife's edge did he strike. His fangs sank into me as his thrusts grew punishing. My orgasm clasped around his thick length and squeezed so hard, he roared into my neck as he drank from me. My vision went dark, the sensations so overwhelming that I had to squeeze my eyes shut and let it all crash over me like a tidal wave.

Laith never stopped fucking me, even as his whole body shuddered and I felt more heat spill inside me. His fangs withdrew, replaced by his tongue laving at my skin as he glided wetly through me.

"Did you just…" I wasn't even sure why I was trying to speak. My lips and extremities tingled. Even a brush of the bedsheet against my hand sent my nerves lighting up.

Laith too seemed barely able to speak. He looked completely entranced as he straightened. A smear of my blood coated his lip, chest heaving and skin glistening with sweat.

"I can't fucking handle how perfect you are." He seemed to be whispering in awe more to himself than to me. "Your blood. Your body. Your scent. How wet you are, how well you take me inside. How could I ever deserve this?"

It took every ounce of strength to roll myself upward, but I did it. I took his face in my hands and kissed him, fighting the tears brought on by all the emotional and sexual release of tonight.

"I never even dreamed I could deserve someone like you," I confessed. "Someone who looks at me like you do, touches me with real desire, and makes me feel like I'm a priority. I'm still wondering if this is a dream I'll wake up from."

Laith wrapped his arms around my back, crushing me to his chest. "I don't just desire you, I ache for you. And you're not just *a* priority, you're the *only* priority. I live to take care of you. The blood mate connection brought us together, but the way I'm obsessed with you is all me."

"I want to take care of you too," I said. "I want to do more than just soak up your attention and give you blood."

"You already do." He pressed a kiss to my forehead. "You're a great listener and you don't expect me to be funny all the time. You let me act out this fantasy that's probably a little fucked up. You make me laugh way more than the dumb losers around here." He paused for a long time, dropping his forehead to mine. "You chose me. Over him."

The significance of those five words needed their moment to breathe.

"It was honestly an easy choice," I said. "I only wish I didn't hesitate for so long. I should have chosen you sooner."

Laith's grin spread slowly. "It doesn't matter. You're mine now."

"I am yours," I agreed. "And you're mine."

"In body, blood, and soul." He brought my hand to his chest, his grin taking on a wicked gleam. "I'll say full vows to you at our mating ceremony. But for now..."

He withdrew from me in one quick motion, then flipped me over onto my stomach. The long, deep press of his cock driving back into me had my eyes rolling back and a guttural moan leaving my mouth.

"Fuck, Laith..."

My vampire bowed over me, wrapping one hand around the front of my throat. The motion forced a deep arch in my back and drew my gaze up, meeting Laith's eyes as he pounded into me with a new ferocity. The new angle hit all kinds of new depths and sensitive spots that I didn't know were possible.

"You're so fucking pretty when you take me." He kissed the top of my head with a tenderness that was in complete opposition with the way he was fucking me. "You're wetter every time I'm inside you. Do you love taking my cock that much?"

"Yes!" I cried out. "Oh God, yes. More."

"Fuck, you make me want to explode." He nipped my ear and dragged rough, biting kisses down my nape and across my upper back. "But I won't until you come for me one more time. Can you be a good girl and do that for me?"

"I can...mm...I can try." He felt incredible but I was so oversensitive everywhere, I wasn't sure I'd be able to again.

"I'll help you. Don't worry." His fangs dragged over my shoulder and I shuddered. "Just relax. Focus on how good you feel. Do you like this position?"

"Mm-hm." He released my throat and I let my head drop, rocking back against his thrusts. "Feels so good."

"You feel amazing." Laith moved my hair off of my neck and I felt the teasing sharpness of fangs once again. "How badly do you want my bite?"

"So bad," I whined. "Please, Laith."

"Fuck, I love the way you beg." His tongue trailed the same path his fangs did. "You make it so hard to say no to you."

"Please, Laith! I love when you take my blood. I need it."

"Do you?" He grunted, driving into me even harder, and I felt the coiling pleasure of an orgasm start to build.

"I need it so much. Please."

"You come harder when I drink from you, don't you?" His teasing was driving me insane. I had no idea how he kept such control while I was a whining, begging mess.

"I never knew I could feel so good," I confessed. "Even before I saw your face, before I knew who you were, I've craved your fangs in me since that first time."

Laith let out a low, ragged groan before he twisted my hair up in his fist. He pulled back, sending tingles of delightful pain down my scalp. My throat stretched out long, my spine bending into an even deeper arch.

When he bit the juncture of my neck and shoulder, I could feel my pleasure hurtling toward the peak like a rocket leaving the atmosphere. Laith fucked me harder, faster. My nerve endings seemed to multiply with each drag of his cock.

He growled as his fangs sank deeper into the muscle of my neck, his hips slapping my ass with enough impact to be painful if I wasn't so far gone with pleasure. I was pinned between his teeth and his cock, the onslaught of sensation never abating until it became too much and crashed over.

The release felt like ocean waves pulling me under before letting me rise for a breath. Over and over the waves came, suffocating and freeing me. I must have passed out for a few seconds, because I came to while lying flat on my stomach and Laith on his side next to me.

He panted hard, his skin glossy with sweat. He looked sated, happy. A lazy grin spread across his mouth when he noticed my eyes peel open. "You back, Science Barbie?"

"Yeah." I lifted my head just as Laith scooted in closer.

"Don't move yet. You're bleeding." He leaned in and dragged his tongue over the crook of my neck, which felt sore and the skin a little ragged. "That last bite might have been too rough."

"No, it wasn't." I closed my eyes in bliss as he soothed the bite with his tongue. Tendrils of pleasure spread throughout my body. It was a calming sensation, like the press of fingers during a massage.

"I didn't hurt you?" Apparently finished with healing the bite, Laith dragged me closer. He pulled my leg over his hip and let his arm fall over my waist. He watched me intently, propped up on his elbow. "Tell me honestly. Was any of it too much?"

"No." I traced the scarring on his chest, not needing to think about my answer. "I loved all of it, in case my many orgasms didn't make that clear."

Laith chuckled, his fingers stroking down the bumps of my spine. "Not even all the things I said to Justin?"

"Not at all. It seems like that was cathartic for you."

"It was."

Laith's palm followed the curve of my butt, kneading gently where it met the back of my leg. Even now, after such intense and emotional sex, he couldn't stop touching me.

"It was for me too, I think."

He gave me a curious look. "How so?"

A rush of shyness came over me and I almost brushed off the question. But this was Laith. I had to remember he would never ridicule me for anything I felt. To be open with him was to be safe.

"Maybe not insulting him specifically, but I've kind of always wished a guy would talk about me like you did. Just...being expressive in how much he wants to fuck me.

Or how sexy he thinks I look. How lucky he feels to have me. In the past, I've always had to guess what he was feeling because I never got any feedback. I've always secretly craved just hearing...anything, really."

Laith took my chin in his fingers and lifted my face up to his. He pressed a long, lingering kiss to my mouth that had me gasping when he pulled away.

"You'll never need to guess with me," he whispered. "You know I can't keep my damn mouth shut. Especially when it comes to how sexy you are."

I wanted to look away, to hide in shyness again, but he kept holding my face to make me look at him.

"Justin is out of my system. I'm happy to never speak his name again. But I'll always tell you exactly what I'm thinking in the moment. You might even become annoyed with it, but I promise you'll never need to crave anything secretly again. Just tell me what you're craving and it's yours. As for expressing how much I crave *you?*" He released my chin, stroking his knuckles against my cheek with a smile. "It's the most natural, easy thing in the world. How could I not?"

No words could accurately sum up the depth and intensity of my emotions then. He made his feelings and actions toward me sounds so simple, so obvious. How could I have spent my whole adult life seeking this kind of romantic validation, and here he was, giving it to me so freely?

"It's easy to crave you too, and get swept up by you." My fingertips drifted over the hard planes of his stomach. "How am I not beating away other women with a stick?"

"Because I'm weird and annoying."

Before I could protest, his fingers paused over the tender puncture marks on my left breast. "Shit, I didn't heal this one. I'm sorry. Hold still."

His head lowered, lips parted and tongue out.

"Wait." I closed a grip in his hair, tugging lightly to stop him. "As much as I love it when you lick me, I want that one to heal naturally."

Laith paused, glancing up at me with an inquisitive look. "It'll take much longer to heal that way. And you might have a scar."

"Good," I said. "Actually, you should bite me there again next time. I want to see your mark in that spot. Right over my heart." I drew his face to mine for a kiss. "Because it belongs to you, Laith."

He brought my hand to his chest again, palm flat over the raised scar tissue. "And mine is yours. Forever."

# Chapter 28

# *Heather*

I woke up to an insistent buzzing, which my half-asleep brain registered as my phone vibrating. Grabbing it from the nightstand with Laith's arm clamped tightly around my waist was another matter.

He spooned me from ankle to chest, his breath puffing softly on my nape. I'd fallen asleep to him kissing me there. Even in sleep, he clung to me. Maybe some people would have found it annoying or too much, but I could never get enough of his affection.

Except, maybe, when I couldn't reach my phone.

"Laith?" I wriggled in his grasp, trying to loosen myself without disturbing him.

"Mmm."

My stirring did the opposite of what I intended. He curled around me tighter, sleepily brushing kisses against my neck and upper back.

I couldn't help but grin. My bloodthirsty, protective vampire was also the cutest snuggle bug in the world. "Laith, honey. I need to check my phone."

"Mmm." His grip did loosen this time, allowing me to slide to the edge of the bed while his hand remained on my hip. "Never had honey, but I bet you taste like it."

If it weren't for the name that repeated itself across my screen, I would have answered him with a cute quip. But my blood turned to ice, rendering me unable to move or think.

Laith sensed my distress immediately, his warmth covering my back as he scooted closer. "Heather?" His hand came to my arm and a kiss dropped to my shoulder. "What's wrong? Is it Justin?"

The phone shook in my hand, as did the breath leaving my mouth. "No. Not Justin."

"Then who?" He rubbed my upper arm, which must have erupted in goosebumps. "Temkra's fate, you're shaking like a leaf. Who's blowing up your phone?"

I turned numbly to face him, dropping the phone on the mattress between us. "I'm so sorry, but there's something I haven't told you."

Laith's face was full of pure concern. "Okay. What's going on?"

It felt like forever before I could get the words out. "I wasn't honest with you in the beginning. The first few times I came to see you...I wasn't really planning on breaking up with Justin. Originally, I had no intention of becoming your blood mate."

Laith's expression turned guarded. "But that changed?"

"Yes, I swear to you." I grabbed the back of his neck and pulled forward to kiss him. "I did leave him and I do want to be with you. I am yours, Laith. Every bit of that is true. I think I had feelings for you from the start, but like an idiot, I was fighting them until you saved me in that alley."

Laith relaxed, although a deep furrow remained etched between his brows. "So, what's wrong?" He pushed away strands of messy bed hair from my face, every touch so tender and careful.

I tried to take a deep breath, but my lungs remained tight. "You remember those bruises on my arms? The ones that looked like fingers?"

Magenta eyes flashed with rage. "Yes."

"They were from a guy named Soren, who's been stalking me because I've made contact with the vampire world several times. He's part of some shadowy government operation in the human world. They know vampires exist and they're gathering information on you guys." I swallowed the lump in my throat. "He wanted me to keep coming back to Sanguine for information. That was why I kept seeing you at first. But listen, Laith."

I touched the side of his face, making his darkening, rage-filled eyes focus on me. "Meeting you at the club was an escape I desperately needed. With you, I could enjoy myself for once and not think about Soren, Justin, or any of the other bullshit in my life. My feelings for you are real, even if my intentions weren't at first. I'm so sorry, Laith."

To my shock and utter relief, Laith leaned in and kissed me deeply. "You have nothing to be sorry for, Heather." He touched his fingertips to the back of my arm, as if reimagining the bruises that had been there. "This Soren guy hurt you. I imagine he threatened you too? If you didn't provide the information he wanted?"

I nodded, the lump in my throat becoming a suffocating knot. "He even showed up at my work. We have really good security, but I guess he has clearance because he's a Fed. I just couldn't get away from him...unless I came to Sanguine."

"And now he's blowing up your phone?" Laith glanced down at my screen lit up with notifications. "What does he want?"

"Well, I basically ghosted him. He's probably pissed about that and wants the information I owe him. I'm pretty sure he bugged my apartment, so he knows I'm not there. But...shit." I raked a hand through my hair. "All my stuff is there. I had to leave so quickly because of Justin."

"We can get you new things." Laith rubbed my arms. "Because you're not going back there. Nothing is worth your safety."

"I know, but it's not just stuff. I need my glasses and contact prescriptions. Some documents and sentimental things. I might need to sort something legally with the apartment manager since it's in my name."

"None of that matters," Laith insisted. "We can set you up fresh here. A brand new start." His hand moved to my waist and squeezed lightly. "You do realize you're moving in with me, right?"

"I figured that." I chuckled. "And I'm excited to, but I'm still worried. What if Soren can track my phone here and find his way to Sanguine? He had some crazy technology that I didn't even know was possible."

"He won't find you here," Laith said on a low growl. "It doesn't matter what resources your human government has. Human-world rules don't apply here. Even if they find their way in, Thorne will be on them if they step one toe out of line."

"I don't know, Laith."

"I do." His hand returned to my cheek. "I bet that's why this guy used you. Because he didn't have the means or was too fucking scared to investigate Sanguine himself."

"Maybe you're right." I sighed.

"I am right." He nipped my nose playfully. "As much as I love having you all to myself, I actually don't want to completely uproot you from your life. Are there any friends or family you want to keep in contact with? We can arrange something."

Grateful for a temporary change in topic, I thought for a few moments. "Honestly, not really. I lost touch with a lot of friends when Justin and I got more serious. Then I got buried in work. My work friends, I only really saw at work."

"What about family?"

I shook my head. "I'm an only child and my parents were older when they had me. They passed when I was in college and I don't have any extended family."

Laith's face crumpled. "Fuck. I'm so sorry."

"Thank you. And it's okay. They hadn't been in good health since I was a teenager. Maybe it's a bit morbid, but I had kind of been preparing myself for years already."

"It's such a shame humans are so short-lived." Laith brought one of my hands to his lips and kissed my knuckles. "The more time I spend with them, the more fascinating and lovely they are."

I thought back to one of our earliest conversations when he explained blood mates to me. "But I'm going to live as long as a vampire now, right?"

"Yes. Once we complete the mating ceremony, your life-span will be attached to mine. We'll age at the same rate and when it's our time, we'll die together." Laith turned my hand over and kissed the center of my palm. "How does eight hundred-plus years sound?"

I shook my head on a soft laugh. "I can't even imagine the next ten or twenty years, let alone eight hundred."

Laith smirked. "How's that for a taste of forever?"

"It's a pretty good taste."

"Fuck yeah, you are." He dragged me into him and went for my neck with his talented mouth.

I shuddered at the memory of his fangs in that same spot last night, although now he only gently nipped and kissed me there, his solid hand and forearm supporting my back. Without his bite driving me to another orgasm, I was able to keep my wits and circle back to our conversation.

"I need to go back to the apartment, Laith."

He groaned against my neck. "No."

"Please? It'll just be a quick trip. I'll pack a bag in like ten minutes."

"And if this Soren guy is watching the place and ambushes you?" Laith pulled back with a hard stare. "He already hurt you once."

"You could come with me," I suggested. "I don't think he'll come near me if you're around."

"Obviously I'd go with you. That'll be the only way I let you go back," Laith bit out. "But I don't want you going there at all."

I chewed my lip. "Okay, look. The only thing I really want is an old photo of me with my parents. It's the only copy I have."

Laith sighed heavily. "You're killing me, Science Barbie."

"Vampire Ken," I cooed, kissing his jaw. "I know exactly where it is. It won't take but a minute."

"What if Justin's there?" he grumbled.

"I don't think he is." I grabbed my phone and scrolled through the messages. "He texted me just once saying he packed his stuff and left for his parents' house."

"Let me see."

I turned the phone screen toward Laith, and he smirked when he read the entire message. "'*Hope you're satisfied*', he says." His magenta eyes lifted to meet mine, hand stroking over my thigh. "Well, are you?"

"You know I am." I leaned into him, our lips meeting in a long, lingering kiss.

That kiss rolled into another one, and then another. Laith grabbed my thigh and drew my leg over his hip, the two of us rolling on the mattress in a tangle of arms, legs, lips, and tongues.

When we parted for a breath, I was on top of him. My forehead snuggled into his neck, legs draped on either side of him. His arms wrapped around my back, palms making soothing passes up and down my spine.

"We'll go back for your picture," he murmured. "And nothing else. In and out."

I kissed his neck happily. "Thank you."

"As if I could say no to you."

My lips pulled into a grin. "Does that mean we could grab my laptop, too?"

A smack on the ass made me squeal with laughter.

"Don't push your luck, Science Barbie."

"Fine, fine." I resettled against body, snuggling into him for the most comfortable position. "Speaking of science, is there any kind of work I can do here?"

"I'm sure there is." Laith curled a lock of my hair around his finger. "Novak would love help with whatever nerdy science projects he has going on. The blood bank would probably have something for you, too." His lips brushed across my forehead. "But only if it's something you enjoy. You don't have to work to live anymore."

"I do enjoy it. Plus I want to stay busy and keep my

mind sharp. And, if I get sick of lab work, maybe I can try a different field of study."

"That's essentially what Bea does. I think she's helping Tavia with the winemaking a lot lately, but for the past twenty years she's just been taking courses in whatever seems interesting."

I lifted my head from his chest. "What is Bea's deal? When I was meeting the girls, she was pretty cagey about whether or not she had a vampire mate."

Laith let out a long sigh. "It's her story to tell, but everyone assumes she and Kalix had a thing."

"Kalix? The friend you're trying to break out of prison?"

Laith nodded. "He's the one who turned her into a brusang. Right before he got taken away."

"Oh...wow. Did he..."

"He did not kill her. He'd never harm a woman. But he saved her life. He got taken away before she woke up so he probably has no idea if the turning worked. A human only awakens as a brusang maybe fifty percent of the time."

I returned my cheek to Laith's sternum. "Wow. That *is* complicated."

"She hasn't been with anyone else, so the unspoken assumption is that she's waiting for him. Sometimes I feel like someone should tell her to move on. Nobody would blame her if she did. Twenty years is a long time, even for us. But we are trying to get him back. Which, even if we succeed, who the hell knows what kind of state he'll be in."

"Yeah." I ran a light touch up and down his torso. "It's a sad situation. I'll do whatever I can to help."

Laith squeezed my shoulder. "Thank you. Assuming we can get him out, he'll probably need some kind of intense drug detox. More than the usual draitrium addicts we see."

"Not my field, but I can get started on the research." I pressed up, as if planning to start right that second.

Laith immediately pulled me back down with a laugh. "Later," he grunted, wrapping around me tightly. "We'll leave at dusk to get your picture. Then we'll get you settled in with your new family."

I smiled against his warm skin. "That sounds great to me."

Heather's hands sat relaxed on my waist as we approached her old apartment complex. So I grabbed her fingers and pulled them forward to clasp over my stomach.

"Don't let go unless you want a spanking," I told her over my shoulder.

"Don't threaten me with a good time, then."

Her voice was muffled through the motorcycle helmet, but I heard the smile in her words. My girl had a mouthy, bratty side to her, and I loved it. I had seen glimpses of it when we first met, but her confidence was growing in leaps and bounds already. I loved that she wasn't afraid to mess with me and push my buttons.

I loved *her*.

The realization hit me like a rush of cold wind. I had known it, felt it for some time, but not in those exact words. I knew she was mine forever, knew that her blood was the most delicious substance to ever pass my lips, but that was run-of-the-mill blood mate stuff. Two people could be bonded as blood mates without ever falling in love.

This had nothing to do with her blood and everything to do with her mind, her laugh. Her warmth and the way she touched me. Her curiosity and how my bed had always felt empty until she was in it.

I wanted forever with her because she was *her*. Heather. My Science Barbie.

My gloved hand remained over both of hers, fingers interlaced on my stomach while I drove the bike one-hand. Heather's chest rested against my back, her body relaxed and at ease.

The covered space in front of her old unit was empty, so I parked the bike there and turned it off. Heather slid out of her seat first and started up the walk, but I kept one of her hands clasped in mine.

"Wait for me. I don't want you out of my sight."

She rolled her eyes but obeyed. We both took off our helmets and I opened my senses to the surroundings. The night was cool and relatively calm. Next to me, Heather's heartbeat was the loudest and clearest. I could sense other heartbeats further away, steady echoes of blood pumping through arteries in the people sleeping in nearby units. Sounds of traffic and typical nighttime activity came through outside of the complex, but everything nearby felt quiet and asleep.

"Okay, let's go."

I remained vigilant while Heather and I walked up to the front door and she unlocked it. Aside from the gentle hum of nearby electrical towers, I didn't sense anything odd in the air. But I wasn't about to let my guard down for a moment.

"Is it okay if I turn on a light?" Heather asked.

"Go for it."

She flipped a switch and the main area of the apartment

came into view. The only thing that looked strange was the empty desk with a distinct dust-free rectangle on it's surface.

"Guess Justin left with his computer." Heather rounded the furniture, heading for the mantle of photos against a far wall. "He better not have taken any of my stuff with him."

"I'll replace anything you need," I reminded her. "You can give me a shopping list."

She tossed me a suggestive look over her shoulder. "Sounds like you want to spoil me."

"I mean, that's a given."

"It'll take me a while to get used to that." She returned to looking at the photos on the mantle.

"You'll have all the time in the world." I approached her from behind and slid a hand from the small of her back to her waist. She visibly melted at my touch, and because I couldn't resist, I moved her hair aside to nibble at her neck.

"What the hell?" Heather muttered, irritated. "It's not here."

I lifted my head, noticing the empty spot where her hand rested on the mantle. "Maybe it fell?"

Together, we searched the surrounding area. It was a small space without much clutter, so we figured out quickly that the photo hadn't fallen.

"That asshole." Heather stabbed her fingers through her hair with an angry huff. "I bet he took it. Or moved it somewhere just to fuck with me."

"Justin?" I asked. "Or the government guy?"

"Justin," she confirmed. "He knew what that picture meant to me. That it would be one thing I'd save in a house fire." Her lip wobbled, eyes shining with unshed tears. "Soren probably dug up my family history, but he doesn't actually know me. Justin *knew*, and..." She let out a shaky breath, continuing, "he always had to have to last word. Always knew what to do or say to hurt me the most."

"Hey." I took her face in my hands and kissed her forehead, then her nose bridge. "Fuck him. We'll find the picture. If I have to hunt him down and take it back, I will do so happily. I'm not fucking kidding."

Heather forced a sad smile, leaning her face into my hands as my thumb caught a tear. "I know you're not."

I brought her into my chest and kissed the top of her head. "Let's keep looking. I won't confront him unless absolutely necessary."

"Okay." She blinked away the remaining tears, determination in her gaze. "Thank you."

"Always." I kissed her mouth once before releasing her. "Should we start with the kitchen? Maybe he hid it in a cabinet."

"Good idea."

The two of us got to work, opening drawers and cabinets and emptying the contents on the floor. In ten minutes, we searched every nook and cranny of that small kitchen with no luck. We moved to the living area next, moving furniture to search underneath and pulling up couch cushions to no avail. Once we finished there, only the bedroom and bathroom were left.

There was a discomforting ball in the pit of my stomach at the sight of Heather's old bed. I hated that Justin slept next to her, even if they hadn't touched intimately for months. This room was a time capsule of Heather's life before me, where she stared at the ceiling feeling rejected and unwanted. If only she knew how much her life would change, how loved and adored she would be.

"Well, at least he left my backpack here." Heather lifted the pack from the floor, unzipped it, and pulled out a laptop. "I might have an old scan of the photo on here somewhere, but I don't remember."

"Keep looking for the actual photo," I said. The sooner we were out of this room, out of this expired part of her life, the better. "You can look for a digital copy when we're home."

"'Kay," Heather muttered distractedly, fingers moving up down the laptop's touch pad.

"I mean it, Science Barbie." I moved to the threshold of the attached bathroom and flicked on the light.

The laptop shut and I heard the zip of the backpack closing as I opened the medicine cabinet. "Yeah, yeah, Vampire Ken."

I grinned to myself, watching her cross the room to pull open dresser drawers. Closing the cabinet, I turned around in the small bathroom. There was not much to it, just a pedestal sink, toilet, and shower stall. I peered into the small garbage can, which was mostly empty besides some wadded up tissue, a q-tip, and a band-aid wrapper. I nudged the can with my foot and noticed something shoved behind it.

It was two thin strips of black wood meeting to form a corner. I moved the trash can further out of the way and saw that it was a picture frame. Crouching low, I picked up the framed photo with my hands.

There was Heather as a child, beaming with wild, golden hair framing her face and one of her front teeth missing. She sat outside on a log between two human adults. They were clearly older, with gray hair, and lines around eyes and mouths. But their joy as they smiled for the camera was so palpable, I couldn't help but smile back.

It was no wonder Heather treasured this photo. The love and happiness shone through the aged photo like a miniature sun in my hands.

"Heather," I called. "Guess what I just found?"

"Oh my God! Did you really?"

I heard her footsteps approaching and turned, eager to show her my prize. But she never came to the doorway.

The next thing I heard was glass breaking. And then Heather screaming.

Forgetting all about the photo, I dropped it and darted into the bedroom. Someone, a human man dressed entirely in black, had one arm around Heather's waist, the other covering her mouth as she thrashed and kicked. He was dragging her through the broken bedroom window.

I lunged for him, fangs bared in a snarl. It didn't matter who he was. This human was dead. Behind a hooded mask, his eyes widened in alarm at my speed. I snatched Heather from his grip and kicked hard enough in the stomach to send him sailing across the patch of lawn outside the window.

Beyond him sat a dark van with no windows. So the government operative *had* been lying in wait. Why hadn't I heard a heartbeat?

It didn't matter. He was here now and needed to be dealt with.

I retreated into the bedroom and carried Heather to the threshold of the bathroom before setting her on her feet. "Lock yourself inside. Don't come out until I tell you it's safe."

Her panicked eyes snapped from me to just over my shoulder. "Laith, look out!"

I spun just in time to see another masked figure hop over the windowsill into the bedroom.

"Lock yourself in!" I repeated to Heather before rushing at him.

My focus was on the human's assault rifle as I closed the

distance between us. I grabbed control of the weapon and pointed it away. Droplets of moisture suddenly hit my face, as if the human had sprayed me with something in his other hand.

On impact, the droplets started to burn my face and eyes.

At first, I could ignore it and wrenched the rifle away from the human. But then the burning grew worse. It felt like acid eating through my skin with steadily increasing pain and intensity.

"What...the fuck?" In my shock, I gave in to the instinct to wipe my eyes, but that only made it worse. I lost the ability to see, my vision clouded with red.

"Huh." I heard the human grunt. "That colloidal silver really worked."

"Told you it would," groaned another human. Probably the one I'd kicked. "Now grab the fucking girl."

"No." I growled out the single word, fighting through the burning pain and hazy vision to stop them.

I was too slow to react to the fuzzy image of the arm lifting and spraying me in the face again. Some of it hit my mouth and I choked at the burning on my tongue. My sudden gasping drew more of the silver substance down my windpipe, setting my throat on fire.

"Laith!" I heard Heather cry out. "No! Put me down!"

"You're dead." My rage burned hotter than the agony in my eyes and throat. "All of you will die."

"Gonna have to catch us first," one of the humans taunted.

I lunged blindly in the direction of the voice, running full-force into a fist at my gut.

The humans laughed while Heather sobbed my name. She sounded further away. I had to reach her.

"Heather!" I went toward her voice, my arms slashing through the air in front of me. Glass crunched underneath my shoes. I swung one hand to the side and promptly felt the edge of the broken window cut into my palm.

"What do we do about him?" I heard one of the humans ask. They sounded even farther away now, and calm, like they had just walked out with her while I couldn't even get a sense of my surroundings.

"Not our problem. Orders were just for the girl."

"Someone might see him. See what he is."

"I don't get paid enough to give a shit."

A car door slammed, abruptly cutting off Heather's screams. An engine started up, sending my panic to a new height.

"Heather!" I ran as far as I dared in this state, which was only a few feet.

I couldn't chase after them, not like this. The sound of that van driving further and further away was a knife carving deeper into my chest. How could I just listen to them take her?

*Don't lose your head. You'll get her back. Just need to calm down.*

I blinked rapidly, fighting the urge to rub my injured, useless eyes. I could catch up to the van quickly on my bike, but could barely see my hand in front of my face.

"Come on." My eyes squeezed shut, teeth grinding in my jaws. "Get it together."

I had never needed my accelerated vampire healing more than right fucking now. But if it really had been silver in that spray, I was at a disadvantage.

"Come on," I repeated. Every blink of my eyes brought on a fresh, stabbing pain, but I had to flush this shit out.

Heather's blood was fresh in my system. As long as

there wasn't enough silver to kill me, I knew her blood should counteract the effects and speed up my healing.

"Any fucking day now," I hissed, pounding my fist into the ground. "Come on."

The pain ebbed slightly, but I couldn't tell if it was due to healing or adrenaline. I blinked some more, and my blurry vision showed what appeared to be red spots on the pavement.

I felt Heather's distress in my chest. It choked me, holding strong like a fist around my heart. What I'd felt that first day I followed her home was an echo compared to this. Our bond had strengthened to the point where her blood showed me what she was feeling in real time.

"Don't worry." I brought my palm to my chest as if that could somehow soothe her. "I'm coming for you. Just hold on."

Time barely moved as I waited. Every few minutes, I lifted my head and tried to make out details in the distance. My vision was healing, albeit slowly. Too fucking slowly.

When I could finally read the numbers on the nearest apartment building, that was good enough for me. I got to my feet, headed to my bike, and followed the call of her blood.

# Chapter 30

## *Heather*

They tied my wrists and ankles in the van, and put a hood over my head. The whole situation was beyond terrifying, but I could only think of Laith. He'd been bleeding from his eyes and face when they dragged me through the window and tossed me in their vehicle.

He had to pull through. He was a fucking vampire after all. Surely he'd be able to recover, find me, and we'd leave this shitty world full of humans for the last time.

Regret filled my chest and burned its way up my throat. This never would have happened if I hadn't insisted on coming to the apartment. He hadn't wanted to come. He'd only agreed because I wanted that photo, which felt so insignificant now. He had found it. I saw it in the bathroom sink when he told me to lock myself inside.

And it was because of that photo that he'd never seen those men coming. So fucking stupid. I shut my eyes against the scalding tears. I'd choose him over that photo in a heartbeat. My parents had lived a full life and were at rest. I had plenty of happy memories with them. If either Laith or I ended up dead, there would be no sweet photo of us to look back on.

The van drove for what felt like hours. It was impossible to gauge distance or make sense of turns and stops without being able to see. The passage of time worried me too. It was early in the night, but Laith only had until dawn to find me. What if these men kept driving past sunrise?

On and on my thoughts spiraled. No matter how much I tried to come up with a rational plan for escape, coherent thoughts turned to frantic worry about the vampire I loved.

*Great time to figure out that you love him.* Of course it would dawn on me now, after seeing him injured and being kidnapped.

I'd known Laith for a fraction of the time that I'd known Justin, and I just *knew*. From the very beginning, he'd been all in. He showed his care in every touch, every joke he cracked, and every single action toward me since we met. I found what had been missing in my last relationship and so much more. A love that could truly last forever.

After what felt like hours of driving, the van slowed to a complete stop and the engine shut off. I curled into a fetal position, bracing myself for whatever would come next. All I could do for Laith now was stall. Buy enough time for him to come find me.

I heard the van doors open. Someone grabbed my leg and dragged me toward the end. I kicked and flailed my arms, and managed to catch my bound hands around some indent in the van wall, probably the wheel well.

"Quit being a pain in the ass," one of my captors groused.

A fist enclosed around the hood at the back of my head, catching a good chunk of my hair and yanking me out of the vehicle. I yelped as he continued to drag me by the hair once my butt hit the ground, never giving me a chance to stand.

"Should have tied her hands behind her," another voice said.

"Yeah, whatever. Fuck you."

I dug my heels into the ground, which felt like slightly damp, packed earth. It wouldn't buy me much extra time, but hopefully it would make an easy-to-see trail as the guy dragged me.

He pulled me across a threshold. Instead of bumpy dirt under my butt, I felt the smoothness of hard flooring. I split my legs wide, trying to catch my feet on the doorframe. My hands also managed to grab one side and hold on.

"Jesus fucking Christ!"

The guy who'd been dragging me released my hair, giving me relief for one split second before something solid slammed down hard on my temple. His fist probably. The impact rocked through my skull and made my head bounce once on the floor, and my body went limp.

A ringing sounded through my head and it was suddenly much harder to stay conscious. *Can't fall asleep. Gotta give Laith time. Stay awake, stay awake...*

"Hey, watch it." I could barely hear the other person over the distorted noise in my head. "Soren wants her alert."

"She's pissing me the fuck off."

"Well, relax. She's out of it now. No more hits to the head, though."

Someone yanked me roughly by the arms and then I was up in the air. Vertigo made me want to kick and thrash, but my limbs wouldn't cooperate.

"Wish I could throw this bitch down the stairs."

The voice was extremely close. The guy who hit me was currently *carrying* me, and the fear of that fact gave me a much-needed dose of clarity. My head continued to pound painfully, but some of the fog lifted.

I was being carried down a flight of stairs and my captor made no effort to be gentle. My head rocked on my neck with each heavy, creaking step. The air became stale and musty, like we'd entered a basement.

Finally, we hit the bottom and a familiar voice spoke up from across the room. "Took you long enough. Put her there."

Soren.

My exhausted, aching body couldn't help but tense up as my captor brought me closer to him. I was deposited in a chair, and then the hood was removed roughly from my head, taking a thick lock of my hair with it.

"Damn it, Hills. You didn't have to rough her up so badly."

I blinked at the sudden brightness, squinting at Soren's fuzzy image as he came closer to inspect me.

"She pissed me off," was the grunted explanation.

Soren made a motion with his hand. "Guard upstairs and leave me alone with her."

Oh fuck. I had expected Soren, but the last thing I wanted was to be alone with him. Even though these men had already hurt me, something about him truly terrified me.

The henchman stomped up the stairs and then Soren knelt in front of me, his face coming into focus and looked like pure evil. How could I have ever thought of him as handsome? He was nothing compared to Laith.

"You ghosted me, Heather. I thought we had an agreement." He shook his head slowly, clicking his tongue as if he were disappointed. "It was only for two months. None of this would have happened if you had just done your part."

My head pounded. I probably had a concussion and could barely hear him over the rushing of my own blood. This wasn't looking good for me, and my fragmented, panicked thoughts couldn't determine if it was better to keep quiet or antagonize him.

*Time. Stall for time. Laith will get here. He has to.*

"You kept changing the rules on me," I choked out. "I felt trapped. I was scared."

Soren laughed dryly. "Come on, Heather. You're no damsel. It was a simple assignment. You could've handled it."

Anger flared. For some reason, his deflection reminded me of Justin. "You *stalked* me. You threatened to make me disappear. You came to my house and my work. You're not my boss. You're just some psycho who showed up out of nowhere."

"You forced my hand when you kept visiting a parallel world we know nothing about." Soren stood to full height, towering over me in the chair. "I've silenced a lot of people for doing exactly what you did. Usually, I only need to do so once."

I swallowed, fighting the sickening idea that he must have stalked and terrified tons of other people.

"When you refused to listen, I tried to give you a break," he went on. "One of their kind seemed attached to you, so my employers thought you might be useful." He clicked his tongue again. "Until you weren't."

My breath sawed in and out through my nose. The seconds dragged by and I tried to listen for any sounds of a motorcycle outside, but I heard nothing. The basement was probably too well insulated.

"We figured you left our world for theirs when we lost all trace of you here." Soren gave me a disgusted look.

"Abandoning your whole life, your own kind, for one of *them*—really?"

"Well, with the choices presented to me"—I gave him a pointed look up and down—"I think I picked the better option."

"They're creatures, Heather. They're not human. Not people."

"They're definitely people," I shot back. "Better people than most of the humans I've met."

Soren sucked his teeth, eyes flickering over me like deciding what he should do. "Too bad."

He walked to a table set against one wall and opened some kind of case. My heart jumped into my throat with a fresh wave of panic.

"What are you doing?"

"If you're really choosing them over humans, there's little chance you'll give us any more intel." Soren's wide back blocked my view, but he was messing with something that sounded metallic. "I have permission to torture you, and while I'm just as much a scumbag as you think I am, I'd prefer not to. It's not something I enjoy, believe it or not."

"What do you even want?" My voice broke with fear. "Why are you doing this?"

"The human world at large will eventually learn about these parallel words, and how they slightly overlap with ours. And when that happens, the United States needs to have full knowledge and control over those places before any other nation does. Wouldn't you agree?"

I stared at his back. "No. Why can't you just leave them alone?"

"And let Russia harness the power of vampires? North Korea to breed an army of werewolves? Leave Iran or China to utilize dragon shifters?" I heard the unmistakable sound of a slide being pulled—a round being chambered into a gun. Soren turned around, holding a handgun fitted with a long silencer. "It really should be us, don't you think?"

Despite the fear running through me, I shook my head. "There is no *us*, Soren. I'm not part of anything you're aligned with."

He looked almost apologetic, but mainly resigned as he brandished the gun.

"I can kill you instantly, make it painless as possible," he said. "Or I can hit a major artery and make you bleed out. You'll die slower but"—his lip curled with disdain—"you can give that creature you love so much a final meal when he finds you."

"Why?" I willed myself not to cry, not to blubber and beg for my life. "Why do this at all? Just let me go. Forget we ever met."

"It's not my decision. I either pass on intel to my employers, or I tie off a loose end." Soren held the gun by his thigh, pointing down. "You don't want to die, Heather? You can talk."

I closed my eyes. There was so much I could tell them at this point. I could talk about the ruling clan, about the vampires' biggest weakness, draitrium. I had enough of a clear mental image of Sanguine now that I could draw out a rough map. I could tell them where the Blood 'til Dawn compound was, the blood bank, and Novak's house.

But when I pictured Laith smiling in bed before he kissed me, his hands on me with reverent affection, I knew I couldn't say a word. It wasn't just him, either. It was because of Tavia sharing her wine with me. Amy chatting with me as we walked to her house, and the way she and Novak looked at each other. It was the gruff sincerity of Thorne and the other vampires when I'd identified the werewolf blood. It was how they'd all helped Laith search for me after I'd been attacked.

Those creatures were better friends and family to me than anyone else I'd ever met, despite knowing me for a fraction of the time. So my choice was made. The only question was how it would be done.

I was still terrified, but did my best to meet Soren's eyes. "Do it quickly, please."

If or when Laith found me, it wouldn't matter if I was covered in blood or not. He deserved the minuscule comfort of knowing I didn't suffer. He would be devastated regardless. Thinking of the pain he'd be in was already breaking my heart.

"You're sure?" Soren asked.

I hesitated for a moment. I could try giving false information, which could buy more time, but I didn't know what they already knew, and they'd probably end up torturing me anyway if they figured out I was lying.

"Yes." I forced the word out through a painfully tight throat, a throat that desperately wanted to scream and sob rather than quietly accept a death sentence.

"Then look up."

My head lifted until I felt the press of the silencer against my forehead. I squeezed my eyes shut, but wasn't fast enough to stop the tears from rolling. I shook so hard from fear, my teeth rattled. But I forced myself to stay there, my final breaths tight and ragged.

I heard the creak of leather as Soren's gloved finger curled around the trigger, and waited for my end.

# *Laith*

My skin and throat stung like hell, but when my vision finally cleared enough to see, it wasn't difficult to follow Heather's trail.

Her blood called to me, pulling me to her on an invisible lead. It had nothing to do with sight but everything to do with instinct and the bond we shared. Her lifespan may not have been tied to mine yet, but her blood was in me. We were already two parts of a whole, never meant to be separated.

Temkra herself seemed to guide me, showing me the correct turns to take with a gentle hand. I drove as fast as I possibly could without laying my bike down on the hairpin turns winding through the mountains.

It wasn't too far from the park Heather hiked through to find Sanguine, although at a much higher altitude.

After roughly forty-five minutes, I spotted the van from her apartment parked in front of a remote cabin, along with a small army of humans, kitted out with guns, masks, and body armor, surrounding the structure.

I cursed under my breath as I counted at least a dozen.

Even in my current state, I could handle three or four humans on my own. The two at the apartment had had the element of surprise, not to mention that liquid silver. If I'd been ready, we would have been evenly matched. I'd been hoping it would be just the two of them again, but no such luck.

Without backup, I couldn't rush in all fangs and fury. I had to go in peacefully. Or least, give the impression I was doing so.

I pulled up next to the van and was immediately approached by the two guarding the front entrance. By the time I dismounted and turned the bike off, they had their assault rifles mere feet away from my chest and spray canisters lifted toward my face.

My hands went into the air, palms open. Surrendering was the last thing I wanted to do, but one hit of that liquid silver would put me at a serious disadvantage. I probably should have called Thorne on the way over, but I'd been too messed up about Heather. Getting her out was the priority.

"I won't fight," I announced. "But I'm not leaving until Heather is released."

"You got any weapons on you?" one of the humans demanded.

I moved slowly, retrieving the silver daggers from inside my boot and my jacket and tossed them in the dirt a few feet in front of me.

One human collected my weapons while the other brandished a pair of metal cuffs. "Turn around. Hands behind your back."

I complied, turning to face the dark, surrounding woods. More humans arrived with rifles trained on me. The bite of metal around my wrists was expected, but the sudden burning heat was not.

I hissed in surprise, jerking against the cuffs which only drew them tighter. The man fastening them chuckled at my reaction.

"Silver alloy. Got those made especially for you, fangface."

He took hold of my elbow and led me into the cabin. For the first time, I felt no small amount of alarm at how much these humans knew about us. The liquid silver wasn't just some hokey experiment based on superstition. They had made cuffs and now had my weapons. What else did they know?

They brought me inside and I scanned the small space. It was a single room, with the barest of essentials. Instead of beds, several sleeping bags stretched out on the floor. The circular dining table's entire surface was covered in laptops, cell phones, guns, radios, and other devices I couldn't name.

No sign of Heather.

"Where is she?" I could feel her nearby, sense her heartbeat and the deep sorrow that overcame her.

The humans didn't answer. They instead patted my legs and torso, inserting their hands into my pockets.

"I gave you my weapons," I snarled, straining against the cuffs. The burning was a constant irritation, but it didn't feel like there was enough silver to burn my hands completely off my wrists. I suspected the liquid silver was also a small concentration. Enough to be a deterrent, but not lethal.

The humans continued to ignore me. One held up my phone that he took from my jacket pocket and placed it on the table with all the other devices. Then they shoved me toward a door at the far end of the cabin. It was pushed open to reveal a set of stairs going down to a basement level.

The air from below wafted up with the scent of salty tears and the woman who made my life complete.

"Heather!" I broke free from the two humans grasping my elbows and hurried down the rickety stairs.

"Laith!"

Her voice was desperate and full of pain, but it made my blood sing with relief. She was alive and well enough to talk, at least.

I hit the basement floor to see Heather sitting slumped over in a chair that was bolted to the ground. Her hands were cuffed in front of her and there was a swelling bump on her head. In front of her stood a man with a gun, facing me with only the slightest surprise on his face.

"Get away from her," I snarled, heading straight for him. Even if I couldn't use my hands, I still had my teeth.

He raised the gun. I dodged. A shot fired and Heather screamed. I wasn't sure where the hit landed. Not until my shoulder blazed with pain.

The shock of it sent me stumbling into the wall. My vision still wasn't fully healed, but I could make out the damage to my jacket shoulder. The smell of burned leather hit my nose. But I couldn't feel any blood dripping and the pain was quickly subsiding. A graze, most likely. And no silver in the bullet, if my healing was already taking over. Thank Temkra.

I pushed off the wall with my opposite shoulder and faced the human. He was about my height, with the coldest blue eyes I'd ever seen. It wasn't that they were the color of ice, but they lacked any emotion whatsoever. Humans usually had instinctive, visceral reactions when meeting the eyes of a vampires. Often it was fear, or at least caution. This human had no reaction at all.

The sound of his heartbeat confirmed that. There had

been no spike of his pulse since I entered the cabin. The pumping of blood through his body was calm, if even slow. As if he were completely at rest. Even his scent held no markers of stress. I'd never run into a human with such flat emotional responses before.

I wanted to look at Heather, to inspect the injuries on her head and make sure she was all right. But my full attention needed to be on this cold human if I wanted to get her out.

"Are you him?" I said after a few seconds of staring each other down. "The one who's been threatening her?"

His face lit up like he was actually pleased. "So she's told you about me."

"Oh yeah." I put on a feral grin. "Enough to make sure that you will absolutely not make it out of here alive."

"How do you figure that, vampire?" The human nodded at the others who stood behind me. "You're cuffed and outnumbered."

"I'm a pretty lucky guy."

If my hands were free and I had access to my weapons, I was pretty confident I could take at least the ones here in the basement. But, right then, my bravado was almost as much for myself as it was for Heather. This shit didn't look good, and Blood 'til Dawn had no idea where we were.

The clan would hunt these humans down and make them pay, but that could be weeks from now. At this rate, I wasn't certain I'd be alive to see it.

But Heather would be. She had to be.

The only solution became increasingly clear as seconds passed.

"Look, I'll do you a solid." The cuffs bit and chafed at my wrists. I felt a trickle of blood run over my palm as I lifted my chin. "Let Heather go and I'll turn myself over to you. No resistance. No tricks."

The human's eyebrows lifted as Heather said, "What? No."

I forced myself to ignore her, focusing solely on him. "I'm what your government really wants, right? A real, living vampire in the flesh. You won't need to do your shadowy intel gathering if you've got me."

"We took his phone," one of the humans supplied. "He can't call anyone."

"Laith, no." Heather shook her head desperately from the chair. "Don't do this."

"We could just keep you both," the cold one said. "It's not like you have any leverage to make an exchange."

I lunged forward faster than he could perceive, raised my leg, and kicked him squarely in the chest. He went down, dropping the gun exactly as I'd hoped. I kicked it away, then pressed my boot down firmly on his sternum before the others could react.

"Pull those triggers and I'll break all of his ribs before I go down," I hissed as they raised their guns.

Heavy footsteps clambered down the basement as more heavily armed humans filed in. The small concrete room soon became filled with various scents, heartbeats, and guns trained on me. But I had their leader at my mercy, which had to count for something.

The human on the ground groaned as I transferred my weight to the foot on his chest. "Hold your fire," he wheezed.

"How's this for leverage?" I looked between him and the others. "If she's in this basement in another five minutes, at least one of you is dead. Maybe two. You might have me outnumbered, but if you don't let her go, you will not get out of this unscathed. Who wants the 25% chance of leaving here in a body bag?"

A long pause followed. The human under my foot's ragged breathing was the only noise.

"Fine," he rasped at last. "Un-cuff the girl."

One of them rushed forward, pulling a set of keys from his pocket. I didn't raise my foot until Heather's wrists were unbound.

"Laith!" She came to me, hands shaking as they ran up my torso and touched my face, then my shoulder. "Oh God, your eyes are so red. And you got shot!"

"I'm okay." I forced a smile, leaning down toward her. "Bullet grazed me. And I can still see my hot Science Barbie."

Her lips met mine in a kiss that was far too brief when I was jerked roughly away from her. Four humans shoved me down into the chair she had just been in, and I heard the click of another set of cuffs attaching me to the slats in the chair back.

"You need to go," the cold one told Heather.

But she rushed at me, wrapping her arms around my neck and bringing her face to my shoulder. I widened my legs to make room for her, wishing I could return her embrace.

"I'm not leaving you," she whispered. "There's no fucking way."

"Listen to me, Heather." The scent of her hair filled my nose and I brought my face closer to hers. "We're not too far from the state park entrance. Get to Sanguine and alert the clan."

"No, I can't go." Her arms wound tighter around my neck. "I can't leave you here. I can't do it alone."

"Yes, you can. It's our only chance." Sweet-smelling,

honey blonde hair tickled my lips as I spoke directly into her ear. "Don't worry about me, okay? Vampire Ken can handle more than just looking good."

My attempt at humor didn't land as Heather cried softly into my shoulder. The humans around us shifted restlessly. Any second now, they would pull her away from me. As much as I didn't want her to let go, daytime was approaching. The sooner she got back to Sanguine, the safer she would be. And the sooner Blood 'til Dawn would bring righteous justice to these thugs.

"There's a road leading down the mountain," I said. "Follow it all the way down to the intersection. You'll be able to get your bearings and find your way from there. I know you can do it, Science Barbie. Your blood is in me so I know exactly how capable and brilliant you are."

Another sob shook Heather's body, but her grip around my neck started to loosen. She pulled back until her forehead rested on mine. If I had my hands, I would have wiped her tears. But without them, I had to kiss just under her eyes, catching the salty droplets with my lips.

"What if I don't..." She swallowed and tried again. "What if I'm..."

She couldn't get it out but I understood what she was trying to say. *What if I'm too late?* The truth would be that Blood 'til Dawn would avenge me, and she'd have a home with them for as long as she desired. The clan would take care of her in the event of my death, but that wasn't what she needed to hear.

"You won't be, because you're my blood mate and we have centuries more to live, okay?" I kissed her brow, hoping I wasn't betraying my own anxiety. "I'm not going home to Temkra until you and I are over eight-hundred years old and we have a beautiful, fulfilling life behind us. It's as simple as that. We've barely just begun. So I *will* be here, waiting for you until you get back."

"Enough already," grumbled one of Soren's men. "Let's go."

Heather's shaking fingers curled into the fabric of my shirt. "Promise me. Promise me you'll still be here when I get back."

It killed me to make a vow I wasn't sure I could keep. It went against everything Blood 'til Dawn stood for. But the most important thing was getting her the fuck out of this cabin and away from these men.

"I promise." Another tear gathered on her lashes and I kissed the corner of her eye. "And when we're home, I can't wait to go dancing with you again."

My brave, brilliant mate tried to smile, but her lips just wobbled. "I'll hold you to that."

"You don't have to. It's done." I smiled back, taking in all her lovely features for possibly the last time.

"Alright, time's up." One of the men grabbed Heather by the arms and dragged her away. She stumbled a little, but didn't resist as her tear-filled eyes remained locked on me. I forced my chin high, keeping a slight smile on my lips as if I had it all under control.

If I didn't make it out of here, which was a real possibility, my one regret would be not getting the chance to see her dance one more time. The elation on her face, the expression in her movements as if she felt the music in her soul. And, if we had the chance, I'd have the freedom to touch her and move with her. Because unlike the first time, she would be truly mine.

"My clan will know if you harm her," I warned the men as they dragged Heather toward the stairs. "And then you'll be outnumbered. You won't have a prayer's chance of escaping them."

"Blindfold her and then let her out in a random spot in town," said the one who'd been under my boot. "No roughing her up. Just take her and ditch her."

My jaw clenched. No matter where Heather ended up, I was certain she'd get to Sanguine. But time was ticking by. The likelihood of me getting out of this alive looked slimmer and slimmer.

Heather's gaze never left me as she was dragged across the basement and then marched up the stairs. The moment she was out of sight, the human with cold eyes held up one of the silver knives that had been taken from me.

"How well does this work?" he mused, carefully thumbing the blade's edge. "Silver is a pretty soft metal. Doesn't it bend when you stab with it?" A chilling grin pulled at his lips. "Guess there's only one way to find out."

With that he plunged the knife into my thigh, just above my knee.

The pain was unlike anything I'd ever felt. Hundreds of times worse than carving my vow into my skin and all of my motorcycle accidents combined. My entire leg burned with an unrelenting fire. It felt like my skin and muscle was being peeled away with a red-hot poker.

I jerked against the chair, my body flailing for relief. Tears burned my eyes. Everything in me wanted to scream, was desperate for some kind of release from the agony.

But I kept my jaws shut, only hisses and groans escaping my mouth while my teeth formed a shield against any other sounds coming out.

Because if Heather heard me, I knew she wouldn't hesitate to run right back into danger.

# Chapter 32

## *Heather*

The van seemed to drive around randomly for hours. It felt ten times longer than the drive up to the cabin, although that could have been my desperation to get out and make a run for Sanguine.

My only cold comfort was that I was sitting in the passenger seat rather than the back of the van. And the driver was the nicer of Soren's two guys, not the one who had dragged me by my hair and slammed my head against the floor. That guy had stayed on guard while Soren tortured Laith in the basement.

Soren might not have wanted to torture me, but he didn't even see Laith as a person. What kind of horrible things would they do to him down there?

Would they even keep him in that basement? Or take him to some top-secret government lab where he'd be experimented on?

*Don't think about that. You've got to keep it together and get help as soon as you can.*

My blindfold was soaked with tears and I sniffled for the thousandth time on that painfully long drive.

"How much longer 'til you let me go?" I croaked. It was the first thing either of us had said anything since we got in the vehicle.

"You asking me that guarantees I'll be driving around for another half hour," the guy groused.

More tears spilled, soaking through my already-saturated blindfold.

At long last, the van stopped completely and was turned off. I let out a shuddering breath of relief. *Finally.*

The passenger door opened and I allowed the man to help me step down to the ground. He took the blindfold off and visibly winced at the sight of me. I could only imagine how big and colorful the bump on my head was.

Bright lights overwhelmed my vision and I blinked rapidly. We seemed to be at an empty gas station. Fuck, how late was it?

I almost said *thank you* to Soren's guy, but caught myself. Fuck him for being complicit.

Without a word, I started toward the little convenience store attached to the gas station. I had nothing on me, no ID or wallet, but maybe the attendant would be sympathetic enough to call a cab for me. Depending on how far I was from home, maybe they'd even cover the fare.

"Wait," Soren's guy called after me.

I wanted to ignore him and keep going, but forced myself to stop and turn around.

He walked toward me, thumbing through bills in his wallet. "Here." He held three twenties out to me. "Get yourself home and, you know, try to forget this ever happened."

I almost laughed. I was supposed to forget that they held the man I loved captive? If I weren't so numb, I would have told the henchman where to shove it. But my fingers closed around the cash instead, and then he was gone, heading back to the van.

Continuing on to the convenience store, the door made an electronic *ding-dong* sound as I stepped inside.

"Welcome in," mumbled the bored gas station attendant, a Black woman with colorful braids in her hair. She barely took notice of me at first, and then did a double-take with a horrified expression, shooting straight up from her lean against the counter. "Holy shit! Honey, are you okay?"

I winced, both from embarrassment and the bright store lights making my head pound. There didn't seem to be anyone else in the store, thank God.

"Hi, um." I approached the counter, swallowing the lump in my throat. "Can I borrow a phone to call a cab?"

The woman blinked once. "Yeah, of course you can." Her tone was considerably softer as she grabbed her own cell phone. "I'll look up a cab company for you." She began a search, then glanced up, her brow furrowing. "Do you need help, honey?"

I did my best to force a smile. "I'm okay. I'm getting help."

The woman frowned but returned her focus to her phone. She held it out to me a moment later. "That's the closest one. I'll get you some stuff for that bump on your head."

"Thank you." I took the phone, noting the time of 12:37 a.m. and that we were still in Eureka, California. A shaky breath escaped me as I hit the call button for the cab company and brought the phone to my ear.

By the time I ordered the cab, the gas station attendant had brought me an ice pack, Tylenol, and a cold bottle of water. I started crying again, simply overwhelmed with the sheer kindness and concern from a total stranger. How could a woman like this exist in the same world as a guy like Soren?

"I can't thank you enough," I said after gulping down half the water bottle. "The cab'll be thirty minutes, so I'll be out of your hair soon."

"Don't worry about it. You're the most excitement I've had all night." She leaned her forearms on the counter. "And I hope to God whoever did that to your face gets what he deserves."

"He will," I said with a nod. "I...I escaped. I got out. And I'm getting to safety and he will be dealt with." It wasn't the situation she believed it to be, but it wasn't like I could tell her the truth. And anyway, violence was violence. She understood enough.

"Good." She nodded approvingly. "You did the hard part already."

She had no idea. Leaving Laith down there willingly was the hardest thing I'd ever had to do.

"Oh, so how much I do owe you for this stuff?" I waved a hand over the water and Tylenol.

"Nothing. It's on me."

"What? No." I put one of the twenties on the counter. "Will that cover it?"

"Don't worry about it. Use it to start your new life." A smile broke out across her face. "Girls gotta look out for each other, right?"

Even if I never stepped foot in the human world again after we got Laith back, I'd remember this woman for the rest of my life.

When the cab pulled up outside, I thanked her again, shoved the twenty into the empty tip jar on the counter, and hurried out of the store.

"You sure this is where you want me to leave you?" The cab driver's gray, bushy eyebrows furrowed with concern in the rearview mirror. He reminded me of my dad.

The trailhead parking lot had only one tall lamppost that was barely strong enough to illuminate the entire lot. My car was parked directly under it, the hood and roof accumulating dust and pine needles. A few sheets of paper notices had been shoved under the windshield wipers, and it felt like a small miracle that the car hadn't been towed already.

"Yeah, this is great. Thank you." I tried to inject cheer into my voice, although I didn't know why I was trying to pretend everything was fine. The driver had seen the state my face was in, although he didn't comment.

I paid the fare and got out, heading to my car like I was going to drive myself home. *Please don't wait for me to get inside the car. Just drive off.*

Gravel crunched as he backed away and headed for the road. I took a steeling breath as I stared down the darkness of the forest. There would be no light to go on. I didn't have a phone or a flashlight. It would just be me and my memory.

*You're a vampire's blood mate. You've been a night owl your whole goddamn life. You can make it through a stretch of dark woods to save him. One foot in front of the other.*

I might as well had been blindfolded again as I walked through thorny brush and nearly headfirst into trees several times. But a deep part of me held this sense of *knowing* I was on the right track. If I got off-trail, I knew how to course-correct. If—*when* Laith made it out of this, Sanguine would become our home. No, scratch that. It already was my home. It was more of a home to me than that apartment with Justin ever was.

I moved with caution, taking care to avoid injuring myself further, while also going as fast as I could. Soren's guy had wasted at least an hour driving me around aimlessly. Blood 'til Dawn needed to find Laith and get him home before the sun came up.

Tears of relief sprang to my eyes as the first landmarks of Sanguine came into view, namely the blood bank. But I couldn't stop to celebrate. As soon as I hit the paved ground of the city, I started running.

Vampires, brusang, and humans all gave me strange looks, dodging me as I sprinted straight for the Blood 'til Dawn compound. My lungs burned when I finally came upon the building, which looked like an ordinary ware-house from the outside. One of the large garage doors was open, light spilling out and music blasting as a few vampires hung around. A couple seemed to be working on their motorcycles. Others smoked or just stood nearby talking.

I was a good dozen or so yards away when they turned around at the sound of my footsteps. Immediately, everyone reacted. The music cut off. Cigarettes and tools were dropped to the ground as everyone ran toward me. There was something about that show of concern that just sapped the rest of my strength, and I crumpled.

"Heather!" Someone grabbed me before I hit the ground. I saw ruby-red eyes and tattoos covering an Adam's apple and slender throat. "What the fuck happened? Where's Laith?"

"They have him," I gasped with labored lungs. "He gave himself up for me and we need to get him out!"

Thorne's eyes narrowed in confusion. "Who has him?

The same people who did this?" His fingers hovered over the bump on my head.

"Yes! Please, you have go now. We have to get him out! They hurt him with silver!"

"Thorne, what are you doing? Bring her inside!"

"Someone has Laith, but I don't know who she's talking about."

Thorne's face floated away, and I saw Tavia's hovering nearby. Multiple voices overlapped, but I heard hers the strongest and clearest.

"Bring her inside, she's hurt. The rest of you, quit fucking barking! She's in shock. Give her some space."

Someone lifted me off the ground and I felt dizzy from the motion. My head pounded, my lungs burned, and everything in my body hurt. All I could think about was Laith, how much time had already been wasted and there was nothing more important than going out to find him. But every time I opened my mouth, my lungs seized up and I couldn't breathe.

"She's having a panic attack. Everybody out. Just leave me and Bea with her."

The noise dissipated, leaving a ringing in my ears. A light touch pressed against my back and rubbed in a soothing motion. It almost felt like Laith, the weight comforting.

"Breathe, Heather. You're safe with us now. Everything will be okay. Just focus on breathing. That's it. Keep it up."

The room came slowly back into focus, as did the woman sitting cross-legged in front of me. Her aquamarine eyes set in black were a stunning focal point.

"Hey, Heather." Bea tilted her head with a small smile. "Are you with us?"

The hands on my back lifted away, and I turned to see Tavia sitting behind me. "How you doing? You okay?"

"I don't, I...Laith—!"

"We'll get to him. I'm asking about *you* right now." Tavia's tone was equal parts stern and loving. "Are you composed enough to tell the guys what happened? Or do you need more time?"

Fuck more time. Laith didn't have that luxury.

"I can tell them." I let out another long breath and nodded. "I'm good. I can keep it together."

"Are you sure?"

"Yes." My voice finally steadied and I said it again. "Yes. Please. Every minute counts."

Bea brought me a glass of water and the two women left to gather the vampire muscle. The men filed into the room with serious expressions, spreading out while maintaining a good amount of distance from me. Tavia had probably told them not to get in my face.

Thorne was the last to come in, but to his credit, he didn't beat around the bush. "What happened, Heather?"

I told them everything, taking sips of water when my breath came too short. Some of the vampires' expressions became drawn when I mentioned the shadowy government operation that was gathering information on vampires.

"Do we know of anything like that?" Rhain asked the question, looking at Thorne.

"Not specifically, but there's been speculation for decades." The clan leader didn't seem particularly concerned. "What time is it?"

"Just after two a.m.," said Des.

"So we've got three hours at the most to get Laith out and back home before dawn comes. To be safe, let's call it two and half." Thorne looked at me. "Heather, is there any way you could locate where they're keeping him? Even a rough estimate?"

"I really don't know." I scrubbed a hand over my face, feeling both exhausted and wired. "It's within driving distance. Probably within an hour of Eureka. But there's so much wilderness. So many hidden mountain roads and so many cabins. I wouldn't know where to begin."

"We'll have to start somewhere. And you have to come with us. If he's in bad shape, he'll need your blood immediately." Thorne scratched his neck. "Worst case, we'll have to call off the search during daylight hours and go out again at dusk tomorrow night."

"Why can't you take that stuff that lets you go out in the daylight?" I said. "Draitrium, is it called?"

All the air seemed to get sucked out of the room. Every single vampire looked to be holding their breath.

"I know you guys don't like it, but this is Laith we're talking about. He's one of you. You're all family, right? If it gives you a few extra hours to look for him, isn't it worth the risk?"

Cyan stepped forward. "I know you mean well, Heather. But the only reason you'd suggest that is because you don't know any better." He glanced at Thorne before speaking again. "Draitrium is a non-negotiable for us. The attack on you by that addict was terrible, and it still only scratches the surface of what that drug has done to our kind. Laith knows that. We all owe centuries of pain and trauma to draitrium. Laith and I were orphaned juveniles together, and I promise you he'd rather die than see any one of us use it, even to save him." Cyan pinned me with an intense look. "Do you understand what I'm saying?"

"Yes. I...I think so." Shame heated my face. "I'm sorry I suggested it. I—"

"You're new to us. You didn't know any better," Thorne cut in sharply. "And you definitely won't suggest such a thing again."

"No. No, of course not."

"Good." Thorne paused, his cheeks hollowing as he took a drag on his cigarette. "I guess the best place to start is the gas station where you were dropped off."

"Heather, can you feel Laith right now?" Cyan asked.

"I don't...what do you mean?"

"You're his blood mate. His blood is in you. Every time he feeds, he also leaves a little of himself in you. The blood mate connection is like an invisible thread connecting the two of you." Cyan's eyes shifted to the side. "Right now, I know that Tavia is nearby, most likely in our suite. She's with someone, probably Bea. She's trying to stay upbeat, but she's worried. Probably about Laith and you. She's holding something warm, most likely a coffee mug." His gaze returned to me. "Our connection has gotten stronger since our ceremony, but it was still there in the beginning. You just have to focus on it."

Des's eyebrows went up as if something dawned on him. "That's probably how Laith found you at the cabin. If he did it, it has to work the other way, right?"

"I mean, wouldn't you guys know better than me?" I looked around nervously at the surrounding vampires.

"It should." Cyan's gaze remained fixed on me. "Focus on Laith, Heather. Imagine where he is. Try to feel what he's feeling at this exact moment."

"She can do it on the road." Thorne exhaled a plume of red smoke. "We need to get going if we have half a chance of finding him. Heather and Rhain will go in the van. Cyan, Des, and I will go on bikes. We'll start at the gas station, then see if Heather can trace Laith from there."

The vampires moved swiftly into action, filing out toward the garage for their vehicles. Des stopped in front of me and held out his hand.

"Come on, girl. Let's get your mate back."

I nodded and accepted his help up from my seat, but struggled to find the bravery and confidence he and the other vampires had.

It felt like we were going in completely blind. How exactly was I supposed to lead them to Laith? What did sensing him through our bond even mean or feel like?

All I knew was I had to figure it out, and fast.

Numbness. Pain. Exhaustion. My perception of the world reduced to those three sensations.

It felt like an eternity. How wasn't I eight-hundred years old already? Why was I still alive?

"Why do vampires carry silver weapons?" Soren, the human with the cold, dead eyes, sat in front of me, examining my silver knife covered in my own blood.

"We're pretty fond of irony." I had refused to scream throughout any of the torture sessions so far, so my voice still worked. My tongue was sore and swollen though from how often I'd had to bite it.

Every injury on my body, even the surface wounds, were healing slower than normal. The silver must have contaminated my bloodstream.

"You kill lots of other vampires?" Soren tapped his index finger on the tip of my knife. "We keep hearing stories about warring clans."

"Whoever's giving you information sucks at it."

"Oh really?"

"Here's something I'd like to know." I licked my cracked lips. "How come I never heard your men's heartbeats?"

Soren grinned coldly. "My men are extremely well-trained. Navy SEAL and Green Beret training are child's play compared to what these men go through. By the time they're done, no amount of stress will trigger a central nervous system response. Doesn't matter if they're fucking, fighting, fleeing. Nothing will make their heart rate rise above resting."

"How do you do that? Torture all of the emotion out of them?" My voice was heavy with sarcasm.

Soren gave a shrug and a nod at the same time. "Works best when they don't have much empathy or emotion to begin with."

How was it not surprising at all that a shadowy government operation recruited psychopaths?

"Here's a question for you." Soren held my blade up toward the light in the ceiling, turning it to make the metal and blood shine. "What's a blood mate?"

I tried not to show surprise at the question, but exhaustion and silver overriding my system delayed my reactions. And Soren was sharp enough to see right through it.

"That's what Heather said she was to you. At least, you believed she was."

I said nothing, keeping my face stoic. He was trying to provoke a reaction out of me by saying her name. Well, fuck him if he thought he'd get it.

"Something about her blood being nutritionally perfect for you, specifically? You got hooked on her and nothing else could compare." Soren leaned back in his chair. "Like a dog after a bone."

I ignored him, focusing on the itch of my skin repairing itself on my face. Three of his men had had a go of using my head as a punching bag for a while. Thankfully no silver was involved there. Just some fuzzy vision, a bit of blood, and a ringing in my ears.

"You wanted her for yourself, and I can't say I blame you." Soren brought his hands together. "And I hate to be the one to tell you this, but she was disgusted at the idea of fucking you."

My gaze returned to him, again unable to hide my surprise. "What?"

His eyes lit up, delighted that he'd baited me, even as his face grimaced. "Yeah. Sorry, man. But she doesn't see you as a person. You're not even the same species as us. She said vampires are closer to animals than human. That's why she worked willingly with us to gather intel from the beginning, and got paid well for it."

Soren put on his best imitation of sympathy. "There's no future with her. I'm sorry. But if you cooperate with us, we'll help you, Laith. Our government takes care of those who sacrifice for this country. Just answer our questions, let us take samples so that our scientists can study you, and you'll be in good hands."

At first, I snorted. The sound morphed into a snicker under my breath that gradually grew louder. And then, because I was too exhausted and weak to school my reaction, I started full-on laughing my Temkra-damned ass off.

Once I started, I just couldn't stop. My brain was probably desperate for some happy chemical shit, because I laughed as if Heather had declared a tickling war on my armpits.

It honestly started to hurt after a while because I couldn't catch a full breath. And when I finally did, the whole process started all over again.

Because Soren just sat there, growing more and more

pissed off. He tried a few times to ask what was funny or make some snide remark but my laughter drowned him out. Everything was morbidly hilarious. The fact that he tried to act like he knew Heather better than me. Tried to act like the sincere and sympathetic Good Cop after sticking my own knife in my leg. The fact that he'd thought I'd believe him. And the look on his face right fucking then, the realization that he hadn't reeled me in at all, and that I was getting under his paper-thin skin, was just the cherry on top.

"Wow. You think you're really good at mimicking human behavior, but damn." My laughing fit subsided and I finally managed to catch a breath. "I bet women can sense how vile you are from a mile away. Is that why you have to stalk and harass them for a shred of attention?"

A vein pulsed in Soren's forehead while his heartbeat hammered in my ears. Oh, *now* he was emotional. The anger and embarrassment came off him in waves. And now that I'd gotten a reaction out of him, I just couldn't help myself.

"You couldn't even get into Sanguine yourself. You had to threaten a woman to collect intel for you," I went on. "Is your tech not sensitive enough to pick up our border magic? Or are you just too much of a coward to be surrounded by *scawy vampiwes?*"

I purposely made my words childlike at the end of my question. Meanwhile, Soren got to his feet, bringing the knife to my neck with surprising speed for a human.

"Careful," I said. "You need me to talk right? Even if you kill me and dissect my body, my corpse will only tell you so much."

He pressed the tip of the knife into my skin and I inhaled sharply, bracing against the flinch of burning silver.

"If I let you live to talk, you have to actually answer questions," he hissed. "Can you do that?"

"Depends on how and what you ask, tough guy."

Soren's jaw clenched. I had pissed him off. Embarrassed him. Crushed his fragile little ego. And it was eerily clear how much he wanted to kill me. That was the only desire I saw in those dead eyes.

But something was holding him back. Maybe he had strict orders from whoever was above him, or the psychopath possibly had a tiny shred of a conscience after all.

He pulled the knife away and returned to his chair, dropping heavily into it.

"How long do vampires live?"

I shifted my weight in the chair. "No one knows exactly." It wasn't a total lie. "But much longer than you. I'll still look the same as I do now when you reach the end of your life."

"Give me an average. Your best estimate," Soren groused.

"No idea. I'm not a math guy."

"Is a year in Sanguine the same as a year in our world?"

"How should I know? I've never compared the two."

Soren looked like he wanted to slap his forehead and drag the knife across my throat in equal measure.

"I know you're not stupid, vampire. You know the information I want."

"Never was the smart one." I inched up my aching shoulders in a shrug. "I'm the funny one, as you probably figured out by now."

"What you're going to be is a lab rat," he hissed. "Kept in a cage. Poked and prodded and experimented on for the rest of your miserable, long life. You'll see generations of scientists come and go, advancing the human species with the secrets of your kind."

"I'm flattered you think so highly of me."

Soren jumped to his feet again and plunged the knife into my other thigh which, until then, had been left uninjured. I bit back my scream but couldn't stop the agony from showing on my face.

"How about I make it so that you can't walk?" Soren twisted the knife and the silver cutting roughly though my flesh and muscle burned with a sharp pain that left me breathless.

"You don't need your legs. Hell, you don't need any limbs to be a vampire guinea pig." He jerked the knife out and plunged it into my shoulder.

When he twisted it there, I couldn't stop from letting a scream escape. My whole body shook like I'd been electrocuted, overwhelmed with inescapable, blinding pain. The silver burned, but my skin felt ice cold. Blood filled my mouth. I knew I must have broken a few teeth. My system just couldn't handle the onslaught of silver poisoning me with every touch.

"You're actually pathetic." Soren gave the knife one more twist before pulling it out, which gave me no relief. "You think Heather will want you without any arms or legs? She'll be even more horrified by the freak you are."

His words were noise, just a distant buzzing while I fought to stay conscious. My blood clotted quickly, but the stab wounds were deep. And with my healing abilities diminishing, I could very well bleed out. At that point, I was starting to prefer it. The drip-drip-drip sound of my blood hitting the concrete floor was becoming quite the lulling melody.

*I should stay awake. I remember telling myself that. But...why? It hurts so much.*

I had done my part already. Heather was gone and hopefully safe with the clan. They would find out what happened and make quick work of Soren and his crew, if not his whole fucking organization.

Soren had a short fuse. I could probably provoke him into accidentally killing me. There was no telling how much time had passed, but I couldn't hold out much longer.

"Okay..." My voice was hoarse with exhaustion as I turned my head and spat out a mouthful of blood. "I'll tell you...I gotta tell you something."

I could barely see, but there was no missing his evil smile. "That's what I like to hear. What would you like to say, vampire?"

"You got a recording device on, right?"

"Yes."

I shook my head, coughing. "Come here. I gotta whisper. This is top secret. Only for you to know."

He lifted an eyebrow, skeptical.

"Your government will want to hear this," I said. "But they're not ready. You gotta hold onto this until the time is right, Soren."

His fucking ego couldn't resist. He leaned in, hovering just above me with the knife in front of us as a warning. "Well?"

"Closer. I need to make sure the recorder won't pick it up."

"You try anything, vampire, and I will rip your fangs out with a pair of pliers."

My flinch at that was not an act. I remembered Kalix's fangs, how they had been filed down flat. If I somehow lived past this moment, I couldn't comprehend the shame and lack of dignity at being defanged.

*Kal endured it. So could you.*

"Got it," I said. "No funny shit, I swear. I just need to speak right into your ear."

After another moment's hesitation, Soren leaned down until the side of his head was right next to mine. He flinched when I turned in his direction, but he stayed put. Waiting.

"I just realized, Soren, buddy, that we're not so different after all," I whispered.

He snorted with disdain. "How do you figure?"

"We both got a thing for Heather. That's why you chose her, right? I might have stalked her a little too. Witnessed some private things. But here's the difference between you and me."

I paused for a breath and he remained still, waiting.

"She chose me because I have more humanity than you ever will." My lips brushed his ear as I said at full volume, "I'm not the one who's pathetic and monstrous."

He snapped straight up, and I had just enough vision to see the outrage on his face. The knife came down again and I was ready. But it wasn't a killing blow. He plunged it into my opposite shoulder, starting the whole cycle of burning ice and blinding pain again.

This time he left it in there while he stomped to the basement stairs. The last thing I heard before passing out was him calling out to the others.

"Come down here and hold his jaws open. I'm about to put some vampire teeth on a necklace."

# Chapter 34

## *Heather*

"Anything?"

I shook my head, fighting tears of frustration. The Blood 'til Dawn vampires and I were sitting in a vacant lot across from the gas station where the kind attendee had let me use her phone. I had insisted on them not making themselves visible to her, considering she'd recognize me and would be alarmed that I was surrounded by a bunch of scary-looking guys.

"I don't know what to feel. How am I supposed to sense him?" I looked at Cyan as if I hadn't asked the question a dozen times already.

"You just do. I'm not sure how else to explain it." He rubbed a hand over his buzz cut. "Like when you know he's in bed next to you without seeing him. You can feel how near he is, right?"

"I mean yes, but there's way more physical and contextual clues to that." I rubbed my leg, nursing an odd ache above my knee that seemed to come from nowhere.

"Can you try turning off the science part of your brain?" Des suggested. "I know it's hard not to rely on logic and what you know to be true, but there is magic to the blood bond. Turn off all your filters and try to tap into the magic."

"There's no fucking magic out in this world." Rhain rubbed his massive arms as though he were chilly. "The air here feels...wrong. Can you feel the difference, Heather? Between here and Sanguine? What if you focused on that?"

It was a good idea. Despite his rough, intimidating appearance, Rhain's suggestion was spoken gently. He hadn't said a word on the drive out here and I convinced myself he was pissed off at me and everything else in the world. But maybe I was wrong.

"It does feel different. I don't know how though. The air in Sanguine does feel...not humid exactly, but heavier somehow."

"That's the magic." Des wiggled his fingers.

"What time is it?" Thorne grunted.

Cyan checked his phone. "3:17 a.m."

"Under two hours." Thorne leveled a heavy gaze on me. "We need something, Heather."

"I know. Fuck! Trust me, I know. I want him back more than anything. I just don't know how."

"Putting pressure on her won't help," Des said. "We're all worried, but she's his blood mate. She's already frantic enough."

"We can just start driving," Rhain suggested. "Split up, take a few different mountain roads and see what we find. Maybe she'll start sensing him if we're closer."

"Great. Sounds like our only option anyway." Thorne turned abruptly and headed for his motorcycle. Cyan and Des did the same, while Rhain and I climbed into the van.

"Fuck." I brought my knees up and rested my forehead on them. "I wish I knew what I was doing wrong."

Rhain's seatbelt clicked into place next to me, then he

turned the engine on. "It's not your fault. You don't know what you don't know."

I turned my head on my knees to look at him. His gaze was on his phone, scrolling through part of a map.

"Do you have a blood mate or...anyone special?" Now that he was talking, it made me realize how little I knew about him. He was definitely the most closed-off one of the group.

"No, I don't." Rhain didn't pause in his scrolling.

"Any reason why?"

"Don't want one." He set the phone in the holder on the dashboard, then started to pull out of the parking space.

Before I could distract myself with more personal questions about him, a shooting pain zipped up my left leg. I clutched it with a small cry of pain, thoroughly confused and alarmed. It was not the same leg where my knee had been hurting.

"Heather, are you okay?"

"I don't know," I gasped. "I don't...fuck...I don't know what this is."

"Muscle cramp?"

I shook my head, squeezing my eyes shut against the pain. It felt worse than a cramp. I'd had plenty of those during my dancing days. It felt like I was being stabbed right in the thigh muscle by a red-hot knife.

"Hey. I'm gonna reach over you and recline the seat, okay?"

"God, what the fuck!" I clutched my leg, trying to sit still as Rhain awkwardly reached over my lap for the lever on the far side of the seat. "Feels like my leg's on fire."

"I'm sorry. I don't know how to help you." Rhain looked truly stricken when my eyes peeked open. His phone was at his ear, his gaze averting when the call picked up. "Hey

Thorne, something's wrong with Heather. She's in a lot of pain all of a sudden. I don't know. Nothing happened."

I started to hyperventilate, my breaths coming in short and ragged while my mind repeated, *What the fuck? What's happening to me?*

"I don't know, but there's no way we're driving up a mountain like this," Rhain said. "She probably needs a hospital, a human one."

"Ah!" Pain exploded in my left shoulder and I clutched it on a choked gasp. It felt like the flesh should be torn and ragged, blood seeping through my fingers, but there was nothing.

"She's having a heart attack or something, I dunno! But I'm dropping her off at the nearest emergency room because..."

My vision and hearing faded in and out. I felt underwater—cold and disassociating but also burning hot and painfully present. The pain was so intense I thought I was going to die.

Just for a second, Rhain and the van melted away and my surroundings changed. It was quick as a flash, but I thought I saw...Soren?

Soren holding a bloody knife and a murderous look on his face.

The pain was so intense but so was my determination to fuck with Soren, to make this psychopathic piece of shit feel as small as possible. He had no fucking sense of humor, so it was honestly pretty easy. At least Heather was far away. That was all I could truly ask for.

Just as quickly as it came on, the pain, Soren, and the basement subsided, and the van came back into view.

But they weren't completely gone.

I felt like I could reach out and touch them. Not with

any physical sense, but with a type of knowing. Like that place and those feelings were on the end of a thread I could tug.

*Laith!* The realization was as liberating as it was heartbreaking. I was feeling Laith. Feeling his emotions and his pain as Soren tortured him.

"Hang on, Heather."

The van started to move again. My hand shot out and landed on Rhain's arm. "Wait."

His heavy foot hit the brake and the van lurched to a stop. "You okay?"

I was absolutely not, now that I knew what Laith was going through. But I needed to go straight there.

"I know how to find him." My voice somehow came out stronger than I felt. "Get out of this lot and go straight through that traffic light."

A smile touched Rhain's lips as he cranked the steering wheel. "Fuck yeah. Now we're in business." He nodded at the cell phone. "Call Thorne and tell him to follow us, yeah?"

I made the call and then sat back, trying to keep my worry in check. We had to make it in time to save him. We just had to.

———

THE VAN'S dashboard clock read 4:21 a.m. when Rhain pulled the van over to the side of the road several houses down from the cabin. Dawn would come just after 5 a.m, and I was a ball of nerves in the passenger seat.

I couldn't see where they kept Laith from here, but knew it was just over the crest of the hill in front of us. My stomach remembered the climbing sensation from when Soren's men brought me, and the descent when I left.

Laith's presence felt close, but weak. I hadn't felt any emotions or even pain sensations from him for at least fifteen minutes. He wasn't dead, though. He couldn't be. I would know, wouldn't I?

"We'll have to leave cleanup for another night," Thorne was saying through Rhain's phone speakers. "And hope human cops don't find any remains in the meantime. Get in, kill them all, grab Laith, and get the fuck out."

"I'm ready." Rhain was strapped with weapons, mostly knives. "Where do you want Heather to be?"

"She stays in the van."

"I'll need to give him blood right away, right?" I piped up. "What's the best way to do that?" I would be useless in a fight, but my blood was literally key to Laith's survival, and I intended to be ready.

There was a pause on the phone as Thorne considered. "Hang out in the back. That'll probably be the safest place to put him."

"Got it. You guys be careful," I said. "I'll be here."

"Keep the van parked and the doors locked," Thorne added. "I don't expect any humans to escape but in case one does, I don't want them getting to you or sabotaging our vehicle."

"Got it."

"Let's go, Rhain."

Rhain ended the call and placed the van keys in the other cupholder. "Unlock only when you see me."

I nodded. "Please bring him back to me."

"I will."

Rhain pulled a small knife from some hidden sheath and pointed it toward a spot on his forearm. Faster than I could blink, he cut two small symbols just below his elbow. His skin reddened and swelled angrily around the shallow cuts.

"In our language, these letters translate to the phonetic L and H sounds," he said, sheathing the knife. "This is my vow, Heather. To ensure you and Laith are together again."

My throat closed up with emotion as I remembered Laith telling me how solemnly his clan took their vows.

"Thank you."

Rhain nodded curtly before slipping out of the van and jogging into the darkness.

Eerie silence settled in as I drew my knees up, hugging around them. The only illumination came from a few dim porch lights in the spaced out cabins. I couldn't see Rhain or any of the other vampires. It was like they'd melted into the shadows.

My hand rested over my chest, the edge of my palm pressing against the tender bite marks I'd asked Laith to not heal. I tried to listen, to feel him through our connection that went far beyond a chemical bond. I didn't know when I'd accepted our connection as something more than physical chemistry, as something magical, even fated, but after he showed me what real love could be like, I'd believe in anything that would get him back.

That connection now felt like a tender thread unraveling while I desperately grasped to keep it in tact. Every eternally long minute I waited in silence put more stress on that thread and brought it closer to severing.

"Laith, I'm here. We're all here." I didn't know if speaking aloud would help, but I would do anything at this point. "Please hold on. We're right here. Just hold on until I can give you my blood."

Only silence and stillness answered me. I was starting to

feel an intensely dangerous urge to jump out of the van and run up to the cabin to see for myself what was happening. But no, that could put the other guys in danger as well. They didn't need an extra liability to deal with.

"Temkra, if you're listening…" I hesitated, swallowing. Faith in a deity had never been my thing. My parents weren't religious and raised me to always be curious and skeptical.

"Cite your sources, young lady," my dad, a history professor, would always say jokingly whenever I made dramatic claims as a kid such as, *you never let me have any fun!* Their influence on seeking knowledge and proof made me the woman I became.

But Laith believed in Temkra. All of the vampires seemed to believe in their deity quite literally. For all I knew, the vampire goddess didn't acknowledge humans at all. But I was Laith's blood mate, which had to mean something.

At this point, I was desperate enough to beg any and all entities beyond my scope of reality to protect him.

"Temkra, if you can hear me," I tried again, "you must know how I feel about him. You must know…how much I love him." The ache in my chest shook my breath. "He is… so pure. He has brought so much joy and light to my life in ways I can't even express. I don't know many vampires very well, but I know he is one of the best. I love him so much, but I'm not asking you to save him for me. I'm just some human asking you to save him because…he's Laith." Tears made hot trails down my cheeks, but I didn't dare loosen my grip on my knees. I was afraid I'd completely unravel if I let go. "He deserves the world just because of who he is. If you have any hand in what happens to him, please…please let him survive."

When I ran out of ways to plead with a deity, I took a shaky breath and lifted my forehead from my knees.

Through the windshield, under a quickly lightening sky, I saw movement in the shadows coming toward the van.

"Unlock!" Rhain hollered, carrying something large over his shoulder as he ran to me.

My fingers shook so hard, it took forever to hit the button on the keyfob. I then climbed between the two front seats, scrambling through the gutted out van to the rear doors.

While still shaking, I managed to unlatch the doors and push them open. A sob escaped my throat as Rhain gently placed a limp and bloodied Laith into my lap.

"Oh my God!" My hands hovered over his face out of fear of hurting him worse. He was barely recognizable with eyes swollen shut, mouth and head bloodied, and so much bruising.

"Cut your wrist on one of his fangs. I need to start driving."

He helped me bring Laith further into the van, then shut the rear doors. Gingerly, I used a fingertip to push up Laith's upper lip, but didn't see a fang. The van was so dark and Laith's mouth so swollen, I couldn't see much of anything.

I ran the same finger over his teeth, trying to find one that was especially pointy, and froze when I found a gap instead. My trembling finger kept going over his front teeth and found another gap on the other side of his mouth.

Rhain opened the driver side door then and buckled himself into the seat. "Is he drinking?"

"No..." The word left me in a whisper of disbelief.

The seat creaked as Rhain turned around. "Is he alive?"

"I don't know...They took his fangs."

"What?"

"They...they pulled them out. He doesn't have them."

Rhain leaned over for a closer look. I was in such shock that I still had Laith's lip pushed up.

"Fucking barbaric," Rhain growled. "We killed them too quickly." With a quick look at me, he pulled out a small knife. "We still need to get your blood in him. Do you want to do it or should I?"

I held my arm out to him. "You do it, please."

Rhain swiped the blade across the blood vessels in my wrist with one quick draw. "There's a first aid kit back there with gauze." He returned to facing forward in the seat. "I'll try not to jostle you too much, but I need to drive fast. Dawn is right on our ass."

"Go as fast as you need to." I cradled Laith's head with one hand while holding my bloodied wrist to his lips. "He's not out of the woods yet."

My blood filled Laith's mouth, but his lips didn't seal around the wound and he didn't swallow.

"Come on." I tipped his head forward in my lap and rubbed at his throat. "Come on, Laith."

A trail of blood dribbled over the corner of his lips and down the side of his face.

"Please, Laith. Please!" My forehead bent down to his. "Please take from me. Please..."

Holding his head steady with one hand and feeding him with the other meant that I couldn't check for a pulse. I brought my ear to his nose and tried to feel any whisper of breath possible. If he was breathing, it was too faint to detect.

"Rhain! Do you know CPR?"

A frustrated grunt came from the driver's seat. "I can't

afford to stop. Keep trying to feed him. Your blood is the best chance he has."

All my blood seemed to be doing was making a mess around the lower half of Laith's face. But I wouldn't give up until Temkra herself told me he was gone.

With a serious amount of effort, I pulled his jaws as far apart as they would safely go. After a quick swipe of my finger down his throat to make sure his airway was clear, I wedged my bleeding wrist between both rows of his teeth.

Rhain's lead foot on the gas pedal and the awkward position of my wrist in Laith's mouth didn't make it easy to move him, but I managed to bring his head up with his chin slightly tucked for an easier swallowing position.

And while I kept stroking his throat, kept pleading with him to give me a sign of life, I prayed to a goddess I wasn't sure could hear me.

# Chapter 35

*Laith*

My entire body felt made out of stone. It took a tremendous amount of effort to crack my eyelids open, and even more to lift my hand to rub them. I groaned with the movement, and my throat rasped like sandpaper.

"Laith?"

My head had felt sluggish, booting up slowly like a computer from the 90s, until I heard her voice. Then everything came online all at once. A familiar bed, along with the scent, voice, and heartbeat I loved most in the world.

"Heather?"

I turned toward her voice and didn't have to reach far. Her hands were already around my neck, soft lips fusing to my dry ones in a hard, hungry kiss. Her whole body pressed to mine, finding contact at every possible point. The feel of her brought life, lightness, and warmth to my stiff limbs.

My hands found her back, her waist, and pulled her into me as if we could meld into one being. There were no words and not enough kisses or intimate touches to express how fucking relieved I was that she was safe and alive.

Her lips broke away abruptly and I chased her mouth for more contact, more of her perfect, beautiful taste.

"How do you feel? Do you need blood?" She pushed her hair aside and lifted her face, extending the most gorgeous neck I'd ever had the privilege of drinking from.

I leaned in, already aching for the comfort of her flavor on my tongue. Her blood would be another reassurance that she was still here, still mine.

But something was wrong. My front teeth touched down on her skin, but my fangs didn't fully descend and pierce through.

"What..." I was still drowsy, my mouth dry enough to stick my tongue to the roof. But I was awake enough to know that the inside of my mouth just felt weird.

"Let me see."

Heather held my face and gently lifted my upper lip. She smiled, looking pleased at what she saw. A hell of a contrast to the memory that hit me right then—the sight of one my fangs held in a pair of metal pliers. Running my tongue over a bloody, sore gap between my teeth.

The pounding ache in my gums, my whole head. The shock settling in as Soren's face came into focus, triumphant and smug as he held up those pliers. And the burning humiliation of it all.

"It's okay, love." Heather kissed me, drawing me back to the present. "They're growing back. It's going to take some time, but I can see your new ones coming in." She edged a fingertip into my mouth and pressed it to a hard, dull point coming out of my gum.

"How?" My voice was hoarse as I felt them for myself. "These are my adult fangs. They're not supposed to grow back."

She smiled and drew her hands back to wiggle her

fingers in the air. "Magic. The others are theorizing it's because we're blood mates. My blood is helping you regenerate damage that wouldn't have been repaired otherwise."

It was only then that I noticed small cuts on the sides of her neck. I grabbed her hands and turned her wrists over. Band-aids covered the delicate blood vessels just below her palms. An overwhelming swell of emotion created a knot in my throat, and the loss of fangs became utterly insignificant.

"You've been hurting yourself to feed me?"

Heather's face hardened. "It's nothing compared to what you did for me. We almost lost you, Laith." Her eyes shone with unspent tears. "I would bleed myself empty if it meant keeping you alive."

I peeled back the band-aid, brought her raw wrist to my mouth, and kissed it before sliding my tongue over the wound to heal it. I repeated the motion on her other wrist, then leaned forward to kiss the tears falling down her cheeks.

"I love you, Science Barbie." My forehead leaned on hers. "And I would face that basement again in a heartbeat to keep you safe."

Heather shook her head. "You didn't expect to make it out of there, did you?"

"It seemed like a long shot," I admitted. "All that mattered to me was that you got away."

She lifted her head, bringing her hands to the sides of my neck. "How about neither of us get involved in dangerous, crazy shit like that again?"

"That sounds like a fine idea to me."

A full-on grin spread across her beautiful face. "I love you too, Vampire Ken."

"Temkra above, I love you so much."

I pressed up to sit against the headboard and drew her

into me. She followed eagerly, sliding her legs over my lap to straddle me. While our kiss moments ago was one out of desperation and relief, this one was unhurried. Slow and melting.

I wanted to show her how grateful I was to be alive by savoring her for hours. But she pulled away, reaching for the small knife on the nightstand.

"No, don't." I pulled the blade from her grip and kissed her again to stop any argument. "You're not using that anymore."

Heather scoffed. "Like hell I'm not. I just want to help you get better."

My arm settled around the small of her back, keeping the knife out of her reach. "How long was I out?"

"Almost a week." A sigh left her mouth. "They think all the silver in your system put you in a coma. Your organs were in danger of shutting down."

I thumbed the tip of the knife. It wasn't silver. Just run-of-the-mill stainless steel. "And how often did you cut your-self with this to feed me during that time?"

"At least once a day." Her chin lifted. Her eyes were defiant but calm. "And I'll keep using it until your fangs grow back."

"No, you won't."

"Laith."

"Heather." My free hand slid up her back to grip the hair at the base of her skull. "The blood bank has better tools. Proxy fangs are used by elderly vampires sometimes if they can't get a proper bite. They're more sanitary and will better replicate the punctures for drinking."

Heather snorted. "You could have just said that." Her fingers dragged deliciously over the back of my head. "Fine. We'll get you some grandpa fangs, then."

"Don't you start with that." I tickled her ribs, loving her surprised shriek of laughter.

"Stop! I'm telling Des," she wheezed, squirming to get away.

"Ugh. You don't love me at all." I held her in place and leaned in to suck at the base of her throat.

Heather's laughter turned to soft moans. Her squirms slowed to a gentle rocking in my lap as I laved on her neck and collarbones. Her skin was the warm, yielding softness I fell in love with at the first taste through that screen. The fluttering pulse beneath the surface thrummed like a kiss against my lips. That beautiful, precious life force that saved and sustained both of us.

When my mouth reached the edge of her shirt, I realized the actual depth of my hunger.

"Take this off." I tugged at the hem of her shirt while my other hand tightened around the knife's handle.

We'd get to the blood bank soon enough, but I couldn't wait for proxy fangs right then. Not while I needed to worship every inch of her skin more than I needed to breathe.

Heather had just lifted the shirt to her bra when a knock came to the door and someone started to push it open.

"Fuck!" I yanked Heather's shirt back into place just as Thorne poked his head in.

"Hey, you are awake. I thought I heard your voice." He stiffened the moment he noticed our position. "Sorry. Didn't mean to interrupt."

"It's okay." Heather, my love, my betrayer, slid out of my lap. "I should have come to get you the moment he woke up."

"No, no. You two deserve alone time while Laith recovers." Thorne's lips lifted in a rare smile. "It's good to have you back."

"Thanks." I arranged the bedcovers to hide my erection. "So, clean-up at the scene went well, I imagine?"

Thorne rubbed his jaw. "Yes and no. We were in a rush to get you out because it was so close to dawn. So we had to do clean-up the following night and..." His eyes flicked briefly to Heather. "One of the bodies was missing."

"What?" Heather and I said in unison. "You're sure?" I added.

He nodded, regret souring his face. "It was obvious. There were drag marks and a blood trail that we definitely didn't leave behind."

"Who was missing?" I could hear the apprehension in Heather's voice.

"The one who was working Laith over in the basement. Seemed like he was the one leading things."

"Soren?" Heather's apprehension turned to outright disbelief. "Only Soren was missing? You're sure he was dead? What if he was injured but escaped?"

"He was dead before he hit the ground," Thorne said. "I saw the light leave his eyes myself. There's no possible way he left that scene by himself."

"Fuck." Heather drew her knees up, distress and confusion on her face.

I scooted until I was pressed to her side and draped my arm over her back. "Maybe the government picked up his body when he didn't check in. An operative is essentially government property right?"

She didn't look convinced. "I guess. But then why not recover all the bodies? Why not have the whole cabin taped off and guarded for an investigation?"

Thorne approached until he reached the foot of the

bed. "I don't want you to worry about it, Heather. It could have been some other person who took him, or he could have been dragged away by wild animals for all we know. Whatever the case, he's not stalking you anymore." Thorne's lip curled into a snarl. "And he sure as fuck is not harming another vampire again."

"Did you get their electronics?" I asked.

"Oh yeah." Thorne's fingers rubbed together like he was itching for a cigarette. "It'll take a while to crack through all the encrypted shit but we'll find out what they know about us sooner or later."

"And Kalix?" I sat up higher. "Where are we on that?"

"Making progress, which we'll catch you up on when you're fully recovered." Thorne settled for shoving his hands in the pockets of his leather jacket. "Get some rest. Plan your mating ceremony. Whatever you lovesick fools do."

"Fucking a lot," I informed him.

He rolled his eyes. "I figured."

"Just wanted to make sure you knew."

"I think I liked you better in a coma."

"Nah. Come on, Dad." I grinned. "Admit it. You're happy I'm back."

"And then you open your mouth and ruin it." Thorne smirked. "Enjoy the time off. We'll need all hands on deck once we're ready to extract Kalix."

"Anything I can do to help, let me know," Heather piped up.

"Thank you." Thorne gave her a grateful look before turning toward the door. "I'll leave you two to rest—"

"And fuck."

With an aggravated groan, he left the bedroom and closed the door behind him.

Tension drained out of my body as I turned to Heather, the brilliant, gorgeous human who had taught me how precious life really was.

Clothes came off and limbs tangled in an unhurried, intimate dance. Feeling her bare skin in the low light reminded me of that night on the dance floor. Little did I know those slow, tentative touches and the unspoken language of our bodies would lead us to right here.

"As soon as I'm well enough to leave this bed," I mumbled into the hollow of her throat, "I'm taking you dancing."

"Oh really?" Her fingers dragged down my back, digging into stiff, aching muscles. "As soon as? No waiting around at all?"

"Hmm." I kissed lower until I found the near fully-healed puncture marks on her left breast. "Maybe I should wait until I'm certain that I can stand and carry you." I drew her leg over my hip, then rolled until she was on her back. "In a multitude of positions."

Heather's grin lit up her whole face. "You know I'm a fan of the scientific method."

"I'm glad you agree." Our lips met and we melted into each other, giving in to our relief and joy to be alive and together.

While I didn't carve it into my skin right at that moment, I made a vow to always run experiments for my Science Barbie. Until my last breath, I would always seek and then implement the best methods for loving her.

# Epilogue

## Rhain

Thorne knew exactly where to find me. I smelled the flavor of his darakt before I heard him climbing the ladder to join me on the compound's roof.

He said nothing at first. Just leaned his forearms on the railing about five feet down from me. After thirty or so seconds, he pulled out his cigarettes and lit up. My own smoke was nearly finished, and I took a final drag before stubbing the end in the ashtray between us.

"They're getting big, huh?" He jerked his chin toward the distance, indicating the orchard of fruit trees Cyan had planted for Tavia.

"Yeah."

The trees were just saplings now, but both Tavia and Cyan, along with a master gardener they hired, inspected them daily for signs of pests and illness. Fifty trees tended to like children. And I found myself oddly protective of the spindly little things. Watching them under a bright moon turned out to be a respite from everything else going on.

"When will they bear fruit, do you think?"

"Tavia said it'll probably be another year for the apples. Three years for the cherries. Not soon enough, in her view."

Thorne chuckled, red smoke billowing from his nostrils. "She'll learn soon enough that three years is no time at all."

I said nothing and waited for him to broach what he really wanted to talk about.

"What do you think of our brothers taking on blood mates?"

I shrugged. "Temkra has chosen well for Cyan and Laith. It's good to see them happy. Amy deserves better than Novak, but nothing can be done about that."

Another dry, smoky chuckle. "Think you're next?"

"No."

"Why not?"

"You know why," I said with more bite than I intended.

Thorne was quiet for a few seconds. "You weren't in your right mind when you made that vow. You were grieving—"

"I really don't want to talk about this with you."

Thorne paused to let out a long exhale of red smoke. "I'm sending you away on assignment."

I forced my fists to unclench the metal railing. "Away where?"

"South of the Ribs, near our border with Shadowburn."

"Where you had Laith and Cy check out the fight club?"

"Yes. There's a dive bar there called Nocturne." He rolled his eyes. "Inessa tells me the owner there is a cousin of her father's. Goes by Vlad."

I snorted. "Seriously?"

"Sadly, yes. He's supposedly the one in charge of running the fights. The bar is a front for the fights and probably big draitrium deals."

"Makes sense. What's the assignment?"

"Find out how to get Kal the fuck out of there. I don't care how you do it. Act like you're an investor. Some big shot gambler. If they sell fighters like humans sell race-horses, buy him. Whatever it takes, but do not let Vlad catch on to you."

I groaned. "So I'll need to become a regular at this place."

"That would be my recommendation, yes."

"What kind of dive is it?"

"Seedy. It has a strip club from what I hear."

"Great." I narrowed my eyes. "That's why you asked me about being next to find a mate?"

Thorne nodded. "I can't send Cy or Laith, obviously. And I'm too recognizable as Blood 'til Dawn. But you, my friend, despite your size, are quite good at flying under the radar. And you're single."

"Why not send Des?"

"He's a good soldier, but he's too young. Too inexperienced for this." Thorne shook his head. "You're the only one I trust to get this done."

"Fine. When do I go?"

"In two weeks. After Laith and Heather's ceremony."

"Right. Wouldn't want to miss that."

"Don't sound so bitter," Thorne scoffed. "Besides, who knows? You might meet someone down south."

"Fuck off with that noise." I dug out my cigarettes, annoyance gnawing at the peace I felt moments before he showed up. "I'll do the assignment, but you need to shut the hell up about blood mates. You know it's not in the cards for me."

Thorne stared at me, his gaze piercing. "You don't still blame yourself, do you?"

I pushed off the railing and got within an inch of his face. To his credit, he didn't flinch. But it took all my resolve to keep my voice low and level.

"You are my friend and the head of my clan. I have only the highest respect for you. But if you keep pushing me on this, I swear to Temkra I will fucking swing at you. And I won't hold back."

Thorne sighed deeply, completely unbothered by my threat of violence. He was lean, even twiggy compared to me, but he had become head of the ruling clan by being a scrappy, cunning fighter. I had him on brute strength, but he could outmaneuver and outsmart me. Whenever we had tussled as juveniles and younger adults, we'd been pretty evenly matched despite our size difference.

He turned to leave, effectively snapping my aggressive tension like a string. I leaned over the railing, grateful to be left alone to watch the orchard in peace.

Just before he went down the ladder, Thorne's voice floated across the roof.

"You always deserved better than her, Rhain."

———

Thank you so much for reading **Taste of Forever!** I hope you enjoyed Heather and Laith's story.

**In the mood for a taste of…trauma?**
Heather and Laith have been through a *lot* of it. How do they balance the joys of their newfound love with the horrors of what they've been through?

Find out in the Taste of Forever bonus scene!
Start reading: **BookHip.com/FHSQVLJ**

---

**Need more vampire romance?**

Read Cyan and Tavia's story in ***Taste of Fate.***

Then you can dive right into Amy and Novak's romance in ***Taste of Death***.

If you're more in a wolf shifter mood, don't miss my Howling Death MC series. The first book is ***Traitor Wolf.***

# Glossary

## Sanguine clans and vampiric terms

## Vampire Clans

**Blood and Truth:** a newly formed clan created when Novak of Rathka's Order renounced his clan to start anew

**Blood 'til Dawn:** Current ruling clan of Sanguine

**Carpe Noctem:** A previous ruling clan, longtime rivals of Blood 'til Dawn

**Marrowers:** Clan and subspecies of vampires with a diet rich in bone marrow and preference for living underground

**Rathka's Order:** A now-extinct clan that succumbed to an unknown illness causing madness and cannibalism

**Temkra's Blood:** Clan and religious order with a strong focus on the vampire's primary deity, Temkra

## Vampiric terms

**Akra:** A term of endearment similar to darling or sweetheart. It can be used for familial affection, but is most often used between lovers.

**Blood mate:** Someone whose blood is considered chemically and nutritionally perfect for the recipient. Once tasted, a bond is created in which all other blood tastes foul and rancid. Can be one-sided or between two parties.

**Blood pet:** Someone who provides their blood to a vampire in exchange for care and protection. Generally expected to be an exclusive arrangement on both ends, unless both parties agree otherwise. Can be platonic or a sexual/romantic arrangement.

**Brusang:** A human who has been given vampire blood near or soon after their death. They awaken after 2-3 days with blackened eyes and adopt vampire traits such as the need for blood, accelerated healing, an 800-year lifespan, and an aversion to sunlight.

**Darakt:** A mixture of dried blood and herbs crushed to a fine power, usually rolled in paper and smoked like cigarettes. Provides a brief, euphoric high like nicotine to humans.

**Draitrium (drae):** A mineral found in the dragon shifter territory that allows vampires to walk in daylight unharmed. Also a highly addictive drug with terrible side effects.

**Half-Century Selection:** Event in which the human community of Sapien gives one of their own as a blood pet to the ruling vampire clan every fifty years. In exchange, no vampires are permitted to feed from Sapien citizens

**Rathka:** Temkra's younger brother, an impulsive trickster deity prone to violence. Patron deity of the clan, Rathka's Order.

**Sapien:** The last remaining human-only compound in Sanguine.

**Temkra:** primary deity of vampires, thought of as the mother of the species. The territory of Sanguine is believed to be the remains of her body when she laid down to die. This is why the regions of Sanguine are divided into body parts (the Heart, the Ribs, etc.).

**Verakt:** A vampire or brusang who claims a blood pet. Responsible for the blood pet's care, comfort, and protection. Generally expected to be an exclusive arrangement on both ends, unless both parties agree otherwise. Can be platonic or a sexual/romantic arrangement

# Also by Sophie Ash

**<u>Vampires of Sanguine</u>**

Taste of Fate

Taste of Death

Taste of Forever

**<u>Gods and Myths</u>**

The Minotaur

**<u>Howling Death MC</u>**

Traitor Wolf

Enemy Wolf

Cursed Wolf

# About the Author

Sophie Ash is a USA Today bestselling author from Northern California, writing paranormal romances with plenty of bite, as well as passionate retellings of myths and folklore.

When she's not writing, she's probably reading, gardening, vacuuming up cat hair, or enjoying a craft beer in the sun.

Sign up for Sophie's email list and get a free standalone novella as a thank you gift: https://BookHip.com/KBRCFWN

facebook.com/Crystal.Sophie.Ash.Books

instagram.com/crystalsophieash

amazon.com/author/sophieash

bookbub.com/profile/sophie-ash

www.ingramcontent.com/pod-product-compliance
Lightning Source LLC
Chambersburg PA
CBHW031239310726
48971CB00004B/1088